W9-BUV-110

A.D. 30

A Novel

TED DEKKER

CENTER STREET

New York Boston Nashville

This book is a work of fiction. Names, characters, places, and incidents are the product of the author's imagination or are used fictitiously. Any resemblance to actual events, locales, or persons, living or dead, is coincidental.

Copyright © 2014 by Ted Dekker

Original maps drawn by William Vanderbush

All rights reserved. In accordance with the U.S. Copyright Act of 1976, the scanning, uploading, and electronic sharing of any part of this book without the permission of the publisher constitutes unlawful piracy and theft of the author's intellectual property. If you would like to use material from the book (other than for review purposes), prior written permission must be obtained by contacting the publisher at permissions@hbgusa.com. Thank you for your support of the author's rights.

Ted Dekker is represented by Creative Trust Literary Group, www.creativetrust.com.

Center Street
Hachette Book Group
1290 Avenue of the Americas
New York, NY 10104

CenterStreet.com

Printed in the United States of America

RRD-C

Originally published in hardcover by Hachette Book Group.
First trade edition: April 2015

10 9 8 7 6

Center Street is a division of Hachette Book Group, Inc.
The Center Street name and logo are trademarks of Hachette Book Group, Inc.

The Hachette Speakers Bureau provides a wide range of authors for speaking events. To find out more, go to www.hachettespeakersbureau.com or call (866) 376-6591.

The publisher is not responsible for websites (or their content) that are not owned by the publisher.

Library of Congress Cataloging-in-Publication Data
Dekker, Ted.
  A.D. 30 : a novel / Ted Dekker. — First edition.
    pages cm
  Summary: "A sweeping epic set in the harsh deserts of Arabia and ancient Palestine. A war that rages between kingdoms on the earth and in the heart. The harrowing journey of the woman at the center of it all. Step back in time to the year of our Lord...A.D. 30. The outcast daughter of one of the most powerful Bedouin sheikhs in Arabia, Maviah is called on to protect the very people who rejected her. When their enemies launch a sudden attack with devastating consequences, Maviah escapes with the help of two of her father's warriors—Saba, who speaks more with is sword than his voice, and Judah, a Jew who comes from a tribe that can read the stars. Their journey will be fraught with terrible danger. If they can survive the vast forbidding sands of a desert that is deadly to most, they will reach a brutal world subjugated by kings and emperors. There Maviah must secure an unlikely alliance with King Herod of the Jews. But Maviah's path leads her unexpectedly to another man. An enigmatic teacher who speaks of a way in this life that offers greater power than any kingdom. His name is Yeshua, and his words turn everything known on its head. Though following him may present even greater danger, his may be the only way for Maviah to save her people—and herself" —Provided by publisher.
  ISBN 978-1-59995-418-9 (hardback) — ISBN 978-1-4555-3345-9 (autographed hardcover) — ISBN 978-1-4555-8920-3 (large print hardcover) — ISBN 978-1-4555-8876-3 (international trade paperback)
  1. Christian fiction.   2. Historical fiction.   I. Title.

  PS3554.E43A64 2014
  813'.54—dc23
                                    2014017802

ISBN 978-1-4555-7854-2 (pbk.)

MY JOURNEY INTO *A.D. 30*

It is said that true spirituality cannot be taught, it can only be learned, and it can only be learned through experience, which is actually story—all else is only hearsay. It is also said the shortest distance between a human being and the truth is a story. Surely this is why Jesus preferred to use stories.

For ten years I dreamed of entering the life of Jesus through story, not as a Jew familiar with the customs of the day, but as an outsider, because we are all outsiders today. I wanted to hear his teaching and see his power. I wanted to know what he taught about how we should live; how we might rise above all the struggles that we all face in this life, not just in the next life after we die.

We all know what Jesus means for Christians on a doctrinal statement in terms of the next life, and we are eternally grateful. But we still live in this life. What was his Way for this life other than to accept his Way for the next life?

So I began by calling Jesus by the name he was called in his day, Yeshua, and I once again set out to discover his Way through the lens of a foreigner—a Bedouin woman who is cast out of her lofty position in the deep Arabian desert by terrible tragedy. Her epic, unnerving journey forces her to the land of Israel, where she encounters the radical teachings of Yeshua, which once again turn her world upside down.

As they did mine.

Although I grew up in the church and am very familiar with Christianity, what I discovered in Yeshua's teachings staggered me. It was at once beautiful to the part of me that wanted to be set free from my own chains, and unnerving to that part of me that didn't want to let go and follow the path to freedom in this life.

I grew up as the son of missionaries who left everything in the west to take the good news to a tribe of cannibals in Indonesia. They were heroes in all respects and taught me many wonderful things, not least among them all the virtues and values of the Christian life. What a beautiful example they showed me.

When I was six years old, they did what all missionaries did in that day and for which I offer them no blame: they sent me to a boarding school. There I found myself completely untethered and utterly alone. I wept that first night, terrified. I don't remember the rest of the nights because I have somehow blocked those painful memories, but my friends tell me that I cried myself to sleep every night for many months.

I felt abandoned. And I was only six. I was lost, like that small bird in the children's book that wanders from creature to creature in the forest asking each if they are his mother.

Are you my mother? Are you my Father?

I see now that my entire life since has been one long search for my identity and for significance in *this* life, though I was secure in the next life.

As I grew older, all the polished answers I memorized in Sunday school seemed to fail me on one level or another, sometimes quite spectacularly. I began to see cracks in what had once seemed so simple.

I was supposed to have special powers to love others and turn the other cheek and refrain from gossip and not judge. I was supposed to be a shining example, known by the world for my extravagant love, grace, and power in all respects. And yet, while I heard the rhetoric of others, I didn't seem to have these powers myself.

During my teens, I was sure that it was uniquely my fault—I didn't have enough faith, I needed to try harder and do better. Others seemed to have it all together, but I was a failure.

Can you relate?

Then I began to notice that everyone seemed to be in the same boat, beginning with those I knew the best. When my relationships challenged all of my notions of love, when disease came close to home, when friends turned on me, when I struggled to pay my bills, when life sucked me dry, I began to wonder where all the power to live life more abundantly had gone. Then I began to question whether or not it had ever really been there in the first place. Perhaps that's why I couldn't measure up.

So I pressed in harder with the hope of discovering God's love. But I still couldn't measure up.

And when I couldn't measure up, I began to see with perfect clarity that those who claimed to live holy lives were just like me and only lied to themselves—a fact that was apparent to everyone but them. Did not Yeshua teach that jealousy and gossip and anxiousness and fear are just another kind of depravity? Did he not say that even to be angry with someone or call them a fool is the same as murder? Not just kind of—sort of, but really.

So then we are all equally guilty, every day.

How, then, does one find and know peace and power in this life when surrounded by such a great cloud of witnesses who only pretend to be clean by whitewashing their reputations while pointing fingers of judgment?

So many Christians today see a system that seems to have failed them. They have found the promises from their childhood to be suspect, if not empty, and so they are leaving in droves, leaving leaders to scratch their heads.

What about you? You're saved in the next life as a matter of sound doctrine, but do you often feel powerless and lost in *this* life?

Think of your life in a boat on the stormy seas. The dark skies block out the sun, the winds tear at your face, the angry waves rise to sweep you off your treasured boat and send you into a dark, watery grave. And so you cringe in fear as you cling to the boat that you believe will save you from such suffering.

But Yeshua is at peace. And when you cry out in fear, he rises and looks out at that storm, totally unconcerned.

Why are you afraid? he asks.

Has he gone mad? Does he not see the reason to fear? How could he ask such a question?

Unless what he sees and what you see are not the same... *Peace.*

Yeshua shows us a Way of being saved in the midst of all that we think threatens us on the dark seas of our lives here on earth.

When the storms of life rise and threaten to swamp you, can you quiet the waves? Can you leave that cherished boat behind and walk on the troubled waters, or do you cling to your boat like the rest of the world, certain you will drown if you step on the deep dark seas that surround you? Do you have the power to move mountains? Do you turn the other cheek, able to offer love and peace to those who strike you?

Are you anxious in your relationship or lack thereof? Are you concerned about your means of income, or your career, or your status? Do you fear for your children? Are you worried about what you will wear, or how others will view you in any respect? Do you secretly suspect that you can never quite measure up to what you think God or the world expects of you? That you are doomed to be a failure, always? Are you quick to point out the failures of others?

I was, though I didn't see it in myself. As it turns out, it's hard to see when your vision is blocked by planks of secret judgments and grievances against yourself and the world. It was in my writing of *A.D. 30* that I discovered just how blind I was and still often am.

But Yeshua came to restore sight to the blind and set the captives free. The sight he offered was into the Father's realm, which is brimming with light, seen only through new vision. And in that light I began to glimpse the deep mystery of Yeshua's Way, not only for the next life, but for this life.

His Way of being in this world is full of joy and gratefulness. A place where all burdens are light and each step sure. Contentment and peace rule the heart. A new power flows unrestricted.

But Yeshua's Way is also 180 degrees from the way of the world and, as such, completely counterintuitive to any system of human logic. The body cannot see Yeshua's Way for this life—true vision requires new eyes. The mind cannot understand it—true knowing requires a whole new operating system. This is why, as Yeshua predicted, very few even find his Way. It is said that nearly 70 percent of all Americans have accepted Jesus as savior at some point, but how many of us have found his Way for this life?

Yeshua's Way is letting go of one world system to see and experience another—one that is closer than our own breath.

It is surrendering what we think we know *about* the Father so we can truly *know* him. It is the great reversal of all that we think will give us significance and meaning in this life so we can live with more peace and power than we have yet imagined.

In today's vernacular, Yeshua's Way is indeed the way of superheroes. In this sense, was he not the first superhero, and we now his apprentices? Would we not rush to see and experience this truth about Yeshua, our Father, and ourselves?

In the Way of Yeshua we will bring peace to the storms of this life, we will walk on the troubled seas, we will not be bitten by the lies of snakes, we will move mountains that appear insurmountable, we will heal the sickness that has twisted our minds and bodies, we will be far more than conquerors through Yeshua, who is our true source of strength.

It is the Way of Yeshua for *this* life that I found in *A.D. 30*. Whenever we find ourselves blinded by our own grievances, judgments, and fears, we, like Maviah in *A.D. 30*, sink into darkness. But when we trust Yeshua and his Way once again, we see the sun instead of the storm.

This is our revolution in Yeshua: to be free from the prisons that hold us captive. This is our healing, to see what few see. This is our resurrection: to rise from death *with* Yeshua as apprentices in the Way of the Master.

So enter this story if you like and see if you can see what Maviah saw. It may change the way you understand your Father, your Master, yourself, and your world.

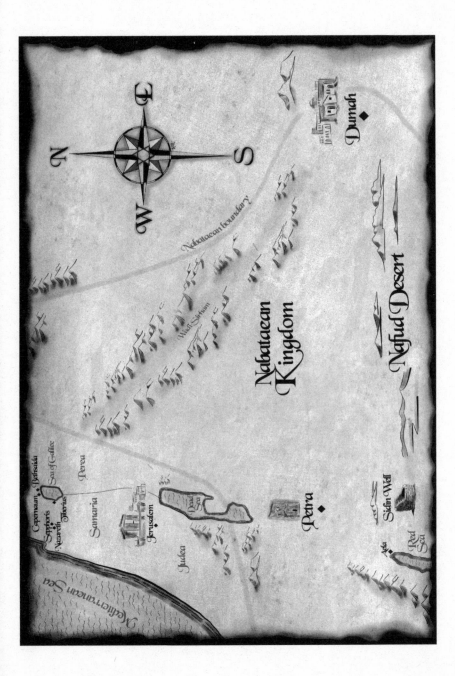

All teachings spoken by Yeshua in A.D. 30
are his words from the gospels.
(See appendix.)

PROLOGUE

I HAD HEARD of kingdoms far beyond the oasis that gives birth to life where none should be, kingdoms beyond the vast, barren sands of the Arabian deserts.

I had lived in one such kingdom beyond the great Red Sea, in a land called Egypt, where I was sold into slavery as a young child. I had dreamed of the kingdoms farther north, where it was said the Romans lived in opulence and splendor, reveling in the plunder of conquered lands; of the silk kingdoms beyond Mesopotamia, in the Far East where wonder and magic ruled.

But none of these kingdoms were real to me, Maviah, daughter of the great sheikh of the Banu Kalb tribe, which presided over Arabia's northern sands. None were real to me because I, Maviah, was born into shame without the hope of honor.

It is said that there are four pillars of life in Arabia, without which all life in the desert would forever cease. The sands, for they are the earth and offer the water where it can be found. The camel, for it grants both milk and freedom. The tent, for it gives shelter from certain death. And the Bedouin, ruled by none, loyal to the death, passionate for life, masters of the harshest desert in which only the strongest can survive. In all the world, there are none more noble than the Bedu, for only the Bedu are truly free, living in the unforgiving tension of these pillars.

Yet these four are slaves to a fifth: the pillar of honor and shame.

And upon reflection I would say that there is no greater honor than being born with the blood of a man, no greater shame than being born with the blood of a woman. Indeed, born into shame, a woman may find honor only by bringing no shame to man.

Through blood are all bonds forged. Through blood is all shame avenged. Through blood is life passed on from father to son. In blood is all life contained, and yet a woman is powerless to contain her own. Thus she is born with shame.

Even so, the fullness of my shame was far greater than that of being born a woman.

Through no will of my own, I was also an illegitimate child, the seed of a dishonorable union between my father and a woman of the lowest tribe in the desert, the Banu Abysm, scavengers who crushed and consumed the bones of dead animals to survive in the wastelands.

Through no will of my own, my mother perished in childbirth.

Through no will of my own, my father sent me to Egypt in secret so that his shame could not be known, for it is said that a shame unrevealed is two-thirds forgiven.

Through no will of my own, I was made a slave in that far land.

Through no will of my own, I was returned to my father's house when I gave birth to a son without a suitable husband. There, under his reluctant protection, I once again found myself in exile.

I was a Bedu who was not free, a woman forever unclean, a mother unworthy of a husband, an outcast imprisoned by those mighty pillars of the desert, subject of no kingdom but death.

But there came into that world a man who spoke of a different kingdom with words that defied all other kingdoms.

Some said that he was a prophet from their god. Some said that he was a mystic who spoke in riddles meant to infuriate the mind and quicken the heart, that he worked wonders to make his power evident. Some said that he was a Gnostic, though they were wrong. Some said that he was a messiah who came to set his people free. Still others, that he was a fanatical Zealot, a heretic, a man who'd seen too many deaths and too much suffering to remain sane.

But I came to know him as the Anointed One who would grant great power to those few who followed in his way.

My name is Maviah, daughter of Rami bin Malik.

His name was Yeshua.

DUMAH

"I tell you, do not resist an evil person.
If anyone slaps you on the right cheek, turn to them the
  other cheek also."

Yeshua

CHAPTER ONE

THE DESERT knows no years. Here time is marked by three things alone. By the rising and the falling of the sun each day, to both bless and curse with its fire. By the coming of rain perhaps twice in the winter, if the gods are kind. And by the dying of both young and old at the whim of those same gods.

I stood alone on the stone porch atop the palace Marid, high above the Dumah oasis, as the sun slowly settled behind blood-red sands. My one-year-old son suckled noisily at my breast beneath the white shawl that protected him from the world.

That world was controlled by two kinds: the nomadic peoples known as Bedouin, or Bedu, who roamed the deserts in vast scattered tribes such as the Kalb and the Thamud, and the stationary peoples who lived in large cities and were ruled by kings and emperors. Among these were the Nabataeans, the Jews, the Romans, and the Egyptians.

Two kinds of people, but all lived and died by the same sword.

There was more war than peace throughout the lands, because peace could be had only through oppression or tenuous alliances between tribes and kings, who might become enemies with the shifting of a single wind.

One of those winds was now in the air.

I'd named my son after my father, Rami bin Malik—this before I'd returned to Dumah and become fully aware of the great gulf that separated me from my father. Indeed, the sheikh tolerated my presence only because his wife, Nashquya, had persuaded him. I might be illegitimate, she'd cleverly argued, but my son was still his grandson. She insisted he take us in.

Nasha was not an ordinary wife easily dismissed, for she was the niece of King Aretas of the Nabataeans, who controlled all desert trade routes. Truly, Father owed his great wealth to his alliance with King Aretas, which was sealed through his marriage to Nasha.

Still, I remained a symbol of terrible shame to him. If not for Nasha's continued affection for me, he would surely have sent me off into the wasteland to die alone and raised my son as his own.

Nasha alone was our savior. She alone loved me.

And now Nasha lay near death in her chambers two levels below the high porch where I stood.

I had been prohibited from seeing her since she'd taken ill, but I could no longer practice restraint. As soon as my son fed and fell asleep, I would lay him in our room and make my way unseen to Nasha's chambers.

Before me lay the springs and pools of Dumah, which gave life to thousands of date palms stretching along the wadi, a full hour's walk in length and half as far in breadth. Olive trees too, though far fewer in number. The oasis contained groves of pomegranate shrubs and apple, almond, and lemon trees, many of which had been introduced to the desert by the Nabataeans.

What Dumah did not grow, the caravans provided. Frankincense and myrrh, as valuable as gold to the Egyptians and Romans, who used the sacred incenses to accompany their dead into the afterlife. From India and the Gulf of Persia: rich spices, brilliantly colored cloths and wares. From Mesopotamia: wheat and millet and barley and horses.

All these treasures were carried through the Arabian sands along three trade routes, one of which passed through Dumah at the center of the vast northern desert. Some said that without the waters found in Dumah, Arabia would be half of what it was.

The oasis was indeed the ornament of the deep desert. Dumah was heavy with wealth from a sizable tax levied by my father's tribe, the Banu Kalb. The caravans came often, sometimes more than a thousand camels long, bearing more riches than the people of any other Bedu tribe might lay eyes on during the full length of their lives.

So much affluence, so much glory, so much honor. And I, the only dark blot in my father's empire. I was bound by disgrace, and a part of me hated him for it.

Little Rami fussed, hungry for more milk, and I lifted my white shawl to reveal his tender face and eyes, wide with innocence and wonder. His appetite had grown as quickly as his tangled black hair, uncut since birth.

I shifted him to my left, pulled aside my robe, and let him suckle as I lifted my eyes.

As a slave groomed for high service in a Roman house I had been educated, mostly in the ways of language, because the Romans had an appetite for distant lands. By the time I had my first blood, I could speak Arabic, the language of the deep desert; Aramaic, the trade language of Nabataeans and the common language in Palestine; Latin, the language of the Romans; and Greek, commonly spoken in Egypt.

And yet these languages were bitter herbs on my tongue, for even my education displeased my father.

I scanned the horizon. Only three days ago the barren dunes just beyond the oasis had been covered in black tents. The Dumah fair had drawn many thousands of Kalb and Tayy and Asad—all tribes in confederation with my father. A week of great celebration and trading had filled their bellies and laden their camels with enough wares to satisfy them for months to come. They were all gone now, and Dumah was nearly deserted, a town of stray camels that grazed lazily or slept in the sun.

To the south lay the forbidding Nafud desert, reserved for those Bedu who wished to tempt fate.

A day's ride to the east lay Sakakah, the stronghold of the Thamud tribe, which had long been our bitter enemy. The Thamud vultures refrained from descending on Dumah only for fear of King Aretas, Nasha's uncle, who was allied with my father and whose army was vast. Though both the Thamud and Kalb tribes were powerful, neither could hold this oasis without Aretas's support.

But my father's alliance with Aretas was sealed by Nasha's life.

In turn, Nasha alone offered me mercy and life.

And Nasha was now close to death.

These thoughts so distracted me that I failed to notice that little Rami's suckling had ceased. He breathed in sleep, oblivious to the concern whispering through me.

It was time. If I was discovered with Nasha, my father might become enraged and claim I had visited dishonor on his wife by entering her chamber. And yet I could not stay away from her any longer. I must go while Rami was still offering prayers at the shrine of the moon god, Wadd.

Holding my son close, I quickly descended three flights of steps and made my way, barefooted, to my room at the back of the palace, careful that none of the servants noticed my passing. The fortress was entombed in silence.

Leaving my son to sleep on the mat, I eased the door shut, grabbed my flowing gown with one hand so that I could move uninhibited, and ran through the lower passage. Up one flight of steps and down the hall leading to the palace's southern side.

"Maviah?"

Catching my breath, I spun back to see Falak, Nasha's well-fed servant, standing at the door that led into the cooking chamber.

"Where do you rush off to?" she asked with scorn, for even the servants were superior to me.

I recovered quickly. "Have you seen my father?"

She regarded me with suspicion. "Where he's gone is none of your concern."

"Do you know when he returns?"

"What do you care?" Her eyes glanced over my gown, a simple white cotton dress fitting of commoners, not the richly colored silk worn by those of high standing in the Marid. "Where is the child?"

"He sleeps." I released my gown and settled, as if at a loss.

"Alone?" she demanded.

"I wish to ask my father if I might offer prayers for Nasha," I said.

"And what good are your prayers in these matters? Do not insult him with this request."

"I only thought—"

"The gods do not listen to whores!"

Her tone was cruel, which was not her normal way. She was only fearful of her own future should her mistress, Nasha, not recover.

"Even a whore may love Nashquya," I said with care. "And even Nashquya may love a whore. But I am not a whore, Falak. I am the mother of my father's grandson."

"Then go to your son's side where you belong."

I could have said more, but I wanted no suspicion.

I dipped my head in respect. "When you next see Nashquya, will you tell her that the one whom she loves offers prayers for her?"

Falak hesitated, then spoke with more kindness. "She's with the priest now. I will tell her. See to your child."

Then she vanished back into the cooking chamber.

I immediately turned and hurried down the hall, around the corner, past the chamber of audience where my father accepted visitors from the clans, then down another flight of steps to the master chamber in which Nasha kept herself.

She was with a priest, Falak had said. So I slipped into the adjoining bathing room and parted the heavy curtain just wide enough to see into Nasha's chamber.

I was unprepared for what greeted my eyes. Her bed was on a raised stone slab unlike those of the Bedu, who prefer rugs and skins on the floor. A mattress of woven date palms wrapped in fine purple linens covered the stone. This bedding was lined at the head and the far side with red and golden pillows fringed in black, for she was Nabataean and accustomed to luxury. Nasha was lying back against the pillows, face pale as though washed in ash, eyelids barely parted. She wore only a thin linen gown, which clung to her skin, wet with sweat.

One of the seers of the moon god Wadd, draped in a long white robe hemmed in blue fringe, faced her at the foot of the bed. He waved a large hand with long fingernails over a small iron bowl of burning incense as he muttered prayers in a bid to beg mercy from Dumah's god. His eyes were not diverted from his task, so lost was he in his incantations.

Nasha's eyes opened wide and I knew that she'd seen me. My breath caught in my throat, for if the priest also saw me, he would report to my father.

Nasha was within her wits enough to shift her eyes to the priest and feebly lift her arm.

"Leave me," she said thinly.

His song faltered and he stared at her as though she had stripped him of his robe.

Nasha pointed at the door. "Leave me."

"I don't understand." He looked at the door, confounded. "I...the sheikh called for me to resurrect his wife."

"And does she appear resurrected to you?"

"But of course not. The god of Dumah is only just hearing my prayers and awakening from his sleep. I cannot possibly leave while in his audience."

"How long have you been praying?"

"Since the sun was high."

"If it takes you so long to awaken your god, I would require a different priest and a new god."

Such as Al-Uzza, the Nabataean goddess to whom Nasha prayed, I thought. Al-Uzza might not sleep so deeply as Wadd, but I had never known any god to pay much attention to mortals, no matter how well plied.

"The sheikh commanded me!" the priest said.

"And now Nashquya, niece of the Nabataean king, Aretas, commands you," she rasped. "You are alone with another man's wife who has requested that you leave. Return to your shrine and retain your honor."

His face paled at the insinuation. Setting his jaw, he offered Nasha a dark scowl, spit in disgust, and left the chamber in long, indignant strides.

The moment the door closed, I rushed in, aware that the priest's report might hasten Rami's return.

"Nasha!" I hurried to her bed and dropped to my knees. Taking her hand I kissed it, surprised by the heat in her flesh. "Nasha...I'm so sorry. I was forbidden to come but I could not stay away."

"Maviah." She smiled. "The gods have answered my dying request."

She was speaking out of her fever.

I hurried to a bowl along the wall, dipped a cloth into the cool water, quickly wrung it out, and settled to my knees beside Nasha's bed once again.

She offered an appreciative look as I wiped the sweat from her brow. She was burning up from the inside. They called it the black fever.

"You are strong, Nasha," I said. "The fever will pass."

"It has been two days..."

"I could have taken care of you!" I said. "Why must I be kept from you?"

"Maviah. Sweet Maviah. Always so passionate. So eager to serve. If you had not been a slave, you would have been a true queen."

"Save your strength," I scolded. She was the only one with whom I could speak so easily. "You must sleep. When did you last take the powder of the ghada fruit? Have they given you the Persian herbs?"

"Yes...yes, yes. But it hardly matters now, Maviah. It's taking me."

"Don't speak such things!"

"It's taking me and I've made my peace with the gods. I'm an old woman..."

"How can you say that? You're still young."

"I'm twenty years past you and now ready to meet my end."

She was smiling but I wondered if her mind was already going.

"Rami has gone to the shrine of Wadd to offer the blood of a goat," she said. "Then all the gods will be appeased and I will enter the next life in peace. You mustn't fear for me."

"No. I won't allow the gods to take you so soon. I couldn't bear to live without you!"

Her face softened at my words, her eyes searching my own. "You're my only sister, Maviah." I wasn't her sister by blood, but we shared a bond as if it were so.

Worry began to overtake her face. A tear slipped from the corner of her eye. "I'm hardly a woman, Maviah," she said, voice now strained.

"Don't be absurd..."

"I cannot bear a son."

"But you have Maliku."

"Maliku is a tyrant!"

Rami's son by his first wife had been only a small boy when Nasha came to Dumah to seal Rami's alliance with the Nabataean kingdom through marriage. My elder by two years, Maliku expected to inherit our father's full authority among the Kalb, though I was sure Rami did not trust him.

"Hush," I whispered, glancing at the door. "You're speaking out of fever!" And yet I too despised Maliku. Perhaps as much as he despised me, for he had no love to give except that which earned him position, power, or possession.

"I'm dying, Maviah."

"You won't die, Nasha." I clung to her hand. "I will pray to Al-Uzza. I will pray to Isis."

In Egypt I had learned to pray to the goddess Isis, who is called Al-Uzza among the Nabataeans, for they believe she is the protector of children, friend of slaves and the downtrodden—the highest goddess. And yet I was already convinced that even she, who had once favored me in Egypt, had either turned her back on me or grown deaf. Or perhaps she was only a fanciful creation of men to intoxicate shamed women.

"The gods have already heard my final request by bringing my sister to my side," she said.

"Stop!" I said. "Your fever is speaking. You are queen of this desert, wife of the sheikh, who commands a hundred thousand camels and rules all the Kalb who look toward Dumah!"

"I am weak and eaten with worms."

"You are in the line of Aretas, whose wealth is coveted by all of Rome and Palestine and Egypt and Arabia. You are Nashquya, forever my queen!"

At this, Nasha's face went flat and she stared at me with grave resolve. When she finally spoke, her voice was contained.

"No, Maviah. It is you who will one day rule this vast kingdom at the behest of the heavens. It is written already."

She was mad with illness, and her shift in disposition frightened me.

"I saw it when you first came to us," she said. "There isn't a woman in all of Arabia save the queens of old who carries herself like you. None so beautiful as you. None so commanding of life."

What could I say to her rambling? She couldn't know that her words mocked me, a woman drowning in the blood of dishonor.

"You must rest," I managed.

But she only tightened her grasp on my arm.

"Take your son away, Maviah! Flee with him before the Nabataeans dash his head on the rocks. Flee Dumah and save your son."

"My son is Rami's son!" I jerked my arm away, horrified by her words. "My son is safe with my father!"

"Your father's alliance with the Nabataeans is bound by my life," she said. "I am under Rami's care. Do you think King Aretas will only shrug if I die? Rami has defiled the gods."

"He's offended which god?"

"Am I a god to know? But I would not be ill if he had not." So it was said—the gods made their displeasure known. "Aretas will show his outrage for all to see, so that his image remains unshakable before all people."

"A hundred thousand Kalb serve Rami," I said, desperate to denounce her fear, for it was also my own.

"Only because of his alliance with Aretas," she said plainly. "If I die and Aretas withdraws his support, I fear for Rami."

Any honor that I might wrestle from this life came only from my father, the greatest of all sheikhs, who could never fail. My only purpose was to win his approval by honoring him—this was the way of all Bedu daughters. If his power in the desert was compromised, I would become worthless.

"He has deserted the old ways," Nasha whispered. "He's not as strong as he once was."

The Bedu are a nomadic people, masters of the desert, free to couch camel and tent in any quarter or grazing land. They are subject to none but other Bedu who might desire the same lands. It has always been so, since before the time of Abraham and his son Ishmael, the ancient father of the Bedu in northern Arabia.

In the true Bedu mind, a stationary life marks the end of the Bedu way. Mobility is essential to survival in such a vast wasteland. Indeed, among many tribes, the mere building of any permanent structure is punishable by death.

In taking control of Dumah, a city built of squared stone walls and edifices such as the palace Marid, a fortress unto itself, Rami and his subjects had undermined the sacred Bedu way, though the wealth brought by this indiscretion blinded most men.

I knew as much, but hearing Nasha's conviction, fear welled up within me. I wiped her forehead with the cool cloth again.

"Rest now. You must sleep."

Nasha sagged into the pillows and closed her eyes. "Pray to

Al-Uzza," she whispered after a moment. "Pray to Dushares. Pray to Al-Lat. Pray to yourself to save us all."

And then she stilled, breathing deeply.

"Nasha?"

She made no response. I drew loose strands of hair from her face.

"Nasha, dear Nasha, I will pray," I whispered.

She lay unmoving, perhaps asleep.

"I swear I will pray."

"Maviah," she whispered.

I stared at her face, ashen but at peace.

"Nasha?"

And then she whispered again.

"Maviah..."

They were the last words I would hear Nashquya of the Nabataeans, wife to my father and sister to me, speak in this life.

CHAPTER TWO

IT IS SAID among the Bedu that there are ghouls in the desert—shape-shifting demons that assume the guise of creatures, particularly hyenas, and lure unwary travelers into the sands to slay and devour them. Also *nasnas*, monsters made of half a human head, one leg, and one arm. They hunt people, hopping with great agility. And *jinn*, some of which are evil spirits, such as *marids*, who can grant a man's wishes, yet compel him to do their bidding in devious matters.

It is said that these ghouls and nasnas and jinn prey on the weak, on children, and on women who are dishonorable. Although I wasn't sure that such creatures truly existed, I sometimes dreamed of them and woke in fear.

The night Nasha left me I dreamed that I was alone with little Rami, wandering in the wastelands of the Nafud, that merciless desert south of Dumah. We were outcasts and without a kingdom to save us, and the gods were too far above in the heavens to hear our cries. Soon our own wailing was overcome by the mocking cry of ghouls hunting us, and it was with these howls in my ear that I awoke, wet with sweat.

It took only a moment to realize that the ghastly wail issued from the halls and not from the spirits of my dreams.

Little Rami slept soundly on the mat next to me, his arms resting above his shaggy head, lost to the world and the sounds of agony.

I sat up, heart pounding, and knew I was hearing my father from a distant room.

I rolled away from my child, sprang to my feet, and raced up the steps and down the hallway, uncaring that I wasn't properly dressed, for it was too hot to sleep in more than a thin gown.

So distraught was I that I flung the door open without thought of seeking permission to enter.

My gaze went straight to the bed. Nasha lay on her back with her eyes closed and her mouth parted. Her lips had the pallor of burnt myrrh, gray and lifeless. No breath entered her.

My father, unaware of my entry, stood beside the bed with his back to me.

Here was the most powerful Bedu in northern Arabia, for his strength in battle and raids was feared by all tribes. Like all great Bedu he was steeped in honor, which he would defend to the death. Nasha was responsible for a significant portion of that honor.

His first wife, Durrah, who was Maliku's mother, had been killed in a raid many years earlier. Filled with fury and thirsty for revenge, Rami had crossed the desert alone, walked into the main encampment of the Tayy tribe, and slaughtered their sheikh with a broadsword right before the eyes of the clansmen. So ruthless and bold was his revenge that the Tayy honored him with a hundred camels in addition to the life of their sheikh, of which Rami had been deserving.

Blood was always repaid by blood. An eye for an eye. Clansman for clansman. Only vengeance could restore honor. This or blood money. Or, less commonly, mercy, offered also with blood in a tradition called the Light of Blood.

It was the way of the Bedu. It was the way of the gods. It was the way of my father.

But here in Nasha's chamber there was no sign of that man.

Rami was dressed only in his long nightshirt, hands tearing at his hair as he sobbed. He raised clenched fists at the ceiling.

"Why?" he demanded.

Tears sprang to my eyes and I wanted to join him in grief, but I could not move, much less raise Nasha from the dead.

He hurled his accusations at the heavens. "Why have you cursed me with this death? I am a beast hunted by the gods for bringing this curse to the sands. I am at the mercy of their vengeance for all of my sins!"

He was heaping shame on himself for allowing Nasha to die in his care.

"You have cursed me with a thousand curses and trampled my heart with the hooves of a hundred thousand camels!"

He grabbed his shirt with both hands and tore it to expose his chest. "I, Rami bin Malik, who wanted only to live in honor, am cursed!"

I was torn between anguish at Nasha's passing and fear of Rami's rage.

"Why?" he roared.

"Father..."

He spun to me, face wet with tears. For a moment he looked lost, and then rage darkened his eyes.

"She's dead!" His trembling finger stretched toward me. "You have killed her!"

"No!" Had he heard of my visit? Surely not.

"You and the whore who was your mother! And Aretas! And all of this cursed desert!"

I could not speak.

He shoved his hand toward Nasha's body. "Her gods have

conspired to ruin me. I curse them all. I curse Dushares and Al-Uzza. I spit on Quam. All have brought me calamity."

"No, Father...please...I serve you first, before all the gods."

He stared at me, raging. "Six months! You have been here only six months and already the gods punish me."

"She was a sister to me!" I said. "I too loved Nasha..."

"Nasha?" His face twisted with rage. "Nasha bewitched me in pleading I take you in. Today I curse Nasha and I curse the daughter who is not my own. Do you know what you have done?"

I was too numb to fully accept the depth of his bitterness. He mourned the threat to his power, not Nasha's passing?

"Aretas will now betray me. All that I have achieved is now in jeopardy for the pity I have taken on the shamed."

And so he made it clear. My fear gave way to welling anger and I lost my good sense.

"How dare you?" I did not stop myself. "Your wife lies dead behind you and you think only of your own neck? What kind of honor lies in the chest of a king such as you? It was you who planted your seed in my mother's womb! I am the fruit of your lust! And now you curse me?"

My words might have been made of stone, for he stood as if struck.

"And you would rule the desert?" I demanded. "Shame on you!"

My father was no king, for no Bedu would submit to a king. Yet by cunning and shrewdness, by noble blood and appointment of the tribal elders, he was as powerful as any king and ruled a kingdom marked not by lines in the sand, but by loyalty of the heart.

His silence emboldened me. "Rami thinks only of his loss. I see Maliku in you."

"Maliku?"

"Is he not your true son? Is not my son only a bastard in your eyes?"

"Silence!" he thundered.

But I had robbed the worst of his anger. Misery swallowed him as he stared at me.

He staggered to the bed, sank to his knees, and lifted his face to the ceiling, sobbing. I stood behind, my anger gone, cheeks wet with tears.

Slowly his chin came down and he bowed his head, rocking over Nasha's corpse.

"Father..."

"Leave me now."

"But I—"

"Leave me!"

Choked with emotion, I took one last look at Nasha's stiffening form, then rose and walked away. But before I could leave, the door swung open. There in its frame stood Maliku, Rami's son.

Fear cut through my heart.

Even so early in the day, he was dressed in rich blue with a black headdress, always eager to display his pride and wealth. He had Rami's face, but he was leaner and his lips thinner over a sparse beard. His eyes were as dark as Rami's, but I imagined them to be empty wells, offering no life to the thirsty.

He looked past me and studied Nasha's still form. I saw no regret on his face, only a hint of smug satisfaction.

Maliku's stare shifted from Nasha and found me. In a sudden show of indignation, his arm lashed out like a viper's strike. The back of his hand landed a stinging blow to my cheek.

I staggered, biting back the pain.

His lips curled. "This is *your* doing."

Neither I nor my father protested his show of disfavor.

"Take your bastard son and offer yourself to the desert," he said, stepping past me to address our father. "She must leave us. We must place blame for all to see."

Father pushed himself to his feet, making no haste to respond.

Instead, as a man gazing into the abyss of his doom, he stared at Nasha's body. Maliku was within his rights. But surely he saw my son as a threat to his power, I thought. This was the root of his bitterness.

"Father—"

"Be quiet, Maliku," Rami said, turning a glare to his son. "Remember whom you speak to!"

Maliku glared, then dipped his head in respect.

Rami paced, gathering his resolve. If Maliku had been younger my father might have punished him outright for his tone, but already Maliku was powerful in the eyes of many. Truly, Rami courted an enemy in his own home.

"Father, if it please you," Maliku said, growing impatient. "I only say..."

"We will honor Nashquya at the shrine today," Rami said, cutting him short. "In private. No one must know she has passed. We cannot risk the Thamud learning of this. They are far too eager to challenge me."

"Indeed."

"Then you will take ten men, only the most trusted. Seek out the clans west, south, and north. Tell them to return to Dumah immediately. I would have them here in three days."

I could see Maliku's mind turning behind his black eyes.

"Three days have passed since they left the great fair," he said. "It will take more than three days to reach them and return."

"Do I not know my own desert? It's our good fortune that many of our tribe are still so close. They will be traveling slowly, fat from the feasts. Take the fastest camels. Let them die reaching the clans if you must. Leave the women and the children in the desert. Return to me in three days' time with all of the men."

Father was right. Ordinarily the Kalb would have been spread over a vast desert, each clan to its own grazing lands.

"If it please you, Father, may I ask what is your purpose in this?"

Rami pulled at his beard. "I would have all of the Kalb in Dumah to pay their respects and mourn the passing of their queen."

"Their queen? The Bedu serve no queen."

"Today they serve a queen!" Rami thundered, stepping toward Maliku. "Her name is Nashquya and her husband is their sheikh and this is his will!"

"They are Bedu—"

"She is your *mother*! Have you no heart?"

Maliku's face darkened.

"I would have my Kalb in Dumah!" Rami said. "To honor my wife!"

Rami stared at Maliku, then turned and walked to the window overlooking Dumah. When he spoke his voice was resolute.

"Bring me all of that might. Bring me twenty thousand Kalb. Bring every man who would save the Kalb from the Thamud jackals who circle to cut me down."

"You are most wise." Maliku paused, then glanced at me. "I would only suggest that she too be sent away."

"You will tell me how to command my daughter?"

Maliku hesitated. "No."

A moment of laden silence passed between them.

"Leave me," Rami said.

We both turned to go.

"Not you, Maviah."

I remained, confused. Maliku cast me a glare, then left the room, not bothering to close the door.

Rami, heavy with thought, turned away from the window. His world had changed this day, in more ways than I could appreciate, surely.

When he finally faced me, his jaw was fixed.

"I see in Maliku a thirst only for power. Jealousy, not nobility, steers his heart. Surely you see it."

I hesitated but was honest. "I see only what you see."

"My son is a selfish man who drinks ambition the way his stallions drink the wind at a full gallop."

I still did not understand why he wanted to speak to me thus, for he rarely uttered a word to me.

"You will remain here in the fortress, beyond the sight of all."

I bowed my head. "Yes, Father."

"If there is any trouble, you will seal yourself in the chamber of audience with your son and answer to no one but me. Do you understand?"

"Trouble? What kind of trouble?"

"You will know if it comes. But you must do this. Swear it to me."

As his daughter I had no choice. "Of course."

"It is of utmost importance. The fate of all the Kalb may depend upon it."

He stared at me for a long time, then dismissed me with a nod.

"Leave me then. I would be with my wife."

I hurried from Nasha's chamber and returned to my room, barely aware of my surroundings, too stunned to cry.

Little Rami, now awake, lay where I'd left him, staring in wonder at the dawning of another day. He smiled, then squirmed and fussed enough to let me know that he was hungry. Light streamed in from the window, but the room felt cold. So I lit an oil lamp, gathered my son in my arms, and let him suckle.

I could feel my life flowing into him as I stroked his cheek and cherished the heat of his small body against mine. In his world there was no knowledge of death. In mine, it seemed to be all I knew. For my son's life, I would die.

Then tears came again, silently slipping down my cheeks. I could not stop them.

CHAPTER THREE

—⟪⟫—

TWO NIGHTS had passed since Rami tended to Nasha's passing. I was not permitted to pay my respects at the shrine, but was confined to the fortress. Maliku had gone to find the Kalb after Nasha's private funeral and the palace Marid was like a tomb, portending the fate of me and my son. Nasha's sweet voice, once ringing through the halls with delight, now whispered only in my dreams.

Father had taken up residence in his tent just outside of Dumah with five hundred of his closest men. He often served tea to guests from the deep desert there, rather than in the fortress. Only after tea had been shared did they partake of the Bedu's greatest pleasure: the sharing of the news.

Where do you come from? Who have you seen? Which clan is raiding? I have seen the tracks of the Tayy, seventy camels strong, traveling east from the well at Junga. My brother has seen a caravan in the west, south of Tayma, plundered by the Qudah tribe. He says more than twenty were killed and over a hundred camels laden with frankincense taken.

And then others' opinions joined these words, each man explaining with unyielding passion his particular point of view, often the same view already expressed but in new words, for every man had a right to be heard.

A hundred times during those two days alone in the palace Marid, I imagined what news might be passing in my father's tent now. No possibility offered me great hope.

The Bedu men told their stories much as they told their news, over and over with great theatrics and without tiring of the same tale, the rest listening as if they'd never heard it. The guest and host would exchange accounts of a time when the locust swarms blackened the sky and stripped the grazing lands of all that was green in Mesopotamia, plunging the region into famine. Or when they and their sons showed their great courage by standing up to a dozen of the Thamud in a raid that would have robbed them of all their women and camels. Surely embellishment was the norm.

But I feared that the stories told of what would soon transpire in Dumah, regardless of the outcome, would have no need for exaggeration.

That trouble came late in the afternoon. I was again high above the Marid, where I often retreated with my son to be in the open air but out of sight. Below the fortress, Dumah slept in silence. I saw the dust then, coming from the east, a silent line of boiling sand stretching across the eastern flat as far as I could see.

A storm, I thought.

Then I saw a speck leading that line. And I knew that I wasn't seeing a storm at all. I was seeing a single camel followed by an army of camels. Far too many to be the Kalb, who would have come from all directions.

East. This was the Thamud. Saman bin Shariqat, ruler of the Thamud, was coming to Dumah.

War!

My breath caught in my throat and I stared at the scope of that army, unable to move.

A call from the slope east of the city jerked me back to myself. Father's lookouts had seen. The call was taken up by hundreds as the warning spread throughout Dumah.

First a dozen, then a hundred and more of Rami's men, mounted on horseback, raced down the slope, toward the trees at the edge of the oasis. They would engage the Thamud there, under the cover of the date palms.

Surrounded now by the sounds of great urgency, I held my son tight and flew down the stairs, thinking only of sealing myself in the chamber of audience as directed by my father.

I hurried down the hall clinging to little Rami, who managed a little laugh. But something in him shifted when I crashed into the chamber of audience, barred the door, and ran to the window. There he began to cry.

I was too stunned by the scene unfolding below to calm him. Like a stampeding herd, a thousand Thamud camels thundered over the crest toward the date palms of the oasis. Then more, flying the yellow-and-red banners of their tribe, flowing like the muddy waters of the great Nile in Egypt.

They were armed with sword and bow and ax and lance, bucking atop lavishly draped camels. The Thamud were a sea of flesh and color intent upon death.

Such a force would have quickly slaughtered Rami's small army had he remained in the open desert. Only by drawing the Thamud into the palm groves and the city itself could his Kalb leverage any advantage of cover.

By riding horses, the Kalb held speed over the Thamud, who'd needed camels to cross the softer sands as quickly as they had. On the harder ground of the city, Rami's horses could outmaneuver the larger beasts.

My father held only these small advantages. How could they possibly offset the superior numbers now swarming into Dumah?

Two days had passed since Nasha's death. The Thamud stronghold in Sakakah lay a hard day's ride east, requiring a full day to reach it and another to return. Now I understood Rami's insistence that Nasha's passing remain secret. The Thamud had surely already received Aretas's blessing to vie for power if his bond with Rami was ever broken.

And now word of that break had reached the Thamud.

Maliku.

It only stood to reason. If the Thamud crushed Rami and the Kalb here in Dumah, the Thamud would give Maliku power as the new leader of the Kalb. Though he would not be a sheikh, his sword would enforce his power among his own people in alliance with the Thamud.

I stepped away from the window, heart in my throat, pacing, bouncing my son in my arms.

"You're safe, Rami. Hush, hush . . . your mother's here. You're safe."

He calmed.

The chamber of audience was large enough to hold a hundred men seated on the floor facing the seat of honor. The ornate camel saddle was placed upon a rise and covered by the finest furs and colorful woven pillows, which provided as much comfort as beauty. Drapes of violet silk hung from the walls, and the room was usually lit by a dozen oil lamps set upon stands.

But they were all dark now, like the rest of the fortress, lit only by the waning sunlight.

I could hear far more than I could see, for camels protest as much in battle as they do rousing from slumber. Their roars reverberated through the city without pause. Shrill battle cries from a thousand Thamud throats accompanied that thunderous camel herd. The punctuating sounds of men and beasts in the throes of death pierced my heart.

The eastern slope was strewn with fallen mounts, camels all of them, taken by Kalb arrows, for the Kalb are known for the bow above all weapons. The sand was weeping blood already.

A Kalb horse raced up a street near the center of the oasis, rider bent low over his mount's neck. No camel could match such speed. And none did, because the fighting was sequestered in the groves along the eastern edge of Dumah, where Rami tested the limits of his every advantage.

I shifted my gaze back to the desert and watched as a camel carrying two riders—one facing forward with reins and one facing backward with full use of his hands—galloped across the slope's open sand. The Thamud warrior at the rear slung arrows into the palms one after the other without pause. Where the arrows landed, I could not see from the palace, but I knew the Kalb were as wise as they were fierce and would not place themselves in the open for arrows to find easily.

A single arrow embedded itself in that warrior's neck, and he toppled unceremoniously from the camel's hump to land in a heap, grasping frantically at the wound. His body went still within moments. I could not deny the thrill of triumph that coursed through my veins at the sight.

And yet he was only one among far too many.

It was the first time I'd witnessed war. In Egypt I'd seen many fight hand to hand with blade or mace or hammer or net, though mostly in training, for my master traded in warriors who fought in an arena for Rome. A brutal business. Johnin, the father of my son, had been among the best, and he had shown me how to defend myself.

But that savagery could not compare to the butchery in Dumah.

Rami would retreat into the city, I thought. The Thamud would abandon their camels. The battle would be taken to the ground. And then to the palace Marid, where I stood.

I closed the shutter, rested my back against the wall, and slid to my seat, uttering a prayer to Isis, who had always failed to listen but might yet, even now. For my sake as much as my son's, I pulled open my dress and allowed Rami to suckle.

Surely my father's noble rule was about to end. Surely the Kalb would not prevail. Surely fate was landing its final, crushing blow.

Unless my father was more god than man.

I could hear the sounds of battle as they moved deeper into the city, closer to me. They ebbed and flowed and at times fell off entirely, and when they did, I would turn my head, listening for stretching silence, hoping against hope.

But then another cry would sound, and the roaring of more camels, and the wailing of another slain. *Thamud*, I prayed. *May the Thamud all drown in their own blood.*

Several times I considered fleeing, but I could not go. Even if I managed through miraculous means to make it to the desert, I would find no home in the sands, for I had no people but these in the palace Marid.

Night came before silence finally settled over the city. Even then I expected yet another cry. Instead a desperate pounding on the door shattered the stillness.

"Maviah!"

I immediately recognized my father's voice. I quickly laid my sleeping son between two pillows and ran to the door.

"Maviah!"

"Father?"

"Hurry, Maviah, there's no time!"

I lifted the board and drew the door wide. My father rushed past me, shoved the door closed, and dropped the timber back into its slot.

He'd discarded his aba and now wore only a bloody shirt and loose pants, shredded along one leg. His face too was red with blood, and his hands sticky with it. A long gash lay along his right arm.

"Father—"

"Listen to me, Maviah!" he interrupted, grasping my arm and pulling me from the door. "There's no time, you have to listen to me very carefully."

He pulled his dagger from its ornate sheath and held the blade out to show me an unmistakable seal etched into the metalwork near the hilt: a circle with a *V* and a Latin inscription, which I could plainly read. *Publius Quinctilius Varus.* And beneath it the image of an eagle.

"This dagger is from Rome and has great significance. It bears the seal of a once-powerful governor—Varus. It is very important that you do exactly what I say. You must swear it to me!"

"Yes! Yes, of course."

"Swear it by your god!"

"Under Isis, I swear it."

He took a deliberate breath. "You must take this seal from Varus to Herod Antipas, the Jewish king in Sepphoris. In Palestine."

I was stunned by this command, unable to comprehend what he was suggesting.

"Take it to him and tell him we can give Rome direct control of the eastern trade route. The Kalb will be a friend to Rome. Tell him we can give Dumah to Rome!"

"Herod of the Jews?" I heard myself say, dumbfounded.

"Herod is the puppet of Rome." He was speaking very quickly. "With this dagger, he will give you audience with Rome."

Rome? The thought terrified me. Rami was beholden to King Aretas, not Rome.

"The king, Aretas—"

"Aretas has turned enemy." He flung his arm wide and stabbed a finger at the window. "*That* is Aretas! He gave the Thamud his blessing should Nasha come to harm!"

I could not comprehend approaching this Herod on Rami's behalf. It struck me as something ordered in a nightmare.

"Then you must send another!" My head was spinning. "I am a woman—"

"I must send my blood for there to be full trust, and Maliku has betrayed me." I'd never seen Rami so crushed. "Shame has been heaped upon the Kalb. Five hundred have been slain; within our walls only the women and children live. We must call the clans to avenge ourselves and return honor to the name of all Kalb! We are thousands! We will rise!"

"Then *you* must go—"

"I cannot leave now—the Thamud won't stop at Dumah. There is only you!"

"How will Herod hear a woman?"

"Because you are my daughter. And because you have *this*." He held the dagger with a trembling hand. "We don't have time now. Saba will tell you everything, then you will know."

I knew Saba to be his greatest warrior and his right hand, a tall black man who spoke with his sword better than with his tongue. All men stood in honor of Saba, sworn servant to my father.

Rami was drowning in the great dishonor heaped upon him. Without honor, there was no life.

But I could not see how I might restore that honor in the world of kings and armies. I was ignorant of the shrewdness required to influence kingdoms and their powers.

My father saw my fear and took my hand, pressing the weapon into my palm. He was reduced to pleading, speaking in a low, rushed voice.

"You must trust me, Maviah. The Romans bend to Aretas only because they have no ally in this desert to match him. We will sustain them in the deadly sands and fight by their side if required. We can give them the Dumah trade route and let Aretas keep the ones along the sea. Today we spit on Aretas."

"Aretas won't allow this..."

"Aretas won't make war on Rome. They are too powerful. You must go to Herod. You must restore the honor of your father and of all the Kalb."

He caught his breath and pressed on.

"You are the daughter of Rami bin Malik, honored of Varus. You are educated and speak the language of the Romans. I will protect your son, who is now my own. I have no other..."

He wrapped my fingers around the dagger.

"Take it. Go to the cave where the eagle perches, north. Saba and Judah have prepared and will take you to Palestine. You know this cave?"

"Yes."

"I trust both men with my life. Saba knows no defeat, nor Judah, who is a Bedu Jew and knows their ways. They wait now with camels."

I knew already that I had to do as he said, for I was his daughter and slave to his honor. But I could not leave my son, despite the honor Rami bestowed upon him.

"My son goes with me. I am his mother."

He stared at me, then nodded. "Then take our son. But you must hurry!" He strode to retrieve the baby. "Take the horse tied at the back. You can get out under cover of darkness. Follow the ravine..."

A thunderous blow sounded at the door and we spun as one. Rami invoked the name of Wadd under his breath.

Then another blow, louder still, shaking the wood to the frame while terror overtook us and we became like stone. There was no escape but through that door, because the window was too high above the street.

On the third strike, the wooden slat snapped in two and the door flew open. There in its frame stood a bloodied warrior dressed in the black fringed *thobe* of the Thamud. But more than this, the dark scowl on the warrior's face marked him as the enemy.

Another Thamud with two behind him stepped past the first, wearing a red-and-yellow headcloth bound by a black agal. By the kaffiyeh's pattern and the boldness in his eyes, I knew that this man was Saman bin Shariqat, leader of the Thamud, conqueror of the Kalb in Dumah.

I glanced at my son, still asleep on the pillows. My son, who was now Rami's only true son.

My father stepped in front of me with one hand pressing me back and the other stretched out as if to hold the Thamud away.

"There's been enough blood," Rami said, his tone now even.

Saman bin Shariqat's brow rose. "There is no more Kalb blood to shed in Dumah. I would not take the life of a sheikh when I can use it for greater gain."

"The blood of ten Thamud mingles with the blood of every Kalb you have slain today," Rami said.

"And yet you are defeated. Payment for many years of robbery, here in the seat of your defiled fortress."

"I've taken only what was mine to take."

"And now I do the same," Saman said, mouth twisted with amusement.

These were words of honor and retribution, expected among enemies. Yet it was absurd that Saman should count this massacre as blood money for Rami's control of the trade routes.

"I will allow you to live so that all Bedu may know my mercy," Saman said. "But I swear in the name of King Aretas, whose daughter now lies dead on your account, that Rami bin Malik shall never again utter a word of command."

"My Kalb will rise up and crush you," Rami said, trembling with rage.

"And yet your son, Maliku, assures me that the Kalb are already mine."

Rami remained silent.

"I now take what I have won," Saman said.

Rami slowly dipped his head, then spoke, voice calm. "As is your right. My life is in your hands. Spare only the woman and her child."

Rami showed no fear. He had been bested by treachery but even this was, in its own way, honorable. He would now accept his fate, wishing only to save me so that I might return his honor by going to the Jews and then to Rome.

But I too was at the mercy of these ruthless Bedu.

Saman's eyes lingered on my face for a moment, then lowered to my right hand, which held the dagger of Varus.

"As the gods will. My son, Kahil, is going to show you my own will. With your blade."

The man who'd broken through the door stepped past my father, took the dagger from my hand, and shoved Rami toward the corner. The two warriors who'd accompanied Saman grabbed my father's arms and slammed him against the wall.

I watched, horrified, as Kahil lifted the very blade in which the hope of the Kalb now rested. I turned my face away.

Still, I could hear the grunts of the Thamud. The slap of flesh against flesh. There was no struggle because Rami offered none— not even an objection, for he was a man concerned only with his honor now.

"Take him away," Saman said. "Keep him alive."

Only then did I dare look. They held up my sagging father by his arms. He trembled with pain; blood flowed from his mouth into his beard. I could see Kahil shoving something into his belt.

Then I knew. They had cut out Rami's tongue.

I would surely have thrown myself at them if I hadn't feared for my son's life. I had no love for my father, but Rami had offered himself for our safety. It was the first time he'd ever shown me any kindness.

He watched me as they dragged him toward the door. In his eyes I saw resolve and pleading both. To see the great sheikh so reduced filled me with rage, but I was powerless.

Saman took my father's dagger from his gloating son, wiped the bloody blade on his cloak, and shoved it under his belt.

Already my mind was spinning with ways I might retrieve it. They were going to spare me and my son, but without the blade, I would have no hope of honoring Rami's wishes. If I failed him, what would I be but bones in the desert, and my son with me?

My only hope rested in that dagger.

Saman strode toward the door, casting me only a passing glance. "Set her free. Take her out of my house."

And then he was gone, leaving me alone with Kahil and little Rami, who still slept.

Kahil eyed me with interest. His lust for blood had been satisfied today, but men have many lusts.

"What is your name?" he asked.

"Maviah."

Recognition dawned on his face.

"Maviah," he said slowly. "So this is the woman they speak about. The whore from the tribe that crushes up the bones of carcasses and makes them into soup." He spit to his side. "The Abysm are worse than dogs. And yet the Kalb keep one in their sheikh's tent."

I had no intention of upsetting him further, but I was pleased to see the desire washed from his face. His eyes now looked me over with disgust.

"How can such a beautiful woman come from the dogs? You defile my father's house."

I saw his hand only a moment before it landed a crushing blow to my face and sent me to the floor. I could have resisted. Though none in Dumah knew, in Egypt I had learned how to defend myself well. But resisting a man was the greatest of offenses.

Take his abuse, Maviah. Say nothing. Save your son. Save yourself.

When I pushed myself up, he was gone, and relief flooded my bones. I would gather little Rami and flee to the cave, where Saba would know what to do.

But then I saw that Kahil hadn't left the room. He was to my right, over my son. Now grabbing him by one foot. Pulling him off the pillows as if he were a sack.

Terror found my throat. I screamed, blinded by rage and revulsion. I clawed at the floor and surged to my feet, throwing myself forward.

"No!"

But I was already too late. As if throwing out garbage, Kahil bin Saman pulled open the shuttered window and flung my baby into the night.

I could not breathe. I could not think. I could only scream and watch, knowing even as I lunged for the window that my son was falling and would never rise.

"Rami!"

When I thrust my head into the opening, it was too dark to see the ground.

"Rami!" I begged the gods for the sound of a cry, a whimper, any sound at all.

But I knew already, didn't I? I knew that my son was dead. And yet my mind could not truly know this, because it was blackened with such torment that it could not make any sense of that dark world beneath me.

I had to save him.

I did not care about the monster who'd thrown him from the window. I was compelled only by the ferocious need of a mother to save her child.

I don't recall running for the door.

I don't remember tearing down the stairs, or rushing into the street.

I only recall seeing Rami's still form on the stone as I raced to him. And then the feel of his warm skin as I fell to my knees and reached for his lifeless body.

A terrible groan issued from my throat and I felt anguish pulling me into the abyss. It could not be! It was a mistake. A nightmare borne by ghouls.

And yet it was real. I could see his broken head.

The greater part of me died then, as I lowered my head to his back, pressed my cheek against his still body, and clung to his little hands and feet, weeping.

I begged Isis to take me. I cursed the world for all its injustice. I despised every breath I took, and yet my weeping only grew until great sobs racked my body.

"My son is still a boy," a low voice said to my left.

I thought it was my father, speaking to me from his spirit.

"And yours only an infant."

I stilled at those words, confused. Then opened my eyes without lifting my head.

It was the Thamud leader, Saman bin Shariqat. He was mounted on a horse, only just leaving, holding a torch in his left hand to light his way. But his presence was of no consequence to the dead, and I was as dead to him as he to me.

Then the man grunted.

A single dismissive grunt.

The sound loosed a torrent of rage deep inside my chest. Though a part of me had died with my son, another part rose from the dead then, with that grunt.

Filled with the darkest storm, I slowly lifted my head and looked at him, not seven paces from where I knelt over my son's dead body.

He shifted his gaze forward, as if to leave.

The moment he turned I was on my feet and sprinting toward him without a sound. My father's dagger was still in his belt, lit by the golden light of the torch.

He clearly had not expected me to move. He had expected even less that I could move so quickly. And even less that I might attack with the ferocity and skill of a trained fighter. He could not know that the father of my son, Johnin, had been among the strongest and bravest of all warrior-slaves in Egypt.

Saman dropped the torch to the ground and was grabbing for his sword when I reached him. But he was far too slow.

I snatched my father's dagger from his waist and thrust at his neck. He jerked back with a surprised cry, avoiding a wound that would have surely taken his life.

Without hesitation, I dragged the blade through his thigh as I dropped to a crouch, then spun and slashed the horse's neck through to the jugular. I could not leave Saman with a mount to give chase.

The beast was already falling and Saman roaring as I sprinted for my son's body. I had to take him with me.

But Kahil, the monster who'd thrown Rami from the window, had entered the street and was running for me. And behind him three others who'd been trailing Saman.

It took me only a single breath to realize that I could not retrieve my son and survive. I would be laden with his body. If I died, Varus's blade, now in my hand, would be taken.

Most in Egypt believed that the body must be preserved for the soul in the afterlife, thus they buried their dead in stone tombs or pyramids, depending on wealth and stature. The Nabataeans also placed hope in great tombs. But neither the Bedu nor I had adopted such beliefs. I prayed now that I wasn't wrong.

"Forgive me, my son." I whispered the words with a last look at his tiny form.

Then I veered to my left, breathing a prayer to Isis for his well-being in the afterlife, and sprinted for the darkness behind the palace Marid.

CHAPTER FOUR

THE DARKNESS was my friend as I fled Dumah on foot, often ducking behind trees and boulders to avoid the pursuit of Saman's men. Had it been day, they would have found and killed me.

I was a bundle of torment, torn between the desperate impulse to return for my son's body and the need to live so that I could avenge him. Rage pushed me, guilt ravaged me, sorrow pulled me to my knees even as I stumbled time and again along the path beyond the city.

It was with a black heart that I found the shallow cave.

The moon cast a gentle light over the sand and the rock, enough for me to see my father's dark-skinned warrior and two equipped camels that gnawed on tufts of desert grass nearby.

Saba was dressed for the desert in long pants beneath a loose cloak that parted at his breastbone, revealing a powerful chest and a necklace of bones and stones that came from his homeland. His head was bald. A bow hung from his back and a dagger from each of his hips, fastened by a sash.

Saba had seen me and waited without coming to my aid. Even when I stopped before him, he only glanced at the dagger in my hand, then studied me with wide eyes.

I could not imagine how he'd survived the battle and retrieved the supplies and camels. Unless the camels had been prepared beforehand, in the event the Thamud attacked and Dumah was overrun.

I looked around for a sign of this Judah but saw none.

"Your father?"

"He's alive," I said. "They cut off his tongue."

To this Saba offered no reaction.

"And your son?"

My resolve to be strong failed me at those words. Tears flooded my eyes.

"They killed him," I said.

He wasn't one to show emotion, but he didn't hide the disgust that crossed his face. "Who did this?"

"Kahil bin Saman. He…" But my throat choked off the telling of how.

"The Thamud are a savage people," he muttered. He took the dagger of Varus from me and motioned to the cave. "We wait. Judah will come soon."

I thought to ask him what he knew about our journey, for my father had said Saba would make all things plain, but my heart was too heavy. I walked to the cave and stood, at a loss, watching Saba, who squatted nearby, studying the night.

I was accustomed to hardship, as are all mothers in the desert. A full third of children perished from hunger or disease soon after their birth. Indeed, among some tribes the practice of discarding female infants was accepted. But nothing can prepare a mother for such a loss. The depth of the night sky could not compare to the black void in my chest.

And yet there was something new in that hollow space where my heart had once beat. A dark power that began to give me life. A purpose that fueled my desire to stay alive. A bitterness that burned hot and lit the path before me.

My resolve to restore my father's honor was now replaced by a terrible need to avenge my son's death. As I thought of his tiny broken body on the street, nothing else mattered to me. I would do as my father willed not for the Kalb, but for my son's honor. My hatred for the Thamud and for Maliku, who had led them to Dumah, became a black stone in my chest.

I cursed Maliku. I cursed Kahil and all Thamud. I cursed the gods who had shown my son no mercy.

Saba stood and stared into the night, and I followed his eyes. From the darkness came a man leading two camels, one of them Shunu, my own. This was then Judah, the Jew. He was perhaps twenty, near my own age, younger than the dark warrior. Unlike Saba, he wore a kaffiyeh on his head.

He approached Saba, spoke quickly in soft tones while looking my way, then gave him charge of the camels and came to me. By the light of the rising moon I saw that Judah's facial hair was neatly trimmed and his eyes were kind, set in a gentle face, distinctly Bedu. He was a handsome man by any standard, and as strong as Saba, though not as tall.

Judah spoke to me with utter sincerity. "As I am the servant of Rami, sheikh of all Kalb, I am the servant of God and now your protector. I will take you swiftly to the land of my people."

I didn't know how to respond.

"I am deeply regretful of your loss," he said in a hushed tone. "The Thamud are dogs." He spit to one side, then raised a finger to the sky. "The God of Abraham, Isaac, and Jacob will avenge you."

He lowered his hand and continued.

"I curse Kahil bin Saman, and his father, and all of the Thamud who share in their treachery. God will smite them with his fist and crush their bones to sand, for they know no mercy."

A passionate man of many words.

"And do your gods?" I asked.

"Do they what?"

"Know mercy?"

He hesitated. "I have only one God, the true God. He shows mercy to those who keep his commandments and crushes those who do not."

He was the first Bedu I'd met who followed the religion of the Jews, though they were not so uncommon in some parts. I'd heard they worshipped only one god.

"And do you?" I asked.

"Do I what?"

"Follow his commandments."

"But of course! As best I can. But I have been known to misunderstand them often and fail some on occasion."

"And when you fail?"

"Then I must once again win his favor."

"How?"

"With the blood of a goat or an offering of wheat."

"So, then, you have only one god who's like all the rest. I would choose many over only one."

"Yes, but my God is far greater! The only true God. He will protect you, Maviah, for his servant is Judah and he has placed you in my charge."

I placed no value in his words, for no god had ever prevailed on my behalf. And if my father could be crushed in the space of one battle, what security was there for any ruler or kingdom, much less me?

Still, Judah's words were kind.

"Thank you."

Saba had gathered the camels and led them toward us. They could not have been more different from each other, Saba and this Judah. And yet all three of us had a common bond. We had all come to Dumah from far away. We were all Bedu, if not by blood then in life. And we now all shared the same objective, to reach Herod.

Judah's eyes shone with pride. "You will see. We will take you to Herod and return to Dumah with the full might of Rome. And then, when the time is right, we will cut Rome off at its knees. You will see."

"Cut Rome off?"

"They are tyrants!"

"You've been there?"

"To Rome? No. A lion cannot sleep with the hyena."

"Have you been to Palestine?"

"My people call it the land of Israel. Call it what you may, the Holy Land belongs only to Israel. And, yes, I have been there. Though only once."

"When?"

"As a young boy. It has been my dream to return. The elders of my tribe in the north traveled there before I was born."

None of this gave me great assurance. But I knew my father was no fool. I would have to trust his choice of Saba and Judah.

"We must leave," Saba said. "On foot to the flint desert."

We had four camels, three she-camels in milk and one younger male. Noisy animals, to be sure, always groaning and moaning and chewing cud with grinding teeth. Although I'd only recently learned the proper way to ride a camel, I found them far more personable than horses. Indeed, my Shunu, a fair-coated camel given to me by Nasha, was like a friend to me, as all camels were to their owners. They were as much pets as mounts and sources of fuel, milk, and meat.

In the soft dunes and sands, the camel was far more adept than any mount, able to cross great distances at a run without need of frequent watering. Such magnificent creatures were indeed the landship of the desert.

She-camels in milk were most valuable in desert crossings, for their milk offered sustenance where there was no water. A good she-camel could travel a full day at a trot and drink only every fifth day, while offering her rider two liters of milk per day. Indeed, so valuable was a she-camel's milk that her udders were often covered so that her calves couldn't drain her. If properly cared for, she might be in milk for well over a year after giving birth.

The male camel, bearing no saddle, carried extra stores and, if needed, could be slaughtered to provide meat. Each animal was loaded with goatskins filled with water, enough water to make me wonder which route we would take. They also carried saddlebags filled with teas, herbs to spice drink and food, and flour and dates to be cooked with whatever meat we hunted along the way. For fuel, camel dung would suffice if there was no wood to be found. I saw blankets for padding and for warmth at night. No tent.

To survive for many weeks in the desert, a Bedu requires only these supplies, a camel, and a knife, bow, or sword.

I approached Shunu and rubbed my hand along her neck as she sniffed my head and flapped her lips near my ear. She was now my closest friend. Perhaps my only. Her calf had long parted ways with her—at times I was convinced she thought I was her calf.

"Come, Shunu," I whispered, taking her rope and guiding her forward.

We walked in silence, single file, first Judah, then me, then Saba, who kept a watchful eye to our rear.

If there was no trouble, it would take us ten nights to reach Petra and another six to reach Galilee, I thought. But much could go wrong in the desert, and the trade route along the Wadi Sirhan was well traveled. Surely the Thamud would give pursuit. These matters I would leave to Judah and Saba. If I died I would join my son; if I lived I would avenge his death.

We mounted when we reached the flint rocks, an endless bed of jagged black stone difficult for even a camel to negotiate. Still, a good tracker could follow the signs even here. The best would know from the dung and hoofprints precisely which camel had passed and when. It was said that some Bedu could remember the track of every camel they had ever seen.

At the very least, a tracker could tell from the depth and shape of the track far more than I could. What kind of camel, whether she was in milk, which clan rode the beast, how long she had walked or run. And by the droppings, where the camel had last grazed, how long since she had last been watered, and where she was likely headed to find water, for they knew all the wells and how long any camel might go without drink.

In this way the sands told the story of all who passed, as clearly as markings on parchment.

But the flint beds would slow down any pursuit, which would have to wait until morning's light. Crossing them was treacherous and the camels protested at nearly every step. My back quickly grew sore for all the jerking and swaying.

Not a word was spoken, and I found no desire to break the silence. Our only accompaniment was the protests of the camels, who grunted and snorted every few steps, urged forward by our sticks, which we struck gently along their necks to keep them moving.

Their objections were quieted somewhat when Saba instructed us to tie their mouths shut, but camels can speak even from their throats, and quite loudly.

The end of the flint desert came suddenly, edging a vast sand that reached toward distant, towering dunes silhouetted by moonlight. There we stopped, gazing ahead in awe.

"The Nafud," Judah said, as if speaking the name of a god.

The Nafud? But we were meant to go northwest toward Petra and Palestine, not south. I had assumed we were taking only a short detour to avoid detection.

Judah offered an explanation even as the concern entered my mind.

"They will expect us to have escaped north, along the Wadi Sirhan. At first light the Thamud will search far and wide for any sign of us, and their best trackers will find it, here, into the Nafud, which will give them great pause." He seemed delighted with this. "Few can pass through this desert without proper preparations. They will assume we are dead."

I nearly said that the assumption would be warranted. The shifting sands of the Nafud were well known to reduce human and beast to white bones. They formed a wall that had long protected all of southern Arabia from the northern kingdoms of Persia and Greece and Mesopotamia, which had long sought her treasures. The few wells were far apart and often dry, the fiery sun treacherous, the blowing sands a storm of wrath that could blind the eyes and strip the flesh. I understood the desire to avoid the enemy behind us, but was the Nafud any less a foe?

As I looked at the distant, immense dunes, a chill cut through my bones.

"I have been across," Saba said quietly. "It is difficult but passable. The stars will lead Judah by night; the sands will lead me by day. Though we both read sand and stars, we have our strengths."

"They will not pursue us here, Maviah," Judah said, smiling. Did this confidence come from his noble spirit or simple stupidity?

And then I remembered what my father had said about Judah. He and Saba both—the best men he knew. Still, I thought they should be very clear about how strongly I'd motivated the Thamud.

I stared ahead and spoke softly. "I slashed Saman's leg and cut his horse's throat," I said. "While he was yet mounted."

I could feel their eyes on me. Their silence stretched.

"He was upset," I said.

"Saman bin Shariqat?" Judah asked, as if still trying to believe.

"I was angry," I said.

"*You* did this?"

"Only because he pulled his own throat away from my blade. The same blade he took from my father after cutting out his tongue with it."

A light sparkled in his eyes. "Then he is now a rabid dog." He faced forward and whistled softly. "God has given us an avenging angel in Rami's daughter."

No, I thought. It wasn't any god's doing.

"Such an insult wasn't wise," Saba said.

"An insult?" Judah scoffed. "And did Bin Shariqat not insult the daughter of Rami?"

Saba looked none too pleased but held his tongue.

Judah did not. "My only envy is that it wasn't my hand at his throat. He would be dead already."

His unwavering self-assurance calmed me.

"Also," I said, "Maliku is allied with the Thamud."

Saba turned his head and stared at me.

"You know this?"

"Saman spoke of it. My father as well."

He grunted. "The fool doesn't yet know the depths of Thamud treachery. What is born of blood will only grow in that same blood. This is Maliku's fate."

"And ours is now a promised land," Judah said. "There we will find the makings of a new fate at God's hand."

And yet neither of them seemed anxious to head into the Nafud to find Judah's promised land.

My mind returned to the dagger I was to show Herod.

"My father told me you would tell me about the dagger, Saba. Our lives depend on it. I would know."

He nodded, then spoke in a low tone, eyes fixed on the dunes.

"Many years ago, long before you were born, before Rami was sheikh, he was well known for his command of men in raiding. The Nabataean king, Aretas, had heard of him and called upon him to prove his might in the land of the Jews."

"Palestine? Rami?"

Judah spoke. "The Jews have always resented the Romans, who rule them with Jewish kings who have Roman hearts. Herod Antipas is king in Galilee now, but his father ruled as a butcher, and when he died, the people rose up in rebellion led by a Zealot named Judas bin Hezekiah. A great man in the eyes of many. It was Judas the Zealot that Rami went to crush." He paused. "And for this I forgive him still."

I knew then that Judah's heart was divided.

"Why would the Nabataean king call the Bedu to Palestine?" I asked. "This is Roman business, not Nabataean."

"These are complicated matters of kingdoms, not best understood by women," Saba said.

Judah wasn't as dismissive of me. "She has a right." He faced me. "Palestine was in the charge of a powerful Roman governor named Varus, who found his charge threatened by the rebellion of the Jewish Zealot, Judas. And so Varus called on King Aretas of the Nabataeans, because Nabataea borders Palestine and would also be threatened if the Zealots could not be crushed. Also, Aretas owed the Romans a favor. Thus Aretas called on the Bedu, through Rami, to aid him. You see how it works...the Romans call on the Nabataeans and the Nabataeans call on the Bedu. There are no warriors so great as the Bedu."

"So my father went on Aretas's behalf, forming an alliance."

"Yes," Saba said. "Rami took a thousand Kalb, the best of raiders, to ride with the Nabataeans into Galilee, to the city called Sepphoris, which had been overtaken by the Jewish Zealots. Together with Varus's army, they crushed the revolt in Sepphoris and burned the city to the ground. The Zealots fled. It was a great victory."

Judah spit to one side.

"For Rami and Rome, not for my people. After he left Palestine, Varus went throughout the south, hounding the Zealots to a bitter end. His army crucified over two thousand in one month alone. Truly, all Jews mourn them still."

I was familiar with the Roman crucifixion—a brutal death sentence meant to terrify those who saw victims hanging on the tree as much as to punish the guilty. I did not relish being witness to such a scene.

"I'm sorry," I said.

Saba seemed unconcerned.

"To honor Rami, Varus presented him with his own dagger. Rami returned from Galilee a victor in the eyes of both the Romans and Aretas, and for this the Nabataean king honored him, years later, with full control over all trade through Dumah, sealed by his marriage to Nashquya, niece of Aretas. In her death, he will now see Rami as enemy."

I understood the rest: the Romans and Herod would give me audience because they owed Rami a debt of gratitude, to be proven by the dagger.

We sat on the camels in silence.

"But now," Judah said, looking into the desert, "our greatest enemy is the Nafud."

He turned his gaze to the stars and I knew he was reading them, for the Bedu trackers find their way at night by the lights in the sky.

"One stage south, then twelve stages west to Aela," he said. "From there, north into Perea, Decapolis, and to Galilee. Perhaps we will find him there."

"Perhaps? Herod is in Sepphoris."

"Yes, of course. Herod." Judah said this as if he'd been thinking of someone else. He lovingly scratched his camel's neck, for he, like most Bedu, was very fond of his mount. Her name was Raza and she leaned into his fingers.

"Herod, who conspires with Rome for the ruin of all Jews," he said absently.

Again he betrayed the conflict in his heart. Though a servant to my father vowed to deliver me into an alliance with the Romans, he despised all that was Roman. He was as much a Zealot as a Bedu, and his desire to reach Palestine was directed by something even deeper than his loyalty to Rami.

"We go," Saba said.

"To glory or to our graves," Judah said. Then he turned to me, eyes bright. "But at my side it will only be glory."

Saba grunted. He slapped his camel with his riding stick and urged it toward the dunes.

I nudged Shunu to follow, keenly aware that our fate, whatever it might be, was now sealed, for there is no forgiveness in the Nafud.

THE NAFUD

"Truly I tell you, unless a kernel of wheat falls to the
    ground and dies,
it remains only a single seed.
But if it dies, it produces many seeds."

Yeshua

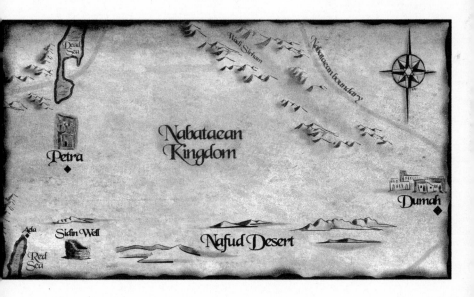

CHAPTER FIVE

ON THE FLAT desert leading up to the dunes, we passed clumps of ghada shrubs. Their white, fist-size fruit is good only for medicinal purposes, for it is a bitter fruit, but the ghada wood burns hot and is used to light the fires of all who live along the Nafud's edges.

I could not keep my sorrow at bay, but I did not wish to appear weak, so I kept my thoughts to myself and mourned in silence. Judah remained quiet as well, though I suspected this was because he sensed my need for solace.

As for Saba, he might have remained mute in any circumstance.

The pale dunes of the northern Nafud rose like mountains and cast shadows even in the darkness. Judah was riding with one leg tucked under him, as was the preferred position for long stretches. We had traveled the flat for over an hour before he began to sing under his breath.

To this, Saba took exception, so Judah went silent again, but within a short time, his voice rose softly in song once more.

Again Saba looked at him with disapproval.

"Do you think my song will carry farther than the roars of these beasts as we climb the dunes?" Judah asked.

"Silence is now our language of choice," Saba said, voice deep and soft.

"Perhaps the language of your choice," Judah returned. "But I feel the camels prefer song. It woos them."

"Beasts are not wooed by song. You've mistaken them for women."

"You don't like the sound of my voice, Saba? How can you pretend to be so stiff? Around the fire, all Bedu love my song."

"I see no fire."

"I will teach you to sing, Saba. Before we reach the Holy Land you will sing and a hundred women will watch you with desire in their eyes."

Saba grunted. "We search for a king, not a woman to keep you warm."

"But I must teach you to sing. Like an eagle in the sky, calling all birds to follow. Like a wolf haunting the night with its call. Song will fill your throat and even kings will stand in wonder."

"You speak too much. Where I come from, silence is the greatest song of the human heart. Only in silence can the call of the sands be heard. Quiet your tongue now and you will still hear the mourning of those in Dumah."

"And does not song comfort those who mourn?" Judah looked at the sky. "I now call for God, who is in the heavens, to hear our song and comfort his people."

Saba spoke evenly in his low voice. "There is no god in the heavens. He sits upon your camel even now."

"Then let God sing!" Judah said.

I had to smile as I rode behind them. The Bedu cannot help but argue. Indeed, even Saba had violated his own demand for silence.

"Let him sing, Saba," I said quietly. "The silence pulls at my heart."

"You see!" Judah said. "We must lift her heart to the sky so that it may soar once again. Sing, Saba! Sing for us."

Saba wasn't impressed, and though he quit his objections he refused to sing.

Judah gave me a knowing smile and began to sing again, softly, in poetic verse, about the desert and the stars and his god, who had made all things with his breath. Judah kept his eyes ahead and looked at the sky often. And after a time, I saw that Saba had settled on his mount, accepting.

When we came to the base of the first dune, I was sure that no camel could climb its steep slope. Surely there was an easier way around. But neither Judah nor Saba appeared bothered by that wall of sand.

"We lead them from here," Saba said, pulling up and dismounting. "Keep the camels moving."

He dropped to the ground, gathered the lead rope, and tugged his camel forward. The unsaddled male trudged behind, tied to the tail of Saba's mount.

I followed directly, and Judah behind me, in Saba's tracks. These cut a line across and up the dune's steep face. The soft sand swallowed my sandals and my feet to the ankles, and I struggled to maintain my balance while tugging on Shunu's lead. She made her displeasure plain, moaning loudly every other step, pulling against her rope.

We were only a quarter of the way up when I stopped, thinking that even a camel knew such a path was madness. To my left the sand rose like a cliff to an insurmountable peak, black against the night sky. To my right it fell away at such a grade that I was sure one slip would send me tumbling to the bottom. It had taken us far too long to reach this unremarkable height, and we had only just begun.

"All is well, Maviah!" Judah cried behind me. "This is not too steep for Shunu." He was pulling his own stubborn beast, and now he placed a hand on Shunu's rump and gave her a shove. "You see? She goes."

So I slogged forward, thinking that there was no turning back to the death in Dumah. My only hope lay ahead, over this dune and all that I couldn't yet see.

With each step I was sure that the sand would collapse under my feet, or that one of the camels would finally tumble down. I often stumbled to a knee, clambered back to my feet, and pushed on. I was tugging Shunu, but in truth she was my anchor. Only my firm grasp on her lead rope kept me from sliding down the slope when I lost my footing.

"It is close, Maviah," Judah would say, pushing against my camel's hindquarters as he pulled at his own mount. "Now we can almost touch the top. And then it will be easy."

He would say such a thing though the peak still rose like a lance far above our heads. And yet his voice soothed me like a warm wind from behind.

It took us nearly as long to climb that first behemoth as it had to cross the flats. But we finally crested the ridge and I was full of triumph until the way before us came into view.

The pale sands extended as far as I could see, hundreds and thousands of towering billows, some as high as the one we'd just ascended. My heart fell. How one could cross such a sea of sand, I didn't know.

"You see," Judah beamed, teeth white by the moonlight. "Not even the Thamud will follow us here."

He was indeed the consummate optimist.

"We go," Saba said.

"We go," Judah echoed.

And so we went. Down at an angle, sliding and nearly falling as frequently as we had during the ascent. But at a much faster pace.

We followed a trough between the slopes and scaled the next dune at a lower point, but even so, my legs could hardly support me by the time we reached its crest. After consulting with Judah, who in turn consulted the stars, Saba led us along several lower dunes over which we could ride mounted.

Then we were confronted with another wall of sand, and once again we plowed our way up its face before sliding down the far side.

And so it went for another two hours before we reached a wide valley of sand. Judah pointed the way and we continued without a rest, mounted once again.

Our tired camels plodded abreast now, separated by ten paces each, too spent to keep up their complaining. A bitter cold had set in, so we wrapped our cloaks and scarves around our necks and arms.

Judah's song, when he began to sing again, soothed me. Saba offered no opposition this time. Indeed, I was sure that I heard him hum a time or two. Judah sang to the stars, he sang to Raza, he sang to his god, he sang to all Bedu and all Jews.

Judah came to the end of a song and pulled his mount close to mine. For a while he rode without speaking, frequently glancing at the sky.

"Does my song comfort you, Maviah?"

His voice was tender and when I looked into his eyes, they were the same.

"Yes," I said.

"All my life I have been singing, as do all Bedu. But not all with their hearts, I think." He looked high again. "The day of redemption is coming. You will see, Maviah. The stars see it already."

I followed his stare but imagined nothing of what the stars could see except three Bedu fleeing through a sea of sand.

"What do you think when you stare at the stars?" I asked.

"I am remembering my own tribe, where the wisest of men read them as easily as other Bedu read the sands."

"Which tribe? May I ask?"

"You may speak to me as you will," he said. And I knew then that Judah was rare among the Bedu. "I am from the Kokobanu tribe, north. The stars foretell all things, though their words are known only to few."

I had heard only once of these distant Bedu who studied the stars. Surely they were a visionary people enamored with dreams and hope. Like Judah.

"And what do the stars say about our journey?" I asked.

"They say nothing about this journey. But they led the elders on a journey many years ago." He spoke with great reverence. "A star led them to a new king, who will deliver his people from their oppression and slavery, as foretold by the prophets of God long ago."

In the desert there is no end to folklore and talk of distant gods.

"Your people have seen this king?"

"Not as king. But the elders saw him and offered gifts. It is my hope that I too will see him."

"You don't speak of Herod?"

"God forbid! Herod is a jackal who betrays all Jews. I speak of the Anointed One, who will see Herod and Rome crushed!"

Saba broke his silence. "We go to Herod with the dagger of Varus for favor. Watch your tongue or he might take it from you."

"Is Herod here in the sands to hear me?"

"If we reach Palestine, he will read the hatred in your eyes."

"They will not read the eyes of Judah! I am far too clever."

Clearly Judah had many hopes. But surely he wouldn't betray my father for this other passion of his.

"He has a name, this king?" I asked.

"This is not spoken among my people, for fear his life would be threatened if he were exposed. At any rate, a true king needs only the name of God."

"Then how will you find him?"

"The sun will rise with him, as with any king. His words will call all Jews out of oppression." Judah used his hands to emphasize his words. "And also, I know where he was born. He is the seed of David, who was also a king."

"So, then, perhaps your king will save us from our oppressors as well."

"But of course! You must only worship him."

Naturally, I thought. And offer him sacrifices or gifts.

"And will he restore honor to a woman sold into slavery?"

"Even as he led his people out of slavery long ago."

"And will he give a mother her child back?"

This quieted him. After a moment he said, "Perhaps not. But I think he could give you many sons."

The sand, for centuries unmoved save to drift back and forth on strong winds, continued to pass beneath us.

"The father of your son, where is he?" Judah asked.

I hesitated, because it was improper to speak of such things to men, even more to strangers. And yet I was in their charge, so I decided then to tell them whom they were escorting through the Nafud. In the wake of my son's death, I no longer had anything to lose.

"You know that I was born to a defiled mother among the Abysm tribe."

My boldness caught even Judah slightly off guard. When he spoke, his voice was gentle.

"Yes."

"Rami sent me away to Egypt when I was an infant, where I was sold as a slave to a wealthy Roman household. My master traded in wares between Egypt and Rome."

The camels plodded on.

"When I was eleven, he began to trade in fighters for the arenas. He purchased strong slaves and trained them to fight with sword and hammer and spear. Gladiators, some call these fighters. My son's father was the strongest of them all. He was given the name Titus by the master. I knew him as Johnin of Persia."

A soft whistle of wonder from Judah. Saba was watching me as well.

"Why did you not stay with your husband?" Judah asked.

"A slave isn't permitted to marry," I said. "In my eighteenth year we grew close in secret. But when I showed with child, our secret was discovered and the mistress became angry. She would have Johnin as her own."

My companions remained silent.

"The master had always favored his best slaves and showed me mercy. But I had to leave. His wife could no longer tolerate either me or Johnin. He was sent to the north and I heard later that he perished in Rome. I was sent to another village, where I gave birth. When my son was old enough to travel, I was returned to Dumah with a caravan."

They said nothing. If I'd been a man, colorful words of praise for my survival and brazen declarations of outrage at my enemies would by now be flowing.

"So now you know whom you risk your life for," I said.

"We risk our lives for Rami's blood," Saba said. "And for his will."

"Then serve Rami well," I said. "Without him, I am nothing."

When Judah finally spoke, there was a new heaviness in his voice.

"It is said that a woman is born into shame," he said. "It is also said by some that a Jew is born the same. And yet there was once a Jew who came out of Egypt and set his people free."

I did not know what he referred to, but I didn't press.

He looked at me. "I think you are wrong, Maviah. You are Rami's blood, yes, but more, you are his will. And as his will, you may return honor to your people." He returned to staring ahead. "Even as the Messiah will restore the honor of all Jews."

"I will return to avenge my son," I said. "Rami has only heaped suffering on us both."

I regretted my words the moment they left my mouth.

"Forgive me," I said. "I speak too quickly."

"As I said, to me, you may speak as you like," Judah said. "I am Rami's servant, and now he sends me home to the Holy Land. If I had not left my tribe and sworn myself to his service, I would still be in the deepest sands. We must both accept God's will. You will see."

It was typical Bedu fatalism.

"Tell her, Saba. It is best to accept."

Saba answered hesitantly. "To accept, yes, though not as the will of any god. We are not his slaves. We are the slaves of those who rise over us."

"And would you not crush those who rise over you?" Judah asked.

"To what end? So that they might rise again? There is no end to uprising and war."

"And yet you swear vengeance for Rami," Judah said.

"He is my master and has expressed his will. I gave myself in service to him and count myself his slave, and so I accept my duty." In calling himself slave, Saba only honored Rami, for he was not owned by Rami as a lowly slave. Truly, he was sworn servant, not slave—Bedu used the term liberally. In fact, Saba was one of Rami's most trusted warriors, commanding the largest raiding parties. "To desire more than service only breeds endless suffering."

"Then I will suffer for my God and be his hand of vengeance against those who crush the Jews!" Judah said.

They went on, back and forth, my son's death already long behind them. Such was the Bedu way in such a harsh land. And in this respect, they were both right: I must accept my fate.

Indeed, I found their argument amusing. In his own way, each was equally right, and they often said the same thing, though expressed very differently.

Coming to no agreement, Judah ended their banter.

"We disagree over little," he finally said. "We agree on our charge, whether from man or God or both. Maviah possesses Rami's dagger, and with it, the hope of honor for the Banu Kalb. For this charge I will offer my life."

"And I," Saba said.

In that moment I felt honored to be in their company.

Nothing more of my past was spoken of that night, but I was happy to have bared my heart and remained in their good graces. And when Judah began to sing again, I wished I knew the songs.

We traveled until we were all too exhausted to remain awake in the saddle, for both Judah and Saba had been in battle that day, and I had lost all my strength to grief. Still we passed the wide valley and several more dunes before Saba finally pulled up at the base of tall, jutting rocks and announced that we would sleep for a few hours.

"We will eat," Judah announced, bounding to the sand.

Saba withdrew a skin and began to milk the she-camels. There was a bundle of wood and dried camel dung in one of the saddlebags, and Judah laid these down for a fire.

There was no tent to erect and I felt strange, watching a man work while I stood by. But Judah was far more practiced with limited supplies and there was little to do. Furthermore, he seemed pleased to serve, which too surprised me. He soon had a small fire burning and was preparing food.

I sat watching with both legs pulled to one side as he mixed flour and water in a pan and coaxed it into a thick dough. After forming six small cakes, he quickly seared each on a bed of hot coals, then covered them with sand and laid the red coals on top. In this way the clean desert sand made an oven that baked the bread quickly and without burning it. Once the cakes were cooked, he brushed away the grit.

"Tell me, Maviah," he said, looking up at me with a smile. "When the Bedu serve food in the camp, who gets the largest portion?"

I hesitated.

"The guest."

"And if there is no guest?"

"Then they cast lots."

"Yes, each man hoping for the smallest portion so as to honor the others. Otherwise the men will fight, insisting they have been given too much food and refusing to eat, for fear they will dishonor the others. I saw once a Bedu throw down his guest's tent in outrage when the guest insisted on eating the smaller portion without casting lots."

And yet in a raid that same man might slit the throat of that same guest to relieve him of his camel, for the Bedu are a raiding people, free to take any man's camel so long as it is taken by force and not stolen unseen, which is shameful.

Upon my returning from Egypt it was at first difficult for me to understand these conflicting ways, but I had come to see that a tenuous balance allowed for survival in the desert, for what was taken by force was also shared with honor, otherwise raiding would soon empty the sands of all living souls. As it was, there was only enough water in the desert to support the strongest.

"The Bedu are most noble," I said.

"Then...shall we cast lots?"

I blinked, unnerved. "This is for men alone."

"And you are Rami's hand. Is he not a man?"

"I am not my father," I protested.

He saw my discomfort and shrugged.

"Then we eat equal shares."

We rolled dates into the baked bread, dipped our rolls into hot goat butter, and ravenously devoured them. Then we washed the tasty food down with a bowl of the frothing camel milk Saba had drawn.

I noted the way Judah looked at me with more than simple interest. He was either taking his charge eagerly or was as attentive to all women. Likely the former, unless Jews generally treated women with more regard than the Bedu did.

"Tea," Judah proclaimed, retrieving the metal pot.

I wasn't as attached to tea as Bedu who'd lived in the desert, so I told them I was satisfied.

Judah would have none of it. "No, Maviah! You must drink tea with us. It will make you strong and take away all of your sadness."

Saba grunted, clearly skeptical. I could only assume he found Judah's attentiveness to me unnecessary.

"Pay no attention to him," Judah said. "In my charge you will drink tea. It will keep you healthy."

So I waited as Judah prepared and then served the tea. It was very hot. And rather bland. But it seemed to bring great comfort to both of them, and I could not deny that it soothed my stomach.

We slept under the blankets at the rocks' base that night.

When I woke, the sun was hot and Judah had already prepared tea and milk with bread. The camels were near, for there were no shrubs or grass on which to graze. We were alone in the camp.

"Where is Saba?"

"He studies the way behind," Judah said. "Drink." He handed me the milk. "Do not worry, Maviah. They will not find our tracks soon, and when they do, they will know they are too late. Our only enemy now is the Nafud. But have no fear. Saba can read the sands by day as well as I can read the stars by night. God will lead us. Now drink."

The milk was still warm and frothy and it calmed me.

Only after Saba had returned and we were mounted and had climbed the first dune did my heart fall. For there, in all its endless, treacherous glory, the vast wasteland that swallowed even the strongest men seemed to stretch to the end of the world. And above, the sun that turned those same men to dust dared us to try crossing.

I had thought our journey the night before marked my initiation to the Nafud. How naïve was I.

CHAPTER SIX

OUR CAMELS PLODDED those searing sands for hours before we found shade beneath boulders during the hottest time of the day. If not for the wide, flat stretches between the dunes we would have had to rest much sooner. In that shade we rested several hours before mounting again and pressing on.

We drank no water, only milk, which was already beginning to sour from the morning's draw. To this end Judah placed a stone at the bottom of a bowl and poured milk to the top of the stone. This much he served to each of us in turn, for no Bedu man will take more than any other, and they gave me the same portion.

Judah and Saba favored the sour milk more than I, but with such a parched throat, I relished each drop. And was this not true also of my parched soul? The thought of how far we still had to travel tormented me.

"When will we reach a well, Saba?" I asked as the sun began to set.

"We pass no wells where we go," he said. "Only when we reach the other side."

I was alarmed. "And how far?"

"Ten stages with good fortune."

"We have enough water?"

"With good fortune. The water is for the camels. We drink only milk."

I had counted the sagging skins of water—there were twelve, each quite large, two of which were seeping moisture. It is said that Bedu can live for a month on camel's milk alone, for it is food as well. I knew that camels could endure five days without water, but struggling over such steep sands, Shunu looked haggard already. Yet if Saba said it was enough water, I would believe that it was enough.

"And with bad fortune?" I asked.

"There will be no such fortune," Judah said. "You are safe with us, Maviah."

But I didn't want his optimism then. I wanted to put my fear to rest with reason, which Saba provided.

"We have enough for eight days," he said. "Then we will be out of water and the milk will no longer flow. We can then travel for another two days. With bad fortune it will take longer."

"Yet we have the male to slaughter," Judah said. "This will give us more time. You will see, Maviah."

My mind then began imagining all manner of bad fortune.

"I've heard that many get lost in the Nafud," I said. "By night you have the stars, but by day only the sun. The desert looks the same to me—only sand and more mounds of sand. How can you know we travel true?"

"The sand speaks," Saba said. He indicated the small dune ahead and to our left. "The wind at this time comes from the southeast, making the horns of this dune point northwest. Our path is now west."

"How do you know the wind comes from the southeast?"

"Because I know," he said. "And when the largest dunes fail to bend with the wind, or we find reason to detour, then three sides is the quickest way around."

I glanced at Judah, who looked at me as if this should make perfect sense. It didn't. But I wasn't leading the way.

I had other concerns and found no reason not to express them in turn.

"What if we meet other Thamud ahead?"

"Then we will avoid them," Judah said.

"What if they see us first?"

"Then we will kill them."

"What if one of the camels breaks a leg?"

"Then we will eat it."

"What if a sandstorm comes?"

To this neither gave a reply.

"You have many questions for a woman," Saba finally said.

Judah ignored him. "If the sands blow, then we will pray."

Unlike most Bedu of the north, Saba rode shirtless in the heat, baring his well-muscled chest, arms, and back to the sun. It is known that a cloak keeps sweat from drying too quickly and so preserves one's water and cools the body, but this wasn't the way of his people, who were Bedu from the far north, he said. I knew that he'd come to my father when his tribe had been slaughtered by the Thamud while he was tending to a caravan far away. Under Rami, he lived only to seek vengeance.

Judah wore a white undershirt and an earthen-colored aba. His headcloth was white as well, held in place by a black woolen agal. And yet even he periodically stripped off his aba and his cloak to bare his skin for a short while.

My own cloak was the color of the sand. I wore my long black hair bound up beneath a dark blue mantle, which kept the sun from my head and face.

That second night we made camp early in a parched wadi, and after eating my meal of bread with dates and butter, I wanted only to sleep. But try as I might, I could not. Judah's camel, Raza, lay close and he reclined against her leg, ignoring her grunts and complaints. The other camels wanted also to be near, so we were surrounded by three of the beasts. I wasn't accustomed to such smells and so much noise so close.

In addition to this, Judah set Saba to talking, and neither showed any interest in sleep. I didn't want to leave the camp, so I turned away from them, closed my eyes, and silently offered prayers to Isis, who might be watching and listening, however unlikely it was.

"Tell me why a man makes himself the slave of a god he cannot hear or see," Saba said.

"God is heard through the prophets and seen in the stars," Judah said.

"And how will you know that what you hear from these prophets is spoken by your god?"

"It is also written on stone and parchment," Judah said.

"And how do you know that what is written are the words of this god, not mere man?"

"Because what is written will come to pass."

"Then you believe blindly in the future as foretold by men who only say they have heard from the heavens. And for this, you will die?"

"I am not righteous enough to know and observe the Law as some do, because I'm a warrior from the desert who only knows a little," Judah said. "And yet I know that my God sends the Anointed One to free the Jew from the Roman. I will find this Messiah and I will wage war in his army to scatter the Roman and restore holiness to our sacred land. You will see. It is written."

"And if he does not?"

"But he will."

"Neither Jew nor Bedu understands that he has made the gods in his own likeness," Saba said. "Gods who become angry and kill and inflict great suffering when offended by man."

"You are Bedu, Saba," Judah scolded. "All Bedu serve the gods. And yet you have turned your back? Why is this?"

Saba seemed reluctant to answer, and when he did his voice was low.

"Before coming to the Kalb, my people in the north traveled the trade paths to the distant east, far beyond Babylon to the lands called China. I took my gods with me as a boy and learned that they did not hear me in that distant place. Only much later did I also learn that they are deaf in the desert as well."

"How can you gaze at a child's face and not see his maker?" Judah pressed. "Or into a woman's eyes and not see a greater truth?"

"No god saved my family when they were slaughtered," Saba said. There was such sadness in his voice.

"But you have a woman, yes?" Judah asked. "A wife in the north?"

"I have no wife," Saba said. "Nor do I long for one."

"Then I pity you, Saba. I loved a woman once. She was killed by the Thamud in a raid, as were my mother and father. As you know, it's the reason I first came to the Kalb three years ago, knowing Rami stood against the Thamud."

All the world was filled with death.

"I long for this love once again," Judah said. "Perhaps the love of a woman surpasses even the love of God."

Saba grunted. "Perhaps."

One of them poked the fire with a stick.

"I think we are in the presence of a queen," Judah said softly. "And one so beautiful I have never seen."

"The Bedu know no queen."

"She is a star in the night sky, I can see it in her eyes. A woman who shed the blood of the Thamud and escaped their clutches." Judah gave a soft chuckle.

"You would do well to remember that it is Rami you serve. She's only a woman. A woman who knows how to draw blood will bring much bloodshed."

"May the Thamud and Roman both drown in it," Judah replied. "Through Maviah, salvation comes to the Kalb."

And this was the last either spoke.

I fell asleep with Judah's tender words whispering through my head. *Perhaps the love of a woman surpasses even the love of God.* I dreamed of Johnin's breath on my cheek in Egypt. Such love felt distant here in the desert. And yet Judah's words brought it one stage closer.

FOR SIX days we traveled through that inferno called the Nafud without any terrible trouble. Each day seemed hotter than the one before. My throat returned to its cotton state within minutes of my taking milk, and from head to toe my skin was surely made of sand. My cloak was dusty and my hair in need of washing. Many Bedu of the deep desert cleanse their hair in camel urine, which kills any flea or mite, but this was not my way. As a slave in Egypt I'd learned to bathe frequently using perfumed soap.

The camels dragged along, one plodding foot after the other. Their humps seemed to shrink, and their bones seemed more pronounced. Perhaps I was only imagining. In many flats I thought I could see water far ahead, but the shimmering waves of heat rising from the sand assured me that this was only a trick of the desert, a mirage promising hope where none waited.

When I complained one day about the oppressive conditions, Saba regarded me graciously. "A fish in the sea cannot help but get wet. As much, a man in the deep sands cannot help but suffer."

Then Judah added, "It seems a woman as well. But this will pass, Maviah. We are almost across."

And yet we were not almost across. I had to smile. Saba the man of the head; Judah the man of the heart.

The scorching sands and the hardship of survival each day put some distance between us and the tragedy at Dumah. I mourned my son's death with each breath but was coming to accept that he was no longer in my life. Nothing would be the same as it had been before. I had to embrace my fate.

Saba guided us by day, keeping mostly to himself except when he engaged Judah, more for sport than for true argument, I thought. He frequently rode to a higher point and studied the sands, searching for the way ahead and for any sign of life on the horizon.

Twice he detected traveling Bedu, and these we avoided in detour. Cutting across the tracks of the second group, Saba and Judah confirmed that they were Thamud—a small group of seven, all men. The camels were from the west, three male and seven she-camels. All had taken water two days earlier. They were headed north, perhaps toward Petra.

Ordinarily such sightings would be welcome, for in the deepest sands even an enemy may offer food and news. Such is the Bedu way. But the Thamud and Kalb were now in open conflict, and even these distant Thamud might know of it. Our food and water, though quickly dwindling, were adequate, and the success of our mission could not be risked.

Judah did not seem to know any form of discouragement, and for this I was grateful. His soft song kept me and the camels and even Saba company during the longest days. Never once did I hear so much as a grunt of complaint or condescension from him.

He had called me a queen and, although he may have been given to overstatement, I believe a part of him truly thought of me as such. He often went out of his way to give me his attention, however small the measure. I was always the first he served. He constantly inquired as to my comfort both in camp and on the camel, offering his own blanket to give my seat more padding and my body more warmth at night.

I was familiar with the courting habits of men. Many in Egypt had shown me small kindnesses in hope of what I might offer them. And I believed Judah found me beautiful, even in my haggard condition. His eyes made his attraction plain.

But his kindness toward me seemed to be rooted in something far deeper than lust. Perhaps he thought helping my mission to succeed would earn him favors from Rami. Perhaps he saw me as his means to reach Palestine and the Romans, whom his new king would crush. Or perhaps he was truly taken with me, as one who could love him in a way that his god could not. Hadn't he said as much?

As the days passed I found myself drawn to the warmth of his hopefulness and the smile that expressed it. When he left camp to scout, I noticed his absence more than I noticed Saba's.

On the sixth day, as the sun set in the west, Saba decided that we should cross a shallow canyon rather than take the time to find another way. We traversed the steep, rocky slope, leading the camels on foot, then remounted and resumed our ride. Without warning Raza, Judah's camel, snorted in pain and stumbled to her knees.

With a cry Judah was off and tugging at his mount's leg, which had been caught in a hole between two boulders.

"Raza!" he cried. "Stupid, stupid Raza!"

Unable to free the leg, he slid around and tugged at one boulder. The stone rolled away but the camel only protested with greater pain, jerking away as her leg flopped beneath her. With a mighty crash, she collapsed.

We could all see the damage, for her leg had been snapped below the knee. The sight made me ill.

"She's broken her leg!" Judah threw his legs under Raza's neck and cradled his camel's head in his lap, stroking her fur. "No, no, Raza. No! Forgive me! I beg you, forgive me!"

I watched as he clung to Raza as he might a child, rocking, distraught. It was the first time I'd seen Judah troubled. We all knew what this meant.

Saba watched, face flat, as Judah poured out his heart.

"Forgive me, Raza…you are the ornament of the sands. There is no camel as magnificent as you. The stars tell your story to the whole world. Forgive your careless master. Forgive me, Raza…"

I thought he might cry, but he gathered himself and hushed his mount until Raza's panicked breathing calmed. Then, whispering a prayer to his god, Judah quickly withdrew his curved dagger and slit the camel's throat.

Raza did not struggle as her blood spilled onto the rocky path. She rested her head on the ground and closed her eyes, as though welcoming the one fate that surely freed her from a harsh existence.

I watched in silence, remembering my son's fate, wondering if my own would be similar. Could I die so gracefully? Perhaps Raza and my son shared the most fortunate fate among us.

Judah was quiet that night. He and Saba harvested Raza's liver and heart, welcome treats after a week of only bread and dates and milk. We did not have time to dry any meat, so we ate only what was most nourishing and left the rest for any buzzards that might venture so deep into the Nafud. Without Raza's milk our daily portions would be cut, but this would not cause a problem, Judah said.

The other camels were by now attached to Raza, and they wandered about the camp, moaning and staring at her corpse near the rocks.

We rose early and left the camp while it was dark. Never had I been so grateful to be out in the open sands once again. Within the hour Judah, now mounted on the male camel, began to sing again.

He would not allow himself to dwell on Raza's passing, for camels live and die at the whim of fate, and man is master over beast. This too is the Bedu way.

But the smile he offered me as a red sun rose over the dunes behind us wasn't as bright as it had been the day before, and I knew that he mourned Raza still.

"We are almost across the sands, Maviah. Soon you will be in Galilee and in Herod's courts."

"Soon," I said, returning his smile. Indeed, we were more than halfway.

But then thoughts of what I would do if I did gain entrance to Herod's courts overtook me.

"How are women seen in Palestine?"

"They will accept you, Maviah. You have the dagger of Varus."

"Yes, the dagger, but I am a woman. How do the Jews count a woman?"

"I am a Jew," he said. "And I count the woman who rides beside me now as a star in my sky."

I blushed. Saba had heard and turned our way. Why I should feel bashful, I didn't know. Perhaps because I was afraid to acknowledge my own longing even though I could not deny that I was drawn to Judah.

"They say Herod's lust for beautiful women knows no end," Saba said. "Rami is no fool to send his daughter."

Judah glared at the dark warrior. "You dare speak this way in front of her? What is this madness?"

Saba's right brow arched. He glanced at me, then faced the sands ahead. "I mean no offense, Judah. Maviah is well equipped to know the truth."

"This is the truth: I will sever the arm of any man who dares lift a finger against you, Maviah."

"Rami does not ask for Herod's arm," Saba said. "Only his favor. At whatever cost."

"Pay Saba no mind. I will not allow Herod to touch even one hair on your head!"

And yet even as the sun rose high, I did pay Saba's statement some mind. Truly, I was even more concerned about this king who had such lust for power and pleasure.

But all my thoughts were swept away that afternoon when the winds rose at our backs. The sandstorm came so quickly that even Judah and Saba were caught off guard.

We were spread wide on rolling white dunes, plodding under a glaring sun. Judah was slumped in the wooden saddle, haggard, I thought. Saba rode far ahead and to my right, cresting the next low dune.

It was then that I looked up and saw Saba waving his hands. His shout was distant but urgent. Judah's cry of alarm joined it. He'd turned his mount and was headed toward me.

"Down! Take Shunu to the ground!"

I twisted in the saddle and saw the storm then, only a hundred paces behind us, a churning wall of sand approaching with such speed that for a moment I thought it was sliding down a large dune.

The hot wind hit my face and I gasped. Even in that gasp, before the chaos was fully upon us, I sucked in the leading sand.

Shunu roared and jumped into a run, nearly toppling me from her back.

"No, Shunu. Slow, slow!" She slowed, and I dropped to the ground, lead rope firmly in hand. But the moment I landed, we were smothered by darkness. The sand swallowed us, and Shunu bolted again, tearing that lead from my grasp.

I screamed at her. "Shunu!" I stumbled in the direction she'd gone, instinctively hiding my face in the folds of my sleeve. "Shunu!"

My second call didn't reach my own ears, for the roar of the wind tore it away from me. I could not see, nor could I breathe. The sand was too thick, swirling around me so that I lost all sense of direction.

And yet the thought of losing Shunu was more terrifying to me than the sand. She was the companion upon whom I depended for survival. It was her milk that I drank, her back that I rode, her nose that pushed against my neck when I was lonely.

So I lunged wildly, praying with each step that I would run into her.

"Shunu! Shunu!"

I had been in storms before, but never without shelter. It is known that the darker sands in the southern Nafud are heavy and do not blow so freely. But we were in the white, and the ferocity of that wind flung the sand at me with biting fury.

It had just become clear to me that I must stop and protect my eyes and face from the sand when the ground beneath me gave way and I tumbled down a long slope.

When I came to a stop, I was sure that a mountain was crashing down on top of me. I pulled my mantle over my face, bowed to the ground, and waited as the wind roared over me.

Where Judah was, I couldn't know. He was surely as blind as I. I understood now that he'd wanted me to pull Shunu to the ground, perhaps even hobble her forelegs to keep her from rising. Any attempt on his part to find me now would be futile. He could not abandon his own mount.

It was dark and difficult to draw clean air, even beneath the covering of my cloak. The finest sand pierced straight through, coating my face and hair with dust. Only by slowing my breath could I manage not to choke, and then only by drawing at the air through clenched, sand-filled teeth. I kept my eyes closed.

There are two kinds of sandstorms. The first and the kindest is called a haboob, which often arrives before a thunderstorm and is short-lived. But in the deepest desert, even a haboob may come without cloud or rain.

The second, called the simoom, brings no rain and may last for days. I prayed we had been visited by a haboob, because I knew that I could not withstand those conditions for long.

The howling wind seemed not to care about the plight of anyone in its path. Many said the sandstorm was the fury of the gods visited on those who had not properly sought their mercy. If so, I knew not how I had angered Isis or Dushares. Or was this Judah's deity, angry at him for showing kindness to a woman who was not a Jew?

But I refused to believe any of these thoughts, and instead I prayed for the mercy of all deities.

For a very long time I remained huddled on the ground, and still the sand blew until, to my horror, I realized that it was building up around me. Indeed, I was already half-buried. So I crawled forward to be free of that grave.

Once again my breathing quickened in panic.

Once again I had to calm myself so as not to suffocate.

I was utterly alone in that storm. My prayers could not reach past the sand. I imagined Judah's voice calling out to me, his arm snatching me from the ground. My heart ached for rescue.

None came.

Once again the world mocked me. In one moment my father and all his great power had been crushed. In one moment my son's life had been snatched away. So in one moment this storm had come from a clear sky to smother us, uncaring of the waste it would leave behind.

What security, then, was there for me?

I crawled out of the sand six times before the wind began to calm.

And then, nearly as quickly as the wind had risen, it departed. And soon after, the dust.

I pushed myself to my feet and looked at my cloak, somewhat surprised to be alive. It was covered in dust, as were my head and hands. Sand was my new skin. Gazing about I saw a desert that I did not recognize—whether the sands had been reformed or I'd wandered farther than I'd thought, I didn't know.

Above, the sky was blue again. There was no sign of life.

"Judah?"

I scrambled to the top of a dune and studied the horizon. To the west I saw receding dust clouds. In every other direction, only white sand.

"Judah!" This time I screamed his name.

I heard a very faint reply.

I stumbled forward, calling out as I plunged down one smaller dune and ran up another, my sandals slipping over the sand.

I saw Judah on his camel when I crested the dune. He rode in a fast trot toward me with Saba hard on his heels. The sight of him striking toward me filled my heart with gratitude.

He slid from his mount and rushed up to me. Not concerned with propriety, he threw his arms around me and pulled me close.

"Thank God, thank God." He drew back and quickly began to brush the sand from my head and shoulders. "I feared you were lost."

He looked like an old man with white hair, white eyebrows— even the hairs of his arms were coated in a film of dust. I laughed, not because he looked strange but because I was flooded with relief. But I blamed it on his appearance.

"Just look at you," I laughed.

"And you! Is it a woman or an ash tree?"

Saba slowed his trotting camel as he approached. "Where is Shunu?"

Silence engulfed us as we looked at the sands for any sign of my camel.

"Two of the skins broke when I went down," he said. I saw the wrinkled waterskins hanging behind his saddle and knew immediately that we were in more trouble than even I had imagined. Shunu had been carrying the rest of the water, except for a single nearly depleted skin on the male Judah rode.

If we could not find Shunu, we would be left with only one she-camel, and without more water, she would not yield much milk.

"She last drank three days ago," Saba said. "We must find Shunu."

"Yes, we must," I said.

But even I knew that finding her would be a significant challenge. The blowing sand had erased all tracks. Shunu might have wandered in circles, disoriented, looking for a way out. To my knowledge she'd never been caught in a dust storm save in the oasis, where shelter was near.

Judah and Saba searched in widening circles for an hour before returning empty-handed.

"I'm sorry, Maviah," Judah said, somber. "We cannot find her sign. She is surely out of the storm and searching for us. We will pray that God leads her to safety."

He was showing me kindness, because I knew as well as they did that Shunu could just as easily be buried at the bottom of a valley. Although the loss of her pained me deeply, I chose not to burden the men with my sorrow.

"If she is meant to find us, she will," I said.

"If God wills it, she will find us," Judah said, dismounting and pulling his camel to the sand. He motioned for me to mount. "You will ride Massu now."

"We can both ride him."

"Yes. But for now I walk."

And so I traveled upon Massu, led by Judah, who walked, and Saba, who rode ahead to scout the way, keeping an eye out for Shunu.

The sun now seemed hotter and each step heavier, weighed down by our knowledge that only the best fortune would deliver us to water before we dried up. This was how the Nafud swallowed its victims and spit them back out as bleached bones upon its dunes.

When Judah began to lose strength, he climbed up behind me and seated himself with one leg folded under him and the other resting on the camel's rump. How he didn't fall off, I could not fathom.

His closeness relieved my anxiety, and when we had the energy, we talked quietly. There, on Massu's back, I listened to his gentle voice as he spoke of adventures that had taken him into more raids and battles than I could imagine, for he was often chosen by my father to champion and avenge clans who'd suffered loss to raiding tribes.

Rami chose him because he wasn't Kalb. Indeed, if Judah had been of Kalb blood, a clan might have been insulted at the suggestion that they needed the help of a single champion. But because he was a bond servant in the service of their sheikh, all clans welcomed his sword and bow.

I learned also of his own tribe and of the woman he'd loved before coming to the Kalb. And Judah learned more about my time in Egypt, of my education and of Johnin, whom I had loved. Truly, I had never spoken so freely with anyone since leaving Egypt, and I found myself wanting to tell him everything. But I didn't want to be tedious, for I knew that he would patiently listen to hours of talk, even if bored by it.

Judah had called me a queen, and yet I felt he was the more honorable.

We had hoped that Shunu might find her way to us while we camped, but when we rose in the predawn hour and detected no sign of her, we knew that she was lost to us. If she was still alive, other Bedu might find her and treasure her, for she was a beautiful animal, friend to all men.

For two more days we plodded on. The stretches of silence between us lengthened, as talking itself robbed us of energy. We would make it, Saba and Judah both said. It is known that a man can live thirty days without food, and only two without water or milk, and yet the Nafud might cut these spans in half. Still, we had just enough for the three days required to reach Aela.

But then, on the following afternoon, our ninth since leaving Dumah, fate dealt us another blow. Saba's she-camel, Wabitu, went searching for a morsel during a short rest and returned with her waterskin torn by a sharp rock or thorn.

The last of our water had leaked out.

Saba invoked the names of many gods in cursing the she-camel, who only looked at him past her long lashes, too dumb to know that she might have just sealed her own death.

Judah looked from the camel to Saba, then to me, then at the horizon. I had come to expect the most positive outlook from Judah, and his silence unnerved me.

"It's too far," he finally said, turning to Saba.

Saba did not dispute the claim.

"We must head south and try for the well at Sidin. There was a rain in that region eight months ago. The well may still have water clean enough to drink."

"South?" I asked. "We are meant to go north, to Palestine."

"We cannot cross the sands without water," Saba said. He regarded Judah. "I have only heard of this well. You know the way?"

Judah looked to the heavens, then thoughtfully at the horizon. "With stars I will know where we are and where we must go."

"If there is no water?" I asked.

Judah said nothing, which meant everything. There were no other wells near the Sidin. If the well was dry, the journey would be our last.

"There is no better option," Saba said. "We rest and wait for the stars."

What struck me even more squarely than the dire nature of our predicament was Judah and Saba's acceptance of it. All surely dread death, but they, who lived so close to it at all times, showed no fear. Facing death was a way of life for them, but I knew that one could walk into the face of death only so many times before being consumed.

We found shade at the base of a jagged cliff, surely the same rock where Saba's she-camel had consigned us all to ruin. She looked sad and wore the same perpetual pout all camels wear, though I was sure she sensed Saba's displeasure with her. Camels are far more sensitive beasts than horses, far more inquisitive and affectionate, always seeking the attention of their friends and their masters. Wabitu had suffered the loss not only of Shunu and Raza, but of Saba's approval as well.

I approached her and rubbed her neck, whispering words of comfort. She sniffed at my hair and smacked her lips near my ear to show her appreciation.

I could only look at her with compassion now, for she did not know the consequence of her mistake. Were we not the same, awaiting the turns of fate at the mercy of ambitious gods?

We rested until dark. There was little to speak of, and even less energy to speak at all. Even so, I wanted to shake off my concerns.

"Are you worried, Saba?" I asked.

"It will be as it will be."

His words offered no peace, so I looked hopefully at Judah, who'd reclined against the rock after offering me the saddle and the blankets on which to rest my head.

"And you, Judah?"

He smiled, but I knew it was for my sake alone. And in his eyes I finally saw fear's shadow.

"No, Maviah. God will see you through."

I briefly thought to ask why his god, if he could see, had led us to this desolate place, but I held my tongue. I was too preoccupied by my fears.

If Judah was afraid, then I should be terrified.

And suddenly I was.

CHAPTER SEVEN

WHEN DARKNESS finally came, Judah climbed the dune and studied the stars for a long time. During the nights he'd shown me how he read the stars, naming many as if they were his brothers and sisters shining for the benefit of all who knew them as he did. And indeed, I was impressed by how he could line up the exact location of each star and then point to a place on the horizon, saying, "There, three leagues distant, is the oasis at Tayma." Or "There, in a twenty-three-hour run on Raza, is the rock of Meidal." But he could be so accurate only at night. The day was Saba's charge.

"We go," he said, briskly returning to us. "We push the camels to reach the well at Sidin before the sun rises."

"It's too far for one night," Saba said. "If we run the camels, they will die."

"We are closer than I first thought."

"No, we are two days."

"No. We can make it in one night if we travel fast."

"It's too far—"

"Do you read the stars so well?" Judah demanded. "Are your dunes more precise than the heavens?"

Saba studied Judah's set jaw and finally dipped his head.

"As you say."

Saba was a wise man, built like a pillar, but Judah when pressed was perhaps the stronger man. If not in body, then in purpose and conviction.

The poor camels groaned as they hauled us step after step over the sands, taking us south, away from Palestine. Once again Judah rode behind me, and his energy returned with the cool air. His stars gave him reason to sing, however softly. And surely in some way he also drew comfort from me, so close to him, warming his sprit, for there was no hiding that Judah was pleased with my company. In the desert a marriage between a man and woman has little to do with sentiment but is meant for the purposes of provision, protection, and the raising of children. And yet I thought I provided Judah with the same warmth of spirit he offered to me.

We did not stop to rest. We did not allow the camels to slow despite their complaints. We did not adjust our course, for Judah had his eyes on the sky all the while.

Judah's elevated spirit lifted my own, and yet I knew that even if we reached the well of Sidin, we would not find life unless we also found water below the surface.

I had been thirsty many times, but I had never felt such a craving for water. My tongue felt too thick for my mouth and my throat was as dry as the sand. I found it unpleasant to speak through a passage so parched.

The eastern sky began to gray and still we had not reached the well. Except for the small thread of water left in Wabitu's torn skin, none of us had taken water or milk since the morning before.

"Just there," Judah said. "Very close now. Just over those dunes."

"Don't say it's just there, when it's never just there," I said.

Judah looked wounded by my accusation. "But it is!"

I wanted to say that with him it was never *just there* unless *just* meant "very far," but I didn't have the energy to explain, so I remained silent.

"It is just there, Maviah. You will see."

It wasn't just there and so I did not see.

Saba finally stopped us by a grouping of rocks. These he pulled from the sand to bare their undersides.

"Lick the dew," he instructed.

"Don't worry, Maviah," Judah chimed in. "This dirt can't harm you."

Though the dirty moisture we managed to lick off those sandy rocks might have filled only one nutshell, it was enough to stay despair.

We remounted and struck south again.

The sun rose over the horizon, promising to bake the flesh from our bones.

"Close now," Judah promised, smiling. "There over that one hill awaits our salvation."

And this time he was right. The moment we crested the dune, we saw the depression below, dug out over many years by men eager for the waters of life.

"The stars do not lie," Judah said.

Farther north the Nabataeans were known for digging great cisterns and lining them with stone, then keeping these hidden from all but their own people. During the rains the cisterns would fill up, to be used when the less fortunate were dying of thirst. Indeed, these cisterns were rumored to be so large that many Nabataeans took to hiding in them when attacked, leaving the enemy at a loss, for their openings were very small and easily concealed.

But this wasn't a Nabataean cistern. It was a well that might be dry.

Yet the camels knew, and already they were staggering down the slope, roaring.

"It's a good sign, Maviah!" Judah cried, bounding behind me. "They smell the water!"

Saba scanned the horizon for any sign of Bedu. Ironically, there is no greater place of death in the desert than about a well, for all men war to control water. But today there were no Bedu nearby.

With water so close at hand, my thirst became intolerable. The moment I slid to the sand, I stumbled after Judah, who had reached the well and was peering down.

A single pole spanned two mounts over the stone lip of the Sidin well. A long rope dipped into the darkness below.

I knelt beside Judah and looked down, nudged impatiently by both camels. The musky scent that filled my nostrils spoke of moisture. Every bit of my shriveled flesh longed for but one sip.

Saba pulled up the rope and tied one of our empty skins to its end, then threw it over the pole and began to lower it. For a long time, the rope snaked downward.

We all listened for the telltale splashing of the skin.

Deeper. Even deeper. Still no one spoke.

And then we heard it.

"Praise be to God!" Judah cried.

"May it be pure," Saba muttered.

He pulled the rope, hand over hand, hauling his draw to the surface. Then out and onto the ground, pushing aside his she-camel, who was nosing for the water.

Saba dipped his hand into the skin and drew some water into the light. It was the color of red sand, but it was wet, and I wanted to shove my head into that skin.

Bringing his hand to his lips, Saba took one sip, looked at me with his deep-brown eyes, held the water in his mouth for a moment, then spit it out.

"It's spoiled."

Unwilling to accept Saba's conclusion, Judah thrust his hand into the skin and sampled a mouthful.

He too spit the water out.

"Bitter."

"What do you mean?" I demanded. "It will keep us alive!"

I reached for the skin, but Judah pushed my hand away. "No, Maviah. This water is poison. You will surely die."

Saba turned and offered the water to Wabitu, but with one sniff the she-camel withdrew.

"Even the camels will refuse this. What a camel refuses to drink, a man cannot."

I stared at them, aghast.

"So, then, we have no water. And there are no other wells close enough to reach."

"Yes. This is true."

I looked between them.

"Then we die here?"

"No." Judah looked at Saba's she-camel. "Now our lives are in Wabitu's udders. We will force her to drink this water. If it does not kill her, she may produce milk. If God wills it, her milk will save us."

I wanted to yell at him and demand he tell me the truth. There was no hope left for us, surely he knew this! I no longer wanted his courage, I wanted only water!

But Saba was already heading toward his camel. So I joined them in deed, if not in hope.

I had heard of forcing a camel to drink, but never had I witnessed nor been a party to it. Only my own desperation for life allowed me to help Saba and Judah hobble all four of Wabitu's legs so that she could not rise. After much pulling and thrashing, they managed to pry her mouth open using sticks, so that I could pour the rancid water down her throat.

In this way we forced Wabitu to drink three skins of water. The other camel stood a long way off, watching and moaning, anticipating similar treatment. But we didn't need him to drink. We needed milk, which he could not provide.

If Wabitu did not produce milk, we could slaughter the camels for their blood, but this was barbaric and would leave us on foot deep in the desert, which itself was death.

We finally released her.

"How long will we wait?" I asked, watching the she-camel happily run off. She wouldn't go far because there was nowhere to go.

"Until the sun is high," Saba said, eyeing her. "By then she will either be sick or begin to make milk."

"Only half a day, Maviah," Judah said, smiling. Like a child, he could seize hope in even the most desperate of situations. Perhaps only a man who has survived so many battles and so many improbable journeys may have such hope.

"And how long before she makes enough milk for us?" I asked.

"Another day," Saba said.

"And yet with milk being made, we will have the courage to survive," Judah said.

I could only swallow. That swallow mocked me, because my need for fluid cut as deeply as my need to breathe. I would perish beside this bitter well, I thought.

I should have expected no other end than to die in the desert. Was this not the fate of all? If my father had failed to protect his kingdom with all his great power, what right did I, his illegitimate daughter, have to expect anything other than death?

The fear that had relentlessly accused me of failure now laughed in my ears.

"You will see, Maviah," Judah said kindly. "God will provide a way. He will not allow you to die in the Nafud."

I turned away.

Wabitu had stopped running and was staring back at us, confused and offended. She awkwardly settled to the ground, stretched out her neck, and moaned in pain as the water, like poison, churned in her stomach.

I glanced at Saba, wondering if he felt as hopeless as I did. But his eyes were not on the camel. Nor Judah. Nor me. They were fixed on the dune behind me, and they were afire with wariness.

I twisted my head in the direction of his gaze. There on the crest, staring down at us, stood a Bedu. An older boy, less than twenty years and yet a man, for all Bedu become men at a young age. He wore a white kaffiyeh with a red agal.

"Thamud," Saba said. His hand was on his dagger already.

"So." Judah stared up at the boy. "We have been found."

The Bedu spun and vanished from sight.

CHAPTER EIGHT

⬥

THE APPEARANCE and departure of our enemy had been so sudden that for a moment both Saba and Judah appeared to be at a loss. But only for a moment.

"He isn't alone," Saba said. "Our camels aren't strong and there's no cover. We must find high ground on foot." He started toward the well, where he'd left his bow and sword.

But Judah had other thoughts. "No, Saba." He looked at me, eyes bright. "They will have camels. Don't you see? They are our means of salvation."

"They are Thamud!" Saba snapped, turning back.

"And even Thamud carry water. I will speak to them." To me, Judah made himself clear: "Remain here with Saba." He strode toward the dune.

"Judah!"

"Trust me, Maviah!" he cried over his shoulder, then broke into a run. "God smiles on us today."

Saba mumbled something and retrieved his weapons.

"Will he be safe?" I asked, watching Judah scramble up the dune.

"He is Judah."

"What does that mean, he is Judah? Of course he's Judah!"

"I have fought by his side many times and would entrust my life to him with all confidence. He thinks more with his heart than his mind, but his sword is true. Judah is as safe as any man might be."

This offered me little comfort.

The moment Judah's form vanished over the dune, I felt lost and utterly alone in that great dust bowl with its bitter well. Abandoned even. I realized then how dependent I'd become on his presence. I turned to Saba, hoping for reassurance, and I found some. But Saba was not Judah.

He still wore his cloak from the long night's journey, and now he stripped it off so his movements might be unencumbered. There was no cover nearby and nothing to prepare, so he crossed to Wabitu and squatted by the camel's head, stroking her neck, perhaps apologizing for our cruelty.

His eyes remained fixed on the crest where Judah had vanished.

"Sit," Saba said without looking at me. "Breathe."

So I did.

My thirst intensified in the hot silence. Judah was like water to my heart, I thought, and without him my thirst became unbearable. I was but dried bones and my tongue like dust.

"Are you sure he's safe?" I asked after too much time seemed to have passed.

"He is Judah," Saba said. His tone told me to be silent once again. But I wasn't listening.

"How many Thamud, do you think?"

"I have not seen their tracks."

"What if they know about Dumah?"

He turned, face flat, and for a moment stared at me. He said nothing with his tongue, but his eyes told me his mind. He had no patience for my questions. Not now.

So I fell silent once again, praying to any god who might hear for Judah's safe return.

And then Judah reappeared at the dune's crest, wearing his customary smile. I sprang to my feet, overcome by relief.

He waved his arms. "It is good! We've found a friend! It is safe!"

"How many?" Saba called, already on his feet.

"They are only two. Come!"

I was already running, stumbling up the slope, and was soon panting with Saba by Judah's side.

"How far?"

"Just over the rise." Judah led us as one who'd found a great prize. "They are a brother and his sister who came to the well in the night and found it bitter, so they made camp behind the sand."

Saba was not ecstatic. "You told them what?"

"That we are Kalb, yet friend of Saman bin Shariqat, sheikh of all Thamud."

"They know nothing of Dumah?"

"No, I don't think so. They have water, Maviah. Did I not say we would be saved?"

"Yes. Yes, you did."

"And now we are."

"Not yet," Saba said. "Where there are two, there are more close by."

I saw the single small black tent as we crested the next dune. It was hardly a true tent, made of only one ragged cloth stretched over two poles hastily set in the sand. A goat was tied off to a post beside the shelter, and it bleated at us. Nearby two camels stood in the sun, watching us through long lashes.

The moment the boy saw us, he motioned wildly with his hand. A girl stood in the tent behind him, younger than he, I guessed. The sister quickly adjusted her tattered tunic. They, like most Bedu in the deep sands, were very poor. But they had water, two skins at least, hanging from the tent posts. Nothing mattered to me as much as water.

"He is Arim," Judah said. "There will be no problem with them."

Indeed, both seemed overjoyed to welcome us into their humble camp. They could not know who we were or what had happened in Dumah, because they greeted us as all Bedu do honored guests and strangers.

The boy, Arim, was thin with scraggly hair and only a few strands for a beard. He might have been sixteen, but his muscle was filling out and already showed strength.

"Thank the gods for honoring us with your presence!" he cried, running up to us. He dipped his head. "You are our guests. No harm shall come to you in our tent." His dark brown eyes, bright as the stars, lingered on me. "I am Arim bin Fasih, great warrior of the Nafud."

His sister was only a few paces behind his heels.

"We are most honored to serve you," he said.

Arim turned and issued a stern rebuke to the sister, flinging his arm with bravado. "Masihna! Go prepare the goat for slaughter! Can't you see we have guests?"

She smiled at me, unaffected by his show. Then she turned and ran back.

"Forgive her, my sister is not accustomed to guests." He swept his arm toward their tent. "Please, you must feast with us."

"We will share your water, Arim," I said. "But you must keep this goat for yourself." I did not want to eat what was so precious to them, but the moment the words left my mouth, I knew I had overstepped, for I was a woman and I had undermined his honor as the master of this tent.

For a moment he looked among Judah, Saba, and me, perhaps

wondering why a woman was speaking for them. But I was from Egypt before Dumah and though a slave, had been allowed to speak to men in common.

"Please forgive her, she forgets herself," Saba said. "We would be most honored to receive food in your tent."

But I forgot myself further, so far was I from the constraints of my father's house.

"Do you travel alone with your sister?"

This time the boy took my boldness in stride. "We are traveling to my father's clan, not a half day's journey from this well."

"And you take this goat for your father?"

"We were sent to the south to take the goat from my cousin, who has offered it to my father."

Saba tried to stop me. "Please..."

"How long have you traveled?" I asked.

"We are gone one week."

"Then you must deliver this goat to your father, lest he be angry the Kalb have eaten his prize."

"It is *my* goat!" he cried. "I am master of this beast!"

He was only seeking the greatest honor by serving his prized goat, as was the Bedu way, but I could not see depriving them of what was surely needed by the boy's elders.

The sister had already gathered the goat and was readying to cut its throat.

"You are most honored to have offered this goat," Judah said, dipping his head. "And we are honored to sit with you and share a meal. We will eat what you serve us, sure that God will smile upon you all of your days."

Judah eyed Arim gently and continued in a reassuring tone.

"We only ask that you keep the goat, and give to us your camels instead. You may restore our health and make your way to your clan."

This request threw the boy into a conundrum, obvious now in his eyes. Judah's tone was bold and the customs for trading complicated, depending on the situation. By offering to take a camel, Judah had given the boy a way to restore any honor lost by not slaughtering his goat, as was his prerogative in his own tent. But a camel was far more valuable.

"We will pay, of course," Judah said.

"You will pay?"

"Handsomely."

Arim stared at Judah as he considered his options.

"I will not see a guest ride on these haggard beasts," he said, referring to his camels. "My clan has many camels close. You must take those."

No, I thought. We could not go into a Thamud camp. It was far too dangerous.

"How many?" Judah asked.

"Many. The strongest and the fastest in the Nafud."

This meant little, for Bedu men are prone to exaggeration.

"Then take us to your clan and see us on our way with camels. Your father will be most generous to you for this."

A knowing smile lit the boy's face once again. "You are wise among all men." His eyes rested on me for a moment, surely curious as to my status as a woman who'd been allowed to speak so freely.

"But we must first drink tea and exchange the news."

He turned and strode toward the tent, and seeing that his sister was already cutting the goat, he hurried forward, followed quickly by Judah.

"No, Masihna! You must *not* slaughter the goat!"

She whirled, eyes wide, blade on the goat's throat. I couldn't see if it was too late, but I saw clearly what happened next. In his hurry Arim rushed to his sister, grabbed the blade from her hand, and jerked it away. By then Judah was close behind, and as Arim scolded Masihna, his arm swept back and his blade nicked Judah's arm.

Startled, the goat bleated and jumped up.

The boy spun around and, seeing blood seep from the small cut, dropped the knife. For a moment they stood stunned—Judah looking curiously at his arm, Arim aghast, and the shocked sister covering her mouth.

Among the Bedu, the master of any tent is liable for the harm of any who enters it as a guest. Indeed, the blood price of a guest is twice that of any man killed in battle—twenty camels, among the Kalb.

Arim threw himself to the ground, hands outstretched on the sand.

"Before Shams I deliver myself as your servant. Tell me the price of this blood, I beg you!"

"It is but a scratch," Judah said.

"My life is yours to command!" Arim cried. "Allow me to restore honor lest I die a thousand deaths and my bones be scattered in the desert!"

Judah looked at me, now beside him, and I saw both compassion and delight in his eyes.

"Then my only command is that you prize your sister as I prize the woman in my own protection," he said, still looking at me.

Arim lifted his head, face covered in sand. "It is not enough! I am liable for your blood!"

And it was true. It was the way of all Bedu that blood must be paid for with blood; eye for eye; life for life. The gods themselves demanded it.

Judah studied the boy for a long moment, then bent and scooped up the knife he'd dropped. Before objection could be made, Judah cut his left palm and held up his bloody hand.

"Then I take your blood upon myself," he said, invoking any

Bedu's right to extend mercy. "This blood is now yours and your debt is repaid in full. This is the Light of Blood."

Arim stared, overwhelmed. The Light of Blood, so offered, set the boy free of his obligation. Judah's heart could not be questioned, though I suspected he wasn't interested in being bound to any Thamud. Best put the incident behind. His wound would heal.

Arim scrambled to his feet, quickly stepped up to Judah, grabbed his bloody hand, and wiped Judah's blood on his own forehead.

"The Light of Blood," he said. Arim clasped both of Judah's arms. "Before the eyes of Shams I beg you be a brother to me and my family."

Judah hesitated. "I am a Jew who does not pray to Shams. How can I be your brother?"

"Ah? It is my debt to offer, not yours to refuse! I accept your mercy and now offer my life. I beg you not leave me in the depths of despair without honor. Do not discard me into the valley of misery, I implore you!"

"I have set you free!"

"And now I offer myself to you as your protector. Am I not worthy?"

When Judah didn't return his agreement, Arim continued, speaking quickly.

"I care not if you are a Jew. My sheikh, the great Fahak bin Haggag, teaches that we are all from the same earth no matter the gods in the heavens, only some are wiser than others. Fear not that my people are wiser, for you will be my brother!"

While Arim made his plea for this blood bond, my eyes were on their water. We were but dust without it, and only Arim could offer it to us, for we could not otherwise honorably take it, even if it meant our death.

If Judah refused Arim's blood bond, the boy would be deeply dishonored. At any rate, how could Judah refuse this plea for kinship while we were in such desperate straits?

I saw a faint smile on Judah's face as he dipped his head. "Then I am honored," he said.

A great relief washed over Arim's face and he smiled like the dawning of a new sun. It was as if he, not we, had been offered life.

With half of my mind still on their water, I was deeply grateful when Arim, having been saved by Judah, immediately retrieved two smaller skins from the tent and proudly offered them to us.

"Now drink life, as you have given it to me," he said.

There are no adequate words to describe the relief I felt as the sweet water slipped past my lips and wetted my parched throat. Water was indeed the lifeblood of the sands. I could feel my dried bones awakening as that water cooled my body.

Arim smiled at me as I drank. "You should slow, woman," he said. "You will not find life by drowning."

His words struck me in that moment. I had been drowning since the day of my birth.

I thought these things with the skin at my lips and then drank again. All the trouble that I had left behind did not exist in those few moments as life flooded my bones.

But once my thirst had been quenched, I remembered who I was, and whispers of dread mocked me once again, for I knew that I had been saved only to face death. If not tomorrow, then the next day, or the next.

CHAPTER NINE

ARIM, THE THAMUD boy of sixteen, proved himself to be a man in all manners, including his interest in finding a woman. After having established his blood bond with Judah, he set his eyes on me.

"She is your wife?" he asked.

"She has no husband," Judah said. Then, seeing the curiosity in Arim's eyes, he added, "Neither is she for you."

This discouraged Arim only for a few minutes. I do believe that most everything he did thereafter was at least in part to impress me.

When I handed the skin to Saba, Arim encouraged me to drink even more, saying that water made a woman shine like the moon.

When he prepared the herb tea, he served Saba and Judah first but looked at me when he spoke of how it had come from Persia and was without doubt the finest tea in all of the Nafud. It was to be taken by only the greatest warriors born to vanquish all who would defy the noble Thamud.

When I was sent to collect our camels, he insisted on accompanying me so that I would know no harm, for he was highly skilled with the sword.

Judah immediately refused. I think he was jealous of Arim's

ambition, and I cannot say that I wasn't intrigued by the small rivalry.

After we revived her with fresh water, Wabitu came to herself with only running stool to show for the foul water she'd taken at the well. By the high sun, we were mounted and headed toward their main camp.

It took us less than half the day to reach the Thamud, as Arim had said it would. Arim rode with his sister on one of their camels, having offered me their second. We carried their goat in one of our saddlebags, which I insisted be my own, as I was riding his camel. It rode behind me with only its head showing, for it was a small goat. I found it impossible to discourage the beast from nibbling at my cloak until Judah tied its mouth with a leather twine.

All the way, Arim angled to ride close to me. He regarded me with bright eyes as he spoke of exploits far too accomplished for any Bedu so young, and of the mighty sheikh Fahak bin Haggag, whom we were soon to meet.

I hoped this mighty sheikh would be more eager to take our money than our heads. Hearing Arim speak of their leader's great might and wisdom, I traveled with some apprehension. But neither Saba nor Judah seemed particularly concerned.

For his part, Judah seemed more bothered by Arim's advances on me. He frequently edged his own camel between the boy and myself, as if to keep me safe, though we both knew Arim himself was no threat. I found the boy's interest endearing.

Judah told Arim that my name was Nada and that I was his sister, because my true name might be known among even these Thamud.

"Just there, over the rise," Arim said, pointing ahead. He slapped his camel's neck with his riding stick as we rode over a wide dune. "I will present my new brother to the mighty sheikh Fahak bin Haggag, the most feared of all Thamud. But do not worry...you are safe with me!"

I crested that dune and stared into the shallow valley with some trepidation.

The camp below consisted of seven black tents, all small save one that had three posts at its center. For all Arim's talk, I had prepared myself for a valley filled with a hundred tents surrounded by many more camels. But here I counted only fifteen camels and no goats.

Arim took his beast to a run, and Masihna beamed her gratitude to be home.

"Hurry," Arim cried, waving us on. "We will feast tonight!"

Saba had ridden in a guarded silence, but now he grunted and made his thoughts clear. "They present no threat."

Judah was more expressive. "They too are the hand of my God to the weary."

And yet Judah's god had not informed this pitiable band of Thamud that they were weak. Indeed, their mighty sheikh, the honored Fahak bin Haggag of whom we had heard so much, was an old man desperately in need of more meat on his bones, though he held himself with pride when Arim presented us to him before his tent. Behind Fahak two wives peered over the tent cloth, whispering.

"They are Kalb from the east, and friend of Thamud," Arim said proudly.

Bin Haggag regarded us with the cold eyes of a hawk, focusing on Judah and Saba. He gave me only a cursory glance. Five other men had gathered, two young and three older. All carried daggers, as did Judah and Saba, who'd left their swords with the camels.

"No Kalb is friend of the Thamud," the old man said in a voice as thin and coarse as his beard.

Arim spoke without missing a step, dipping his head in respect.

"None but these two, whom I have captured and delivered. And now I have made them my friend and my brother."

Arim's feat did not impress the mighty Haggag, whose frown

appeared fixed. I felt a pang of anxiety, and yet surely the sheikh knew that such powerful warriors as Saba, who carried twice the meat on his bones as any other man in the camp, and Judah, who stood unworried and unflinching, could slaughter every man in the valley with daggers alone. They were at our mercy, not we at theirs.

"There are whispers of war in the east," the sheikh said, eyes fiery. "In our grace we may let you pass with your lives, but all Kalb are now enemy."

"Then I too am your enemy," Arim said. "For I am now bonded by the Light of Blood to my brother."

"What madness do you speak of?" the sheikh demanded. "Have you exchanged your mind with that of the goat we sent you to fetch?"

"I offer you no offense, most honored sheikh of the mightiest among all Thamud," Arim said, words flowing like honey. "In my taking of these men into my tent as guests to bring to you for your wisest consideration, my knife cut Judah's arm, and we are now bonded by the Light of Blood as is most noble. Now he is under my protection."

The sheikh appeared stumped.

"Your knife has a mind of its own?"

"No, honored sheikh. It is surely an extension of my own arm."

The elder grunted.

"And who is this Judah?"

Arim stepped over to Judah and placed his hand on his arm. "Judah, the Jew who is Kalb. My brother."

"A Jew, no less?"

"The most noble of all Jews, who are filled with nobility," Arim said.

"Quiet down, boy."

Arim dipped his head.

The gathered Thamud waited for a verdict, for a sheikh is measured by his wisdom and shrewdness in impossible situations.

The old man studied Judah with new interest.

"I have heard that the Jews believe that any who refuse to worship their god will be consumed in fire," he said. "Is it true?"

Judah dipped his head. "You have heard a lie."

"This is not true? How can I trust a man who would demand I leave my gods for his to escape death?"

"This is not believed by so many," Judah said.

"The Jews have only one kingdom, ruled by one god," the old man persisted. "Any who do not convert are to be counted evil and consumed in fire."

"No, no, this is a lie," Judah reassured him.

"It is not true that your god is for only your king?"

"Yes, this is true. And yet we have no king now."

"A Bedu serves *no* king. None. How then can you serve a god who curses those who are not of his kingdom? Perhaps you are not Bedu after all."

"The Jew is no better than any who is not Jew. Even now I am your humble servant."

The sheikh regarded him with suspicion, and Judah pressed on.

"Most honored sheikh, I would speak."

The sheikh offered a shallow nod.

"It was when Saman bin Shariqat, sheikh of all Thamud, overtook Dumah for all of its plunder not ten days ago that we rose with him. Indeed, he now commands those Kalb who do not wish to perish. We were to bring the news to the farthest clans in the Nafud, but we lost two camels in a storm and the well at Sidin is putrid. If it please you, it is our honor to be welcomed into your tent to exchange the news and be on our way to fulfill the wishes of Saman bin Shariqat."

The sheikh did not respond.

"Also, Judah is now my brother," the boy Arim said.

The sheikh gave him a harsh glance. So Arim upgraded his claim.

"My brother, Judah, will pay ten times the price for each camel we offer him. It was for this I took him captive."

"You have taken your brother captive? Which is it, boy?"

"It is both."

The old man looked at Arim as if he were daft, but then regarded Judah.

"You would attempt to have our camels for ten times their value, Arim says. Is this true?"

No such promise had been made, but neither Judah nor Saba objected. I didn't know how much coin they carried, only that Judah kept it on a belt around his waist. Surely Rami had anticipated great need.

"We had not discussed a price."

"And yet I heard one," the old man said. I saw then that Bin Haggag was far more shrewd than he was strong.

Judah glanced at the boy, who gave a quick nod as if to encourage him.

"Yes," Judah said. "Ten times."

"Ten times," the sheikh said, lifting his hands and spreading his fingers.

Judah nodded. "Yes. The price of thirty camels."

"For three camels."

"For three."

After a moment Fahak bin Haggag, mighty sheikh of the Nafud, used a walking stick to slowly push himself to his feet. He stared at me, frowning, then at Judah.

"She is your wife?"

"No. My sister." He cast me a side glance.

"She is Nada," Arim offered. "She is not claimed."

"Nada." The old man nodded. Then his face softened and a sparkle came to his eyes. He found no displeasure in looking at me.

Employing great drama, Bin Haggag spread his arm toward his tent behind and offered a thin smile. "You, Judah, brother of Arim, are indeed a friend of all Thamud. Drink my tea with..." He paused. "And what is your name, black warrior?"

"Saba." My father's servant dipped his head.

"With Saba, the great bald-headed warrior, and allow us to share our great fortune as the gods have willed."

There was a murmur of approval at such wisdom.

To his clan the sheikh lifted a bony fist in triumph. "We will slaughter the goat and a camel to honor our guests! Though they come from the Kalb, who know less than the Thamud, we will make them wise. This is the will of your sheikh, who is myself, and the will of the gods!"

A great cheer arose in that valley and I knew then that we, for the moment, were saved.

SABA WAS NOT eager to spend more time in the Thamud camp, but Judah insisted that we rest at least until the late night so as not to offend our host. We were only a week from Sepphoris and we needed the rest. So we remained, I with the women, watching and aiding in preparing a feast that made quick use of the goat and an old camel slaughtered for the occasion.

As with any Bedu feast, great pride was taken in the preparations. Foods that surely had been carefully saved were brought to the pot, for the measure of any Bedu is found in what they can serve a guest.

The Thamud cooked in cauldrons in which every part of the goat was put to use——its liver, its heart, its ears, feet, eyes, even its tail, for the tail may be chewed to clean the teeth. These all mixed with spices and the marrow boiled from bones to make a broth to be poured over meal.

The meat of both goat and camel were cooked over a fire on spits, then cut off the bone in thick slabs and served with dates. I could not recall such a delicious feast, though I must confess that after ten days in the Nafud, I might have eaten raw meat and found it satisfying. We then feasted on buttered wheat cakes with honey and drank tea. Many cups of tea.

More than the Kalb, the Thamud women mixed with the men, who expressed their appreciation unabashedly. I was reminded of Egypt, where in my experience women were regarded more highly than in Arabia.

We ate until we could eat no longer, laughing at the antics of Arim, who had not given up his quest to impress me, and those of the rest of the tribe, who seemed as enthusiastic as he. Indeed, they only followed the lead of their sheikh, who was at once perfectly grave and as mischievous as a child.

After much banter the sheikh regarded Judah seriously.

"So...a Jew." He waved his old hand in the direction of a servant, one of three attending the sheikh. "Hashem has come to us from Syria not so long ago. He too knew many Jews there. Is that not right, Hashem?"

"Yes, my lord."

"You are a Jew?" Judah asked.

The servant looked at his master, who waved him on, permitting him to speak freely.

"I served in a household of Jews before I was traded."

"Hashem has been with me one month," the sheikh said. "He is well versed in the news of the world. It is good that you are from the desert rather than Palestine. There Rome has made all Jews slaves. Is this not so, Hashem?"

I saw Judah's attention fixed on the servant, who nodded.

"I have only heard," Hashem said.

"What have you heard?" Judah asked.

"That the kings now, Herod and Philip, are no better than their father, who butchered his people to win the favor of Rome. It is said that all Jews are stripped of their land and wares to pay Rome its taxes."

"You see?" the sheikh said, spitting to one side. "No Bedu would stand for it."

"Nor any Jew," Judah said.

"Rome came once into the desert with all of its might, and the Bedu sent them home like dogs."

"As my people in Palestine will one day send Rome home."

"And yet they have allowed these foreigners to rule them for many years. Have they no stomach to overthrow tyranny?"

The sheikh could not know how deeply his speech offended Judah. I took it that most Jews of Arabia were not as invested in Palestine as he. Judah had come from a tribe of stargazers who longed to see their new king rise to power and set his people free.

Careful not to betray his own passions, Judah looked at the servant for an answer. "If you served in a Jewish house, then you know there are many Zealots who stand against Rome."

"Many, yes. And all are crucified."

"The Romans are indeed dogs," the sheikh said.

"And have you heard any news as of late that might give my people hope?" Judah pressed.

"I am only a servant," Hashem said, "who hears the talk among a few noblemen who eat and drink too much. There are rumors of the Zealot who speaks of the kingdom of the gods."

"Which Zealot is this?"

"They say that he is a great sage, obeyed by even disease. A wonder-worker who commands the jinn and ghouls. Some as far as Syria have taken their sick to him."

"But you say he speaks of a new kingdom?"

"A kingdom, yes. From his Jewish god."

"What is this Zealot's name?"

"Yeshua. Of Nazareth, I believe."

Silence visited us until the sheikh dismissed the whole thing with a flip of his wrinkled hand.

"There is no end to talk of the gods," he said. "These matters do not concern the desert." His eyes rested on me and he smiled. "It is far more rewarding to speak of what does. Tell me, Judah, what price would Nada's father accept?"

The request for my bride-price caught Judah off guard.

When he didn't respond, Bin Haggag pressed. "The price of thirty camels, perhaps?"

Judah remained silent.

"No, this is not enough for such a beautiful woman," the sheikh said, eyeing me. He nodded. "Sixty then. It is settled...sixty camels and I will take her as my wife. I have only two others."

"Forgive me, honorable sheikh, but Nada is not for marriage. I fear she has caught the eye of another."

The old man, who might have passed as my grandfather, arched his brow. "Oh? By another Jew? I would hope not, for only here in the desert is the value of a good woman known. Not even the Kalb know how to be gentle with women. We, the whole world agrees, are the men whom women cherish with such passion as to die without."

To this the men made clamorous agreement. But I doubted that the Thamud were any more caring toward women than the Kalb.

"She is to be mine," Saba said.

"Yours? You can afford such a price?"

"When we have returned to Bin Shariqat in Dumah, she will become my wife."

The sheikh looked between Saba and me, as if undecided whether to believe this revelation. Then he lifted his cup and dipped his bearded head.

"May you have many children, all of them but one boys. And may the one girl be your twin to shine as only a star can on the faces of all men."

He drank deep with the rest, and I caught Judah's smile. In his smile I imagined the light of a star, for he was the gazer of stars and I the one he watched.

"Now be gone with you women!" the sheikh said. "I would rob Judah of his money!"

It took a full hour to negotiate the price of three camels and the supplies we required for the balance of our journey. In my estimation Judah was indeed robbed. But he also acquired fine clothing for me to wear—at no additional cost, he said—for the Thamud were known for their weaving and the Nafud had worn my cloak to a dirty rag.

We slept until the moon was high, then mounted our new camels and slipped out of the camp, headed south under the pretense of taking our news of Dumah's fall to other Thamud. When we were sure that no one followed, Judah turned us west and then north.

Only then did we speak.

"How far?" I asked Judah.

His eyes were on the heavens. "Six days. Perhaps seven."

"So we will have no more trouble?"

"There is always trouble in Palestine."

He seemed introspective and I wondered where his mind was. But then I knew.

"You think of this mystic who speaks of a kingdom of the gods," I said.

He faced me, jaw firm. "He is the one," he said.

A mystic, one who spoke of the mysteries beyond earthly matters—matters of the heart and spirits and unseen forces at work. Yet Judah seemed more interested in the restoration of his people.

"How can you possibly know he is the one merely from the talk of a servant who repeats rumors?"

"The moment he said it, I knew. And if it is not, then I will know as well."

I could not trouble my mind to believe in a mystic who worked magic. Neither did I have any faith that Judah's tribe of stargazers had ever seen a child-king, much less that this mystic was he.

But I would not dash Judah's faith in the matters of his people.

"We go to Herod," Saba said. "Nowhere else."

"Herod's palace is in Sepphoris," Judah said.

"Sepphoris. Yes."

"There is a small village on the way to Sepphoris. It is called Nazareth."

Neither I nor Saba spoke.

"We will go through Nazareth, and there I will inquire."

To this Saba said nothing.

I straightened upon my camel and swayed with its plodding gait in the cool of the night.

"Then you must, Judah," I said.

"I must, you understand."

"Inquire of your king."

"I must," he said.

Thoughts of kings and kingdoms shifting and destroyed at the whims of fate filled my mind, but I pushed back the fear rising in me and spoke with my shoulders squared to the horizon.

"And then take me to Herod."

GALILEE

"You have hidden these things from the wise and intelligent
and have revealed them to infants.
Truly I tell you, unless you change and become like little
    children,
you will never enter the kingdom of heaven."

Yeshua

CHAPTER TEN

PALESTINE. What might I say of such a contradiction to my way of thinking?

I cannot say that I experienced the breadth and width of that legendary land, for our journey took us north, east of Perea, through Decapolis and into Galilee toward Nazareth from the east. We avoided many well-traveled roads and skirted cities for fear of being challenged by any authority. But I learned much from Judah, who was acquainted with the way of the Jews and had questioned several Jewish travelers on the journey.

In the wealthy Roman house I served in Egypt, all was orderly and we remained clean in the sight of both man and the gods. In Dumah too, that rich oasis overflowing with water and date palms, the gods were satisfied with our cleanliness, if they indeed cared for such things. Except among the poorest, the nomadic way was noble and there was little concern about being unclean.

But in Palestine, I saw that the people were enslaved by all that was unclean before their god. Man and woman alike were dishonored by the oppression of Rome and those wealthy Jews who'd joined with the Romans. The people were surely hated by both their

Roman masters and their god, who lived in a temple in Jerusalem. This then was cause for terrible misery.

The women in particular were hated, for they, like me, had been born into shame and were the most unclean before their god.

Upon first entering Galilee at the sea that stretched north, Judah had been overwhelmed with joy. He was like a boy who'd finally returned home, and his exuberance was infectious.

"Have you seen such water, Maviah?" he cried, flinging his arm toward the sea. "The purest and cleanest in the world."

It was magical to see this water after weeks in the sands. I wanted nothing more than to run to its bank and fling myself in.

"We must bathe!" Judah said.

"We will reach Sepphoris by day's end," Saba said, looking about. "We will bathe there."

"Maviah must enter the city as a queen from the desert, dressed in linens and perfumed for a king."

"You forget where we are," Saba said. "A woman may not bathe in the same waters as men. If she is seen——"

"I know precisely where we are! And I also know that we might not find suitable public bathing for Maviah in Sepphoris precisely because she is a woman. If she is to go as a queen——"

"I would bathe here," I interrupted, eager to be clean. For many days I had fixed my mind on approaching this king—thinking on what I would say and how I might represent my father. But I'd given little thought to how I might appear or even smell when first before him.

The men looked at me.

"I must! I can't go on smelling like a camel."

"You smell nothing like a camel," Judah said. "And I have frankincense."

"You're saying that I *do* smell like a camel?"

He was flummoxed. "No. I only say that if you do——"

"I would bathe. Now."

"As I said." Judah looked to Saba and offered an apologetic smile.

But we did not bathe there, for Saba was right about the danger of being seen. Judah found a small cove down the road, and there we both bathed, separated by reeds and beyond the sight of any who might approach. Saba kept watch at first, but seeing no one, he too plunged beneath the waters and splashed about like a child.

I could see between the reeds. The sight of two such powerful men frolicking about, all care drowned in that water, made me laugh. This they heard, and then we were all laughing, until Saba scolded us for risking unwanted attention.

I dressed in the clothing Judah had obtained from the sheikh Fahak bin Haggag. A white linen dress and a scarlet cloak, simple and yet fine. I had combed my dark hair and tied it back to best show my high cheekbones, as favored by many men. The sash about my waist was the color of olive leaves, as was the mantle I wore over my head. Judah had also acquired strings of black stones to be worn about my forehead and neck, but I would not wear them here in the countryside. I wasn't comfortable in such luxurious appointments.

Both Judah and Saba stared at me when I stepped beyond the reeds and approached the camel.

"Is it too much?" I asked after neither spoke.

Saba arched a brow. "Herod will be pleased," he said.

This gave Judah a moment's pause. Each day he'd become more comfortable and easy in his tone with me, and I with him. We had not spoken of our affection for each other, but to deny it would have been deceitful. And in the wake of my loss, I had decided to accept his affection in whatever form it took.

Judah smiled and dipped his head. "You are perhaps the most beautiful woman Palestine has yet seen."

I felt a blush rise to my face. "Then I should take it off."

"But why? You are a queen!"

"I have been a slave most of my life. Have I suddenly become what I never was? I don't want to be noticed in this strange land."

"You go to Herod," Saba said. "He must notice you."

Judah could not hide the pride in his eyes. "You are no longer a slave, Maviah, but a queen. And now it is plain."

I cannot deny that I was flattered. And Saba was right—it was Herod who would first decide my fate and then take the plight of the Kalb to Rome. Herod's decision now depended on me.

My thoughts returned to treachery of the Thamud. To the screams of the Kalb being slaughtered on the streets. To the face of Kahil bin Saman as he cut out my father's tongue and then threw my son from the window as if he were a bone for the dogs. My people in Dumah were enslaved by butchers. Their hope rested in me. I did not feel up to the task.

And yet there I stood, a woman of wonder before Judah and Saba.

It might be said I was plunged beneath the waters of the Galilean sea a dirtied slave and emerged a queen fit for any king, at least by Judah's reckoning. But that would only be true of appearances.

Palestine offered us its own illusions.

We put the sea behind us and passed through small villages along the road. At first I saw the many fields of grain and the vast groves of olives tended by farmers. Then villages made of stone-and-reed houses cobbled together with mud and dung. Everywhere I looked I could see abject poverty forced upon the people by the Roman taxes. As Judah explained with growing consternation, in the occupation of Palestine, Rome demanded a heavy tax to support its empire. Up to fifty percent, but paid in coin, not grain or produce. Many farmers had to sell their land to rich Jewish landowners in order to pay their tax. Most who had themselves once been landowners now worked in those same fields for new masters, to make the coin owed in taxes. Fishermen and tradesmen were robbed in the same fashion.

The people walked about with heads bowed. Judah explained they suffered so because the Jews of Palestine were by nature exceedingly pious and clean. It seemed to me that the Jews were no more soiled than any person I'd seen in Egypt or among the Bedu. But they could not attain their standards of cleanliness amid the filth of poverty.

And I could feel an even deeper oppression in the air. Something else seemed to have overshadowed this land that Judah called Israel.

By late afternoon we came to Nazareth on a narrow path rarely traveled. My mind was consumed with Sepphoris, which lay only an hour's walk north from this poor village. Had it been mine to decide, we would have bypassed Nazareth, for I was a foreigner and Judah had been clear that all foreigners were considered unclean.

And yet Judah was thoroughly committed to finding this Yeshua, and he'd convinced himself that Nazareth would lead him to the man.

"We must not remain long," Saba said, staring at the dingy huts.

"With only a few questions, they will know," Judah replied. "Only a few hundred live here."

There were perhaps fifty houses by my reckoning, all of stone and mud, many sharing a common courtyard. I could not imagine any king living in such a state of poverty. I wasn't eager to enter the town dressed as I was.

"You should go, Judah. Saba and I will wait."

He looked over at me. "No, I would have you with me. You must see as well."

See what, I did not bother to ask.

So as not to appear lofty in this place of squalor, I replaced the olive mantle over my head with the threadbare one from Dumah.

Judah prodded his camel forward and we entered Nazareth on the single dusty road that passed through.

It was true, only a few hundred could live here. Most were gone, presumably to the fields or to nearby Sepphoris. Three small children squatted on the roadside, dressed in what might pass as rags. The moment they saw us, the youngest boy, perhaps eight years of age, jumped to his feet and raced our way, yelping with delight. There was no mistaking his announcement for all to hear.

"Foreigner, foreigner, foreigner!"

It appeared he was too young to realize that this designation was meant to be shouted not with delight but with scorn, to warn others.

Judah only chuckled. "You see, they love you, Maviah."

All three wide-eyed children had now reached the camels and were hopping about, slapping at the camels, tugging on their ropes, hands extended as they chattered and bickered.

"Do you have denar?"

"I will brush this camel!"

"They are from the city."

"No, they are from the desert!"

"From Jerusalem!"

"What do you know?"

"Do not touch her, it is forbidden!"

"Do you have honey?"

Judah slid from his mount, dug out a small jar of honey from the bags, and handed it to the first child, only to be descended upon by yet more children who'd heard the commotion and magically appeared from the houses—no fewer than a dozen.

A woman emerged from the nearest door and cried out, shooing the children frantically. "Leave them! Have you no decency? Get back to your mothers!"

They scattered, surprisingly obedient. An old man with a cane had appeared from behind one of the mud homes, and it was to this man that Judah went without giving the woman a second look, for among the Jews a woman could not be easily approached by a man.

He quietly spoke with the man for a few minutes, likely explaining that he too was a Jew and was looking for this Yeshua. I kept my eyes on the children now peering at me from the sides of the road, several still holding their hands out for food or money, some daring to call out.

"Do you need a guide?"

"You must be careful of the robbers on this road!"

"I can guide you!"

"Can you give me honey?"

The woman, now joined by another, offered even more pronounced scolding.

I sat upon my camel next to Saba, and for a few minutes I felt a terrible pity for these young children.

Except for the aged, there were no men that I could see. Others who saw us watched for only a few moments before ducking from sight.

"Come!"

I turned to see that Judah had returned and was eagerly tugging at his camel by its rope.

"What is it?"

"Did I not say it? He is from here! Yeshua ben Joseph. His father is now passed, but his mother, Miriam, lives at the end of the village near the spring. She will know."

Miriam. I knew the name, also called Mary among some. It meant "star of the sea." I could only imagine what Judah, the stargazer, might make of this.

"How can anyone of royalty come from this village?" Saba said. "This old man said that your Yeshua is a man of high standing?"

"Not in such words."

"Then how?"

Judah glanced back at the old man, who frowned at us. "He says Yeshua is a mystic who has left his family to be with his followers, because no one will pay him mind in Nazareth."

Saba's brow arched. "And this brings you courage?"

Judah dismissively flipped his hand. "What do they know? Don't you see? My elders spoke of his mother. When I tell her this, she will remember. Then we will know this is the same child. You must trust, Saba!"

Saba grunted but made no objection.

Most of the houses adjoined others in walled courtyards and had thatched roofs. High windows prevented any from seeing inside the homes while still allowing for ventilation. I would have preferred the open tents of the Bedu.

It took us only minutes to travel that dusty path to the western edge of the village, then a short way up another path to the far corner.

When we came to the house of Miriam, mother of Yeshua, Judah told us to remain by the road while he inquired. He hurried to the wooden door and called out. A woman's voice answered and when Judah explained that he was a Jew from the desert who'd come to find Yeshua, she was silent.

"Miriam? It is I, Judah ben Malchus, who searches for the one who will liberate the Jews. I beg you hear me."

The door then opened and a woman peered out cautiously, then stepped into the sunlight. She was dressed in a simple, dirtied tunic and a brown mantle, which she held closed with one hand.

The woman was slight and fair, but it was her eyes that struck me, for they stared at me upon my camel, not at Judah. I saw a woman who bore the weight of the world on her shoulders, and yet those eyes understood all of that world. A woman of sorrow and grace at once.

"You are Miriam?" Judah asked.

Only after watching me for a long moment did she turn to Judah. "I am."

"Then you must know that I am of the Kokobanu tribe from the east, the great Bedu who read the stars. Our wisest elders came many years ago and offered gifts to you and your son, I am certain. Do you remember?"

Miriam did not need to respond because her face had paled and I knew at once that Judah had found the mother of his king.

He did not wait for her to speak, but immediately stepped back and went to one knee in a bow. "It is my honor to stand before you."

"No, you must not." She glanced down the street, but no one was in sight.

"Among the Kokobanu, you are blessed among all women, for you are the mother of the one who will..."

Before he could finish, she stepped behind the wall of the court-yard, leaving him on his knee. He glanced back at me, then quickly stood and followed, vanishing from our sight for the moment.

I turned to Saba, who wore a curious look. "He was right. What do you make of it?"

He didn't quickly respond. At the very least, this woman and her son were those Judah's elders had found. But as far as I was aware, Miriam might be wary of Judah and his tribe of stargazers, for such men put their trust in what is not of the earth.

Yet I knew that Judah was a sane man.

"It isn't good for him to be alone with a woman in this land," Saba said, glancing down the street.

But it was she who'd drawn him aside, I thought. And none had seen him enter the courtyard.

The moment held the quality of a dream. I had come to avenge my son's death by begging favor in Herod's royal court, and yet here

I was beside a house made of mud and dung as Judah paid homage to the mother of his king.

Saba was right to ask how a king might come from such a home.

I do not know what Judah spoke, nor Miriam, only that when he strode from the courtyard, his eyes were on me and aflame with hope.

"She will speak to you," he said, taking the lead rope and tugging my camel down to its knees.

"Me?"

"I've told her who you are. She would speak to you in the house."

"Why? I have no business with these people."

"Because you now know what I know about her son. It concerns her."

"I know only what is claimed."

Judah set his jaw. "What I've claimed is now made certain. Miriam's son was the child. Herod's father tried to kill him. No one must know Yeshua is this same child. She will speak to you."

I slid from the camel and saw that the door was still open.

"Hurry, she wishes not to be seen with us."

So I walked to the door and glanced back at Judah, who motioned me forward. Then I stepped into the dimly lit house.

Miriam stood by the oil lantern, watching me. Here in her own home, she appeared far more at ease.

The moment I looked into her eyes, I felt like a servant. I could not understand, for she was not a man to command me, nor was I a slave in Egypt to be commanded by a woman. But I did not resist her influence.

I dipped my head. "You have asked to speak to me?"

"Judah tells me that your son was killed in Arabia," she said.

For weeks my loss had been my constant companion, silenced by the resolve that compelled me to avenge him. For all the Kalb, I had been obliged to remain strong, for they now depended on me as much as my son had, and I could not fail them as well.

But with Miriam I was again a mother. The emotions that swallowed me came unbidden.

I saw my baby cooing at me with a full belly, milk still on his tender lips. I saw his little arms grabbing awkwardly at the air, only just learning what it meant to be alive.

I saw Kahil bin Saman casually walk over to my sleeping child, pluck him from the ground by his one leg, and throw him from the window.

I saw my infant son lying facedown on the stone, head crushed.

I saw it all and I could not speak. I could hardly breathe.

Miriam, seeing my pain, stepped up to me and brushed a strand of hair from my face.

"I'm so sorry, sweet Maviah." Her eyes were misted. "I am so very sorry for your loss."

Her words, spoken as if from my own soul, washed over me and I felt rivers of grief rising. Then flowing. I didn't want to cry there in Nazareth, but she had given me permission and I could not remain strong.

My head fell and my body shook as I began to weep.

I felt my mantle eased from my head. Miriam's arms encircled me and I lowered my forehead onto her shoulder.

"Weep, my child," she whispered. "Weep for your son."

Judah had told me to hurry, but I was undone by anguish and I could not move. Nor did Miriam seem to want me to. For long minutes she soothed me and held me as if she were my own mother.

Indeed, in my mind's eye, she was my mother, and sobs racked my body. I placed my arms around Miriam and clung to her as only a daughter might, and I could not stop weeping.

I wept for my son. I wept for my father. I wept for the fear that lurked in my breast like a tiger waiting its turn to tear out my throat.

But I wept mostly because I was offered deep understanding and comfort from a mother who knew of suffering and fear.

When I finally began to settle, she wiped my tears from my cheeks with her mantle.

"You must weep for your son," she said. "Even as I weep for mine."

I felt I should say something, but no words came.

Miriam walked to the table, where she'd been kneading a lump of floured dough. She picked up a vessel and poured water into one of two chalk cups on the table.

I glanced around the humble room. Light filtered in from small windows near the thatched reed ceiling. Two oil lamps on the mud walls produced flames that filled the room with the scent of olive oil. Mats covered the dirt floor. A passage to my left with only a sheet for a door led into what must be the sleeping room. Several large earthen vessels sat in the corner, presumably holding wheat to be ground by hand.

It was by all accounting a poor home.

Her eyes found mine as she handed the water to me. I drank.

"Among my people, you are seen as unclean. It is forbidden to break bread with a foreigner. Even touching you has defiled me in my people's eyes. My son never saw it that way. He was always beyond the simple ways of religion and tradition, seeking instead a far deeper knowing. And I know now that he was right. I suppose I knew so even from the time we were in Egypt."

"Egypt? I grew up there as a slave."

She hesitated. "Our people were once slaves in Egypt. Now we are slaves in our own land."

Miriam took the cup from me and placed it back on the table. When she faced me, urgency had claimed her expression.

"Judah tells me that you travel to Herod."

"Yes."

"That you seek his favor."

"Yes."

"Then you must know that Herod knows no more mercy than the one who took your son's life."

I didn't know what to say, so I agreed. "No king understands mercy."

"You must say nothing of my son to Herod. Not even that you were here to see me. It is all that I ask from you or from Judah."

"Yes. Of course."

She held my eyes longer, then smiled faintly as if believing my intentions.

Miriam looked at one of the oil lamps on the wall. "They have rejected him, you know," she said. "He not once spoke a word of disrespect to any in Nazareth, and yet they could not understand him. His brothers still believe him to be out of his mind. Just a quiet boy who liked to spend time alone in the hills and speak of another world in the tradition of the spiritual teachers. He was more interested in being with the birds than in learning his father's craft. He often went to Sepphoris with the others to work with his father, but even there his fascination was with the synagogue. And with Herod's grand theater."

It was clear to me that Miriam rarely spoke of her son and yet had found reason to confide in me.

"Your husband was a craftsman?"

"Joseph was a simple man who worked with wood and stone, trades needed in rebuilding Sepphoris. He traveled there an hour every morning to return upon the evening."

She faced me again. "His brothers thought Yeshua out of his mind, but they do not know him. One cannot truly know my son and remained unchanged. Perhaps the world will see that one day. But today I fear they will try to kill him."

"The Romans? Why?"

"Because they fear the kingdom of which he speaks. Even the Jews may try to kill him—I have seen hatred here in Nazareth."

"It is true then...that Yeshua is a great mystic who works wonders."

"You've heard this? Where?"

"From a man in Arabia."

She studied me for a moment and spoke very quietly. "He works wonders. And far more."

The notion intrigued me, because I had known of holy men who traded in the world of wonders, but I had lost my belief in them.

"Then eventually they must embrace him," I said.

"Perhaps. But Yeshua rises above even the Jewish way of mystery. And above all the ways of the world. I pray for his safety."

"Then he should leave Palestine," I said. "You are his mother, he will listen to you."

"He is bound to the world of spirit, not to me. My son will do what he was born to do. Even as you, Maviah, must do what you were born to do for your people. And I will do what I was born to do."

"You know what I was born to do?"

"Judah tells me that you will be a queen of the desert one day, uniting all that divides. That you will bring salvation to your people."

"I fear Judah is a man taken by impossible dreams."

Miriam hesitated. "I would not discount dreams so quickly, Maviah. Do what you must do. Only be careful of Herod."

In that moment her words compelled me even more than my father's, urging me toward my purpose, because she understood my place in the world as a woman and as a mother.

"I will."

A knock sounded at the door. Judah, surely wondering what had become of us.

"Then go and take my blessing with you."

I thought that Yeshua was fortunate to have a mother such as Miriam. And in small way, I thought of her as a mother to me as well.

"Thank you. You are very kind."

She smiled at me and turned toward the door.

"Maviah..."

I turned back. "Yes?"

"You will find that Yeshua loves you."

CHAPTER ELEVEN

SOMETHING IN me shifted in my short time with Miriam there in that desolate town of Nazareth, but I did not know what. Perhaps it was only the fact that Miriam, mother to a boy who'd been rejected in his home, had embraced my mission.

But in expressing concern for her son's safety, she'd sown worry in me for my own. I found myself overwhelmed as we approached the city of Sepphoris, that city looming on the hill so close to Nazareth, yet I kept my thoughts to myself.

When Judah asked me what Miriam had spoken to me, I told him that she'd consoled me for my loss and asked that we make no mention of her or Yeshua to Herod. And yet both Judah and Saba could tell I had been deeply affected by my encounter with her.

"So now you know, Maviah," Judah said as we left Nazareth. "The stars tell us only the truth."

I could not deny it. "Yes."

"And you, Saba. There can be no doubt."

"Your stars have spoken," Saba said. "What they mean, no one can know."

"What more is there to know? For out of Bethlehem will come a ruler who will shepherd Israel, as it is written. Now we know that Yeshua is this ruler, even as my elders have seen. Rome will fall."

"And what is a ruler? In the east, a man seeks to rule his own heart, not a land or a people."

"In the east, perhaps, but you are in Israel. Here it is the land and God's chosen people." He turned to Saba. "At the least, you now know that the stars have conspired to give us a sign."

Saba finally nodded. "What I know even more is that Rami is in need of Rome, and I serve Rami. As do you. And we serve Maviah, who is now the voice of Rami."

"Yes," Judah said, settling with his attention fixed forward once again. "Of this too there can be no doubt."

We made camp in a shallow, dry wadi just before the city, for it was too late to make any entrance to Herod's palace that day.

That night we spoke little, each enslaved by his own thoughts. But the voices in my head kept sleep from me, so I finally rose and walked around an outcropping of rock near the bedded camels.

The night was silent and lit only by starlight, without a moon. No creature stirred and still my mind would not join the calm.

When I reflected on Miriam's kindness I fell further into the hopelessness of my predicament. Like Miriam, I too was only a woman. Like her and her son, I too was an outcast.

And Miriam, though mother of Judah's mystical king, was afraid of Herod. As was I, and for the same reason as she. As she herself had made plain, Herod was ruthless and could not be trusted. I became certain that I would fail miserably in the task set before me.

Who was I to walk into Sepphoris to request the Roman armies for my father's sake? The notion now struck me as preposterous.

Dread shadowed me.

Who are you, Maviah, to sway a king?

Who are you to seek vengeance against the vast Thamud?

Who are you but a slave still, no more free than upon your first breath?

My father and Judah and Saba had all made a terrible mistake in entrusting me with the dagger of Varus, for in my hand it was only a worthless relic, sure to draw little more than a chuckle from Herod.

I was pacing on the sand with my arms crossed, mired in an unprecedented fear, when a voice spoke.

"They are like you," it said.

I turned to find Judah staring up at the stars.

"No thought can remove them from the sky." He looked at me with a smile.

"What are you doing?" I demanded, disturbed by his appearance.

"I saw that you were unsettled," he said, coming closer.

"Of course I'm unsettled. This entire mission is absurd."

"And yet it's the only way. You will rise like the sun."

"What do you expect from me?" I snapped at him. "I am only a woman!"

His smile softened. "I expect nothing more from you," he said.

"Nothing more?" I could have told him that he might take this *nothing* and choke on it, because it was a lie. Instead I only grunted and turned away to avoid heaping my frustration on him.

"Maviah...what Rami has asked of you...it's far too much for any common woman. But you—"

"Stop it!" I turned, face hot.

"Stop it?"

"Stop it! Do not ply me with your silver tongue."

He blinked and I knew immediately that I had hurt him. But I only crossed my arms again and turned away. Judah as much as my father had placed the weight of the world upon my shoulders.

For a long while, he said nothing. Then I heard his feet on the sand. I felt his hand take mine.

I turned and saw that Judah was on his knee, face lifted, tears brimming in the dim light.

"I beg your forgiveness," he said, voice strained. "If I have harmed but one hair on your head, I stand condemned. I see you only as the brightest star in the heavens. I worship you as that queen. If my tongue hurts you with even a whisper, you must cut it out, so that I would be as silent as your father now."

The boldness of his approach took me off guard and I glanced into the night, expecting to be seen, but we were alone.

"I beg you, Maviah. Do not cast me away."

How could a man speak in such subservience to me? I was unaccustomed to such extravagant praise. My first instinct was to pull away.

But the sincerity in his eyes stilled me. Judah truly did see me as one who had great power, if not over the world, then over his world. It was then that I first realized the true nature of his heart. I had known we shared affection, but this... this was far more.

Judah was not only drawn to me.

He loved me.

"How could I cast you away?" I said quietly.

He pulled my hand closer and gently placed a kiss on my fingers.

"Then I remain your humble servant. For you I would lay down my life."

For the second time in that same day, overwhelming emotion swallowed me and tears sprang to my eyes. I did not feel worthy of such words. I did not know what to make of them. Instead of gratitude, fear rose into my throat.

And yet how could I refuse the love of such a man, who had never spoken a word of anger to me? How much had I hurt him by raising my voice?

I dropped to my knees in that sand and I threw my arms around his neck, so that his beard pressed against my cheek.

"No, Judah," I wept. "It is I who serve you." I kissed his cheek and his hair. "Please forgive me. Forgive me, I beg you."

"Maviah." His arms were around me. In both Bedu and Jewish ways, we had crossed those lines called forbidden, but neither of us cared. "You are the——"

Without forethought, I kissed his mouth, silencing what was sure to be yet another utterance of my majesty, not because I objected but because I was carried away with affection for him.

For a long moment, we lost ourselves in that kiss, drinking like thirsty souls who'd stumbled upon a well in the most desolate sands. And then I withdrew, breathing hard.

I stared into his eyes and he into mine, stunned.

"Forgive me, I——"

He silenced me with another kiss. I had known that Judah was a zealous man, but I had not felt his great passion until then.

He pulled away, held my face in his hands, and spoke gently. "I will not forgive what is freely given. Nor must you."

"No," I said. "Do not forgive me."

"Nor you me."

"I won't."

"Then it's settled." Judah released me and sat back, grinning like a boy who has discovered his first secret. "Now tell me what concerns you so deeply."

So I sat beside him, staring into the night, and I told him my deepest fears. That I was too common to win the favor of a king, that I was too weak to avenge my son's death, that now the Kalb and my father relied on the very slave girl they themselves had saddled with shame.

When I finished he remained quiet for a long time, arms on his knees, gazing at the stars on the horizon.

"In Arabia and in Palestine both, they say that a man is more honorable than a woman," he finally said. "But this I know is a lie. In truth, all of man is first born of woman, then, when grown, slave to woman. Think of Yeshua. Born of a woman whose love and nurturing make the way for him to be king."

"Yes, but——"

"Think of Herod, then. Would even a king not give away his kingdom for a woman? You underestimate your true power, as a woman. So who says a woman is born with less honor than a man?"

I could not properly appreciate his words just then. I thought them prompted by affection. And yet they pulled at me, deep within.

"Even the gods recognize the power of a woman," he said. "Is not your god Isis?"

"I no longer serve a god."

"But do men not bow to Isis? Do they not beg Al-Uzza for her good fortune?"

"You believe in neither," I said.

"True, but what do I know? Sometimes I don't believe in my God, though he be one. And for this I beg his forgiveness in sacrifice, only hoping for his mercy. But what good is any god, be he man or woman, if he cannot give his people bread?"

"None."

"In Israel the king has also been called the son of God, appointed by the divine to rule. And now even as Israel begs her son of God to restore her land and the bread of that land, so the desert begs her daughter of God to restore her honor. Is this not true?"

"I don't think I can give it to them."

"But you will, Maviah. You will see and then you will believe."

"And if I don't?"

He shrugged. "Then it was not meant to be. And this too is life. I only ask that you begin to see what I see in you. Tomorrow you will stand before the king, Herod, who will only see you as you see your-self. And then he will offer you his favor."

I remained silent, wondering if I could see myself with such favor.

"Herod is a man," Judah said very quietly. "There is no one to win his favor like a woman such as you."

I felt myself blush in the darkness.

"I have no interest in appealing to the man in him."

"And yet Saba is right—you come for your people, and so you will do what you must."

"This doesn't bother you?"

He responded slowly.

"It isn't my right to speak on this matter."

This was true.

"I would, however, advise against marriage," he said, with a hint of mirth. "His wife, Phasaelis, is the daughter of Aretas and surely filled with as much pride as her father."

Phasaelis. I had given little thought to Herod's wife, for surely she wouldn't have a voice in Herod's court. If so...she was the daughter of Aretas, whom I sought to betray even as he'd betrayed my father. It was his endorsement of the Thamud that had led to my son's death.

"Could she present a difficulty? Surely this wife won't be party to his decisions."

Judah's brow arched. "Do women not turn the heads of kings as I said?"

"Then I can only pray that this Herod isn't such a weak king."

"No, Maviah. We will pray that he *is.* Do you not intend to turn his head as well?"

I saw the challenge and for a moment felt loath to embrace it. But then I let my fear go, because this was the path before me, regardless of where it led. What other choice did I have now?

None that offered any hope.

"I will do what I must do."

"And you will do it as a queen."

I put my hand on his head and ran my fingers through his hair. It was strange to feel so honored by a man. There in the desert, I truly was Judah's queen.

"Enough about kings and queens," I said. "Tell me about the stars, Judah."

CHAPTER TWELVE

⸻

THE CITY OF SEPPHORIS in Galilee was by any standard expansive and stunning. Saba knew the city well enough, having been twice with caravans from the Far East across the northern trade route, which ran through Mesopotamia.

My only adequate comparison was that majestic city called Memphis, which lay south of my Roman master's country estate. As a slave I had been to Memphis twice.

Though smaller, Sepphoris was just as grand. There could not have been a greater disparity between the tiny hole called Nazareth and that modern city on a hill called Sepphoris. Saba said more than thirty thousand lived here, nearly half as many as lived in Jerusalem.

Where Nazareth consisted of a few humble homes made of mud, dung, and reeds, couched together with common courtyards for communal cooking, Herod's ornament of Galilee was a walled city of Roman design, newly constructed of limestone blocks and the hardest woods.

But it was the makeup of the population that set Sepphoris apart from Nazareth. Before entering the city, I had seen only the poor; Sepphoris was inhabited also by those of great wealth.

The poor were nearly all Jewish. They mingled with the rich only in the markets and on the streets.

According to Saba the rich were in equal parts rich Jewish land-owners and foreigners—Arabians, Greeks, and Romans, the latter being primarily soldiers.

We approached from the east along a low ridge. Here a covered aqueduct flowed with clean water from a massive limestone reservoir farther east. Then we passed through the eastern gate, which was flanked by two tall, square towers guarded by Roman soldiers. These were dressed in leather skirts, breastplates, helmets, and red capes.

A soldier gave us a cursory look, then turned away, evidently seeing no harm in three Arabians on camels with only saddlebags.

Guards were posted upon the wall at long intervals around the entire city. No one could possibly approach Sepphoris without being seen or challenged.

"Do not worry, Maviah," Saba said as we passed into the city, for he could see that I was unnerved by the scale of it. "Remember that you are protected by Varus and are friend to Herod."

"These soldiers are yours to command," Judah agreed, but this was only his bravado speaking, for I commanded no one but him, and then only in private.

Beyond the gate the stone-paved road took us to a plaza where Jewish farmers sold their produce—mostly beans, melons, olives, wheat, and lentils from what I could see. The city was made of many houses, apartments, and shops constructed along the main street, which ran east-west and ascended a switchback rise to the towering wall at the city center.

My eyes were on this wall as we passed through the market. The towering structures of Herod's acropolis, a royal city within a city, were clearly in view beyond the wall.

We were surrounded by the hustle and bustle of merchants, many of them aided by young boys, each urging us to buy his produce or wares. It was a larger, louder version of the scene that had greeted us in Nazareth.

"Ignore them," Judah said, eyes on the acropolis. "Remember who you are."

Yes, of course. I was a queen. And so I rode on, shoulders fixed, head straight, breathing calmly though my heart raced. Even so, I could not hide my interest in certain distinguished men who wore long white robes, and shawls with tassels and blue stripes. Small black boxes were strapped to their foreheads.

"They carry scrolls with prayers," Judah said, noticing my interest in the boxes. "These are the holy men of Israel who follow the Law without error."

And were proud to do so, I thought. I dared not attract their attention. Women were not permitted to look men in the eye, Saba had said.

We had discussed our entry into Herod's courts. Aware that once we reached the gate to the acropolis we would be challenged by the guard, we had decided that I, not Judah or Saba, was the one who must show authority. Saba had given me the dagger of Varus, now at my side. And so it was with my role in mind that I directed my camel to the Roman guard who stood before the massive oak gate.

One wearing a red cape stepped forward when it became clear that my intention was to enter. "What is your business here?" he demanded. His eyes flickered over Judah and Saba behind me.

"My name is Maviah, daughter of Rami bin Malik in Dumah," I said. "I have come for an audience with Herod, tetrarch of Galilee and Perea."

A faint smile crossed his face. "Herod?"

"Does he not rule here?"

"You are a whore?"

A guard behind him chuckled. In that moment I reached inside my mind and traded myself for the Roman mistress I'd served as a slave in Egypt—a powerful woman unlike any I had since known.

"Does the daughter of a king look like a whore to you, Roman?"

He appeared unimpressed, so I continued.

"And if I am Herod's whore, would you deny him his lusts?"

"Then you don't know that Herod has no whores who pass through this gate. Nor queens without Roman guard."

"I have no Roman guard because I have brought my own slaves, each with the strength of ten Roman soldiers, as you can see."

I held his gaze, boldly challenging him. Was this not what a queen would say?

The guard's lips flattened. "You should watch your tongue here."

"And you yours," I said.

His expression soured and I knew I'd pushed the boundaries. So I calmly withdrew the dagger of Varus from my sash and held it out.

"Since you doubt my honor."

He glanced at it, then took the knife and inspected the hilt, which clearly showed the crest of Varus. Another soldier had approached and peered at the dagger.

"What is it?"

"The insignia of Varus." My interrogator looked up at me. "Where did you get this?"

"My father, ruler of Arabia, was given it for audience with Rome as required. It was Rami bin Malik's victory with Varus at his side that allowed Herod to build Sepphoris."

There was still doubt in the soldier's eyes, but his contempt was gone, for he was surely familiar enough with the city's history to know it had been burned to the ground before Rome gave Herod charge over Galilee.

He passed the dagger to the other soldier. "We will see if Herod agrees."

"Of course. We will wait."

As the second soldier headed for a horse tied by a smaller gate, I nudged my camel to turn. Then, on second thought, I glanced back.

"We've been on a long journey with urgent business and the sun is hot today. Please keep that in mind."

I did not glance at Judah or Saba until we retreated to the shade of a palm, out of the guard's hearing. Even then I turned my gaze to the gate, where the soldier looked my way, having dispatched his companion to Herod's court.

Judah whistled under his breath. "And now the star shines."

I fought my worry. "It wasn't too much?"

"It appears not."

"Be careful," Saba said. "Such men shouldn't be crossed."

His words pricked me. "Then I overstepped."

"Don't fill her mind with worry, Saba," Judah hissed. "She does only what comes naturally."

He was wrong. I felt no more natural here than I might have stepping from a boat into the sea having never learned to swim. And yet I sat still and erect. The soldiers were watching.

Neither Judah nor Saba made mention of my calling them my slaves, which had come from me without forethought, because it was natural for a queen to be accompanied by such strong men. Judah would have no trouble, but Saba surely swallowed the notion of being slave to a woman with some difficulty.

Still, he played his role in service to his master, Rami, with grace.

We waited for nearly an hour before the soldier who'd been dispatched returned and gave his verdict to the other, who then motioned to us.

Again we approached, and this time he waved for the gate to open. "Quintus will take you."

And so we entered the acropolis, inner city to Herod, Jewish ruler of Galilee under the authority of Rome. The soldier rode in silence several lengths before us, leading us over the clean-swept streets, in no hurry.

We passed magnificent villas like none we'd yet seen. Herod had indeed built his seat of power using impressive Roman and Greek architecture. Tall palms swayed in the wind along narrow canals and around pools. I felt as though I had entered an oasis, though we were high on a hill.

The cobbled way led past a massive circular theater with towering walls. Johnin, father of my son, had been killed in one such Roman arena.

A team of slaves worked at a wooden structure the height of fifteen men, an irrigation waterwheel. Its buckets lifted water from an aqueduct on the acropolis wall to suspended troughs, which I assumed fed pools and cisterns at the palace's highest point. Many stone columns rose along the causeway, supporting covered walkways.

According to Saba, Herod had spent thirty years building the city, and I could now see why so much effort had been required, surely on the backs of Jewish workers. Perhaps Miriam's son, Yeshua, had learned a disdain for Roman oppression here, on these very streets.

When we came to the entrance to the royal court, Quintus handed us off to another soldier, this one in black leathers. The palace guard, I guessed. Quintus dipped his head in respect, uttered the man's name, "Brutus," then turned his horse and left.

By the scar over his right eye and another visible below his sleeve, this one called Brutus appeared to have seen his share of battle. He had limbs like small trees and towered over a normal man. He was as tall as Saba. But he did not possess Saba's placid demeanor. The scowl on his face looked fixed.

"Leave the beasts here," he ordered. "With your weapons."

We offered no objection, though I knew that both Judah and Saba might just as well have been asked to disrobe in public. I could see Saba's jaw flex as he removed the two knives at his waist and the bow upon his back and carefully placed them in his saddlebag.

Thus stripped, we followed the brute past armed guards, up a sweep of marble steps, and to a great atrium. Its towering dome was supported by columns that surrounded a fountain and pool. We kept going, up another wide staircase also flanked by guards in full regalia, then through the entrance into Herod's villa.

The grand room into which we were led had a polished marble floor with yet another, smaller pool at its center. Herod clearly had an obsession with water, which was life. A curved stairway on either side of the expansive hall rose to the second-story walkway, which encircled the room. Ahead, yet more steps led to what I assumed would be the inner sanctum.

Everywhere I looked I saw frescos and tall decorative vessels. The railing was trimmed in silver polished by servants. The frescos were embedded with precious stones and framed by velvet curtains.

My first sight of Herod's palace took my breath away, and I stopped for a moment. This then was what so many taxes had purchased for the ruler of Galilee.

"This way," Brutus said.

Neither Judah nor Saba spoke, but I could hear them breathing close behind, surely as impressed as I. Or as affronted.

We were led around the pool, up the broad steps flanked by yet more guards, and into Herod's living quarters. By the looks of the long carved dining table to the right and the groupings of upholstered chairs about the room, he met with dignitaries and entertained private guests here.

The oil lamps on the tables and the walls were all silver. Copious draperies of rich red and green velvet were suspended from the ceiling between windows that peered out on an expansive view so high above the city.

Herod stood by a table with his back to us, pouring wine from a pitcher into a silver chalice. He wore a purple robe with a golden sash and his feet were bare on the polished floor. Apart from the guard and two servants who worked over the table, freshening offerings of grapes, olives, and cheese, we were alone with him.

"As you requested, my lord," Brutus announced. "The Bedu." He stepped to one side.

I had applied the frankincense upon rising and Judah had helped me with the strings of black stones about my forehead and around my neck, then assured me that I was a stunning sight to behold. But in this extravagant palace, my white linen dress and olive mantle only humbled me.

"So..." Herod's voice filled the room. Back still to us, he picked up the dagger of Varus, looked at it curiously for a moment, then unceremoniously dropped it into a chest by his feet.

"Maviah, queen of the desert."

He turned slowly, then lifted the chalice to his lips, his piercing amber eyes never leaving mine.

By any measure Herod was a handsome, powerfully built man. His trimmed beard and wavy hair were nearly black, though I knew he'd lived fifty years.

His robe hung loosely over his shoulders, as if he'd only just risen and shrugged into it, but his hair was oiled. Two golden rings, one with a ruby, the other ornately fashioned, hugged strong fingers. He held his goblet with grace.

He wore his authority with careless confidence, like a man who was bored with his command. I was immediately reminded of how powerless I was in his court. Fear whispered through my bones, mocking me.

You are a fool, Maviah, a powerless woman in this world of king-doms ruled by ruthless men.

But I refused to show my fear.

The tetrarch lowered his silver goblet and glanced briefly at Judah and Saba behind me, but his eyes returned to me immediately. I thought wine might spill to the floor for the way he let his cup dangle from his fingers.

"And tell me, queen where there is no queen, what brings you to this godforsaken land?"

I was taken aback.

"Hmmm? An old dagger that appears to be from the Roman governor who handed me this razed city? That is why you have come? To give me what is mine?"

"No, my lord. I come for audience with you."

"An audience? Rami sends his daughter from so deep in the desert as a gift for me? To what end?"

"Not as a gift. Only to present his word."

"And yet Rami doesn't present himself. You think I don't know the way of the Bedu? A sheikh would never send his daughter to do his bidding unless he had no other choice. Or is it that your father thinks so little of Galilee?"

"He thinks of you only in the highest terms," I said. "Or I would not be standing before you after so many weeks of travel. You mis-understand who I am."

For a moment I thought I might have offended him. But then a coy smile twisted his lips, and he approached slowly.

"Is that so? Then tell me more about yourself, Queen Maviah.

I know all about your father's valiant efforts under the command of Aretas, who served Varus. And as you can see"—he spread his arms—"I have not wasted his victory. Tell me, do you like my city?"

He spoke in a different way from those of the desert, more like the Romans, I thought.

"As you say, you haven't wasted my father's victory."

"Nor has your father wasted his bravery. You know, I assume, that Aretas is the father of my own wife, Phasa."

"Yes."

"As I understand it, he repaid Rami well. Your father now controls the great trade route through Dumah, living comfortably on the taxes he imposes."

Herod stopped not three feet from me, studying my face and my shoulders with eyes that saw through me. I could smell the luxurious ointments that bathed his skin. He lifted his hand and ran the back of his fingers over my cheek. I immediately thought to withdraw, but I dared not.

"I had no idea such beauty could come from so deep in the desert," he said softly, as if speaking to himself. "With a proper bath and a little care, my slaves would transform you into the most stunning woman in all of Palestine."

He lowered his hand.

"But we were discussing why Rami would send his mysterious daughter, not to Aretas, his advocate, but to me, whom he does not know. What business could your father possibly want with me, other than to woo me?"

I did not know Herod's full history, only what Saba had told me. Whereas this tetrarch's father, also called Herod, had been a tyrant, Herod Antipas was by comparison a gentle man who had caused no great trouble. And yet among kings even the gentle might be ruthless.

I had expected a display of power, not such a smooth tongue.

He glanced over my shoulder in Judah's direction. "And he sent you with a warrior who doesn't like me touching you. Tell me, is it common among Bedu queens to so easily love common Jews?"

Whether he was mocking us or merely playing with us, I didn't know, but I could imagine the storm boiling in Judah's veins, and my instinct was to protect him.

"My slave is none of your business," I said.

He lowered his hand. "No? Now you misunderstand *me*, Queen. You see, *everything* in Galilee is my business. Not the least of which is the presence of such a beautiful woman in my courts."

He looked at Judah again. "You are a Jew. I am your king?"

Judah answered slowly, only to keep peace.

"Yes."

"Good. Then you know your place." He addressed me, mirth gone. "Now, let's stop playing games. Tell me what has happened in Dumah to cause Rami to send a slave to do his bidding."

He knew that I'd been a slave? My anger fell from me, replaced by dread. But of course he knew. Herod was as shrewd as any sheikh. If I had felt humbled before, I now stood as if naked before him.

I found that I could not speak. The full reality of my true identity had been exposed before not only his eyes, but my own.

He turned his back to me and walked to the window. "Join me, Queen."

I glanced at Judah, who offered me a slight nod and an encouraging smile. His self-restraint made him as strong as Herod.

I crossed to the window and my gaze followed Herod's. Below us lay the large theater. Its rows of seats sloped up to a covered colonnade that faced not grounds for battle, but a stage with tall columns and arched entrances from the side and the back.

"Do you like it?" he asked.

"It is a wonder to behold."

"I built it after the Theater of Marcellus in Rome, designed by Marcus Vitruvius Pollio, architect to Augustus, the same architect who designed the waterworks under Rome." He looked at me. "Did you know that I was educated in Rome when I was young?"

"No."

"No. But then you hardly know me at all. That must change if I am to trust you." He nodded at the arena. "Tell me, have you ever seen good hypocrites on the stage?"

"I've heard of them."

"There is no finer entertainment in all of Galilee. Only the best of all hypocrites may take my stage. They take their roles seriously and perform perfectly, so one forgets that the role they play is not who they truly are." He paused, then spoke softly. "You, on the other hand, are not the best of hypocrites. But I like you, so I will accept you as a queen." He looked at me. "Fair enough?"

"I am grateful."

He reached up and slipped my mantle off my hair so that it rested on my shoulders.

"If you are here to play the part, then you must look like a queen, my dear. These clothes will not do. And we must have you properly bathed."

"Yes." I was mortified and attempted to say what I'd come to say so that I could leave. "My father—"

"Did you know that my mother was a Samaritan? An outcast in the eyes of most Jews."

He put his hands on his hips and stepped alongside the window, gazing down at the workers who slaved to repair the massive water-wheel behind the arena.

"Forgive me, I did not."

"My mother was a Samaritan and my father was a monster who

killed more Jews to maintain his seat of power than might die of natural causes in any year. My wife is a Nabataean. So you see, I am ruined from the start." He turned to me. "Wouldn't you agree?"

Herod's words sought to trap me, I thought. Or perhaps he was only looking for acceptance from someone who, like him, wore the cloak of shame among his own. I decided to offer grace to the man.

"I'm sorry."

"Do you know the problem with most Jews, Maviah?"

"No."

"They are terrified of being unclean. Even my insistence that you bathe is a part of the curse of my religion."

"I too would bathe," I said, hoping to move past his confession. "Is it so wrong?"

He ignored my question, for Herod heard only himself.

"Our God demands the highest forms of cleanliness. To be unclean is to be cursed and punished by God himself. He judges the unclean and commands his children to resist any who want to take his Holy Land. It is said that any illness or misfortune is God's punishment for uncleanliness. And do you know what makes one unclean?"

"Only what—"

"Many foods are unclean and cannot be touched. No food may be eaten without first the washing of hands. Breaking bread with sinners and the unclean also makes one unclean. All foreigners are unclean and must not be touched. Menstruating women are unclean. Anyone who touches a menstruating woman is unclean. Women who have given birth are unclean—forty days if they have a son and eighty if they have a daughter, because daughters are not as valuable as sons, it is said. Anyone who touches a corpse is unclean. Anyone who touches someone who's touched a corpse is also unclean. Anyone with a rash or fungus or skin disease, all such conditions which they call leprosy, is banished from the household and forced to wear rags and walk about crying, 'Unclean.' The laws are endless. For a rich man to follow them all is difficult enough; for the poor it is nearly impossible. What do you make of this?"

I chose my words carefully, because I knew that Herod, as well as Rome, was responsible for that poverty.

"I think that perhaps the Jewish god is the most demanding of all gods. Better to have the choice of many gods so as not to be victim of one who offers so little mercy. And yet the Bedu, too, resist any who take their land."

He raised his brow. "So the queen is as insightful as she is beautiful. You see? It is always this insane fear of one god or another that precipitates conflict. If the Jews weren't enslaved to their code of conduct for fear of their God, they wouldn't harbor such vitriol at this Roman occupation. It would make my life so much more simple. Truly, they are more enslaved to their fear of God's disfavor than to Rome, which occupies many lands that don't hate it so much. Rome builds roads and provides security and opportunity in exchange for a simple tax. Still the Jews insist on rebellion for fear of God."

"No man takes kindly to being under the fist of another," I said. "The Bedu must remain free or they die."

"Yes, the Bedu. And the Jew. And you, Maviah, for you are a woman under the fist of all men."

I felt unexpectedly appreciative of his insight and this attempt to find a common ground between us.

He sighed. "But take courage. I don't take the way of the Jews so seriously as their religious leaders. To touch a foreign woman does not sentence me to suffering but to passion."

He smiled at me, then walked to the table that held his wine.

"Now . . . tell me about your father's problems."

Judah and Saba stood still, hearing all of it without any outward reaction, for they too were hypocrites now. Their presence gave me courage.

I stepped to the room's center, glanced about to be sure no one else had entered, and saw that none had. My audience included Herod, Judah and Saba, the guard Brutus at the entryway, and the silent servant by the table. I could not allow his wife, daughter of Aretas, to hear what I was to say.

"Go on, Maviah." Herod waved his cup at me. "Don't be shy. Play your part."

I ignored his barb.

"You know that my father's control of the trade route was sealed with his marriage to Nashquya, niece to King Aretas?"

He eyed me and took a drink. "Those crafty Nabataeans—always with the upper hand. Of course I know this."

"Did you also know that Nasha took sick and has passed?" I said. "And that the Thamud accepted Aretas's blessing to attack Dumah for control of the trade?"

He stilled with the revelation.

"And Rami?"

"Is taken," I said. "But he is sheikh of all Kalb and would have his honor restored."

"Then you've come to the wrong king. Petra is your destination."

"I do not come for Aretas. I come for Rome."

He spoke after a long pause, cautious now, for there was no end to backstabbing among rulers.

"A slave asks for the world," he said.

"As you said, we are all slaves. Giving Rome what she has always wanted would not be without its reward. With Rome's help, all the Kalb under Rami will regain control of Dumah and the trade route. Together the Kalb and Rome would conquer."

He paced to his left. "And Aretas?"

"If the Kalb and Rome were to join in the desert, no force could stop them, not even Aretas. He would accept the loss to protect his other interests in the west. Furthermore, you would not be harmed. I seek only an audience with Rome."

I could tell that the idea intrigued him, but Herod was shrewd.

"You underestimate Aretas," he said. "He is a worthy adversary with more wealth than he knows what to do with. Why do you think Rome keeps going back to him for assistance?"

"Perhaps you underestimate the Kalb, who are as worthy. It is clear that Rome has ambitions beyond the Nabataeans. Perhaps you do as well."

I could not read him.

"This was Rami's plan or yours?"

"Both," I lied. "As you said, though slave, I am queen."

A voice cut my thoughts short.

"A queen?"

I turned to see a woman walking into the chamber, dressed in a long white gown with a golden mantle draped over her shoulders. Her arms were accented with gold bracelets. She wore a stunning pearl necklace over her breastbone and a band of pure gold about her forehead—appointments that made my own appear as if they'd been drawn from a river. Her skin was olive, betraying her Nabataean heritage, and her eyes were brown, set in a kind face. I thought her to be at least twenty years younger than Herod.

"And who is this beautiful queen gracing Herod's court?" she said, eyes twinkling like Judah's stars.

Herod quickly set his goblet down and walked toward her. "My dear Phasa. You brighten my day already." He swept his arm toward me. "This is Maviah, queen of Arabia."

Phasaelis glided to me in slippers strapped to her feet with golden ties. "I had not known there was a queen of Arabia as of late."

I dipped my head. "I am from the Kalb, as far as Dumah."

"The Kalb. I have heard of no queen among the Kalb. But the Kalb are friend to my father and so friend to me. It is my honor to know you."

I had to tread carefully. "The honor is mine."

"What then brings you to this pit of despair called Galilee?" she asked.

Herod caught my eye. "She comes with a gift from her father, Rami."

"A gift?" Phasa studied me, then let her eyes linger on Judah and Saba before looking at her husband. "For me, I hope."

"Of course...if you wish." For a moment I thought she meant Saba and Judah, but Herod set my mind at ease. "She brings the very dagger that Varus gave him when he aided Aretas in driving the Zealots from Sepphoris thirty years ago."

"I see. A dagger. And to what end is this...gift?"

"To the end that Rami knows how valuable my relationship with your father is," Herod said. "And his ties with me as well. To the end that we be a family of kings and queens to rule this godforsaken desert."

Phasa approached me, speaking to her husband without regarding him. "Don't be silly. You've shown no interest in me or my family for years. I doubt that a dagger will change that."

He stood still, unwilling to challenge her directly in our hearing.

"Please, Phasa...be a good wife and prepare our guest," he said. "Maviah has traveled many weeks. Tonight we would dine and show our appreciation for her."

"I'm sure you will."

I was as surprised by her offhand dismissal of him as by his tolerance of it. She struck me as a woman who accepted but had not yearned for her position here. She, like me, was trapped in her role as a bond maker.

Phasa touched my face with long, slender fingers, perfectly manicured. She smiled. "My dear, you have such fine bones and skin. Don't you worry, I will make you shine like the stars. If my husband intends to enjoy your company, then I will as well."

She took my arm in hers and steered me toward the side entrance. "You will see, Maviah...we have the most beautiful baths."

"And what of my slaves?" I asked.

Herod turned to Brutus. "Take them to the stockade for safe-keeping," he said. "See that they are watered and fed."

I stopped and turned, horrified by the thought. Saba stood unmoving, as he had since entering. Judah only nodded at me. At their side, Brutus's smirk expressed a measure of contentment.

"Don't worry," Herod said, brow raised over a whimsical grin. "I'm not going to kill them. Only keep them safe."

CHAPTER THIRTEEN

PHASA, DAUGHTER of Aretas and wife to Herod, proved to be a delightful woman, far more intelligent than her cavalier attitude suggested. She flitted about with a goblet of wine always close at hand, thoroughly embracing all the advantages she enjoyed as Herod's wife, seemingly uncaring of anything political—not for lack of understanding, I suspected, but because such matters would offer her nothing but worry.

Rather, she seemed determined to enjoy her wine, and her gowns, and the lavish palace, and the servants who waited on her hand and foot, and, yes... me.

I should say she seemed determined to care for me. Although the Nabataeans and Bedu are distinct, she swept aside formalities and treated me as she might a long-lost sister.

She whisked me away to a wing in the palace reserved for her, speaking in no uncertain terms of how beautiful I would be. She immediately began to issue commands to her servants: draw a bath, prepare the soaps, bring cheeses and grapes and pomegranates. And more wine, the best from Zachariah's vineyard, which she assured me was twice the value of any wine from Rome. Indeed,

Rome imported Zachariah's wine at a premium—one of the few good things besides gold and silver that flowed from Galilee to the Roman monsters, she said.

She possessed both love and hatred for those who gave her husband power. Strangely, so did I. I was at once appreciative that Herod seemed receptive to my mission, and deeply bothered by his dismissal—indeed imprisonment—of Judah and Saba.

Surely both Judah and Saba were safe, but why had Herod seen fit to treat them with such disdain?

I asked Phasa this as she hurried me to my bath.

"Don't you worry about your slaves, dear Maviah," she said, patting my arm. "If my husband wanted them dead, they would be already."

This offered me no comfort.

"Though I will warn you to stay clear of his chief, Brutus. He despises all that is pleasant, not the least of which is me. He lost a brother to the Nabataeans. Among the soldiers Brutus alone hates me, but he is head of the palace guard. At times I wonder if my husband entrusts his safety to such a hateful man foremost to protect himself from me."

She laughed at this, then looked at me, curious.

"I see a fear in you, Queen. What is it?"

My mind spun, searching for an answer. "I care deeply for my slaves," I said. "I cannot stomach the thought of any harm coming to them."

At this she lit up. "So, then...you have taken one of them into your bed?"

"No. By Isis, no."

"But you love one. Tell me which. The black one, perhaps. He is a magnificent beast, that one, apt to rip the head off his prey with his hands rather than use the sword."

"No! It's not that way."

"Then the one with kind eyes. He's as strong as the beast, but a lover! I can see it in his hands and his face."

"A lover does not concern me."

"And yet you found one. This is the prerogative of queens, my dear. I see you have much to learn."

She wasn't wrong, but neither did she know that I was a queen in Judah's eyes alone. And this thought gave me pause, for in Judah's eyes I might indeed have such a prerogative.

"Then it is also my privilege to refuse your husband," I said.

"Herod?" She released my arm and smiled. "So you see that Herod is more in the line of kings like the ancient Solomon than his father. Have you read Solomon's songs?"

"I don't think so, no."

"Scandalous. Sometimes I think my husband was born a thousand years too late. He was educated in Rome, you know, where men are known to die for women. They are called romantics by some."

It was heard of, but not so common, I thought. Mark Antony and Cleopatra came to mind. Clearly, however, Herod and Phasa were not of typical stock either. I found their forthrightness unnerving.

"He would be a fool to force himself upon you. If he tries, scratch his eyes out. Or put a knife in his belly, that will teach him a lesson."

She laughed, but I didn't believe she could mean such words. Still, they gave me courage because I had no intention of allowing the king to touch me.

"Don't you worry, my dear," she said. "My husband is bound for Rome tomorrow on urgent business. I'm sure he'll set your lover free before he leaves. And the beast for me, if he will have it. What is his name?"

"Rome? Tomorrow?"

"Yes. What did you say his name was?"

I knew then why Phasa seemed so overjoyed—she was soon to be free of her husband's presence. I had to leave for Rome with Herod.

And, with me, Judah. A voyage to Rome and back would take many weeks. The thought of being parted from Judah for so long filled me with dread.

"His name is Saba," I said. "He would likely tear your eyes out."

Phasa laughed once more. "Then I must tame him."

She led me to a drawn bath that might fit four, the tub of white marble, the water steaming and milky. I had taken a hot bath only three times before, and my memory of the experience drew me like a moth to a flame.

"You're pleased?" Phasa said.

"It appears inviting."

"Inviting? It is heaven on earth, my dear! I can see you have much to learn from me. I've heard that there is a mystic or a madman—no one seems to knows which—who tells the Jews that the kingdom of heaven is among us already, and I know he speaks the truth. I swim in it every day."

"A mystic? By what name?"

Phasa regarded me with brightened eyes. "Yeshua. You've heard of him?"

I remembered my promise to Miriam.

"Yeshua? No."

"Evidently he's from Nazareth and follows in the way of the Baptizer. You've heard of the Baptizer?"

This time I didn't need to lie. "No."

She stared at the window, distracted by her thoughts. "The people flock to the Baptizer by the hundreds. He is a thorn in Herod's side, but I rather like the idea of a sage speaking out against the Romans with so much boldness."

"Herod knows of this Yeshua?"

"Of Yeshua? He worries only about threats to his kingdom, and Yeshua is no such thing. I am Nabataean and more disposed than my husband to ponder the claims of mystics. And yet"—she turned to me—"my heart also takes offense on behalf of these Jews oppressed by Rome."

"Oppressed by Rome or by Herod?" I said, and then wondered if I had spoken too boldly.

"By both," she said without so much as blinking. She turned to one of three Jewish chamber servants awaiting her direction. "Disrobe her, Esther. Let us show Maviah how to bathe as a queen."

"Yes, mistress." The girl smiled.

The slaves seemed as eager to serve me as Phasa was to have me served. And serve me they did, like mother hens. I did not lower myself into the bath—they eased me into it, one under each arm. When I reached for the cloth, they took it and spread the warm, soapy water over my shoulders. Then they gently scrubbed every inch of my skin, using a scented soap and a dried sponge from the sea.

Having served a mistress in Egypt, I was familiar with giving baths, but those had not been so lavishly conducted or involved as many ointments as what Phasa's servants rubbed onto my skin.

I rose from the water smelling of lavender and stepped from the bathing room dressed in a blue silk robe.

Phasa treated me royally the whole day. She talked endlessly about all the appointments of her palace, and of clothing and jewelry, and feasts, and her spoiled husband.

And all the while, half of my mind was on Judah, my powerful Bedu protector from the desert, who was surely pacing in a hot cell, trusting in me.

I did not see Herod again until the evening came. We met in a private dining room off of his chambers. I was presented there in a turquoise silk gown. My long hair was cleaned, brushed, plaited, and glistening with ointments that made it appear even darker than it was naturally. I had relied on Phasa's choice of jewelry, and after much deliberation she'd insisted on silver-and-black-onyx bracelets around my wrists and at my elbows, a silver necklace with a single onyx stone, and across my forehead a simple silver band polished so that it could be used for a mirror.

For the first time I felt like a queen, even if only as a hypocrite playing on Herod's stage.

Herod was already reclined against cushions on one of the ornate couches. The marble table before it was constructed in a semicircular fashion, like a waning moon. This I knew to be a Roman style, allowing easy access for the servants who stood at the ready.

"As you requested," Phasa said proudly. "Is she not beautiful?"

Herod stood and approached, eyes sparkling by the light of a dozen candles. He took my hand and dipped his head.

"As I said, the most stunning in all of Galilee. Come, sit. We have food, wine, and dancers to come."

I reclined between them. The food came and went, only to come and go again. Flatbread with fowl and fish and figs and cheeses and eggs and plums and grapes and squash and pears and olives and sweet sauces. And wine. Much too much wine, which I only sipped at, unlike my hosts, who seemed intent on dulling their senses with it.

The Bedu know how to feast, but this banquet consisted of far more variety than I had ever encountered.

The dancers, too, came and went, much to Herod's delight. We talked of everything and nothing, avoiding the true nature of my mission, which could only be discussed alone with Herod, a prospect that I could not remove from my mind. Nor could I displace thoughts of Judah, who was surely eating only bread with water, or perhaps a soup.

"Now then, my dear Phasa," Herod finally said, fully fed. "Give me some time alone with our guest to discuss her father."

Phasa rose agreeably. I suspected that she was too pleased about his departure the following day to object to anything.

"As you wish. Remember what I told you, Maviah. Go for the eyes." She smiled at me, then left without a second look at her husband.

Herod dismissed the servants, who closed the doors upon exiting. So then, I was finally alone with the king of Galilee.

"I trust your day with Phasa was pleasant," he said.

"Yes, thank you."

"She isn't one to hold her tongue."

"I appreciate your delicacy regarding the matter at hand."

"And what matter is that, my dear?"

"Rami's request."

"Yes, of course. The great betrayal in the desert." He reached for a burgundy grape. "Fortunately for you, Phasa isn't terribly interested in politics. Anyone else would take great offense at your intention to betray her father."

This surprised me. "She wouldn't be put off?"

He shrugged. "Perhaps, but she leaves her father's business of state to him as long as she is set in good stead. If something were to happen to her, on the other hand, Aretas would not sit quietly, as you know." He spoke as though the thought weighed him down. "Loyalty runs thick among the Nabataeans, at least as it pertains to blood."

"And among the Bedu," I said.

"And the Bedu." He glanced at me. "Your father is a brave man."

"He is."

"Such bravery often ends in a premature death. But what is a ruler to do? The whole world conspires to rip power from those who have it. It's a merciless business, pitting son against father, father against son. My father was the worst offender. You have heard?"

"I know that he was ruthless. And that you owe your kingdom to him."

"Don't we all owe what we have to our fathers?" He plucked another grape and stared at it between his fingers. "He had ten wives in all, you know. Not all survived his jealousy and wrath. He killed more than one son—until his death, I didn't know if I would be the next. All this to protect his throne."

"And yet he still died."

"Of disease, which finally destroys us all. But my father was a great man in his own way. His reconstruction of Jerusalem stands as a marvel—the temple, of course, but also the hippodrome for chariot races and games in Greek fashion. Did you know he paraded victors through the streets naked? Gladiators, even, trained in the amphitheater he built beyond the city wall. Bloody business rejected by many Jews but loved by plenty of others. He even built caged houses for exotic beasts to be viewed by all who came to his games. It is no wonder the world loved him. My father spared no expense to impress, either in coin or in blood."

"And his son?"

He grinned. "His son loves women and theater more than blood."

He'd charged me to speak like a queen, so I did.

"What good is it to rule over a people if they hate you?"

He hesitated, either intrigued or offended. "I see Phasa has given you more courage."

"None that a queen isn't entitled to."

"And did my queen suggest that my people hate me?"

"No, my lord."

He leaned back, looking off.

"We don't see eye to eye, Phasa and I. Our union honors my treaty with Aretas—that is all, and this we both know. You see my problem, dear Maviah. What good is the throne if I cannot find love in the arms of my own queen? And yet what good is a wife if I have no throne?"

He was thoughtful, considering his own question.

"So you will understand that I cannot afford to further upset Aretas. With this in mind, I must regretfully decline your request."

He said it all without looking at me, and I was too stunned to respond.

"I have decided instead to send you to Aretas."

"Aretas?" I sat up quickly. "He's now the enemy of my father."

"And so you are enemy to me, are you not? I will send you as my gift."

He meant to betray me.

"How dare you?" I cried. "I offer you all the Kalb under Rami to wrest back control of the northern trade route with Rome's help and you would send me to my death?"

His face showed no anger, only amusement.

"You do have spine. I like that. But I have no desire for more gold. Love is the only gift I long for."

He was asking for my love? Confusion spun through my mind as I considered the possibility that this was only Herod's way of wooing me. Even so, I knew that Herod wasn't interested in a whore's love. He wanted a woman's heart, and he surely knew that threats would not buy him mine.

I saw then what I assumed to be the truth about the tetrarch of Galilee. Herod Antipas was a complex man of the heart, whose own had been turned to stone by a wife who could not reciprocate. He was indeed sick for love. He might risk his bond with Aretas for a woman who loved him, but not for glory or gold.

If so, I had to offer him my heart, or I would be sent in chains to Aretas, who would learn the truth of Rami's plans to betray him.

For the sake of my people and my son, of Judah and my father, I felt compelled to change Herod's heart toward me by whatever means necessary.

I reached for the wine and filled my chalice. Then his, to the brim. Without waiting for him, I drained my own for courage and set the goblet down.

Herod looked at me from beneath an arched brow. "You mistake me. I do not long for your love."

"But you must." I picked up his glass and held it out to him. "Drink."

I only hoped that my boldness, born of fear more than experience, would play to my favor. He hesitated, then took the chalice, amused.

"Drink it," I said.

Surprisingly, he did. All of it. "Is that all you offer, Queen? Wine?"

"No. I offer far more, but you seem incapable of appreciating the weight of my offer. So my first gift to you will be proper thinking. You've studied the Greeks, I'm sure."

"Of course. I'm surprised you have."

"Then you know the value of proper lines of thought. Proper thought would suggest that letting Rome decide what to make of my offer would gain you far more than making the decision for them."

I slipped off my sandals and settled down to my belly, propped up by my elbows, calves bared. Surely I could speak Herod's language.

"Proper lines of thought would suggest you have nothing to risk in taking me to Rome—it is your duty. Aretas would accept that much. Rome would demand it."

None of this seemed to influence him. I reached for the wine and filled his goblet yet again.

"Proper lines of thought would also suggest that for a lovesick man to ignore the company of a beautiful woman while taking such matters under consideration is foolish." I handed him the wine. "As you said, what good is a throne if you cannot enjoy its spoils?"

"Wine is not conducive to proper lines of thought," he said.

"Not for the common man, but I've heard it properly lubricates any king's mind."

"Well then...you are more queen than I had thought."

"You see? Now you are finally thinking. So drink. Enjoy your last night before setting off to Rome."

He drank, only half this time, but by now he'd had five or six cups and I was sure that even he could not withstand its powers.

"I'm not convinced," he said, warming to my game. "Show me more of your...thoughts."

I lowered my hand and traced his knee with my finger, daring him with my eyes to resist. "First you will show me yours. Tell me what you are hiding from me. You have nothing to lose by taking me to Rome, and yet you refuse, thinking that Rome will never learn you rejected my gift of the trade routes. But you are wrong. Rome will learn."

"Oh?" He reached for my hand and stroked it lightly, which gave me pause, for I didn't want his touch.

"Of course they will learn," I said. "You'll send me to Aretas, who may well kill me, but not before I explain to him why he must immediately inform Rome of your betrayal."

I saw the hesitation in his eyes.

"Aretas stands to gain if he tells Rome of your failure to take Rami's offer to them," I continued. "That offer will be useless by then, because Aretas will have time to defend against the threat, and this will only infuriate Rome more."

It was clear by his look that he had underestimated me.

It was also clear that he wasn't terribly bothered about that. There was something else that played on his mind. What was he hiding?

Another thought occurred to me.

"You might also think that killing me this very night and letting my offer die with me will save you," I said. "But again, you would be wrong."

"By the heavens, you have thought of everything, haven't you? Then tell me how I would be wrong?"

"First you will tell me what else you are hiding," I said, running my hand across his thigh. "You are too intelligent to ignore such an opportunity for gain."

"The only gain that interests me now is love," he said.

In the space of one breath, I knew what he was hiding. Herod had his eyes on another woman. Not me, but someone he already knew. I was only a distraction.

The king of Galilee was in love with another woman.

Only Phasa stood in his way, for any betrayal of her would be a betrayal of Aretas. He was trying to win favor from Aretas in the event he sent Phasa back to Petra. It was the only thing that made sense to me.

"Who is she?" I asked.

"Who?"

"The woman you love."

His eyes shifted from mine, confirming my suspicions. I had stumbled upon a terrible secret. I could not afford to antagonize him.

"It doesn't matter what her name is," I said. "You're a king; this is your prerogative. And as you said, for a man to be king but not be loved is a terrible thing. I can see the distance between you and Phasa."

Herod stared at the candles without speaking.

"Is it wrong, then, to seek the love that a king deserves?"

His eyes moistened, surely aided by the wine. When he spoke, he did so as a man smitten, not as a king.

"Who can know what it's like for a king to live so long with a woman out of obligation? To be starved of love is like death for me."

I didn't tell him that most marriages among the Bedu, as well as in Palestine, had nothing to do with sentiment. As a man of privilege he apparently expected love.

And who was I to blame him? His obligations to Rome and Nabataea, and, indeed, to his own heritage, had imprisoned him. I knew something about such obligations. Herod might well be a monster, but one I then pitied.

"Then starve yourself of love no longer. I would think Phasa is as much a prisoner to this marriage as you."

Herod settled, undone now by the baring of his true heart.

"During my years in Rome, I learned to see a woman in ways most among my people do not," he said. "Too many rabbis, indeed the whole of the Jew, now embrace the teachings of Ben Sirach. He claims that a woman, indeed a daughter, is nothing more than a constant source of shame."

He knew that Rami had sent me into slavery, so he knew that he was pulling at my heart. My mind returned to my conversation with Judah and Saba about how women were treated in Palestine.

" 'Do not sit down with women,' he writes. 'A woman's spite is preferable to a woman's kindness, for women give rise to shame and reproach.' "

Herod took a deep breath.

"But there was once a king named Solomon whose heart I share." He looked at me with cheerless eyes. "Phasa is a good woman, Maviah. I wish her no harm."

"No. No, of course you don't."

"But I feel nothing for her."

Herod lay back on the cushions and rested the back of his hand over his eyes, reduced to sorrow. I thought of my father, a ruler without his tongue, and here Herod, a ruler without the woman he longed for.

So, then, what good was it to be king if what you craved, either power or love, was out of reach?

Still, Herod was slipping away and had not yet agreed to take me to Rome. So I rose and sat beside him, stroking his hair with my fingers. In that moment I felt like a mother to him. But one with her own mind.

"Listen to me, my lord. You must not send me to Petra."

A tear slipped past his temple. I had not envisioned such an outpouring of emotion from such a powerful man.

Unless, I thought, he was hiding something else.

But I dismissed the notion. I leaned over him and placed a gentle kiss on his forehead.

"You must not send me to my death," I whispered. "It will only cause you more suffering."

He let out a long breath. "Yes. You're right."

"Instead, you will take me to Rome with you."

Herod lay still.

"You must, out of obligation to the emperor."

"No. I can't."

"Why not?"

"It's not possible."

Although I could not understand why it was impossible, his tone made any objection hopeless. So I let the request go.

"Then take my offer to Rome for me," I said.

"Of course." He relaxed further and lowered his hand, eyes still closed. "Yes, I will," he breathed.

Was there more to be said? I saw that I had few choices in the matter but to trust him. I had won at least this much through persuasion, hadn't I?

"Lie down with me, Maviah," he said. "Comfort me."

Strangely, I did not find his request objectionable, for he was being gentle with me and was not forcing himself. But there wasn't room on the couch, so I leaned over and lay my head on his heaving chest.

There I heard Herod's heart beating in all its terrible sorrow. His hand settled on my head and stroked my hair for a few minutes, but he encouraged nothing more.

Finally his hand stilled and he began to snore softly.

When I was sure that he was in deep sleep, I eased from his chest and, unsure of what to do, walked to the door.

When I opened it, two posted guards faced me. One of them looked over my shoulder, saw Herod's chest rising and falling on the couch, and motioned me back.

"You will remain here."

"Phasa—"

"Use his bed."

With that, he motioned me back again and closed the door. So I walked to the door that led into Herod's chambers with its large bed dressed in silk and stuffed cushions. Just one oil lamp lit the room. Then, disrobing but for the simple white tunic, I lay down and closed my eyes.

I had prevailed. Judah would be proud. My father, even.

We would have to wait, yes, but tomorrow Herod would leave and I would once again be with Judah. It was enough.

Heavy with wine, I fell asleep on Herod's bed and dreamed of Judah.

The sun was already bright when I woke, and for a moment I was surprised to find myself on a soft bed rather than on the sand, as I had slept for so many nights. Only then did the events of the day before return to me. I glanced about the room.

The first thing I saw was the guard Brutus posted by the door, watching me with a satisfied glint in his eyes. I saw no sign of Herod. Or Phasa.

"Where is he?" I asked.

"Where he is meant to be. To Rome."

I sat up, surprised he had not awakened me before leaving.

"Where is Phasa?"

"In her chambers," he said. "Where she should be."

I threw the sheets from my body, intending to rush from the room.

"Such an eager one." He offered me a twisted grin.

"I must go to Phasa," I said, setting my feet on the marble floor and rising, holding my dress closed at my throat.

"You're mistaken. You will remain here."

"Here? For what purpose? For how long?"

"Until the witch comes for you."

Here was the disdain Phasa had mentioned.

"You call your queen a witch? I am her *guest*!"

"Then let her fetch her guest. Until then you will remain." He smiled. "You wish, instead, to contest me?"

I saw that Brutus could not be bent, for he despised both Phasa and me.

"Then bring Judah to me," I said.

"Judah?"

"My slave. The Jew, Judah."

"Of course. Your slaves. They will remain in the cells until Herod's return."

The blood drained from my face.

"What can you mean? Don't be absurd! I wish to see my slaves at once!"

"Now the witch's guest orders me to betray Herod's orders? Are all queens from the desert so unwise?"

"Why would he order this? Judah is *my* slave, not Herod's!"

"Because he knows you care for him."

Judah was being kept in the dungeon to ensure my loyalty.

"You will not leave before Herod returns."

With that he turned his back to me, left the room, and shut the door.

CHAPTER FOURTEEN

FOR TWO WEEKS I lived in Herod's castle, separated from Judah and Saba, lost in a sea of uncertainty, never able to dismiss the whispers of fear that chased my every thought. I was no less imprisoned than Judah. We were all at the mercy of Herod and his guards, and the thought of waiting so long for his return from Rome only increased my unease.

The moment Phasa learned I was awake that morning of Herod's departure, she had swept in to collect me, joyous as a bird on the banks of the Nile. Her husband was gone and she could fly. But her high spirits in the days that followed could not put the wind beneath my wings.

I told myself that I was in Galilee only to avenge my son's death and bring salvation to the Kalb, not to be with Judah. But I failed to convince my heart to join my mind in this matter.

In much the same way that Herod seemed enslaved by his need for love, I was caged in that palace and my heart was captive to Judah more than to my greater purpose.

Who was this man who'd swallowed my heart? I had known Judah only for a few weeks, and passion was not a sign of strength among women in the desert. Perhaps I had bonded with him only because I'd lost my child and needed comfort. Perhaps I sought in such a strong man a new father to replace the one who'd rejected me. But I thought neither of these possibilities pointed to the greater truth.

For in greater truth I was a woman so thirsty for companionship that she could no longer keep her mind fully fixed on the journey ahead.

Was this not true of all? Of Herod and Phasa and me? Did not we all long for what we could not have? So, then...I pitied us all.

It was Brutus who had ordered my separation from Judah in Herod's absence. Phasa told me this. Herod had only insisted that I remain in the palace and that Judah and Saba be kept in their cells. There was no reason except spite that Brutus would prohibit either Phasa or me from visiting the dungeons. My bitterness toward Herod's guard grew.

The daughter of Aretas smothered me with kindness and lavish comforts, insisting that I sleep in her chambers and bathe in her bath, attended by her servants. I put on my bravest face, relishing her comfort as much as I could, for I would not allow my heavy heart to unseat her from her perch.

So I spent my time listening to her speak of Petra, which she missed terribly, and of Galilee, which she tolerated, and of the Jews, whom we both agreed had always been an enslaved people—whether under the Egyptians or the Babylonians or Rome, always in the chains of a troubled god who demanded bloodshed in exchange for cleanliness. The Jews, it seemed to me, followed this god out of fear that he would smite his children with the rod of disease, death, and punishment.

Truly, the whole world was enslaved by belief in troubled gods.

Phasa, like me, had little use for religion.

We spoke of the theater and her favorite hypocrites, whose antics sent her sprawling across her bed in fits of laughter as she mimicked them. And of her beautiful jewelry, any single piece of which was worth more than all of Nazareth might gather in a year. And of her servants, whom she loved, I thought. And of Sepphoris, which we both often gazed upon from the high tower.

From our protected perch, the political troubles spoken of by Judah and Miriam were difficult to fathom. There were many slaves at work about the grounds, and poor begging on the distant streets, but the world was full of slaves and poor, was it not? And by Phasa's own accounting, Herod was a decent king, unlike his father, who had butchered thousands of his own people to protect his throne.

It was also clear to me that Phasa hated her husband no more than he hated her——she only felt enslaved by him and, indeed, by Aretas, who'd sent her to Galilee for his own gain. In this way, too, Phasa and I were like sisters.

We ate more food than I had known to exist and took more baths than we possibly needed and applied more fragrances than I thought was healthy for the flesh.

During all this, Judah and Saba were captive in dark dungeons beneath the ground. A Bedu might prefer death. I could not find peace.

And so, on the fifteenth day, I conspired to take whatever risk necessary to see that they were alive and safe.

"Phasa...may we speak alone?" I said, stepping into her chamber that late afternoon.

She waved her hand at Esther. "Give us a moment, Esther."

"Yes, mistress." The young servant who was like a shadow to Phasa dipped her head and left the room, easing the door shut.

"What is it, dear?"

"Only a question."

I had considered my approach all through the day.

"Why does a queen have slaves?" I asked.

"To serve her, of course." She paused, studying me curiously. "You would like your own in my chambers? Surely you know that my slaves are yours."

"Is a queen not obligated to her slaves, so that they might serve her?"

"But of course."

"She must see to it that they are well cared for."

"Even more," she said, "to be sure they want for nothing. I have always said, Maviah, treat a slave like a queen and she will love you like one. Did I tell you about Esther's mother?"

She had and I didn't wish to hear again the story of how the woman had died of illness, leaving Esther like a daughter to Phasa. So I ignored the question.

"And if a queen wished to fulfill this obligation here, in this palace, knowing that her slaves were in the dungeon, how would she go about it?"

Phasa stared at me. She knew what was on my mind, naturally, and that I aimed to protect her from crossing any line that might later be questioned by Herod.

A knowing smile lit her face and she crossed her arms, pacing now.

"It would be very dangerous, of course."

"Of course," I said.

"Because here there is a dog named Brutus who hates the queen and has made it his business to keep her in misery."

"Yes."

"Then the queen must find a way to her slave while Malcheus, who is a Jew of good heart, takes charge. A time when Brutus is gone from the palace, drowning his own misery and guilt in drink."

My heartbeat quickened, for Phasa hadn't rejected the idea outright.

"And when might this be?" I asked.

"After the twelfth hour, naturally. When it is dark." Phasa lifted a finger. "She would not go as queen, however."

"No?"

"No. As a servant. In the event she is seen by the wrong party. She would enter the tunnels through Herod's court and slip unseen to the dungeon on the east side." Phasa eyed me with one brow arched. "But she could not enter the cell. This would require the theft of a key and constitute a breach of Herod's will."

"No, of course not. She would only see that her slaves are well."

"Herod cannot be crossed," she said.

"No, never. It would be madness."

"Madness."

Truly, I could not jeopardize Herod's trust in me by defying his will, any more than Phasa could.

Matter settled, Phasa continued.

"After the twelfth hour, if the queen were to be caught entering the dungeons dressed as a servant, she would be turned over to Malcheus, who serves me as well as Herod. I would find a way to protect her."

Phasa's eyes sparkled and I decided then that I would do precisely this. So I asked her to tell me the way in the event the queen would see her slave. She only too willingly plotted with me.

It was as much a game to her as it was a matter of life and death to me, but when the hour approached and she helped me dress in the simple white tunic and blue mantle worn by her servants, she grew somber.

"You really mean to do this, Maviah."

"Would you not?"

She took me by the arm.

"I will call the servants to my chambers so none will see you going to Herod's court. Remember, down the stairs and through the underground passage. I cannot tell you the danger if Brutus or any loyal to him were to find out."

"I understand."

"Danger for Judah," she said. "Not only you."

The thought had not occurred to me.

"The guards there don't know you, and the way through Herod's passage should be clear, but swear to me that if you see anyone, anyone at all, you will turn back."

"I will. I swear it."

She gave me her most earnest stare, then smiled.

"It is a scandal, isn't it? Sneaking right past the nose of that beast."

By now I was unnerved, thinking how Judah might be punished if I were caught.

"This is no game, Phasa."

"No, which makes it that much more terrifying. Wait here a minute while I call the servants, then use the back passage to Herod's court as we discussed."

She walked toward the door, but stopped and turned back.

"Maviah?"

"Yes?"

"You will pass my good will to the black one?"

"Saba?"

"Yes, to Saba. Tell him that the queen finds him... I don't know... how would you say it to such a man?"

"You ask me?"

"Tell him the queen finds him powerful." She started to turn but thought better of it. "No, magnificent. Tell him the queen finds him exotic."

I was flummoxed by this, for I wasn't risking so much to indulge her fantasies. "Well, which is it? Magnificent or exotic?"

"Like a stallion," she said. "That's it. Tell him the queen sees him as a stallion. Can you do that for me, my dear?"

What was I to say? But Phasa was of the Nabataeans, who were extravagant in all matters.

"If I can. Yes."

Phasa smiled and swept from the room with the grace of an eagle.

I followed Phasa's instructions with great caution. I went to the same room in which I'd first met Herod, then slipped through a side door that led me down a flight of stairs hewn into the rock. I used an oil lamp to guide my way, careful to keep it from going out, stepping lightly in bare feet.

The passage beneath the palace led me directly to a large cavern. I could hear two guards talking out of sight to my right. But Phasa had told me to go left, so I hurried to that passage, holding my tunic close so that it caused no sound.

It was here that I found the main tunnel lined with smaller cells and barred iron doors. At the end of the tunnel, another door. And in the last windowless cell before that door I found a man seated on the rough ground, leaning back against the rock wall. There were wooden stakes embedded in the surface above his head, made to strap up prisoners for punishment, I assumed.

Even in the darkness, I recognized Judah immediately.

His face was covered in dust and he was naked except for a dirty loincloth girded up around his thighs. He looked to have been starved, but his was a body bound in muscle and accustomed to harsh living, and he would not be easily weakened.

He stared at me, momentarily at a loss.

"Judah?"

He blinked, unbelieving. My face was in the shadow, so I slid my mantle from my head.

"It's me. Maviah."

He came off the ground like a lion and rushed to the bars. His wide eyes skirted the cavern beyond me.

"I came alone," I said.

He snatched a finger to his lips and peered down the passage again. "They know you are here?" he whispered.

"Only Phasa."

"But not Brutus?"

"No. I...I had to see you, Judah." I was unsure whether to feel relief at the sight of him or rage that such a noble Bedu was caged like a dog.

"Are you well?" I asked.

He hesitated, then made himself plain.

"I am Judah," he said.

I can't say why those words struck me to the core as they did, but I could not stop the tears that flooded my eyes.

He was Judah—a towering rock who could hardly think of his own safety, much less fear for it.

He was Judah—eternally bright like the venerated stars in his sky.

But more, he was Judah, who, though a man, saw beyond my shame.

I impulsively reached through the bars, seized his arm, and pulled him as close as possible, my cheek pressed against the iron.

"I was so afraid for you," I whispered.

I felt his hand grip my tunic. Though the bars separated our flesh, our hearts were one, I thought, and we held each other for a long moment before looking into each other's eyes.

"You are well," he said.

"I am."

"Then tell me...what has been decided? You bring me good news?"

"You know that Herod has gone to Rome?"

"Rome? They've told me nothing."

"Nothing?" I said.

"They've refused the many requests of a slave to see his queen, no matter how persuasive my words."

I could imagine him bending their ears with his winsome speeches.

"And Saba?" I glanced down the passage.

"Past the door. They've prevented our speaking, but he's unharmed."

Phasa's request seemed as preposterous now as when she'd made it, but I had given my word.

"When you can, tell him I have a message from Phasa."

"For him?"

"Yes. She wants him to know that he is a stallion in her eyes."

Judah stared at me, then smiled. "It will be a great gift to him."

"To Saba?"

"Don't be fooled by his mask of stone. He is only a child behind it. Now tell me the news of Herod. He's gone to Rome on your behalf?"

I told him everything, speaking in soft tones that could not reach far. I told about my night with Herod and about my time with Phasa and how we had become like sisters from the desert. In whatever delighted me, Judah would reflect that same joy. Then he offered me a warning, reminding me of the dangers of Aretas and Herod and even Phasa, for he did not know her the way I did.

Each moment I lingered increased the risk of my discovery, but I relished this encounter.

He agreed that Herod's departure must be taken as a good sign, even if kings were known for their betrayal. There was no better option for us than to wait as Herod's guests, in strict accordance with his wishes.

"It will be many weeks," I said. "I cannot possibly go so long without seeing you."

"Nor I. But you must understand, Maviah...this too will pass. It is what happens after Herod's return that concerns us most. I would have you safe with Phasa, beyond any threat from the guard. Brutus is a vile man."

"How can you remain here, caged like an animal?"

"Me? I've spent many months in the Nafud until only my bones were left under the scorching sun. I have waged battle with a thousand arrows and blades, many cutting into my flesh. I've seen the worst and now the best that this world has to offer." He opened his palm and indicated the cell. "Do you think a few nights here will harm me? It's cooled by the earth and my bed is smooth. Herod's dungeon is my place of peace and rest. He only makes his guest stronger."

Then he reminded me who he was once again.

"I am Judah."

"Yes. You are Judah."

"Son of Israel."

"Son of Israel."

Satisfied, he turned from me and stroked his beard, pacing.

"I have only one request of you, Maviah."

"Of course. Anything."

"You say that Phasa has an eye for Saba?"

"Clearly."

"Then perhaps you might convince her to do what you cannot."

"To do what? Comfort Saba?"

He took one of the bars in his hand and spoke in a very soft voice.

"No. To go to Capernaum. To see Yeshua."

Yeshua. I had put the mystic from my mind, worried only for Judah.

He continued, speaking quickly in a whisper. "Miriam told me that her son travels sometimes to Judea. He was by the sea in Capernaum when we saw Miriam, but he's not likely to remain long."

"You fear that he will leave before Herod returns," I said.

"Yes."

I felt oddly irritated in that moment. Surely Judah could find his mystic after we were out of danger.

"You want Phasa to find a way for me to find—"

"Never! Herod has forbidden you to leave. But Phasa might go. On account of Saba."

"For Saba? Hers is but a passing fantasy! She would never go on his account."

"You could speak to Phasa. She might be swayed."

It was absurd. Judah was grasping for his stars. Perhaps I was bothered by the awareness that his obsession with finding his sage consumed him more than our present danger. His fixation on Yeshua seemed to have deepened here in the dungeon.

"Speak to Phasa on this," he said. "A way might be made, you understand. Perhaps Phasa would want to see Yeshua for herself. Do only this and I would find great comfort here in my cell."

I had promised Miriam that I would say nothing to Herod's court of Yeshua. Judah had made the same promise. Still, his imploring eyes drew me.

"And if she agreed, what would Phasa say to this sage?" I asked.

He blinked. "She would tell him about me and my elders who came to him. She would ask him if I could be of any assistance."

"To join with him in overthrowing Rome? She is Herod's wife. You ask the impossible."

"Then she might only see him and report for me. You say she is a friend to Jews and to you...ask her. Or perhaps she knows of another who will go on my behalf."

It was madness.

Then again, Judah was Bedu. It is said that the greatest Bedu feed on madness, for it makes one strong enough to defeat the greatest enemy in the desert. Or perhaps his time alone in the dungeon had pushed him beyond reason.

"I only ask that you speak to her about—"

"Yes," I said.

"Yes?"

"Yes, I will speak to Phasa."

"You will, then?"

"For you, I will find a way."

I was so taken with Judah's passion for his king, and he was so engrossed in the prospect of gaining news of him, that neither of us heard the sound from the passage until it was upon us. Only the scrape of a sandal on the floor, but unmistakable.

We turned as one, breath caught.

At first I could not make sense of what my eyes saw. A guard, yes, but not just any guard. My heart crashed into my throat.

For it was Brutus who stood in the passage, face like a stone.

CHAPTER FIFTEEN

WHAT EVENTS had conspired to me pluck me from the heavens and thrust me into the deepest abyss? Perhaps I had been seen after all, and a report made to Brutus. Perhaps he had never left the palace, or had returned by chance. Perhaps my plotting with Phasa had been overheard.

Any explanation for how Brutus came to be standing in the dungeons would do nothing to remove him.

"Judah?" My voice came in a trembling whisper.

"Say nothing."

No, for there was nothing to be said. Except by Brutus.

"So." His low voice sent dread through my bones. "The whore from the desert seeks misery."

Two guards approached from behind him, one of whom held a torch.

A nightmare unfolded before me, too quickly and too slowly at once. And as in a dream, I was powerless to alter events.

Even if I had been able to influence Brutus, he was beyond the place for words.

Calmly withdrawing a knife from his side, he walked up to me, grabbed my hair, and pulled me against him, blade at my neck.

Judah gripped the bars and his knuckles turned white. "She is under the protection of Herod!"

Brutus ignored the warning. "Restrain the slave."

The guard with the torch set it in the wall and approached the cell, keys in hand.

"If you resist, I will cut her," Brutus said.

With those words we both knew what Brutus intended. Judah looked into my eyes, offering me strength. But I knew then that it was he, not I, who would need it.

My vision blurred. "Judah..." The blade pressed against my neck.

"Do not resist him, Maviah," Judah said. "He cannot hurt you." The warrior in him hid any panic he might have felt. "Remember who I am."

He was Judah. Judah who would now suffer on my behalf.

Brutus, breath heavy and thick with the scent of drink, said nothing as his men unlocked the cage and with swords drawn forced Judah to the far wall.

"Remember, Maviah!"

But I found no courage in the thought that Judah could withstand great suffering for his queen.

I guessed that Judah could have easily overpowered both guards, for he was a warrior unequaled and by appearance alone much stronger than either. Instead he turned willingly and lifted his hands to the posts jutting from the wall. With leather thongs they strapped one wrist to each post, then stepped back.

Torchlight danced over scars from old battles on Judah's bare back.

"Make sure he bleeds," Brutus said.

The guard closest to me took a whip from his belt, stood back, and laid the leather strap across Judah's back, grunting with the exertion.

The crack of whip on muscled skin echoed through the chamber and I winced.

Judah did not. He might have been made of stone.

The guard drew his arm back and struck again, then again. The first two lashes drew welts. The third cut Judah's flesh outright.

Still he showed no sign of pain.

I closed my eyes and stilled my breathing as Judah's tormentor beat him without mercy. An eerie silence enveloped me but for the breath of Brutus in my ear, the grunting of the guard with each blow, and the crack of the whip.

I did not count them, but the guard laid the whip across his back at least twenty times before Brutus stopped him.

Perhaps if he'd taken less drink that night, the terror would have ended with the last blow. Perhaps if Judah had cried out, Brutus's thirst for blood would have been satisfied. But neither was the case.

"Now the whore," Brutus said.

I opened my eyes, not sure I'd heard correctly. Judah was sagging, his back a bloody mess. The guards were staring at Brutus, unsure.

"Tie her to the bars."

"Sir—"

"Do you question me?" I flinched at the voice that thundered in my ear.

"No, sir."

Judah slowly straightened, but he did not speak.

The guards feared Brutus as much as they feared the king, surely. Judah was restrained, and I was without the means to defend myself. Nothing could stop Herod's beast.

"Strap her up and bare her back," Brutus said.

Judah remained silent, but I could see his flesh trembling as he stood. Fear washed over me.

Brutus shoved me toward his men, who grabbed me by the arms, spun me around, and shoved me against the cell door. They lifted my arms and began to tie me to the iron bars as ordered by Brutus.

I could see Judah to my right, chest heaving, facing the wall. He knew that any objection would only gain both of us more suffering. He was powerless to save me.

I realized that to resist in any way, even in my heart, would only offer me more pain. In this way too, Judah and I would share our lives. We would both leave Galilee with scarred backs. This was now our fate to accept.

A strange calm settled over me.

"Judah..." I whispered.

His resolve broke then, as if my faint call had beckoned a jinn deep within him. One moment Judah stood still, strapped in silence to the wall inside the cell, and in the next he was twisting, baring all his strength, voicing his outrage with a thunderous roar.

The leather restraints did not pull free; they simply snapped. Both of them, as if made of thread. And then Judah was in the air, mouth stretched wide, eyes on fire with hatred.

It was his ferocity more than his boldness or strength that took my breath away. For in that moment, Judah was not the man I knew. He'd been transformed into a warrior the likes of which I had never seen, not even watching Johnin fight for his life as a gladiator in Egypt.

I was restrained already, with my back to Brutus and his guards, so I saw only the first blow of Judah's fist as it slammed into the side of the guard's face like a hammer. The unmistakable crack of breaking bone cut off the man's surprised cry.

And then I saw nothing except the bars before me.

But I heard. I heard the raging grunts of men fighting off death. I heard the heavy landing of fist on bone and the distinctive sound of a blade piercing a body. The slapping of flesh on a stone floor.

And then I heard only the heavy breathing of one man.

I twisted to see Judah standing over three dead Roman guards, staring down at his handiwork, stunned. The blade in his right fist dripped with blood.

"Judah?"

He straightened and looked up at me, as if only now remembering where he was.

Judah rushed to me and sliced the blade through my restraints, freeing me in the space of two breaths. I would have thrown my arms around him but for the blood on his chest and the painful welts upon his back.

"I've killed Brutus," he said, looking at the still body. A gash in the chief's neck continued to bleed. I could summon no remorse for the beast.

"You have."

"I wasn't thinking."

Indeed. He had been acting only from his heart, I thought.

"What have I done?"

"You have saved your queen," I said.

Judah hesitated, then dipped his head. "Then it was my honor."

I knew then that I would always love Judah. He was the savior not only of my heart, but of my body. His eyes lingered on my face, and slowly his full senses returned. The brutal warrior in him retreated into the shadows as the more gentle part of him emerged.

"We must free Saba," he finally said.

"And tell Phasa."

"You are sure?"

"Perfectly."

PHASA PACED before us, glancing first at Saba, then at Judah, with equal parts awe and interest. To say that she was worried would be to lie outright. Although she'd feigned great concern over what Herod might think of such a dramatic turn of events, she could not hide her awareness of her own good fortune.

Brutus, her enemy, was dead.

We'd quickly freed Saba from his cell beyond the door using the guard's keys. Saba had stared at Judah's carnage without asking for an explanation, having heard enough. It had taken us only a few minutes to make our way unseen back up to Herod's court and, from there, to Phasa's chambers.

She'd expressed shock at the appearance of both Saba and Judah, then insisted we clean Judah's back and apply salve. Only when he was properly treated did she stand before us for a full accounting.

"Now tell me," she said, crossing her arms. "Whom did you kill?"

I told her what had happened, precisely as it had. And when I finally explained that Brutus and two of his guards were now locked in the dungeons, robbed of life, a thin smile slowly replaced her initial shock.

"So, then...it appears that the gods have finally come out of hiding."

"I see no gods," Saba said. "Only trouble."

Phasa walked up to him with a twinkle in her eye. "Sometimes even trouble can bring the most pleasant surprises, my stallion," she said, tracing his bare chest with her finger.

I had not yet told her that Saba knew nothing of her message.

"Do you think you can trust me? Can you lay that wild man at my feet and give me charge?"

He glanced at me, taken off guard.

"I ask you, not your queen," Phasa said. "If I bite, it is only for your own pleasure as well, I can assure you."

This wasn't the way of the Bedu, and though Saba was well traveled, I doubted he had experienced the sensuous ways of royal Nabataeans like Phasa.

"Well?"

"If I must," he said.

"But do you want to? If I could promise you the world, would you let me bend your ear?"

His eyes flitted to Judah.

"Not him either," she said. "It is I who speak."

"Yes," he finally said.

"Good. It's a beginning."

Phasa stepped away from him and faced us all.

"Maviah, I know, will trust me. What about you, Judah? Will you?"

I suspected that he too had been taken aback by Phasa's brazen words, but he was quick to respond. "Yes."

"Good. Then wait for me in my bedchamber." She faced Saba. "Both of you."

She turned her back and swept toward the outer door, gliding in her long gown as though on a cloud. "Your queen will remain here with me until I call for you. Make no sound."

"Go," I whispered to Saba, who in particular still appeared unsure.

They went without another word.

Phasa pushed wide the heavy door that sealed her outer chamber. "Esther, my dear, please fetch Malcheus. Tell him that I must see him immediately on a matter of life and death."

"Yes, mistress." I heard her feet pattering away in a hurry.

When Phasa turned she was smiling. "That will get him here quickly."

And so it was that Malcheus, who was second only to Brutus among the palace guard, presented himself within minutes at Phasa's door. He wore the dark armor of Jews in service to the Roman order.

He stared between us, curious. "You called, my queen."

"I did. Thank you for coming so quickly."

"Of course."

She took his arm and led him in, which made him appear awkward, for this wasn't the way of a queen with her guard.

Phasa released him. "You know that I've always liked you, Malcheus."

He said nothing.

"And you know that I have always seen the Jewish people as unfairly oppressed, even though I am the beneficiary of their oppression. Is this not true?"

Malcheus looked at me, even more confused now, for he was on quicksand, serving both Jews and Romans.

"Speak freely, Maviah is from Arabia and can be trusted."

"I can't say that I was aware of your thoughts on this matter."

"No, of course not. I am merely the wife of Herod, whom you serve first. And yet, Herod knows my heart. And now you do as well, for your ears alone."

He offered a curt nod.

"And you also know that there is no room for error in executing Herod's orders."

"I do."

"None at all."

"None," he agreed.

"Good. Then you should know that Brutus has betrayed my husband's orders and placed himself in the most dreadful condition."

"Brutus?" His attention, though fully present before, was now acute.

"Yes, Brutus." Phasa swept to her left, regal and bold. "That beast of a man has defiled his charge in the most egregious manner. Tell me, what was Herod's charge regarding the queen Maviah?"

"That she be forbidden from leaving the palace."

"Only this?"

"Yes."

"I would add only that in accepting her as queen from the desert, explicit in his order was that she be treated as a queen in his palace."

"Yes, of course."

"And what of her slaves?"

"That they be held in the dungeons."

"Did Herod, on any occasion, forbid the queen from seeing her slaves?"

Malcheus answered with caution. "I believe this was an order from Brutus."

"Brutus. The vilest of creatures who believes in nothing but his own self-importance and miserable existence, which he lords over all who cross his path."

She let the bitter indictment settle.

"And what would you say if you were to learn that this vile creature defiled Herod's will by ordering Maviah—my sister at heart, from the noble Kalb, who are like brothers to my father, King Aretas—to be whipped?"

Malcheus surely knew that he was being led but could see no way to shift Phasa from her course.

"I would say he has misjudged."

"You put it with too much grace, but it will have to do. If you had been present, I have no doubt that you would have stopped Brutus from such a heinous act against his king. Not doing so would only implicate your own conspiracy with that monster. Surely."

His nod was slow to come and only half-assured.

"No need to fear, dear Malcheus. Fortunately for you, another man stepped in to stop Brutus while his arm was still drawn with whip in hand. But Brutus's aggression against Herod's guest cannot be ignored."

Again, Malcheus's response was slow.

"It cannot."

"The one who stopped Brutus must be kept safe until my husband's return so that Herod can make the appropriate accounting."

"Yes," Malcheus said. Then his concern got the better of him. "But, as you know, this may present a challenge for Brutus. If I understand correctly, the queen wasn't whipped. Is Brutus truly at fault?"

"This is for Herod to decide, not you," Phasa snapped. "And yet we all know that Brutus is at fault. Why else would he now be dead?"

"Dead?" The second in command paled.

"Dead. Killed by Judah, Maviah's slave, after Brutus whipped him and then turned that same whip on my sister. Dead in the dungeon as we speak. Don't look so shocked." Phasa stepped up to him. "On my word, this is the day of your own deliverance."

"I must know what happened!"

Phasa quickly explained the order of occurrences, meticulously laying blame at the feet of Brutus. As she spoke, Malcheus relaxed, seeing his opportunity in Brutus's death.

Aretas's blood flowed in Phasa's veins, I saw, for she was as shrewd as any king.

"So you see, Malcheus...Judah did only what one most loyal to Herod would have done. And he cannot be faulted for being a Jew even as you are a Jew. And now you, as ranking officer, must assume charge of the palace guard until Herod can express his will. Under my hand, naturally. Do you not agree?"

He offered no further hesitancy. "I see no other way."

Phasa paced. "Good. Then you will also understand why Judah and the other slave, Saba, must be my guests and will remain under my protection. I will not suffer the retaliation of any Roman guard loyal to Brutus."

"Yes, of course. I shall place two of my own men at their cells immediately. They will not be touched."

"You mistake me, Malcheus. Your dungeons failed the king once. Saba and Judah will remain in my chambers, as I see fit." She arched her brow, inviting him to challenge her. "Or would you rather I tell Herod that it was your gross misjudgment on the hour of your own watch that led to his favorite guard's death?"

My heart leaped within my breast. I could have kissed Phasa's feet.

"I see," Malcheus said after a few moments.

"You will leave them in my charge, to be done with as I see fit. They are no longer your concern."

"They must at least remain—"

"They will remain where I see fit. If I choose to walk naked through the streets with them, it is none of your concern. Do you understand?"

He finally wiped his hands, one against the other, disowning any further responsibility. "Then they are on your head."

"Precisely." Phasa walked up to him and brushed his bearded cheek with her thumb. "Don't worry, my dear Malcheus. As I said, I like you. I'm sure you will do nothing to dampen my affections in such a dangerous time."

She turned and called for Judah and Saba, who appeared from her chambers, eyes fixed upon Malcheus.

"I am happy to inform you that Malcheus has risen in station to chief of the palace guard. He has insisted that both of you should be placed under my charge, as I alone see fit, because his dungeons have failed to protect you." She turned back to Malcheus. "One Jew to the other, swear that neither you, Malcheus, nor you, Judah, will undermine my will in this."

They showed agreement by the dip of their heads.

"Swear it," Phasa said.

Judah reaffirmed his agreement. "I swear by the God of our fathers that I will not undermine your will in this."

"And you, Malcheus."

"I swear the same."

"Thank you, Malcheus. I will speak only the best of you to Herod. You may leave us now."

He hesitated, then left us.

I could scarcely contain the joy in my heart. The moment his form vanished from our sight, I hurried to Phasa, lowered myself to one knee, and kissed her hand.

"Thank you."

Then I threw my arms around her body and held her close.

"Thank you, thank you."

She laughed, delighted, hand on my head. "Thank your slave, dear Maviah. It is he who has shown himself to be a lion. Go to your slave. I will go to mine."

By this she surely meant Saba, but I knew that Saba would not be enslaved to her so easily. Even so, my mind wasn't on Phasa's plotting.

I rushed to Judah, already knowing how I would repay him. I kissed him on his cheek and then tenderly held his face in my hands.

"We will go to your king, Judah," I whispered. "I swear it. I will find a way for you to see Yeshua."

CAPERNAUM

"The kingdom of God does not so come that you can
watch for it.

Nor will they say, 'See here,' or 'See there.'

For the kingdom of God is within you."

Yeshua

CHAPTER SIXTEEN

I WOULD prefer to claim that it was I who persuaded Phasa to help Judah find Yeshua in Capernaum, but it was Saba. He, though slave in appearance, was not easily swayed by Phasa in any regard. He did not resist her playful advances, but neither did he yield to them, and this only seemed to delight Phasa more. She was not the kind to make demands in matters of men, clearly preferring the distraction of the game.

Though stiff and quiet for several days, during which he was ever by her side, Saba began to accept his role after I suggested in private that he consider himself her honored guard.

"Saba," Phasa would say, "please bring me the grapes. Thank you, my stallion."

"Saba, have some wine with me. It will soften your skin."

"Will you walk with me, Saba? To the tower. The sun will do us good."

At times I think he even found his role appealing.

When I first approached Phasa with the request that Judah and perhaps I take the journey east to Capernaum while we awaited Herod's return, she was immediately agreeable.

"We will have to find a way, Maviah. Soon."

"Then perhaps tomorrow."

"Tomorrow? No, no, that won't do, my dear. You are under my care. It has to be planned. There are bandits out there!"

"They are no match for Judah."

"Indeed. Still, it has to be planned. Soon." And then she was off.

But soon was not so soon, and a week became nine days, and Judah began to grow impatient despite my assurances. It was only after I asked Saba to see if he might help Phasa hasten the journey that she approached me on the tenth day, lit like the sun.

"I have wonderful news, Maviah! We go to Capernaum tomorrow. Saba and I have made all the plans. We will travel by camel as Bedu six hours east to Tiberias, on the Sea of Galilee—it's a wonderful city, you will see. From there we'll take a boat north to Capernaum. We leave in the morning and will be in Capernaum before the sun sets."

"You as well? It's far too dangerous! You will be seen..."

"I go as Bedu with only my eyes uncovered. Saba will be by my side. No one will know. Not a soul."

She appeared delighted. I suspected her shift in disposition resulted from the prospect of a daring adventure with Saba.

As for Malcheus, Phasa explained that we would be gone to the countryside for one night and return the following day. No one was to know that we had left the palace. After some convincing, he made the arrangements for the guard to be otherwise occupied for a brief period early the next morning, before the city awoke.

So it was that we found ourselves on the road to Tiberias when the sun rose the next day. We rode on camels, four common Bedu, yet our aspirations were anything but common and our spirits were high.

Judah's, for he was to finally see this king his elders had spoken of for so many years.

Saba's, for he was mounted as a warrior once again.

Phasa's, for she was a new woman, free of the clutches of royalty, if only for a day.

And mine, for I was repaying Judah for saving me.

He was quiet, but his eyes were bright and his smile fixed. We had spent many hours together in the palace, always aware of each other's presence, and yet I suspected that the larger part of Judah's mind had remained on his greatest passion.

Saba positioned himself between Phasa and the edge of the road, watchful eyes always on the countryside, a fact that did not escape her attention.

"You are such a good slave to me, Saba," she said with a smile. "With you I have nothing to worry about. You must consider staying when Maviah leaves us."

He offered no response, nor was he expected to.

In the seventh hour we came to Tiberias, a glorious new city on the sea. Tiberias was Herod's truest pride, Phasa insisted, built and named after the emperor of Rome. His walled palace within the acropolis there was even more grand than the one at Sepphoris. He remained mostly in Sepphoris only because of Phasa. If Tiberias was Herod's, Sepphoris was hers.

But we avoided the city itself, making our way instead to the shore south of the wall, where fishing boats lolled in the blue waters after the morning's catch. The vessels were small, no more than ten paces long. Surely a larger one would be fetched for us.

There, while Saba, Phasa, and I waited on a hill, Judah took coin to hire a boat to take us north to Capernaum. He returned soon, beaming.

"It's arranged. Elias will take us, and his wife will see to the camels until we return."

"How much?" Saba asked.

"Twenty days' wage."

"Twenty denari?" Phasa said. "It's nothing. Tell him we will pay him a hundred when we return to find our camels in good stead."

"You would inform him we carry so much?" Saba said.

"It's not so much. Tell him, twenty denari now, eighty upon our return."

Judah raised a finger. "And he assures me that this is the best boat on all of the Kinneret." Galileans called their sea by this name. "Built to withstand the strongest winds."

"Which boat?" Saba asked.

Judah pointed to one of five down in the water.

"These?" I asked. They all looked dilapidated.

For a moment none of us spoke. We were all from the desert—our seas were the sands and our ships the camels. But Judah seemed confident.

"It's a strong boat. Elias speaks truth."

So it was settled, despite my misgivings.

Elias was a stout man with thick, callused fingers, a large nose, and a beard that had surely never seen a blade. But Judah was right, his eyes were kind and he seemed confident, and when offered the prize of a hundred denari, he could not have been more exuberant had he found a chest full of gold.

"This way then!" Elias cried. "This way, watch the stones. I will lay down a plank so your feet stay dry. Samuel!" He glanced at his boy of perhaps fifteen years, who stood on the shore with our camels. "Tell Martha to feed the camels from our grain stock. If she questions you, tell her not to."

He spun back to us. "This way. Just this way."

"We need no plank," Saba said, for he saw that the man intended to stretch one of considerable length from the shore to the boat, but traversing it would take some skill. "Bring the boat close."

"But you will get your feet——"

"Bring it."

"Of course." Elias tugged on the boat's lead rope until the shore stopped it firm.

Without waiting for instruction, Saba plucked Phasa from her feet, waded to the boat, and hefted her over the bow. Then he returned for me.

Elias watched. According to Herod, this man's god would have rejected him and demanded repayment in blood or offerings for contact with a foreign woman.

"So, then," he said. "We are off!" And he slung himself into the boat as easily as any Bedu might mount a camel. Judah and Saba, on the other hand, made a splashing mess but managed.

"Sit," Elias instructed. "Sit here. Do not move. I will take care of you."

Using oars, then a single small mainsail, he guided the boat out into a gentle breeze and turned it north. The sea was placid, and we moved at a crawl. I wondered if it might take us a full day to reach the distant northern shore.

After Miriam in Nazareth, Elias was only the second common Jew from Galilee I'd met. I'd passed many and exchanged a few words with merchants and children, but I had yet to know any.

"How far? There is no wind," Judah said, gazing north. A tall mountain Saba had called Hermon rose on the distant horizon, in the direction of Syria.

It was the only invitation Elias needed to impress us with his knowledge of the sea from which he made his living.

"This is little wind. With little wind, as much as three hours to Capernaum. But do not worry, the wind comes. In the winter it may be like stone, and then the bitter winds sweep in from Mount Hermon to throw about waves twice the height of a man. Many foreigners gaze upon the Kinneret and claim it sleeps always, but what do they know? Great skill is required to fish this sea, I tell you. It's like a bowl, you see, catching the wind in terrible circles that cast over many boats. For this reason they build the shore walls to protect Tiberias. Even so, the waves have swept the streets there as well. I have seen it with my own eyes. The sea is a terrible monster when it becomes angry."

I stared at him, struck by horrifying visions of danger. Dusty sand I understood, but how wind could stir heavy water to deadly heights was beyond me, and I had no desire to investigate it further.

"Only in the winter," Phasa said. "And not so often. Must you frighten us so?"

Elias saw his mistake.

"No, no, you must not be afraid. Mine is the strongest boat in this sea, they all know this. And there is no strong wind in the summer, as you say. The sea is very kind to me. It knows me by name, surely. I have taken many, many fish from her waters. Many. If not for the Romans I would be rich."

His mention of the Romans shifted his disposition. He spit over the side.

"Rich, I tell you."

His antics made me smile. If Judah, Miriam, and now Elias were any representation of Jews in general, then I would surely love them all.

As Elias guided the boat farther from shore the wind did pick up, though only enough to toy with the small square sail and push us along gently. All the way Elias talked, mostly with Judah, who was predisposed to hear the news, as were all Bedu. And like all Bedu, he soon steered the talk to matters of politics.

I cringed at Elias's lengthy expressions of frustration in Phasa's presence. Judah tried to temper the man's outrage over the Roman occupation and Herod's compliance with such subjugation, but Elias, thinking we were all Bedu who lived to be free, made his points with great passion.

"It's an outrage, I tell you! They take half of my catch each day if I do not have the coin to pay the taxes, yet how am I to have coin if they take half of my catch? And these fish they sell to fill Herod's coffers. Why? So that he can build yet another palace where he can languish in luxury? So that he can impress Rome while defiling God by building Tiberias on the graves of our ancestors? It is no wonder God himself now spits on the Jew."

"And yet you live in Tiberias, built on the graves," Judah said.

"Would you have me starve?"

Phasa listened impassively.

"And what do the teachers of the Law say of this?" Judah asked.

Elias tugged at the rope to tighten the sail. "The Sanhedrin say only what fills the temple coffers and protects their villas. They are all the same, save the Pharisees. The Pharisees speak of a resurrection from the dead and give alms to the poor, which, as you know, makes them friend to all who suffer under Rome, and all who hope for a better life when this miserable one ends."

"And you?"

"Me? What do I know? But in this life, I want to throw out the oppressors and catch fish."

"No religious leaders support you in this?"

Elias shifted his eyes and stared at the steep, jagged shore to the east. "The Baptizer in Judea. And the rabbi who follows in his way and speaks of a new kingdom." He turned to Judah, suddenly calm. "You go to see him?"

"Who?"

"The one who works wonders. The rabbi Yeshua." Elias searched Judah's eyes. "They say he heals the sick. That he can make wine from water. Then I wonder why he cannot make coin from dust and save all of Israel. We have too many drunkards already."

"He is in Capernaum?"

"You go to see him then?"

We had agreed that we would not speak of our purpose, but I saw that Judah was at an impasse. If he lied, he would need another sound reason for our visit.

"Yes," Phasa said.

Elias regarded her suspiciously, for she had spoken boldly though covered from head to foot save her eyes.

"You are unclean?" he asked her.

"She has no illness," Judah said. "It is a private matter, not a religious one."

Elias accepted the explanation with a simple nod. "Then you are in good fortune. I have heard he is in Capernaum."

"Where in Capernaum?"

"Does it matter? It is only a fishing village—a few hundred. They come from all of Galilee to see him, any might know where he sleeps. But you must be careful. It is said that he eats with the tax collector there, a scoundrel called Levi. It escapes me why a Zealot would befriend any tax collector unless his intentions were to conspire with the Romans. So you see, even through this rabbi, we Jews are betrayed."

Judah only nodded, but I saw the fascination deep in his eyes.

The sun was already sinking low in the west when we approached the village of Capernaum, nestled on the northern shore where several dozen small boats rocked gently. They would soon go out for fish, Elias said. He could join them once he put us to shore and perhaps sell the fish—not to worry, he would have his boat clean for our return. But he must join them for he was sure to bring in the largest catch.

Judah stood with one hand on the mast, gazing at the sunbaked

mud homes that shared courtyards, as was common in the countryside. These groupings were scattered along the rising shoreline and
clustered between olive groves. I could see only a few people on the
streets between houses. Yet Capernaum was twice as populous as
Nazareth, and spread out. Two hundred dwellings, perhaps.

The wind lifted Judah's hair and his eyes remained fixed ahead.
Here then he might see the end of his long journey, one that had
begun thirty years earlier when his elders discovered the child who
would be king.

If there was a king in Capernaum, this humble village by the sea
appeared unaware of it. I could not help but wonder if Judah's search
might bring him to great disappointment.

Then again, if there was a rebellion gathering in Palestine, would
it not stew underground, hidden from prying eyes? Had not Dumah
been asleep when the Thamud storm arrived on a thousand camels?

Judah, my courageous lion, was surely thinking of what could not
be seen with the eyes alone, and I too wondered what mystery and
power hid behind the mud walls of this sleeping enclave.

AND YET no wonder greeted us when we finally set to shore and
stepped out of the boat onto a dock in need of repair. Instead a fisherman who, upon learning from the boisterous Elias that his passen-
gers had come from Tiberias to see the rabbi Yeshua, inquired about
his cousin who lived there. Elias knew of the man and an immediate
friendship was thus consummated. The fisherman quickly directed
us to the house of Levi ben Alphaeus, who was also known as Matthew.
Also, he told us, Levi was a tax collector and as such should not be
trusted, although many said he had become more friendly of late.

No wonder greeted us as we followed Judah to the tax collector's
house on the outskirts of that quaint village. Only the lingering
scent of dead fish.

None as we waited on the street for Judah, who entered the house. Only a donkey and several children, but these were shooed away by women who recognized us as foreigners and stayed clear. The sun sank and the cold set in.

And when Judah did emerge, though his eyes were full of anticipation, he offered us little encouragement.

"They say he's gone to the hills," he said.

"To the hills?" Phasa demanded.

"To rest and pray. Don't you see? He's here!"

"He rests in the hills?" Phasa said. "It's far too dark for us to go to the hills!"

"He will return." Judah's excitement refreshed me. "Come, I have persuaded them to allow you to wait in the courtyard." He motioned us toward the gate that led to the homes' common area. "Come. Come."

"Wait how long?" Phasa asked. "Did we travel so far to wait in a courtyard?"

Judah turned back and spoke sternly. "You must be patient, Phasa! We are not in the palace. If you announce yourself as Phasaelis, wife of Herod, I am sure they will give you immediate entrance."

"Never," Saba said.

"No," Judah said, having made his point. "So, then, today you are only a common woman and a foreigner. They now entertain a Pharisee from Judea who would surely object to your presence in the room. But they assure me the wait will not be long." He headed through the gate.

"And you?" I asked, following quickly.

"I must speak to them, you understand." His mind was already back in the house.

"How many?" Saba asked.

"There is Peter and his brother, Andrew. They share news with a Pharisee who has come from Judea in secret. Something is in the wind, I tell you. I must return. Wait here. You will be comfortable. Saba will see to you. Watch over them, Saba."

And then he was gone, leaving us in a cold courtyard without a fire. I had expected signs of women and children, for Levi was a tax collector and children were a sign of wealth among the Jews, Phasa had told me. They might have been tucked away in one of the other houses.

"This isn't what I expected," Phasa said, crossing to a dead fire pit on the far side. "Not in the least."

I tried to reassure her. "As Judah said, we aren't in Sepphoris. But we are with Saba—no harm will come to us."

"I don't fear harm. I only resent being left out in the cold while these men plan my downfall." She was referring to the Zealots who plotted the demise of all things Roman, which included Herod and, by extension, her. No one would recognize her, covered as she was, but I too would have felt the rejection. Still, the choice to come had been hers. "I can scarce keep my head atop my shoulders, and Judah leaves us without so much as a bed? It is not what I expected."

"He's taken with this sage," Saba said. "You must be patient. In agreeing to come, we agreed to this."

Phasa looked at him, then settled. "Then be a good slave and keep me warm."

Saba hesitated. "We are in a Jew's home. I cannot be seen like this."

She sighed. "So now you too are a Jew."

"If I must be. To keep you safe."

We waited for a long while, until I too felt growing frustration. Judah seemed to have forgotten us entirely. The absurdity of our situation became more plain as the darkness deepened. I had left Dumah on matters of life and death for my people, and yet here I stood in a tiny fishing village, risking that very mission for the sake of a man who seemed to have forgotten that I existed. The reasoning I'd harnessed to visit Capernaum for Judah's sake vacated my mind, and my irritation strengthened.

"I will check," I finally said. "Saba, stay with Phasa."

"Maviah, this is not wise."

I ignored Saba's objection, walked to the door, and eased it open. Firelight from a room beyond a short hall flickered on the walls. Soft voices reached me. I slipped in and carefully approached.

There in the shadows I stopped, wondering if I'd been seen. But none of the five men reclining at the table seemed to notice, so I withdrew far enough to guarantee my concealment.

Firelight lit a vessel and chalk cups used for wine on the wooden table, which, unlike Herod's table fashioned in the Roman style, was surrounded by simple wooden stools and a stone block along one side. Food also waited, covered by cloth. The men were too engrossed in their talk to pay food or drink any attention.

"But by saying *kingdom*, he can only mean Israel," Judah said in a low, urgent voice. "As you say, Andrew, the Baptizer also spoke of the kingdom's restoration. It is this the prophets foretold, is it not? And it was of this the elders from my tribe surely spoke."

"So it seems." Andrew sat across from Judah—a thin laborer or fisherman who looked to eat too few of the fish he caught.

At the far end of the table, a heavily bearded man with gray hair wore a clean robe and a blue mantle over his shoulders, and I took him to be the guest Pharisee. Which would make the man next to Andrew his brother, Peter. Also a fisherman, I guessed. And across from them was a well-dressed man I thought must be Levi, for the trimmed beard on his chin.

They did not appear to be the kind of men a great leader would gather for any reason, much less for an uprising.

Miriam had spoken about her son as a teacher, not a warrior, but I felt as though I was witness to the heart of a conspiracy.

Andrew continued: "But the master's speaking of this kingdom is different from the Baptizer's."

"Different?" Judah said. "What can you mean? A kingdom is a kingdom."

"Yes, of course."

"The kingdom of God is Israel. And his rightful seat is in the temple."

"Yes. Yes...but no..."

Judah spread his hands. "How can this be yes and no? It is either yes or no."

"And yet with Yeshua it can be both. It depends on——"

"What my brother means," the one I assumed to be Peter interrupted, "is that we don't know. Yeshua says the kingdom is at hand."

"Of course. Meaning upon us."

"Meaning it is now at hand. And *among* us, he says. Among us already. This is what he says everywhere he goes."

"But of course! We are the very seeds of that kingdom! This kingdom will come from among the true sons of Israel. And it will come now!"

"And within," Peter added. "He says the kingdom of heaven is not here nor there, but within."

"Within?" Judah asked. A moment of silence passed. "Within what?"

"Within the heart."

"Inside a man?" Clearly this was a new concept to them, as it was to me. "But of course this must be merely symbolic," Judah said. "It's the spirit of Israel rising up to take her rightful place in the Holy Land."

"Yeshua says the kingdom is not of flesh and blood but of spirit," Andrew said, taking up from his brother. "And is now among us."

Judah stood and paced to his left. He spoke as much with his hands as his voice. "And yet he heals flesh and blood. He says he has not come to bring peace, but a sword to divide even a man from his father. Is this not what you have said?"

"Yes . . . but no. He carries no sword and speaks only of peace."

"You just said he speaks also of the sword! Which is it?" Judah weighed his hands, one and then the other. "Yes or no, this way or that way, blood or no blood? You've been with him for many months, how can you not know these things?"

"Please," Levi said. "Speak with grace in my home."

Judah placed a hand on the table and leaned forward. "I have come to you with news from my elders that surely confirms what you have wondered. Yeshua is to be king. The way must now be made plain."

Andrew looked at the Pharisee, who watched without comment. "You must understand, Judah, in Yeshua's way, nothing is plain. What he speaks makes little sense to the common man."

"Are you a common man? Surely his way must be plain. Why would you follow him otherwise?"

Peter abruptly stood and addressed Judah in no uncertain terms. "Yes! We *are* common, and still, he chooses us. We only say as much as we do because of who you are. Do not judge too quickly. When you see him you will know why we follow him. Then you will also know that what he says is *not* easily grasped. Everywhere we go he speaks riddles that leave the mind amazed, yet with little understanding. Many times he says one thing and then immediately seems to offer its contradiction."

I was certain by now that I did not belong in the house, but I was fixed. I couldn't see Judah's eyes, but I feared for his heart. What if his king was only a madman?

"What kind of riddles?" Judah asked.

Levi spoke in an even, calculating tone.

"He says that he did not come to abolish the Law, but to fulfill it. That until heaven and earth themselves pass away, not one jot nor tittle shall pass from the Law. Any who annuls one of the least of the laws given by Moses shall be called the least in the kingdom of heaven."

Levi picked up a cup and absently turned it in his hand.

"And yet he himself commands all who hear him to break these laws. It is dangerous talk. The Sanhedrin won't stand for it."

"Impossible," Judah said. "You are hearing it wrong. What law does he command you to break?"

"Sit!" Levi looked between Judah and Peter, who both took their seats.

"Thank you. Now..." Levi nodded at the Pharisee. "Ask one who is friend and knows the Law well."

I could only assume that they had not used the Pharisee's name because he wished to be unknown. A friend to Yeshua might cause problems among his peers in Jerusalem.

"You are a teacher of the Law," Judah said. "Does Yeshua command his followers to break the Law?"

The Pharisee hesitated, then spoke in a smooth, calming voice.

"So it appears. Some laws are only interpretations of the Law, but many are directly from the scriptures, as given to Moses word for word from God."

"Then tell me just one Yeshua breaks. I would know."

"From Exodus, anyone who strikes a man so that he dies shall be put to death. He who strikes his mother or father shall be put to death. He who kidnaps a man shall be put to death. He who curses his mother or father shall be put to death. As it is written, you shall appoint as penalty life for life, eye for eye, tooth for tooth, hand for hand, foot for foot, burn for burn, wound for wound, bruise for bruise. This I quote."

An eye for an eye was the code of all people in the desert, but putting a child to death for a curse struck me as cruel beyond measure. Surely Judah would never adhere to these particular laws of his religion.

"This is the Law given by God to Moses," the Pharisee continued. "And yet Yeshua, who in one sitting insists every law be followed, countermands his own teaching when he says in that same sitting: 'You have heard that it was said, "Eye for eye, and tooth for tooth." But I tell you, do not resist an evil person. If anyone slaps you on the right cheek, turn to them the other cheek also.'"

Judah had no reply. The contradiction was apparent even to me.

"So you see," Andrew said, "his words are not easily understood."

"Surely he does not mean this of Rome," Judah said. "He is misunderstood. And concerning his talk of the kingdom, he surely means the restoration of the kingdom of Israel here on earth, not merely in spirit or after death."

To this no one responded.

"Why does he not simply state his purpose? When you ask him, what does he say?"

"That we will not understand yet," Andrew replied.

"He is a teacher of the *moshel*, using teachings of wisdom in the tradition of the Merkabah," the Pharisee offered. "You know of the Merkabah?"

"The desert is full of the whispers of sages. I have heard."

"Mystics," Andrew said.

"And what is a mystic, as you understand?" Judah asked the Pharisee.

"One who directly experiences the world of spirit beyond common reason. One who engages through experience that which is mystery."

"And this is Yeshua? He comes from the Merkabah?"

"No, no. I only say that he speaks in the manner in which they speak. They are masters of wisdom who challenge all with teachings meant to confound the mind, so as to offer a path for the heart to know God beyond the mind. These mystics see with the eyes of the spirit and speak in parables and riddles meant to infuriate a man's thoughts. They say one is not meant to know the full meaning of their teaching before the mind is unmade and made again."

"And yet he is surely more than a mystic," Judah said.

The Pharisee swept away any concern with his hand. "This is only a word. There are those among the Greek who speak in the gnostic way. They say that salvation comes through secret knowledge and that the flesh is evil. They too are mystics, but Yeshua defies their teachings."

"The gnostic way?" Judah said. "I've never heard of such a thing."

"I only say this because you ask what a mystic is," the Pharisee said. "The gnostic way is also mystic, and yet Yeshua seems to say that man will find salvation through faith, not through knowledge. And he makes no attempt to shun the flesh, but rather eats with prostitutes and sinners. He loves what is human."

"And yet you call him a mystic."

"A new kind, then. His authority cannot be denied. He speaks *Gevurah*—from the mouth of Spirit. All the teachers of the Law in Jerusalem recognize it, but they say it must come from Beelzebul, not God, for it defies the Law given by Moses."

"And you?"

"Beelzebul does not restore sight to the blind and speak of being born yet once more, though born already."

"You see?" Peter said, lifting a hand in exasperation. "What is a fisherman to make of this? Words upon words that mean what they do not mean. Born but not born—it makes my head spin."

Judah appeared perplexed. The Pharisee regarded him and offered more, but his voice softened, as if he was now sharing a deep secret.

"I went to Yeshua not so long ago in private to ask of these matters, that I might see, because he speaks of a new kind of sight. He told me then that one cannot *see* the kingdom of God unless he is born—not once—but yet again. The same kingdom that is now among us and within us cannot be seen with human eyes. He said it is like the wind, which cannot be seen, and yet is here, now. Only with new eyes can one see it."

"Reborn? As a Jew?" Judah pressed.

"Born of spirit, in the world of spirit, which is this kingdom of heaven. As I said, this is the way mystics speak. I believe this is what he means when he speaks of eternal life. Not simply a place in the resurrection, but also a realm within us at present. The eternal has no beginning and no end, you see? It is already. His power comes from this eternal realm. Heaven. And he invites all to follow him."

"He said this?"

"Not in so many words," the Pharisee said. "But as I've pondered his words, it's the only explanation that sits with me. Few will find this kingdom within, he says. To do so, one must follow him, because he is the way to the Father. Those who follow him will have this same power as they are birthed into this eternal realm of heaven within."

Judah seemed at a loss.

The Pharisee spoke barely above a whisper now, as though afraid his words might carry beyond the walls. "With Yeshua, God seems to be intimate, as though breath itself. The rabbi calls him even *Abba*. And we his children, to be born not of Abraham but of Spirit. Such things are not spoken elsewhere. And yet he asks us to follow."

"But to follow *where*?" Judah demanded.

"This too is a mystery." The Pharisee sighed. "You must understand... to have faith is to let go of knowledge as the means to salvation. To do so, one must embrace trust and mystery rather than make knowledge one's god, as the Gnostics wrongly do. It is not *where* that matters so much as simply following. Faith, you see? Trust, like a child. It confounds the mind."

Something in the Pharisee's soft-spoken words struck a chord of intrigue deep within me. Such concepts were far too lofty for me to understand. And yet they pulled at me like an ancient memory.

"What good is a path without a destination on earth and what good is a kingdom if not made real to overthrow the Romans?" Judah said, standing once again.

"Perhaps he means this as well," Andrew said.

Judah paced, hand in his beard. "He must!"

"Yes and no," the Pharisee said. "Not yet and already. Paradoxes all, understood only by the heart, beyond the mind." He paused for a moment, perhaps expecting Judah to challenge him, then pushed on.

"But what can I know, for I am only a teacher of the Law, and Yeshua fulfills that Law by overturning it always. If he is from God, then all we think we know is now suspect. His is a dangerous path to follow, requiring trust, not knowledge."

"And you," Judah said, "do you see this kingdom you describe so well?"

The Pharisee was careful with his reply.

"No. I only say what has come to me upon much reflection. In the larger part, his words offend all that I once knew. But I cannot deny the authority with which he presents himself, and so I dare find myself here yet again. Surely it's why we're all here when we might be in our appointed places, breaking bread."

They grew silent. It occurred to me that Judah might come to check on me. So I returned to the courtyard door and quietly eased it open.

"You are missing something," Judah said, sitting. "A kingdom requires a king and a king rules on earth. I did not come to find one who turns the cheek while Rome punishes God's children."

Then I was out in the cold, knowing that Judah had found less than he'd hoped for. I was thankful that Phasa, who paced beside Saba across the courtyard, had heard none of this talk.

She stopped and faced me as I approached. By the light of the rising moon, I could see that her mood had not brightened in my absence.

"Well?"

"Nothing. They talk of religion."

"Then you must return and tell them we would have a place to sleep. I find this intolerable. Ten hours under the hot sun on camel and over the sea—"

"It's nothing compared to two weeks through the Nafud," I said. Only a week earlier I wouldn't have dared speak so boldly, but our familiarity had rid me of my fear. "Forgive me, Phasa, but we are all worn."

She stared at me for a long moment, then offered a conciliatory nod and crossed her arms. There was nothing more to say.

Truly, I felt as drained and as hopeless as she, for after such disappointment we did not have even a fire to warm us. Judah had all but forgotten us, so taken was he with his Messiah, who, by the sound of it, would only lead him to unanswerable riddles and nonsense.

I was lost in a moment of self-pity when the gate behind us

creaked and I turned to see a man of average height step into the courtyard and close the gate behind him. My first thought was that the sage had finally arrived, but by all appearances this man in his simple tunic was yet another fisherman. A mantle was draped over his head for warmth, shielding his face.

We watched from the shadows as the man walked toward the house in even, measured steps, arms folded with a hand buried in each sleeve. He did not hurry. He did not look up. He did not seem to notice that he wasn't alone. He moved like a man who bore the weight of a long day upon his shoulders. Perhaps he was another disciple who'd been summoned.

Perhaps they were all beginning to wonder who their leader really was.

The man reached the door and stopped, his back to us lit by a full moon. For a long moment he remained perfectly still, as if trying to decide whether to enter.

Slowly his head turned toward us. Moonlight lit his face as he stared at us from beneath his mantle.

The moment I looked into the brown eyes of this man, I knew that Yeshua of Nazareth could surely see into my soul and know my every thought.

I knew that he could see into my soul because I felt it being laid bare before me. I knew that he was Yeshua because I was sure that only the most powerful mystic could at once pierce me with such a singular gaze and leave me feeling perfectly safe and unscathed.

The night was still.

He knew me. He knew me through and through and he found no shame in me.

"Two queens sit out in the open," he said in a soft, rhythmic tone. "And yet the fox who hunts you is not so far away."

He knew who Phasa was? I thought to glance at her, to see if she saw him as I did, but I could not remove my eyes from his gaze.

He offered a faint smile and dipped his head. "It's warmer inside. Come. Eat at my table. I will give you food."

Then he turned, opened the door, stepped past the threshold, and vanished into the tax collector's home.

Judah's king had arrived.

CHAPTER SEVENTEEN

—◆—

I COULD NOT see the fox so far from the desert, nor understand how grave was the threat that hunted me, as I stood speechless with Phasa and Saba under the moon.

My mind was taken captive by Yeshua's presence, not by his words. My first encounter with him, all through that evening and the next day, was characterized by something far greater than wisdom or knowledge.

After all, I was not well versed in the religion of the Jews. How could I understand all their clever talk? I was only a woman from the desert. I heard Yeshua with my heart far more clearly than with my mind. I can't say that I even made much of an attempt to understand his meaning. If such a thing was beyond the grasp of the learned Pharisee, it was for me beyond the stars, cloaked in mystery.

But it made no matter, for it wasn't Yeshua's words that made him.

It was the power of his presence. And how great was that power indeed.

I don't remember following Yeshua into the house with Phasa and Saba, only entering the room to find all five men standing in silence as Yeshua embraced each in turn. Behind me Phasa and Saba breathed steadily, watching over my shoulder.

But Yeshua did not simply offer the customary greeting. His embrace surrounded each man as if only they two existed. He the master and each his sole devout follower. Each bowed in turn, offering only one word.

"Master."

He neither sought nor rejected the title, but dipped his head in simple acceptance. Even the Pharisee, so esteemed in Jerusalem, might as well have been a cub before a lion here in Galilee.

Yeshua turned to Judah, who had backed away from the table and there stood as stone, eyes like moons.

"You too are from the desert," Yeshua said.

Judah appeared too struck to speak.

"It's been a very long journey, my Bedu friend," Yeshua said, wearing the hint of a smile. "Judah is a good name. I am honored."

How he knew Judah's name, I could not guess.

Overcome, Judah fell to his knees and bowed his head.

"I am your humble slave! Send me and I will go. Call for me and I will come. My sword is yours and my heart rests in your hands. Use it as you will."

Seemingly intrigued, Yeshua raised his brow and turned his eyes toward the one called Peter. Despite the fisherman's questions regarding his master, they shared a special bond, I thought. Peter seemed to be a simple and kind man, filled with more passion than knowledge. Evidently Yeshua found his qualities appealing.

"Then lift your head and give me your heart as brother, not slave," Yeshua said to Judah.

Judah did so immediately, eyes misted. He grasped Yeshua's hand and kissed it.

"I am yours," he said. Then kissed the hand again. "I am utterly yours."

Yeshua gently placed his hand on Judah's head. "Rise and eat. Tomorrow brings its own temptations and troubles. Tonight we break bread and drink wine."

Yeshua looked at me and the others at my back, and then, without so much as casting a glance to the Pharisee standing at the far end of the table, spoke to him.

"Before I came tonight, you were inquiring of the kingdom of heaven, Nicodemus?"

The answer came haltingly from the Pharisee, for they knew Yeshua could not have heard them.

"Yes, Rabbi."

Yeshua kept his eyes on me until I thought I might not breathe.

"We are honored to have guests from another kingdom so distant. Honor them with your seat, my friend, and I will tell you what you long to hear."

I might have protested had I not been so disordered by my own emotions. According to Phasa, foreigners could never sit at a Pharisee's table, much less take the seat of honor, for in their tradition all foreigners were gentiles and evildoers. And we, two women, all the worse. Neither their customs nor their god would look upon it kindly.

"Of course," Nicodemus muttered.

Yeshua nodded at Phasa. "You will be safe here. Your covering is not required." He passed a bowl of water but did not wash his own hands before sitting on the stone bench across from Judah.

Levi ushered us to the table without making eye contact, allowing Saba to sit at the end and Phasa and me to sit on either side, at the corners. Phasa moved haltingly, without removing her covering, surely terrified that she was known and at the mercy of conspirators.

To all this Yeshua paid no mind, occupied instead with uncovering the food and pouring the wine. He gave me a glance and an encouraging smile as we were seated.

His eyes were brown, but to describe them so misses the point. They did not look at me; they swallowed me. They cherished me. With even one glance from him, the world seemed to still and shift. How can such a thing be described with mere words?

I don't recall their blessing of the food, only that there was one. Nor can I recount the small talk, for there was little. Nor any weighty talk, for they all seemed to be waiting. Yeshua did not immediately offer any teaching on the kingdom, occupied for the moment with each bite of his food.

Phasa finally slipped the covering from her face so that she could eat, but she left the mantle over her head. She looked at me with the eyes of a child but remained silent, as did Saba.

I watched Yeshua's strong hands as he tore off bread and dipped it first into olive oil, then vinegar before eating. I watched his throat as he swallowed, and his mouth as he chewed. His light-brown eyes, glinting warmly by the firelight. The way he lifted his cup and drank.

I didn't see him the way a woman sees a man, but as a mystic who had seen things I couldn't begin to fathom—one who could affect my heart from across the table without so much as a look.

And yet certainly a man, perhaps not yet thirty.

One who was hungry and thirsty and enjoyed food, particularly the ripest of the olives and figs.

A man with dust on his cloak and hair, tangled by the wind in the hills where he'd gone for his contemplations. A man who looked bone-weary save for his bright eyes, which shone with a life that could not be extinguished. I wondered what was in his mind as he ate. What had his childhood been like? What did he think of his mother, Miriam? Why had his brothers dismissed him as a madman? What kind of suffering had delivered him to this place? What kind of woman had he loved or married, if any? What was he like when he became angry or when he wept?

I dared watch him, wondering if he knew my thoughts as well, not caring if the men thought my gaze offensive, for I knew that their master did not.

I knew men to exchange the news while eating food, always, but in that room even Judah remained silent. There were only the sounds of eating and the occasional comment regarding the food or the weather. Few remarks were added except a "Yes, of course," or a "Very good, yes, very good indeed."

They were waiting. Waiting for Yeshua. We were all waiting.

We were this way for perhaps half of the hour before matters of significance were finally set upon the table by Judah, the lion who had anticipated this night for so long.

"Master…" He leaned into the table, voice low and intent. "I have come from—"

"Yes, Judah," Yeshua said, lifting his intriguing eyes to him. "And you too wish to know what Nicodemus has come to understand."

Judah glanced at the Pharisee. "Yes."

The master reached for a fig and turned it in his fingers. Not a soul stirred.

"My Father has hidden these things from the wise and intelligent and revealed them to infants. Truly I tell you, unless you change and become like little children, you will never enter the kingdom of heaven."

In response to this Judah only stared. I assumed Yeshua meant that one could not enter this kingdom of heaven without first becoming like a trusting child. Did an infant have great intellect? Then the mind must be changed to be like that of a child who simply trusted.

This then was his way, as the Pharisee had suggested. And even if I was mistaken, I could not doubt that he spoke the truth because of the unwavering surety and gentleness with which he uttered each word.

Yeshua looked from one of us to another, gathering each of us in his gaze.

"And yet you wish to know more of the kingdom of heaven." A mischievous sparkle lit his eyes, daring us to hear. "Then know that it is like treasure hidden in a field. When a man found it, he hid it again, and then in his joy went and sold all he had and bought that field."

This then was one of his parables—these *moshel*, as suggested by Nicodemus earlier—and the master said it as if its meaning should be unmistakable.

But he said more.

"Again, the kingdom of heaven is like a merchant looking for fine pearls. When he found one of great value, he went away and sold everything he had and bought it."

In the shortest order Yeshua had chided the great wisdom of Nicodemus, first by suggesting that he must indeed become like an infant yet again, to see with new eyes. And then by suggesting that the kingdom was within, buried from sight, found only by those who would forsake all for its value.

"You have heard me say, 'Do not store up for yourself treasures on earth where moths and vermin destroy...but store up for yourselves treasures in heaven...for where your treasure is, there your heart will be also.' And so it is. But have I not also said that the kingdom of God is within you? And have I not said that you cannot enter unless you change your mind? For I have said often, repent, for the kingdom is at hand. Then you will see and know that what I say is true."

To repent meant to go beyond one's way of thinking, this I knew also from the Greek of the same word, *metanoia*. In his own way, Yeshua was throwing into madness all that was held dear about wisdom, thereby making it foolish to the learned, and wise only to the infant.

"Faith," he said with a twinkle in his eyes. "If you have faith as small as a mustard seed, you can say to this mountain, 'Move from here to there,' and it will move. Nothing will be impossible for you." He paused. "If anyone steadfastly believes in me, he will himself be able to do the things that I do; and he will do even greater things than these."

If there had been a mustard seed in his fingers and he'd dropped it, I think we might have heard it strike the table in that moment. What did it mean to trust steadfastly in him? I did not yet know.

"Hear what I have said and you will know. Yes, Nicodemus?"

The esteemed teacher dipped his head. "As you say, Ra—"

"Good. Now let me tell you a story of another kind," Yeshua said.

He took a small bite from the fig and leaned against the wall at his back.

"The kingdom of heaven is like a man going on a journey, who called his servants and entrusted his wealth to them. To one he gave five bags of gold, to another two bags, and to another one bag, each according to his ability. Then he went on his journey."

He paused, letting the scenario settle in.

"The man who had received five bags of gold went at once and put his money to work and gained five bags more. So also, the one with two bags of gold gained two more. But the man who had received one bag went off, dug a hole in the ground and hid his master's money. After a long time the master of those servants returned and settled accounts with them. The man who had received five bags of gold brought the other five. 'Master,' he said, 'you entrusted me with five bags of gold. See, I have gained five more.' His master replied, 'Well done, good and faithful servant! You have been faithful with a few things; I will put you in charge of many things. Come and share your master's happiness!' The man with two bags of gold also came. 'Master,' he said, 'you entrusted me with two bags of gold; see, I have gained two more.' His master replied, 'Well done, good and faithful servant!' "

Yeshua turned his eyes to me now, and I was certain that he spoke only to me, though I knew it could not be.

"Then the man who had received one bag of gold came. 'Master,' he said, 'I knew that you are a hard man, harvesting where you have not sown and gathering where you have not scattered seed. So I was afraid and went out and hid your gold in the ground. See, here is what belongs to you.' "

A hard master who was unfair. My mind immediately went to all the men who had used me for their gain. He was speaking of the hardship of life. And yet the last servant had done well to preserve what had been entrusted to him, as had I, and for this he would surely be praised.

Yeshua leaned into the table now. He spoke in a soft tone, so that each of us clung to his every word, but his eyes were on me.

"His master replied, 'You wicked, lazy servant! So you knew that I harvest where I have not sown and gather where I have not scattered seed? Well then, you should have put my money on deposit with the bankers, so that when I returned I would have received it back with interest. So take the bag of gold from him and give it to the one who has ten bags. For everyone who has will be given more, and he will have an abundance. Whoever does not have, even what he has will be taken from him. And throw that worthless servant outside, into the darkness, where there will be weeping and gnashing of teeth.' "

So harsh was this master? But yes—we all knew the world to be a cruel master. No one moved and I was sure they were looking at me.

Yeshua pushed himself back from the table, stood, and rounded to my side. I was so astonished by his approach that I began to panic. I thought I must kneel as Judah had, and I began to move off my seat, terrified that he had come to rebuke me.

But before I could, he held out an open hand. There was no rebuke in his soft eyes, only acceptance and understanding. So I placed my hand in his, aware that mine was trembling. His fingers, warm and strong, gently closed about my hand.

A surge of heat spread up my arm and swallowed my mind, and with it came a low hum, like a breeze softly moaning through a window. Perhaps it was only the blood rushing through my head, but I suddenly felt as though I could not breathe.

"Do not allow fear to bind you up, dear one," he said. Immediately tears sprang to my eyes. "You will only lose what you already have. Accept what is given now."

I had until then thought shame to be my greatest burden, but the moment he said "fear," I knew the truth. For fear had followed me all my life. Though I masked myself in my role as a woman, my heart trembled always. I was lost in fear.

Fear of not being worthy. Fear of being outcast. Fear of failing my father and all of the Kalb.

Fear of being worthless.

Tears rolled down my cheeks, an overflow of the courage poured into me by his words. I meant to respond with gratitude, but my throat would not speak.

Before I could collect myself, he turned to Saba. Then he released my hand and looked at Phasa, who could not tear her eyes from him.

"When you hear of the coming wrath, you must pay it mind and flee."

She offered him a shallow nod, though surely as lost as a fox at sea.

Yeshua turned from us and sighed. "Now I must retire, my friends. The day is late and many will come tomorrow."

With that he walked to the short hallway that led to the door, and only there turned.

"Judah."

"Yes, master."

"Seek first the kingdom of God. All else will be added."

"Yes, master. I will. I swear it by the heavens themselves, I swear it!"

"Only a yes or a no will do."

Judah hesitated. "Yes."

Yeshua offered him one final nod, turned, and left the house.

More than I saw him vanish from our sight, I could feel his presence leave the room.

"You see what I mean," Nicodemus said when the silence grew thick.

And I did, I thought. I saw.

I SAW all that night and all the next morning with the eyes of my heart.

Phasa and I were given room in a far part of Levi's house and there lay in the darkness, left to our thoughts. I held Yeshua's face in my mind, as if he were yet gazing across the table with those haunting, kind eyes that swallowed my soul and brought me such comfort.

I saw why Peter and Andrew and Levi had left their tasks to follow him. I saw why Nicodemus, an esteemed member of the Sanhedrin, had sought him out and risked so much to meet him yet again in Galilee.

I saw why Judah had been obsessed with meeting this mystic, whose powers were beyond comprehension.

"What could he have meant?" Phasa asked as we lay in the dark.

"About being hunted by the fox?"

"Yes."

I had meant to leave the love-sick Herod to his own misery, for matters of marriage among royals weren't mine in which to meddle. But emboldened by Yeshua, I felt no compulsion to hide what I knew.

"Herod is in love with another woman," I said.

"This is not a revelation."

"Did you feel his presence, Phasa? Did you feel Yeshua's power?"

She was silent for only a moment.

"He seems to know what cannot be known. So I ask again, what must I flee?"

"I think Herod intends to take another wife. He seems consumed by his need to be loved as he would love."

"Another? My father would never have it!"

"So, then, perhaps danger awaits."

"Did Yeshua not say that you too were in danger?"

My mind returned to our first meeting, in the courtyard. *Two queens sit out in the open*, he'd said. *And yet the fox who hunts you is not so far away.*

I could not understand how or why Herod would hunt me. Only if I fled, but I had no intention of doing so. Perhaps then Saman bin Shariqat and the Thamud had pursued me after all and were now close. Or what if my brother, Maliku, had been sent to destroy me? But they would not hunt Phasa as well.

Who was this fox?

"Yes," I said. But we spoke of the warning no more that night.

The next morning hundreds came to the hillside beyond Capernaum like ants traveling to the mound for food.

Yeshua's food was the same he'd offered me, not bread for the belly, but sustenance for the soul.

His words from the previous evening came to me all through the day. *Do not allow fear to bind you up, dear one. You will only lose what you already have. Accept what is given now.*

Now I was on a mission to save my father and restore honor to the Kalb. I, a woman who brought no shame to this teacher of such repute.

And were his words about fear not also true for all those oppressed under the fist of Rome? Do not resist but accept, he would surely say. This is the lot given you. Do not cringe in fear, for you will only lose what you already have. Rome is a harsh taskmaster, as is all of life. Do not fear it.

Judah remained with the other disciples, Jews all. Peter, Levi, Andrew, and several others whom I did not know. They stayed close to Yeshua, hurrying to help like servants of a king.

Nicodemus had left in the morning, I was told, for he could not be seen with Yeshua in public.

I remained with Phasa and Saba under the shade of a tree, within hearing of Yeshua when he spoke for all to hear.

What I heard remained for the most part mystery to me, but I didn't care. I knew that I was witness to the turning of some great tide.

Happy are the poor in spirit, he said, speaking of humility, *for theirs is the kingdom of heaven. Happy are those who mourn, for they will be comforted. Happy are the meek, for they will inherit the earth. Happy are those who hunger and thirst for righteousness, for they shall be satisfied.*

But this made little sense. He was speaking of what was seen as weak as leading to fulfillment. It was the way of the world turned on its head.

Then, speaking in my direction so that I was sure he could see me as he spoke: *Happy are the pure in heart, for they shall see God.*

As when he'd told the story of the treasure in the field, I knew then that a pure, undivided focus was required to find Yeshua's treasure. Like that of a child fixated on a simple task with the faith that it could be done.

But he said more.

You are the light of the world, he said to all the people gathered—young and old, men and women, diseased and whole, clean and unclean. *Let your light shine before others, that they may see your good deeds and glorify your Father in heaven.* And when he said "in heaven," I immediately recalled that this kingdom of heaven was now at hand and within me.

But was I also the light as he claimed? How could I be? I saw only darkness in my life.

The eye is the lamp of the body, he said. *If your eye is clear, your whole body will be full of light. But if your eye is bad, your whole body will be full of darkness.* And more: *How can you say to your brother, "Let me take the speck out of your eye," when all the time there is a plank in your own eye? You hypocrite, first take the plank out of your own eye, and then you will see clearly.*

The problem with my life, then, was my own eyes, I thought. My perspective of the world determined whether I saw light or darkness, offense or mercy. I was blinded by a plank of grievance and saw only darkness.

Give me new eyes, I found myself begging. *Remove this plank from my eyes that I might see the same light that you see.*

Yeshua's Father was near, shared by all, for he said "*your* Father," which made Yeshua's Father my true Father, did it not? Was I then this god's daughter? And if I had been a man, would I not be his son? Why else would Yeshua call him my Father?

His affection for the Father was plain even in the way he gently said that word, *Father*, sometimes using the more intimate expression *Abba*, as little children might call their father. *Unless you become like a child...*

His intimate union with his Father was a mystery to me, for I could not conceive of such a father. Yet his words and his presence pulled at my heart in ways that stilled my breathing.

And his compassion for the children was unlike any man I had seen. When others tried to send them away as was the custom for all peoples in the desert, Yeshua bid them come. And the moment he smiled and stroked their hair they calmed and returned his gaze with wide wonder in their eyes.

He was a father to them, I thought, and seemed to hold them in the highest regard, for it was to simple minds like theirs that Yeshua's Father revealed himself.

I thought of my own son and prayed that he was now with a Father so loving. With Yeshua's god, which he claimed to be the only god. In that moment I prayed it to be so.

As Nicodemus had said the previous evening, Yeshua often recited their sacred law given by their god, speaking for all to hear, "You have heard it said..." and then speaking of a different way, saying, "But I say to you." And each time I wondered if he invited great danger by speaking blasphemy against their religion.

But surely no one could stand against a man with such power.

You have heard it said, "Eye for eye, and tooth for tooth," he said. *But I tell you, do not resist an evil person. If anyone slaps you on the right cheek, turn to them the other cheek also.*

Love your enemies, he said. But these teachings I could not comprehend, for they crushed my need for retribution. Even so, I was in awe of him.

Do not judge or you too will be judged, he said. *For in the same way you judge others, you will be judged.*

Who could go through life not judging the Thamud or the Romans? It seemed impossible to me. But he said even more.

The Father judges no one, but has given all judgment to the Son. And then immediately of himself as judge, *Do not think I will accuse you before the Father. Your accuser is Moses, on whom your hopes are set.*

Then I would know this Father, I thought. Not a god who demanded the stoning of a shamed woman. Nor the gods of the Bedu, full of retribution and punishment. But this Father who was Yeshua's Father.

And further, I would gladly allow Yeshua, this Father's son, to judge me, for he would not accuse me before the Father. The sytem of the law on earth was their judge and mine, and a false one at that, surely. In either case Yeshua would not condemn me but surely follow his own teaching and turn his cheek if I offended him, just as he taught others to do.

To be so loved without condition was beyond my comprehension.

Perhaps I was misunderstanding. Who could love in such a way?

He spoke also of dividing the sheep and the goats—those who loved the outcasts and those who did not. Those who did not would endure terrible suffering. This I knew to be scandalous to the Jews, because their religion taught that if a person was outcast or unclean or ill or poor, it was punishment from their god for sins and uncleanliness.

Yet Yeshua said to treat those same poor and outcast with love and kindness, for this was how the Father loved them all.

But he went even further, having the audacity to personally identify with those outcasts and downtrodden, saying: *Truly, whatever you did not do for one of the least of these, you did not do for me.*

He was equating himself with those their religion said were deserving of their punishment. Truly he loved them as himself. Was he then saying that I should look at the hungry and downtrodden and see them as if they too were Yeshua? It seemed to stand all reason on its head.

But I was naïve about their customs and could not know the intricacies of his teachings. I only heard what I heard and made of it what I could, overwhelmed by the good news that fell upon my ears that day.

Everyone who hears these words of mine and puts them into practice is like a wise man who built his house on the rock. Everyone who hears these words and does not put them into practice is like a foolish man who built his house on sand. The rain came down, the streams rose, and the winds blew and beat against that house, and it fell with a great crash.

The teaching returned to me thoughts of the shifting sands of the Nafud and how easily one could sink. And of Petra, that renowned city of rock from which Phasa had come to marry Herod.

His preoccupation seemed to be this: We were to see the world with new eyes, and with a new heart of love as the Father loves. We were to love the unclean and clean alike rather than judge them for their sin; to love even enemies; to live as the Father's children by loving as he loves, without judgment, for the Father judged no one.

This was how Yeshua and his Father loved me, and it was too staggering to comprehend.

Yeshua spoke of many things, but always it was his presence that spoke with even more authority than his words. Indeed, I did not speak to him that day, for the demands on him were great, but I felt no need to—being close to him and listening to such powerful words flow from a place deep within him were enough.

Later I saw for the first time Yeshua undo what had been done in the physical realm. I was standing with Phasa and Saba, gazing out at the waters, for Saba was searching for our boat captain, Elias.

"He is there, tending the boat," Saba finally said, pointing. "The sun is high, we must leave soon. We cannot be gone yet another night or the palace guard in Sepphoris will grow suspicious. We must leave—"

"Look!" Phasa cried.

I turned to follow her gaze. A woman dressed in rags lay prostrate on the grass before Yeshua, who knelt on one knee before a young boy, hand on the boy's cheek. The mother was weeping, begging for her son, who looked to be starving, for his arms and legs appeared as sticks. But it was the boy's hands that caught my eye.

They were crooked and withered at the wrists, like broken branches.

Yeshua took the young boy's hands in his own as I watched. He then put one hand behind the boy's neck and pulled him close to his breast, as a father might his son.

I could not hear the words he whispered in the boy's ears, but I saw the boy begin to sob as Yeshua held him. And I watched the boy's crippled hands as he attempted and failed to clutch Yeshua's cloak.

Before my very eyes, the hands began to straighten. I could not fathom what I was seeing, but neither could I deny it. Like trees emerging from the earth, the boy's hands grew. Even Saba gasped.

Yeshua's words whispered through my ears: *You can say to this mountain, "Move from here to there," and it will move.*

It took only a few moments, and then Yeshua kissed the boy on the forehead and whispered something else in his ear.

The boy looked at his hands, aghast. His mother was scrambling to her knees, stunned. Then the boy began to cry out, not with fear or sorrow, but with shock and joy, for his hands were those of any boy's, perfectly formed. He wriggled his fingers before his face, surely for the first time in his life.

"How is this possible?" Saba whispered.

Indeed, how? I could not contain my smile.

Pandemonium broke out about Yeshua, but I will never forget what he did next, for even as they expressed their wonder and praise, he calmly looked over to where I stood not twenty paces distant on the hill.

The breeze lifted his hair and swept the cloak about his feet. I saw a man who was tired, though the day was young. A man who bore more than the weight of this world upon his shoulders. Who knew far more than he could possibly say.

And I saw a man who loved me as he loved the boy, in a way that none other had nor could. For this love I would die.

Then Yeshua smiled at me.

Just one slight, knowing smile, but it delivered to me more comfort and revelation than even his undoing of a crooked limb. He was indeed the Father's son, I thought. And was I not his sister?

He loved all as if they were his brothers and his sisters. How he loved them, equating himself with those who were downtrodden and unclean, demanding they be treated as though they were he. All of life had enslaved me, for I too had been the lowest of the low. Yet Yeshua loved me as his own.

And as he looked into my eyes, I loved him in a way I had not known was possible.

Judah had come to find his king, and he had. But Yeshua had found me.

And yet I was still blind to his way of seeing the world.

CHAPTER EIGHTEEN

OUR SAIL south to Tiberias took only an hour, for the wind was blowing steadily. Elias was his boisterous self, bragging of his catch the night before and inquiring about our visit. But none of us was of the mood to offer the fisherman more than simple words with little meaning, and he soon quieted with the rest of us.

Phasa remained stoic though smothered by fear, I believe, for Yeshua's knowledge of her identity, along with his warning, haunted her still.

Saba had used strong words in persuading Judah to leave Capernaum, mind ever fixed on our mission.

And Judah had surely left part of his heart on the Sea of Galilee's north shore, with his new master, for he appeared like a water bladder deflated until we had reacquired our camels and set off once again for Sepphoris.

Only when we had covered half the distance to Sepphoris did Judah open his heart to me.

"Maviah..."

I looked over at him upon his camel.

"Now you see, yes? Now there can be no doubt. He is the Anointed One."

I was not looking for a messiah as in the Jewish tradition, but my heart had been taken captive.

"I see that there is none like him."

"And none ever to be."

"His followers," I said. "They will be like him. Even greater, he said. How is this possible?"

His eyes were bright. "Those who follow will know. My destiny is now set. I must return."

As would I some day, I thought. "You heard what he spoke to me."

"And to all of us," he said, lips curled in wonder.

I lifted my voice. "And you, Saba. You heard. What do you make of it?"

Saba's camel made several strides before the man responded in his thoughtful way.

"Fear is the devil, always, and throws one into darkness. To accept is the best way—this is the teaching of all the sages." He paused, then offered his verdict. "He is the greatest man I have seen." And then, after a breath, "Perhaps he is more than a man."

High praise from the stoic black warrior who'd traveled farther than any other I knew.

"And this power he speaks of?" I asked, my mind on the wonder that had overcome me at his mere glance.

Saba stared ahead at the horizon.

"It is beyond this world."

"How might one find it?"

"In following," he said.

"Yes, but how does one follow?"

But Saba had no answer, for we all understood that this was yet the mystery.

"I must join him," Judah said, swaying with his camel's slow gait. "I cannot wait, you understand. Herod will be another month in Rome, perhaps two. I cannot waste away in the palace while Yeshua gathers his disciples. I must return immediately and then come back to you when Herod arrives."

He was going to leave me? Though held safe in the embrace of courage, I felt stung.

He would leave me now? So soon? Then what was I to him?

I nearly said so much, but then the worlds of Yeshua came to me and I held my tongue. I was to accept my path. Did this not mean I must allow Judah to follow his path as well?

Saba, however, did not accept.

"Return now? This would be a fool's turn."

"How can you say?" Judah challenged. "Was it not Yeshua himself who said we must follow?"

"Your duty is first to Rami and the Kalb, to whom you gave your word. There is trouble yet—this he said as well."

"Only while we wait, Saba. Did you not hear him speak to me? Seek first the kingdom and all else will be added. Am I a fool to seek that kingdom first? It was for this I was born, I tell you. I am from among the Bedu who followed the stars to find this king. I must do the same. And when he calls for it, I will offer my sword."

"Your sword?" Saba said. "He speaks of peace."

"I was also told by his own disciples that he claims he did *not* come to bring peace, but the sword, even to divide."

"Then perhaps they misunderstand," I said.

"There is nothing to misunderstand," Judah said.

His way seemed set and it didn't seem to include me. I had made it possible for Judah to see Yeshua as a means of returning the affection he'd shown me. And now he would leave me for his greater passion.

Once again I felt the fear of being abandoned, as I had been abandoned my whole life.

"You must not jeopardize our mission, Judah," Saba said quietly. "If you think with your heart, then remember that Maviah also is in your heart."

"I would never allow any harm to come to Maviah!" Judah cried. "Please, Maviah, you must hear me in this."

"Are you not in my service first?" I challenged.

He hesitated. "Yes, of course." Then he turned his gaze ahead. "I will return for you and together we will follow Yeshua. You will see."

"No, Judah. I must return to Dumah. This is the task before me."

He remained silent. My heart softened for him, because I knew that he could not abandon Yeshua any more than he could be separated from himself. Or from me. But had he not dreamed of Yeshua longer? I had only just become his charge.

"I will never abandon you, Maviah," he said. "God forbid."

"You are right, Judah. Go to Yeshua while you can. Seek the council of your brothers. Saba will keep me safe."

I said it, but my heart ached with his rejection, and I think he knew it because he could not respond.

We rode in silence, strangely deflated after our powerful encounter with the master. I could only set my mind on what I knew to be my course. I was to put aside any fear of failing to restore honor to the Kalb and to myself. Fear was my greatest enemy.

I remembered the power that had passed up my arm upon Yeshua's touch, and I released all my self-pity, setting my shoulders squarely to the west. Surely his lingering presence gave me the courage to be who I was.

And was I not a queen?

The sun was hugging the western sky when we finally approached

Sepphoris and made our way to the palace. Phasa began to come into her own with the high walls in sight, and when we entered the gates to the acropolis she laughed with delight.

"What I will do for a hot bath tonight. It is good to be home, is it not, Maviah? You must admit, the ways of the countryside are harsh. Tonight we will dine and drink."

"We will, Phasa." I offered my best smile. She had been born into the house of the Nabataean king, Aretas, then traded in marriage to Herod. Did she not deserve her bath and wine?

Phasa cared not that the guard saw us returning. We were home safe, this was what mattered to her. And when she saw Malcheus waiting at the steps that led up to the palace, she hurried her camel to greet him.

"Well, Malcheus, what did I say to you? We have returned without harm. Call the servants to my quarters at once. We would bathe and dine."

But Malcheus did not appear relieved.

"Of course, my lady. As you say. But you should know that the queen, Maviah, has a guest."

"A guest?" Phasa slid from her camel, which Saba had couched. "So late? What kind of guest?"

"He will not give his name. I only know that he is from among the Sanhedrin in Jerusalem."

"The Sanhedrin? What can those scoundrels want with us?"

"Only Maviah. Alone, he said. He waits in Herod's court."

"Impossible!" Judah said. "Maviah will take no guests."

Phasa looked at me. "Whom do you know from Jerusalem?"

"No one. It must be a mistake."

"Saba, what say you to this?"

But it was Judah who pushed forward to my side. "She has many enemies in the desert. I absolutely forbid this. It is not safe. I will go."

"He's from the Sanhedrin, not the desert," Phasa said. To Malcheus: "He's a Jew?"

"There can be no doubt. There is no danger in a teacher of Law."

"And he specifically asked for Maviah?"

"Specifically."

"Then play your part as queen, Maviah. See to your guest. I must have a bath drawn. Saba, you will join me in my chambers. Judah, call the servants for food."

"She cannot go alone!" Judah insisted. "She is my charge."

"No, Judah," Phasa said. "Your charge is now this sage. Did I not hear correctly?"

I could see that her words cut him, but she spoke before he could protest.

"Malcheus, take Maviah." Her tone left no room for argument.

"I will wait for you, Maviah," Judah said. "I will wait—"

"Judah!" Phasa glared at him. "Now."

He was not pleased, but he followed her command, for he was in her court.

Malcheus led me to the same court in which I'd first met Herod. There, staring out the window with his back to me, stood a religious leader in dress I had not yet seen. A long white robe and blue mantle with many tassels draped his form in priestly fashion.

Play the queen, Phasa had said.

"Who comes to meet the queen of Dumah at such an hour?"

He turned and I saw then that it was the teacher I already knew. This was Nicodemus, who had left Capernaum for Jerusalem only this very morning. He had come to Sepphoris first.

But why?

"I would speak to you alone," Nicodemus said.

"As you say." Malcheus left us and closed the doors.

"Forgive me," Nicodemus said. "It was the best way to bring you the news I have. I cannot be accused of speaking to Herod's wife."

"You could not have told me in Capernaum?"

"I did not know of your connection to her until late. I think you will understand. Trust me, I come as a friend."

I might have felt discomfort, alone with a religious teacher in his regalia. Instead I felt at ease, as if I had known him for a very long time. We shared Yeshua in common.

"Why do you not speak to Judah?"

"It must be this way."

"Yeshua sent you?"

The teacher of the Law did not respond.

"Do you know who I am?" I asked.

Nicodemus came closer, glancing at the doors. "I know that you are from the desert. I know that you are close to Phasaelis, daughter of King Aretas of the Nabataeans, and that she will listen to you. I cannot speak directly to her—there are too many complications in these matters. Neither can Joanna, for her life would be in jeopardy from Herod."

"Joanna?"

"The wife of Herod's chief steward, Chuza. You did not know? Joanna is friend to Yeshua and provides for his needs. She can be trusted."

Joanna—a friend to Yeshua who was married to a man in Herod's courts. His steward no less!

"Are there others here whom I might trust?"

Nicodemus considered the matter. "Stephen, son of Gamil. My nephew. He too is from Sepphoris and follows Yeshua. I know no one else here who follows. But Stephen is wise beyond his years and is one to trust."

"And what message do you have for Phasa?"

"For you," he said. "I say this only to you. What you say is your concern, not mine, you understand."

"Then what do you have to say to me?"

He glanced once more at the doors and spoke quickly.

"It has come to my attention that Herod intends to marry Herodias, the wife of his brother Philip, tetrarch of the north."

My discussion with the love-sick Herod flew through my mind. "Marry her?"

"Yes. He was with her in Rome six months past and is with her now, along the sea."

"That's impossible. Herod has gone to Rome."

"No, I'm afraid not. He's with his brother's wife, Herodias. And he would return in three days' time to make a way for his marriage to her. For this he must rid himself of Phasaelis, you understand? Herodias would never stand for a second wife."

My mind spun with the revelation.

"You're certain Herod isn't in Rome? How can you know this?"

"I'm certain. We may be oppressed but we are not without our means."

My heart rose into my throat. Herod had no intention of delivering my cause to Rome. He never had.

"This is all I can say, for anything more would be speculation," he said. "But you surely know, as Herod does, that to divorce Phasaelis would be tantamount to declaring war on Aretas."

The blood had left my head. I had been played for a fool. All was lost! Any semblance of courage I had fell away, and I felt a great fear swelling in my breast.

"So he will kill her?" I said. "This is less of an offense than divorce?"

"Where Rome is involved, yes, and Herod is Rome's puppet. Arranging Phasa's inconvenient death would earn Herod less trouble than casting Aretas's daughter aside in divorce."

Nicodemus must have seen the pallor of death on my face, for he softened his voice and spoke deliberately.

"But I've said too much already. Remember the words Yeshua spoke to you, Maviah. You will know what to do. Save Herod's wife. Take your path. Do not hear the voices of fear that would push you into even deeper darkness. This is Yeshua's way."

And with that, Nicodemus, perhaps fearing that he had overstayed his time alone with a woman, stepped around me, walked to the doors, and left without another word.

I cannot fully express what consternation poured over me when the import of the Pharisee's message fully set into my mind. Where I had been riding with such courage and purpose only an hour before, I felt crushed there in Herod's courts.

But I could not run to Judah for comfort. Nor advice. Not yet. I had to consider why Nicodemus had come to me and not Judah or Saba. Yet who was I to restore honor to the Kalb and avenge my son's death? Who was I to save Phasa or Judah or Saba or myself?

I hurried to the chest in which I'd seen Herod place the dagger of Varus upon our arrival. Not once had I thought to check to see if he'd taken it, assuming he had.

Dropping to one knee, I opened the chest. There it lay, among golden goblets and ornate bowls. Anger rushed through me. He'd never had any intention of taking it.

I quickly withdrew the dagger and stood. Herod had betrayed me. My mission had been no more than a fool's errand. I paced, dagger tight in my fist, washed with indignation.

You are the light of the world.

The thought came unbidden and I blinked.

Do not be afraid.

I turned to the window and stared at the distant horizon, which ran with ribbons of red from the setting sun.

Breathe, Maviah. Breathe.

There between breaths a new thought entered my mind and instilled an even deeper fear.

It wasn't true that the dagger had gained me nothing. It had led to my alliance with Phasa. And Herod would rid himself of Phasa, because to divorce her would unnecessarily inflame Aretas. Herod would surely have her overcome by an accident. He didn't fear Aretas's wrath the way Rami had when Nasha died, because Herod had Rome at his back. After Phasa's death, he would marry Herodias. It was what Nicodemus had meant.

And if Herod intended to kill Phasa, I too was in grave danger, because I was allied with her and could voice my suspicions should any harm come to her.

So, then, Herod would kill us all.

Do not allow fear to bind you up, dear one. You will only lose what you already have.

Surely I now understood his teaching in a way that perfectly applied to me.

I thought about my son being dashed upon the rocks.

I thought about weeping on Miriam's shoulder.

I thought about the trust my father had placed in me.

I thought about Yeshua, who had found me.

Fear gripped my heart, and yet slowly, like moonlight reaching across dark waters, a path came into view. And then I knew that I must follow this path no matter what fear threatened my way.

"THIS IS MADNESS!" Phasa hissed, pacing in her outer chamber, which was now lit by the flames of four lanterns. With only one hearing of what I knew, she agreed that I spoke the truth.

Indeed, she directed her initial rage at herself for not suspecting Herod's devious plotting sooner. Had he not carried that distant look

of desire in his eyes ever since his return from Rome six months earlier? Had he not made the thinnest excuse for such a hasty return to
Rome? Had he not refused to touch her for the better part of a year?

When I told her the extent of my intention to solicit Rome's help
to overthrow the Thamud in Dumah, she seemed unconcerned,
despite her father's support of those same Thamud. These were matters of state.

Phasa was overcome instead by the betrayal of her heart.

I carried my head high, for I did not want her to see the depth
of my fear, but even as I watched Phasa rage, my fingers trembled.
Judah and Saba stood to the side, having expressed their outrage at
Herod's betrayal in short order.

"What that wench has to offer him that I don't is impossible to
imagine! Does he realize for a moment the kind of terror he brings
upon his own head? My father will storm Sepphoris and crush him!"

"No, Phasa, you don't hear—"

"Divorce me! For that witch? And what of her husband, Philip?
But no...Philip is a coward and will quickly hand Herodias to him
along with that contemptuous daughter of hers, Salome. What does
Herod see in that woman?"

"Only desire, I'm sure, Phasa, but you must listen—"

"I should have known! How blind of me! While I play the fool
in his palace, he lies by the sea in the arms of a whore." She shook a
finger in the air. "Don't think the religious leaders won't cry out over
this one, not for a moment."

"They will object?" I asked.

"She is his brother's wife! Yes, this will cause an outrage! He's so
sick in his head as to heap this trouble on top of my father's rage! He's
lost his mind, I tell you!"

"Phasa—"

"Let him divorce me! I despise this cursed land anyway! I have wasted my life languishing here as his pawn for far too long. I cannot—"

"Phasa!"

Cut short, she spun to me. "What?"

"You must listen to me carefully," I said. "It only stands to reason that Herod has no intention of divorcing you. The danger to him would be far too great. Rome might withdraw its support."

"I don't understand. You said he would marry Herodias."

"I told you what was said. He means to be rid of you." I approached her, lowering my voice. "By what means, I don't know, but if you were to fall ill and die, his trouble would be far less."

I watched the blood drain from her face, for she knew her husband well.

"A man as obsessed as Herod will stop at nothing," I said. "Does his blood not run with treachery?"

"You're saying he intends to kill me—"

"Would you risk thinking otherwise? If you die then Herod, after a show of great sorrow, will be free to marry Herodias. And if she is the woman you say, would she not encourage such a plot?"

Phasa paced again, staring at the floor, hands clenched to fists.

"You're right. You're right!"

"You must be very careful," Saba said. "These are words that make wars."

"Yes," Judah said. "If Aretas's daughter were to die, God forbid such a thought, Rome would protect Herod from Aretas's rage. But if Herod throws his daughter aside in divorce—for this Aretas would wage war, and Rome might not come to Herod's defense. Maviah is right."

"Even if I am wrong," I said, "there is now only one course you might take, Phasa."

She looked up at me, nearly frantic. "To flee."

"To flee now, before Herod returns. Once safe with your father, you will force his hand. He will have no option but to divorce you if he wishes to marry Herodias. She will insist. This is what Yeshua spoke over you in Capernaum. You must flee, Phasa."

She stared at the window as her predicament settled about her. "I must. And fleeing will not be so easy."

"No. But with us, there is a way."

I looked at Judah and continued with assurance.

"We will take you to Petra on the safest route. Judah and Saba cannot fail you."

"Petra?" Judah had gone still. "To Aretas, enemy of the Kalb? Impossible!"

"Do we have any better choice?" I snapped, bothered by my own fear. I took a breath to settle myself. "Our mission with Herod is crushed. If he intends to kill Phasa, then he will likely put all of us to death. Tell me this isn't so."

"It is," Phasa said. "You stand to betray him."

Saba exchanged a glance with Judah. "And Aretas will favor us? He backs the Thamud, who crushed Rami. To go to Aretas is to invite more death. Better to go to Rome with the dagger ourselves."

"Rome?" Phasa said. "Herod has Rome's ear. They will crucify you before they would give you audience."

"Rome is too great a risk without an advocate," I said, watching Phasa. "But Aretas will hear me. Phasa will ensure our safety in exchange for her own."

She did not hesitate. "Yes. Of course I will. You will take me to Herod's fortress, Machaerus, in Perea, only a stone's throw from the border with Nabataea. Once we cross, we will be safe. Take me away from this cursed palace and I will be your advocate."

"And what will you tell Aretas?" Saba demanded. "You will beg for mercy?"

"Phasa and I will decide," I said. "You will only deliver me to Petra as charged by Rami."

"My charge was to bring you to Herod," he said.

"And Herod would have our heads," I snapped. "I say now, Petra."

My strong tone gave him pause. I had to be strong or else capitulate to my own worry.

"She says Petra," Judah said.

"Yes, Saba," Phasa agreed. "She says Petra."

But Saba was loyal to Rami.

"Herod will know that you have betrayed him," he said. "Rami cannot afford to have an enemy in both Aretas and Herod, who speaks for Rome. It is treacherous ground you tread."

I crossed my arms and walked to the window, then spoke, looking out at the night.

"True. Which is why we must be forced by Phasa, under her demands for our obedience."

I turned back to them.

"Phasa, you will leave a letter for Malcheus, explaining that you have discovered Herod's intention to marry Herodias."

"Malcheus will never stand with me now!"

"It won't matter. We will be too far gone by the time he sees the letter. I ask only that you claim to have taken me by force to ensure my slaves' aid in your escape. Ten of your most loyal warriors are no match for Judah and Saba."

They stared as one, uncertain.

"He will accept this. Don't you see? Even Malcheus knows that neither Judah nor Saba would threaten the life of Aretas's daughter. This you will explain in the letter."

"This was your thinking?" Saba said.

"Tell me it is flawed."

He could not.

"It is brilliant," Phasa said, eyes now fierce. "To see the look on that oaf's face when he learns…" She headed toward her inner chambers. "Saba, come! We must leave immediately."

"Leave by way of your chambers?"

Phasa spun back and shoved a finger toward her door. "My entire *life* is in that chamber! That beast can have his palace but I will not leave without my jewelry."

She turned back, cloak swirling, and marched into her chambers. "Come, Saba!"

Saba. The black stallion so accustomed to freedom and respect in the deepest sands, now caged by Phasa.

"Go with her, Saba," I said.

With one last glance at Judah, he dutifully followed, then stopped and regarded me.

"Aretas is no fool. Herod is but a child next to him. You court a dangerous storm."

"And you, Saba, will keep me safe!"

He hesitated, offered a shallow bow and walked into Phasa's chamber, leaving me alone with Judah.

I had spoken with far more courage than I could feel, and the strength was gone from me. But what I had started, I had to see through.

For a moment neither of us spoke. And yet, by the forlorn frown upon his face, I already knew that Judah was courting remorse.

"Maviah…"

"It is well, Judah."

He rushed up to me and fell to one knee, grasping my hand.

"Forgive me, my queen. My place is with you. I lost my mind in thinking that I would leave you for Yeshua."

"No, Judah, there's nothing to forgive. Please, don't kneel before me." If he only knew the depths of my worry.

"I long for what my elders have spoken of all my life. But I can't possibly leave you. I will be your lion to Petra and beyond, I swear it by the sun and the moon."

"There's no need to swear."

He rose to his feet, soft eyes swimming. "Forgive me, Maviah. Forgive this Jew who——"

I impulsively leaned forward and kissed him on his lips, cutting him short. I did it more for my comfort than his and I knew that he could feel the tremble in me as I pressed close to him.

I knew what a sacrifice he was making, abandoning his great obsession for an unknown future. But in truth, I could not bear the thought of continuing without him at my side.

I would be lost without Judah.

"It is I who thank you," I said, pulling back. "Never leave me, Judah."

"Never."

"Stay with me always."

"Always."

"Swear it."

"There is no need to——"

"Swear it!"

His eyes were bright. "I swear by the heavens and the stars and the moon and the sun . . . I will stay by you always."

"Thank you, Judah." I swallowed a knot that had formed in my throat. "Thank you. We will find Yeshua again when the time comes."

"Together," he said. "And soon."

But Judah was no prophet.

PETRA

"The eye is the lamp of the body.

If your eye is clear, your whole body will be full of light.

But if your eye is bad, your whole body will be full of darkness."

Yeshua

CHAPTER NINETEEN

LIKE A STORM in the desert, the events surrounding our departure from Sepphoris were full of flurry and motion.

In her letter, carefully crafted with my help, Phasa made her claims explicit. She had no choice but to find safety with her father, King Aretas of the Nabataeans, until all rumors of marriage to Herodias were settled, because she feared for her life. Distrusting any Roman or palace guard, she had forced Maviah, daughter of Rami bin Malik of Dumah, to accompany her. Upon reaching Petra safely, she would send the slaves back for Herod to deal with as he wished, for they were of no concern to her.

"It will eat at his gut," Phasa said with triumph. "If he denies his love for Herodias, she will quickly spit him out. He's crossed the threshold. He will have to divorce me."

"Then it is to your benefit," I said.

"It is! You have come as my savior!" She kissed me on the cheek. "My only regret is that you did not happen by ten years ago."

Phasa was willing to face any danger in flight for the prospect of freedom in her father's courts. I, on the other hand, was fleeing to my enemy's stronghold, and whispers of impending doom refused to be silenced.

Our journey would take us six days if we traveled light, and it took considerable persuasion on Judah's part to pare down Phasa's mounds of jewelry to two saddlebags' worth. Each saddlebag of gold would surely give any pursuer a half day's gain on us, he insisted. Phasa could live with less treasure easily replaced in Petra or die with gold enough to fill her coffin.

She acquiesced, taking only the most expensive pieces.

We left in staggered fashion so as not to raise suspicion, then reunited outside the city—four Bedu on camelback, supplied for a week's journey.

If not for Saba, who knew of ways far off the traveled paths, we might well have been intercepted by a dispatch on horseback. As it was, he led us south through little-known wadis toward the encampment of Nabataeans east of Machaerus. We slept in the heat of the day, far from any sign of human life, and traveled by night into morning at a trotting pace.

By the second day we knew that we had escaped the greatest danger of pursuit and slowed our pace to save the camels.

By the third day we knew that there was nothing now to stop us from reaching Petra, and Phasa's spirits soared.

By the fourth day, with exhaustion now working into our bones, Saba's words concerning Aretas began to overtake my mind like heavy boulders. But I said nothing. I rode with my shoulders square to the horizon, clinging to the words Yeshua had spoken to me.

Do not allow fear to bind you up, dear one. You will only lose what you already have.

And what did I have?

I had a love for Judah that I clung to with my every thought. I was a queen because of him and only with him. We spent many hours talking quietly to the rear of Saba and Phasa, and with each day our bond grew. Although it was true that our mission rested on my shoulders, I rested the strength of my heart on his. From the first day we entered the Nafud weeks earlier, he had been the rock upon which I had built my house.

I had the authority given me by Yeshua, though I hardly understood it.

I had the fate of the Kalb in my hands.

I had myself. Maviah, daughter of Rami, once honored sheikh of northern Arabia.

Could it be true that I too was the light of the world, as Yeshua had said to us all? Was it true that those who followed him would do greater works than even he? Was it true that a kingdom full of power and light resided inside me even as I rode atop my camel?

Or had he meant something else? For no one seemed certain of his meaning, only that he called all to follow.

Yet what did it mean to follow him?

Judah and I spoke often of Yeshua. In Judah's mind the kingdom was at hand to deliver Israel from oppression from Rome. The way of Yeshua, he said, was to use the power of love and goodness to free all people from tyranny. Evildoers must be thrown into outer darkness for their treachery. Because the day of restoration would come any day now. Even now. And what was outer darkness but their own misery? They would reap what they had sown.

"We must love, of course!" he said. "And, yes, we must turn the other cheek, but only to our brother. This is what he meant when he said he had not come to bring peace, but a sword to divide, even brother from brother if they will not join him."

"It doesn't seem to fit with the man I saw and heard," I said.

"Because you do not know the way of the warrior as I do. We must also protect the widows and the orphans and those who cannot protect themselves from those who refuse love. Let the Romans reap the same end they have sown. If a man comes to take your life, am I to allow it?"

No, I thought.

"If a warrior comes to slay the innocent among us, are we not to discourage him with the sword?"

I thought of my son.

"Yes."

"There you have it," he said. "Love first even the enemy, but if need be, love them finally with the blade!"

It made sense to me. So, then, perhaps we had heard the same. But it bothered me still.

I abandoned such difficult thinking and concerned myself instead with the Father Yeshua had spoken of so intimately. That Father who did not judge. The god of the kingdom of heaven now among us. Indeed, within me.

Was it possible to be the daughter of such a Father? I had never before heard of such a god. Isis certainly wasn't so gracious.

If it was possible that Yeshua's Father god could also be mine, could his power come to my aid as I stood before Aretas?

As we drew near to Petra, my only consolation was that Phasa had sworn to be my most spirited advocate. Her father would listen, she said. As for Shaquilath, his hotheaded queen, she could offer no assurances.

We arrived at Petra on the sixth day. I had not adequately prepared myself for that great city of stone.

Upon our approach we encountered a caravan southeast of the city. At least a thousand camels plodded in line, heavily laden with spices from Hadhramaut in the deep south, we were told. For many months they had traveled the southern trade route parallel to the Red Sea. I was immediately taken back to Dumah, where I'd witnessed the arrival of many such caravans.

Once again I was surrounded by the roar of a thousand camels as they were couched outside the city while the traders made entry. The scents of their frankincense and myrrh, mixed with the odors of the beasts that carried it, offered me some solace. And the Bedu who smiled as they lazily guided the camels...

These were my people. Though raised in Egypt, I was Bedu. I could not help but ponder what role I would play in their lives and they in mine.

We parted ways with the caravan as we approached the grand entrance to Petra—four travelers unnoticed, for there many were coming and going from that great pillar of trade.

Towering red sandstone obscured my view of the city. Tall columns were built directly into the face of the mountain. These rose a hundred feet, hewn into the cliff wall.

"It is a temple?" I asked.

"A tomb," Phasa said. "A facade only, to mark the burial of a royal. We are Nabataeans, Maviah, lords of the world, you will see. This is nothing, I will show you."

And she was right. We passed many such monuments to the dead, as well as an expansive arena carved from the mountain, large enough to seat five thousand, she said. It was new, the pride of her father.

Yet none could compare to the magnificence of Petra's heart. We entered the main stone colonnade, a perfectly ordered street bordered by towering columns that faced the Jebel mountain, from which more great monuments had been cut, glowing red in the sinking sun. Merchants everywhere traded their wares—sparkling treasures and spices and fabrics from the farthest reaches, some having undoubtedly passed through Dumah.

We were soon in a red canyon carved with many channels that collected and diverted water into massive cisterns. The big rains came only a few times each year, but Petra's people had mastered the art of collecting and preserving water long before any other, Phasa told us.

Only in this way could such an impenetrable city survive in the desert. Many had come against Petra for her wealth. None had succeeded. Not the Romans, nor the Greeks before them. None ever would.

And none could enter Petra and not wonder at the power of her king. To build such structures had surely taken many lifetimes.

Everywhere I looked I saw majestic architecture, greater by far than any in Sepphoris, if only because it had all been carved into the rock itself. Phasa insisted on showing us the city's greatest features before making entry into her father's courts.

The walled city itself was not so large, for most homes were on the slopes above the city, and the thousands who came and went by camel couched in massive camps to the south. Not so large, but glorious.

And unique in another way. The women dressed casually, at times scandalously, baring more skin than I was accustomed to. Their fabrics were rich in color and they were free to laugh on the streets. This place was more Greek and Roman than of the desert. Everywhere I looked I saw wealth. Petra was drenched in it.

This was the seat of Aretas, and the Bedu were a mere footstool to be kicked aside.

"But now you will see where the true power of Petra sits," Phasa announced, and she led us toward what appeared to be a great temple.

Steps rose to a huge terrace with three rows of columns on either side. I assumed this to be the temple to the Nabataeans' patron gods. Did Aretas then rule from a temple?

I glanced at Judah, who had remained silent, as had Saba, for they both knew that their lives were now in the hands of Phasa. He saw my look and offered an encouraging nod.

"Remember Yeshua's words, Maviah. Remember who you are."

"I am the enemy of Aretas," I replied.

"You are the savior of Phasa, his daughter. And Saba is her pet."

Saba glared at him but said nothing. His muscles were taut under dark skin glistening in the sun.

"Do not fret, Maviah," Phasa said, turning on her mount. "We are home."

And yet I did worry.

We reached the foot of the steps and Phasa angled for a guard on station there. "Send word to Aretas," she said. "Tell him that Phasaelis, his daughter, has arrived from Galilee and would seek his audience immediately."

The guard stood still.

"Are you deaf?"

He glanced at two others, one of whom must have recognized her, for he took a knee.

"My lady." He bowed his head.

"At least someone recognizes the daughter of their king when she presents herself. Have these camels quartered and bring the packs. I carry valuable cargo."

They hurried then, four of them running not as guard but as slaves—three to the camels and one into the courtyard to relay her message. The guard in Herod's courts did not jump for the queen as they did here.

"Come," Phasa said.

I held myself erect as I followed by Judah's side, aware that I was not dressed for my role. The clothes I wore were Phasa's, made for travel, not for court. The fitted blue-and-brown tunic was made of the finest hide, and loose gathered slacks fell to sandals strapped to my calves with leather binding. My hair was braided and tied back with a blue band about my forehead.

At my waist I carried the dagger of Varus.

Judah and Saba were dressed as warriors and carried both knives and swords. Only Phasa wore a cloak—black—but not one so extravagant as to bind her as she rode.

She walked now with fire in her eyes and head held high, directly up the steps and into the courtyard, which stretched between the towering columns to another series of steps and the inner courts.

"This is the palace?" I asked.

"This is where my father conducts all of his affairs. He lives elsewhere. You will see, Maviah." She looked at me. "Only let me speak. Say nothing out of turn."

"Of course."

We were halfway to the inner courts when a servant dressed in a white tunic hurried down the steps and ran to Phasa, bowing. "Phasaelis, daughter of Aretas, friend of his people. The king awaits."

"Lead us."

The servant lifted his head and glanced at Judah and Saba.

"They are my slaves. Lead us!"

"Of course, my lady."

He led us up the steps into a grand room that at first appeared to be a theater. Or a court. Seats ran on either side, facing a bare marble floor, finely carved and inlaid with rich colors. Everything my eyes saw spoke of exquisite workmanship and vast wealth, from the rich drapes to the golden lions positioned on either side of the entrance.

Light streamed in from windows near an ornately tiered ceiling arched in the Roman way.

"Phasa!" The voice thundered from a raised platform across the theater, and I lifted my eyes to see the true seat of power in Petra.

There, beyond yet another flight of five steps and four columns, stood two thrones made of silver and wood. On either side, fixed stone tables ran the length of the landing. Sculptures and tall lamp-stands made of silver appointed the platform.

"Phasa!"

A man with graying hair rushed down the steps. His beard was drawn to a point and tied with cords. He was dressed in a loose multi-colored robe, untied in the front to show white undergarments. His feet were bare and slapped on the marble floor as he hurried forward.

By the golden rings on his fingers and the silver bands on his wrists and forearms, I knew immediately that this was Aretas.

He stretched out his arms and cried out as if he'd found his only treasure.

"Phasa, love of my life! You have returned to an old king before his death. Al-Uzza has answered my prayers!"

He threw his arms around her and held her close, and for a moment I thought he might weep for his joy.

She kissed his face and beard. "Father, how I missed you!" I thought she too might burst into tears. Arabian blood ran thick in their veins.

I glanced up and saw that a woman of elaborate tastes, taller by a hand than Aretas, had left the table where they were feasting with several other royals and was striding to the edge of the platform. Unlike Aretas she was dressed in perfect fashion, red and purple silk drawn tight around her slender frame. Jewels sparkled where skin was to be seen, and her dark hair was piled high, bound in place by thin golden cords.

She did not hurry down the steps—doing so might have caused her to trip, for her gown was narrow to her sandaled feet.

This then was Shaquilath.

Phasa was the daughter of Aretas by his first wife, born before Shaquilath had become queen.

"Shaqui!" Aretas cried, turning back. "You see who has come to visit us."

"I see." The queen's mouth formed half of a smile. "And to what do we owe this pleasure?"

Phasa offered a slight bow, but her tone was less exuberant with the queen. "It is my greatest pleasure to see you as well, Mother Queen."

"You are well?" Aretas demanded of Phasa.

"Of course, Father. And now that I am in your court, I am the most favored daughter known to the world."

Aretas took Phasa's hand and pulled her toward the landing. "Join us in drink and food. You must tell us about your journey. Everything. We weren't told of your plans. Why did you not send word?"

Saba, Judah, and I were left standing in the middle of the floor. None of us had thought to bow. Unsure, I remained still.

They had reached the foot of the steps leading up to the thrones and banqueting table when the queen spoke.

"Aretas?"

He stopped and glanced up. "Yes?"

"Who are they?" Shaquilath stared at us without pointing.

Only now did Aretas become aware of our presence. He looked back and stared at us, then at Phasa for explanation.

"They are my slaves," Phasa said, smiling. "My guard. How else would you have me cross such treacherous ground to reach my father?"

"They are Phasa's slaves," Aretas said, satisfied. Then to a servant, "See that they are fed and bathed." Then to Phasa, "Come."

"And why are your slaves Bedu from the desert?" Shaquilath asked, not in an accusing voice, but still firm. "Where is Herod's guard?"

Sweat clung to my brow and my heart beat heavily, for it knew too well the danger at hand.

"Judah and Saba could slay ten of Herod's guard," Phasa said. "There is no match for the Bedu save the Nabataeans."

Why was she delaying the simple truth?

"There you have it," Aretas said. "Judah and Saba. Only the strongest for any daughter of mine."

"And the woman? What is her name?" Shaquilath pressed.

Phasa hesitated, but would not lie.

"She is Maviah. Daughter of the desert. As strong as any man."

Stillness fell upon the room and I knew immediately that my name was known.

"Maviah," Aretas said, slowly turning back to me. His countenance had shifted. "And where does Maviah come from?"

"From Dumah," Phasa said.

"From Dumah. Who is your father?"

I, no more than Phasa, could undermine my character by lying, so I did not hesitate.

"I am Maviah, daughter of Rami bin Malik."

Aretas released his daughter's hand and glared. He strode toward me, glancing first at Judah and Saba just beyond me.

"The daughter of the sheikh who fails me comes to my court with my own daughter?"

"The daughter of Rami, the great warrior who brought you great honor at the side of Varus. Rami, the conqueror whom you yourself once celebrated with great—"

"How dare you!" he thundered, eyes fired. "Do you think that I do not know what happens in my kingdom?"

"You fled Dumah with the dagger of Varus," the queen said.

How much they'd learned of my mission I could only guess, but I was now wholly at their mercy.

"I did. And I have now come to you of my own free will."

"Then you have come to your death willingly."

"No, Father!" Phasa rushed to Aretas. "You must listen to me. Whatever you think you know, it is only half. If not for Maviah I would be dead. How can you have so little mercy on the one who is the savior of your own daughter?"

"What absurdity is this?" Shaquilath demanded. "Where is Herod's guard?"

Phasa ignored the queen, pleading instead with her father.

"Did you hear me, Father?" She pointed to me, growing more bold. "If not for this woman who is like a sister to me, I would be dead. She and her slaves have saved my life."

He was slow to respond, eyeing me with great suspicion. "Nashquya, my niece entrusted to your family, is dead," he said. "In what manner has Rami angered the gods? He has betrayed me, and my blessing now remains only with the Thamud, who even now grace the courts of Petra. And yet here stands the daughter of Rami bearing the dagger of Varus, begging favor."

The Thamud were now in Petra? An image of Kahil bin Saman throwing my son from the window flashed through my mind.

"Nasha was my dearest friend," I said, unable to still the tremor in my voice. "I mourned her passing more than any. And I—"

"A slave *cannot* mourn the passing of Nasha like her own blood!" he thundered.

"And did I not also lose a father?" I said, knowing that it was too bold.

"Your father? Rami is in chains, begging for his death, a just punishment for the death of Nasha!"

"I am your *daughter*!" Phasa cried. "And Maviah has saved this daughter of yours from certain death. I beg you hear her."

Shaquilath's voice cut through the hall. "Where is Herod's—"

"Herod's guard is with *him*!" Phasa cried, spinning to the queen. "And with the woman he would take to be his wife."

Her voice rang out to rob the room of breath.

"The pig took me as his wife only to satisfy you, Father, but you know this already." Her jaw was taut as she leveled each word in accusation. "Now his longing has been satisfied with Herodias, the wife of his brother, Philip the tetrarch, and he conspired to have me die of illness, fearing that to divorce me would enrage you."

"Impossible!" Aretas roared.

"Is this not in keeping with the ways of his father, Herod the butcher? He has cast me aside and I would surely be dead, but for Maviah. It was she who learned of this plot and demanded that I return to you with Judah and Saba to save me from death. She came even knowing that you would despise her. For this she should be celebrated, not accused of betrayal!"

The revelation had taken them all by storm, and neither Aretas nor his queen could immediately speak.

"You must hear her, for she is—"

"Divorce?" Where Aretas had been angry before, his face was now pale.

"How can we know this is true?" Shaquilath demanded. "She told you this?"

"You question my word?" Phasa demanded.

"I question her!" The queen pointed at me as she approached. "She was the one who told you that the king would take up with another woman and divorce you. How do you know this is true?"

"Because I know my husband," Phasa cried. "I should have known many months ago, but my eyes were blinded by my own captivity. Herod would have me dead. He will take up with Herodias, you will see."

Aretas seemed not to hear their exchange.

"They think I am too old to defend my own honor?" His hands were fists and he paced away, staring at the floor. "They have forgotten what we did to the Greeks when they tried to defy the Nabataeans? To the Romans when they sought to suppress our control?"

He spun back to us and thrust a finger in the air, face scarlet. "No man can defy the power of the Nabataeans and live! I will crush that insolent little bastard. I will crush his armies and scatter their bones. How dare he cast aside his covenant with me for his own lust!"

"We cannot know this to be true," Shaquilath said. "Herod may be weak but he is not such a fool."

"Do you know him?" Phasa demanded. "Have you bathed him and fed him too much wine?"

They were lost in passion and I knew that unless reason was brought to bear, the outcome might not favor me, so I stilled my heart and spoke in a calm voice.

"All will be known soon enough. If our words lie, then judge as you see fit. But I am sister to Phasa and have delivered her to safety at my own peril. For this I ask only that you hear what I have to say. There is a way to deal with Herod for his treachery."

"How dare you tell the king how to deal in matters of state!" Shaquilath hissed.

Phasa glared. "Is a queen's word so worthless, Mother?"

"She is no queen!"

"I am," Phasa said. "And I say that she is."

"Silence!" The king's jowls shook. He caught his wife's angry stare, hesitated for a moment, then regarded Phasa, speaking in an even tone. "Mind how you speak to your queen."

Phasa thought better of pushing the matter.

"Yes, Father." Then, to Shaquilath, "Forgive me."

"If what you say is true," Aretas said, "then I swear before Al-Uzza that all of my fury will rain down upon Herod and all of his armies."

"If what she says is true," Shaquilath said. "We will not take the word of a slave from Dumah."

Aretas glanced at me. "No, we won't."

"Put her in chains until we have word."

For the first time since our entering the courts, Judah's passion took over and he stepped forward.

"I beg you, as Judah, mighty warrior of the Kalb who does not know the meaning of a deceitful tongue, what my queen speaks is true. I beg you have mercy and honor her as your guest."

"She is your queen?" Shaquilath said. "And you, a Jew who knows only treachery. How dare you speak in my court!"

"Forgive me, I only——"

"Do not speak to my queen," Aretas said. And then, to the guard behind us: "Put them all in chains."

"Father——"

"Separate them," Shaquilath said, turning back to the platform.

Aretas glanced at his daughter but did not defy his queen.

"Separate them and put them in chains."

CHAPTER TWENTY

MY FIRST THOUGHT when the guards seized me and pulled a hood over my head was for Judah. He would go gracefully, I knew, because Judah was not threatened by any dungeon. But I was the cause for this, his second imprisonment far from his true calling in the hills of Galilee.

I did not cry out. I did not resist, but beneath the dark cloth my eyes were wide with fear.

"Remember who you are, Maviah. Remember!"

They were the last words I heard from Judah before a blow sounded on his flesh. Phasa protested, but her father obeyed his wife.

Confused and terrified, I was led from the courts and away from the city bustle, then down a long flight of steps into damp air where keys rattled and gates were opened. They threw me into an earthen cell, moist but not muddy, that smelled of moldy straw.

Not a word was spoken to me.

After waiting for the sound of the guard's feet to leave me, I pulled the hood from my head and stared into the darkness. The sound of a distant gate clanking shut reached me, and then I was swallowed by silence.

"Judah?"

My prison rang hollow. I could make out the bars of the cell, but barely, like faint shadows in the dark. There was no source of light, no matter which direction I looked.

I pushed myself to my feet and slowly approached the bars. Peering beyond, I could not make out the passage—it was too dark.

"Judah!"

The only reply was the pounding in my own chest.

So, then, I was alone until Phasa could convince Aretas and his queen to believe my claim. A day at the most, I told myself. Phasa had her father's blood and would not remain silent. Had I not been like a sister to her? One day, perhaps two.

I felt my way along the stone walls, found the corner, and settled to the ground, hugging myself for comfort.

I had suffered much in my life, both as a daughter and as a slave, but I had never been imprisoned in the dark with only my thoughts to keep me company. And my thoughts, I soon learned, were my greatest enemy.

You see what you have done, Maviah? You see how hopeless is your life? You see how fear stalks you in the dark? You see that you are only a slave?

The thoughts were lies, of course, merely fear tempting me. I must face that fear and weather its storm. Had I not received this word so powerfully from Yeshua?

But his words now seemed to speak from another world, as far from me as the heavens themselves. I tried to keep my mind on his voice, and I managed for a while.

Without day or night, there was no way for me to keep track of time. Light came in the form of a torch, many hours later, but only long enough for a guard to shove a bowl of water and a lump of bread into my cell before retreating.

I clambered to my feet. "Wait! May I speak to Phasa?"

He offered no response.

"Please, call Phasa, I beg you!"

The outer gate slammed shut.

Then it was too dark to see and I mistakenly knocked over the bowl.

Be strong, Maviah. Only a day or two and Phasa will come for you. It is only a short time and you will stand before Aretas and he will hear your plea.

I'd rehearsed my request many times as we approached Petra.

The guard once again brought food and water many hours later. Once again he shoved it under the gate without looking at me. Once again I called out to him without receiving a response. But this time I grabbed the bowl in the diminishing light.

Just one more day, Maviah. They are discussing it this very moment. Soon Phasa will come.

Had it been only a day, I think I would have retained my full courage. Even two days. As best I could calculate, I was given food twice each day, and it was after the sixth time they brought food that I finally submitted to the truth of my predicament.

Phasa had failed to persuade her father to hear me. Aretas, influenced by his queen, would wait for the truth from Herod himself before considering his options.

How long would it take to secure word from Galilee? A week at best. Two weeks. And how quickly would Herod make his intentions known?

I might be in waiting for a long time, living like a rat in this dark cell.

The thoughts filled me with dread as three days became four. And then five.

The uncertainty of not knowing when or how I would be heard

affected me more than any belief that I would *not* be heard. Aretas would surely give me audience when the time came.

Unless Nicodemus had been misinformed about Herod's intentions to marry Herodias.

Unless Herod reversed his course.

Unless the Thamud—Kahil or his father, Saman—were now in Petra, conspiring to seal my fate.

Unless no one really cared what happened to me, for who was I but a slave? Unless this was my just reward for having courted the belief, however thin, that I was more than a woman deserving of her fate.

My mind began to ravage me.

I tried to hold on to my surreal encounter with Yeshua in Capernaum. But his power was not with me in my cell, and though I tried to follow his teaching to release fear, I could not find a way to shift my mind. With each passing day, my memory of him seemed to fade.

I spent many hours also thinking of Judah, my lion who had saved me more than once. Surely he would save me again. Surely I would find a way to save him. Surely he would not end his days in a Nabataean dungeon on my account. I would not be able to live with such terrible guilt.

A week passed. Or was it eight days? I lost track. I curled up in a ball on the dirt when it became cold, hating myself for feeling so powerless.

And then I felt the first significant shift in my mind. Though I had attempted to accept my fate, the first sparks of anger ignited deep within me.

I cannot say that my anger resulted from any particular thought, but the moment I felt that heat in my chest, I clung to it, then fed it with deliberate thoughts.

Had I ever betrayed anyone for my own gain, that the gods would have cause to punish me?

Had I not done my best to serve as a slave?

Had I not loved my son and nurtured him with life from my own breasts? Had I not honored my own father, even in his rejection of me? Had I not followed his wish in taking the dagger of Varus to Herod?

Was it my fault that I had been born a woman?

For hours the thoughts pounded through me, growing in their strength. I stood and paced, blood flowing hot through my veins. I despised any god who would visit such suffering on any mortal.

Yeshua had spoken of turning his cheek, and of a Father who did not judge, but my father knew only judgment and was made in the image of gods who loved only those who obeyed their every wish.

My thoughts turned again to Judah. To the way he'd led me through the desert and held me tenderly and saved me from Brutus. The moment an image of him being whipped filled my mind, I gripped my hands to fists and screamed into the darkness. Not once but many times.

My fury did not free me from the dungeon, but perhaps some god somewhere heard me, because the next day they came for me.

They came for me, but I felt little relief, so numb had my ravaging thoughts left me.

Four guards—two with torches, and two to shackle me and lead me from the cell. None offered a word of explanation.

I shrugged from their grip and walked upright, jaw tight, blood still hot.

They led me up the steps into the blinding sunlight. Only then did I come to myself and remember my true purpose in Petra. I stopped. Stunned that I'd drifted so far in my thinking, I allowed the sight of the sun to flood me with hope.

"Move!" One of the guards shoved me and I walked on.

My entire body was covered in filth and my hair was thick with dirt and sweat. But I was beyond caring what any might think of me. I was going to be heard. That was all that mattered.

Still, they delivered me to a washhouse, where three servants stripped and washed me using buckets of cold water, then dressed me in a plain white tunic and brushed my hair. Satisfied, they passed me to the guards, who shackled my hands once again.

They must have been under orders not to speak, for they were silent. Neither did I have anything to say to them.

Once again I was led into the great court that resembled a temple. Once more up the steps and into the inner courts of King Aretas, my head held high, for I had weathered their torment and was Maviah still, unharmed.

The open floor that I had taken for a theater was now set up as a court of law. Three wood tables formed a three-sided square with ornate chairs behind each table. Candle stands were set upon long silk runners, and bowls of fruits and nuts had been placed before nine members of Petra's ruling class.

Presiding at the head was King Aretas, dressed in regal purple, adorned with gold bands and heavy rings. Shaquilath, his queen, hair piled high, wore a sheer, close-fitting white dress. She sparkled like a jeweled tower.

The others I did not know, except Phasa, who bolted to her feet the moment I was led into the court.

"Unshackle her!" she snapped, hurrying to me.

The guards complied, then stepped back to the wide doors and took their place next to four others. I scanned the room but saw no sign of Judah or Saba.

"Are you well, my dear?" Phasa grabbed my hand and kissed it. "Tell me they treated you well as I was promised."

She spoke clearly for all to hear, and in her sincerity I found courage.

"Where is Judah?" I asked.

"They refuse to release him until they have heard you."

"Please, Phasa," Aretas said with a wave of his hand. "Sit."

"Be strong," she whispered, gripping my hand. "Show them you are a queen." She nodded a final encouragement, then retreated to her chair next to her father.

Aretas leaned back with one hand on the table and eyed me past bushy eyebrows. In his dark eyes I saw a lifetime of cunning and struggle, knowing that the Nabataean were world-renowned for their delicate strategy and brute force. They alone had managed to form strong ties with the Bedu sheikhs, who yielded to none but this man, for the great wealth he provided, for truly, only gold was thicker than blood.

For a long moment, we looked at each other without speaking. He drummed the table with the tips of his ringed fingers.

"Maviah, daughter of Rami. Do you know what happens now in Dumah?"

"Only that the Thamud butchered many Kalb for position and wealth," I said. "Only that Kahil bin Saman threw my son to his death for sport."

This seemed to give him pause and I knew he'd not heard of my son's death.

"My condolences," he said. "But now know more. The Thamud raid the Kalb as far as the Kalb can run, because the Kalb are headless. Your women are taken and your men killed. There is no mercy for either. Saman bin Shariqat ignores the Bedu code of honor and takes life where none is owed. The desert flows with blood." He took a deep breath. "This is what happens when my daughter dies in the care of Rami bin Malik. This is the consequence of defying Aretas, king of the Nabataeans, friend of his people, and his people alone. Without my direction the Bedu only butcher each other. So be it. But make no mistake, one word from me and my army would crush the Thamud where they stand."

I blinked, taken aback by the extent of the devastation.

"And yet Dumah pays me my full tax," he said.

"My father?" I asked.

"Awaits execution at my word. So you see who it is that you stand before now?"

I dipped my head in respect. "I stand before the king to whom I entrusted my life in coming."

Shaquilath flung a dagger from the table. It clattered to the floor and slid to a stop three paces from me.

The dagger of Varus.

"And what was your intent in presenting this to that snake, Herod?"

I studied her before speaking. "So you have heard from Sepphoris?"

"Answer my question."

Before I could, Phasa spoke for all to hear. "We have heard. Herod has announced to his advisers plans to marry Herodias. As you said, Maviah. I live only because of you."

"Phasa..." Aretas warned.

She sat back and crossed her arms, satisfied for having said her piece.

"Well?" the queen demanded. "Answer my question. The dagger."

I addressed her with care, knowing that she was the one who would decide my fate.

"I was thrown aside by my father when I was born, and sold into Egypt as a slave, where I served a Roman house. But the mistress sought revenge when I loved a slave whom she desired, though her passions were unknown to me. I was cast out again and sent to Dumah with my infant son. There only Nashquya loved me and called me her sister, though Rami was shamed by my presence. Being the stronger, she persuaded Rami to keep me." I looked at Aretas. "When Nasha fell ill, she feared your retribution on Rami and begged me to flee. But I could not abandon my father and be shamed once again."

"And what does this tale of gloom have to do with Herod?" the queen snapped.

"Suspecting that his son, Maliku, might betray him, Rami sent for me. When the Thamud descended upon Dumah, he gave me the dagger of Varus and begged me to find Herod."

"To what end?" Aretas said.

"For the purpose of securing an alliance between the Kalb and Rome. He would offer Rome the northern trade route if they would drive the Thamud from Dumah."

The king's right brow arched. "The Thamud and their Nabataean allies."

"Yes," I said without pause. "Rami saw no other way to restore his honor."

This much I guessed they knew, but my forthrightness was unexpected, judging by the stretch of silence that followed.

I pressed on while I had their ear.

"So I made my way to Palestine as any honoring daughter would do. I entered Herod's courts and presented Rami's offer. It was there that your daughter, Phasa, and I became like sisters as much as Nasha and I had been sisters."

"Yes, yes, of course," Aretas said. "Sisters all, so we have heard. We have not heard, however, how you learned of Herod's intentions."

"What the king is asking," Shaquilath interrupted, "is how we know this courageous act of yours isn't some elaborate plot between you and that snake, Herod, to undermine the Nabataeans."

I blinked, confused by her line of thought.

"But my queen——"

"I am not your queen. I am Shaquilath, queen of the Nabataeans, not the Kalb."

I felt my anger rise, but dipped my head. "As you say. How could I conspire to undermine you by rescuing your daughter? Surely there is no longer any question of my own risk in saving her."

"Is it so difficult for a slave to understand?" Shaquilath spoke through twisted lips. "Herod's purpose was to rid himself of Phasa. Yours was to gain our support to reclaim Dumah for your father. Isn't this what you have said?"

"Yes."

"So, then, you conspired with Herod to convince Phasa to flee him. He may now say that Phasa fled because she wanted to be rid of him, not he of her! Having been abandoned by his wife, he is free to find comfort in another woman's embrace." She paused. "As well, you may now claim you rescued her from Herod, and so win the grace of Aretas for your return to Dumah. Both you and Herod get what you want, and we are left the fools."

I had never considered such a convoluted plot, but I immediately saw how a cunning mind might.

"So, then..." the queen said. "Your plot has been uncovered."

"This is absurd!" Phasa cried. "I was with Maviah day and night and this was not in her heart!"

"By Isis, I swear no such thought passed my mind," I said. "I found Herod to be a greedy man, smitten by lust for another woman. I am a Bedu, bound to my father, a slave who knows how to serve a master, a woman who seeks honor. I am not one to deceive a king or his daughter!"

Shaquilath studied me.

"Herod has been with Herodias for many months," I continued, adamant. "This you will learn. I only met him the day before his departure from Sepphoris, just weeks after Dumah was overtaken by the Thamud. Did Herod and I conspire to this elaborate scheme in the few minutes I was with him the night before his departure? I am a mortal, not a goddess to work such spells."

A thin smile curved the king's lips.

He nodded after a moment. "I think she has made her case." He set his elbows on the table and touched the tips of his fingers together. "So, then, Herod has defied me of his own will. And for this he will feel my full wrath. I will crush him, you must know. No one can be allowed to defy my kingdom. Not one."

"I would expect no less," I said. Shaquilath glared at me. "And to this end, I have no doubt that you will succeed. All I ask is that you grant me grace by returning Dumah to the rightful control of the Kalb in return for saving Phasa."

"Ha!" The queen scoffed. "What Kalb are left to control Dumah?"

"If they knew that King Aretas, friend of his people, supported the Kalb, they would rise from the sands and crush the Thamud," I said. "Who would you prefer control the northern desert? Rami, who showed no aggression, or the Thamud, who are treacherous and will surely bite the hand that now feeds them?"

"Now you tell the king how to conduct his affairs?" Shaquilath demanded.

"I only speak what a woman might know, which is nothing."

I let the statement settle upon her, for she too was a woman.

"What you ask is impossible, naturally," Aretas said, but I believe he was intrigued by me. "Dumah has found its fate with the Thamud. My only concern now is Herod."

"Herod, yes," I said. "But if your eyes are only on the north, the south may—"

"Silence!" Shaquilath snapped. "Matters of state are none of your concern. Remember who you are!"

I looked at Phasa, who smiled, clearly encouraged by all she'd heard. And I remembered who I was. Judah had told me. As had Yeshua.

"I do remember who I am," I said to Aretas. "I am Maviah, who crossed the Nafud and made her way to Herod's courts. I am Maviah, who found the favor of the king. I am Maviah, who delivered Phasa from certain death. And now I will be Maviah, the servant of King Aretas in his bid against Herod."

No one spoke, for they had not expected such a bold statement.

"How so?" Aretas asked.

I glanced at the others seated in silence, each one watching me intently. Not one of them so much as coughed.

As I now understood my predicament, I had not the slightest leverage except grace from Aretas, which Shaquilath would never condone.

Even if Aretas released me to the desert, I would return only to bloodshed and bitter enemies. My only hope was in gaining Aretas as an advocate, and the only way to gain his trust was to prove myself further. Saving Phasa was not enough.

"I will prove myself to you further, my king."

He did not protest my use of his title.

"And?"

"You now have an enemy far greater than Rami. Herod defies you to your face for all the world to see. I will return to him."

Even the queen seemed intrigued now.

"You are under the impression that I need your help?" Aretas said.

"No. But I have my ways with Herod. He has a fascination with women, as you know. I will return in great distress, claiming to have been taken by force, as Phasa's letter to him has said."

"Brilliant!" Phasa cried, standing to her feet. "That's it! Maviah will be a spy in his bed and learn of his plans, then betray him as he betrayed me."

"Sit!"

"She's right about the pig," Phasa said. "His lusts know no bounds."

"Sit down!"

She sat.

"She might be right about Herod, but Maviah doesn't know Herodias," Shaquilath said. "I've heard of this witch. It will never work."

"I will worry about Herodias," I said. "Herod will surely expect retaliation from you. I might lead him astray."

"How so?"

"I would tell him how I was treated like a slave and mercilessly thrown in a dark pit for many days." This much was true. "I would convince him that I know of your plans for the harshest retaliation."

Aretas frowned and then stood. He paced. "She's right, Herod will expect retaliation. He knows that I cannot allow his insult to stand."

"Surely he prepares already," I said.

He turned to me. "You know this?"

"Would you not prepare?" I continued before he could respond, moving to my right only to match his movement. "But I might persuade him that you will accept a lesser penalty than war."

"I would never accept a lesser penalty."

"Of course not. But he won't know this. By agreeing to a lesser payment, he will lower his guard."

"Allowing me to strike effectively."

"Precisely."

Shaquilath stood, incensed. "We are discussing matters of state with a slave from Egypt? We are in this predicament *because* of her."

"I am *alive* because of her!" Phasa snapped, standing to match the queen.

The gathered elders alone remained seated, watching the four of us with interest.

"What kind of lesser payment?" Aretas asked of me, ignoring both daughter and wife.

"Whatever Herod might expect the king of Nabataea to demand," I said. "The changing of the border to Perea, perhaps."

Shaquilath sat, looking on with suspicion. But the king was curious.

"Perhaps a large payment in gold, enough to show the world his guilt."

"It's brilliant," Phasa said.

"You must understand," I said to Shaquilath, for I knew that she too had to be convinced. "You have nothing to lose. I take all the risk. Whether I succeed or fail, you will one day crush Herod, as is the Nabataean way. If I fail, Herod will be prepared, for he prepares already. But if I succeed, you may crush him when he is least prepared, at a time of your own choosing. What is there for you to lose in using me at my own risk?"

They said nothing.

"As well, what might I learn while in Herod's courts that might benefit you? Did I not learn of his intentions to kill Phasa? No emissary from you could hope for that much."

They studied me, fully curious. "And if you succeed?"

"Then you would restore my father's honor in Dumah."

"You cannot succeed in this," the queen said.

"Then Herod will put me to death and you will be rid of me."

For a long while, no one spoke. Then Aretas sat and spoke to the guard.

"Take her out and bring her when we call."

I bowed my head and followed the guard beyond the doors, which they closed behind me.

So, then, I had cast my lot. And having done so, I began to imagine the task ahead of me. Faced now with their possible agreement to my plan, I wondered how I could possibly approach Herod with such a proposition and succeed.

He was no fool. As cunning as Aretas. He would as likely put me to death or use me for his own pleasure as believe a word I said.

I was a slave now to both Aretas and Rami. But I knew only slavery.

I heard passionate voices beyond the door but could make out no words as I waited for long minutes. And then the door was thrown wide.

"Come."

Without waiting to be led, I walked in and stood before them once again.

Aretas sat beside his wife, who regarded me with arms crossed. It was she who delivered their verdict.

"We have not come to an agreement," she said. "But we will consider this plan further and with care. In either case you could not go to Herod soon, or he would surely expect foul play. These matters take time. No hasty demand for payment will be taken seriously."

I felt a moment of relief, for time would serve me well in preparing my thoughts, should they agree.

"You will be returned to your cell and wait for our decision," she said.

To the cell? The air thickened inside my chest.

"Until we decide, you stand in defiance as your father's daughter."

"How long?" I asked.

She shrugged. "We shall see. No less than two months."

My mind descended into a pit of despair.

"This was not what we said!" Phasa cried. No—it was Shaquilath's way of exerting her will. And Aretas made no objection.

"Don't worry, Phasa," the queen said. "She will be fed well."

"I will be alone?" I asked.

"Naturally," she said.

"And Judah?"

"Will remain where he is as well. You are fortunate to be alive...
no need to panic."

"This is preposterous, Father!" Phasa cried, pushing herself to her
feet. "You cannot allow it!"

"The whole world is preposterous, Phasa," Aretas said in a tired
voice. "She will be kept in good stead, you have my word."

Phasa looked at me, eyes desperate. Then spun to her father.
"Then I demand you release Saba to me. As my slave."

"Whatever for?" Shaquilath demanded. "We have many slaves as
beautiful."

"I will have the slave who delivered me to Petra and no other.
And if any harm comes to Maviah, I swear I will seek vengeance.
Saba under me, as a guarantee that she is well treated."

The implied threat could not be mistaken. If harm came to me, a
warrior such as Saba could surely do harm if not caged.

"Agreed," Aretas said, giving both wife and daughter their fancy.
He rose to his feet. "Give Phasa the black slave. Keep the Jew in
chains. Isolate the daughter of Rami bin Malik in the dungeon and
see that she is fed well."

Having made the matter clear, he turned and walked from the
court.

I felt ill.

CHAPTER TWENTY-ONE

THERE IS little to say of the weeks I spent in my cell with only cruel loneliness for company.

They put me in a larger cell lit by an oil lamp. It had a stone floor, a passable bedroll with straw for my head, a pot for waste, and a wooden bench to sit upon. And they offered me two meals each day—both with bread, some meat and vegetables in the form of a stew, and water.

All my physical needs were tended to, as Aretas had commanded.

But as the time passed, my thoughts began to slip away. I could feel my good sense leaking out, like water from a skin that had sprung a leak in the desert. And I seemed powerless to patch up that hole.

I had never known such deep loneliness as I did in those weeks, waiting without any knowledge of my fate. Worse still, I began fear *whatever* fate awaited me. The more I considered the matter, the more I became convinced that returning to Herod would end in my death.

Perhaps my fear was heightened by my appearance, for I was coming to look nothing like the queen who'd first made his acquaintance. In that cell I began to stoop like a lowly slave, a scavenger from the desert, a memory of my mother eating the bones of the dead for sustenance.

I was trash to be thrown out at the earliest convenience.

Perhaps my fear was heightened by the knowledge that even kings could be crushed in a single day. What hope was there for a woman such as me, imprisoned at the whim of such a king?

All the courage I'd found at Judah's side soon left me. The words and presence of Yeshua, once so powerful to me, drifted away, as distant as a long-forgotten dream. When I did remember his words, they only mocked me, for Yeshua must have known that fear would be the end of me. Why else would he have singled me out over the others in the room that night?

I saw only three guards, each in rotation, all warriors of lesser strength. They were taller than most Bedu and well fed, but not as well muscled, perhaps because they faced no danger in the dungeons. Of the three, only one, the oldest and thinnest—who wore a pointed gray beard and carried no sword—seemed even to notice me. He alone offered me a kind, half-toothed smile each time he set my dish through the bars and removed the waste.

It was my impression that he might be daft. But not even he spoke a word to me, regardless of what I said. They were all under orders.

So I spoke only to myself.

At first I did so only in my mind, as I had always done. But after two weeks in isolation, I began to whisper aloud, if only to hear the words.

"Pull yourself up, Maviah," I would whisper, pacing. "You must hold yourself together. Your father depends on you. The Kalb depend on you. Only you can avenge your son's death. You must stay strong!"

But then I would think, *Who is speaking to Maviah?* I was speaking to myself, naturally. But who was *I*?

"Your fate is your own doing, Maviah. You are the slave of an angry god who has already sent you to the underworld."

Then I would again wonder, *Who is this* I *who is speaking to* you? My mind began to twist around itself like so many snakes trapped in a box.

Time became a blur to me, defined only by the second meal each day, when I placed a mark on the floor with a small pebble. Two months at the least, Shaquilath had said. It could be much longer, for the Nabataeans were known to bide their time, striking only when all was known and prepared. This was the way of cunning.

If I had known that my wait would be only thirty or forty-five days, or sixty days, I might have counted the marks on the floor with hope. But how could I have any hope when I knew nothing of what was happening above the ground? Judah could be dead, and I would not know it. Phasa could have taken Queen Shaquilath's view that I was a conspirator with Herod, and left me to rot.

A month passed and I settled into a numbing routine of pacing and talking and eating and sleeping. And thinking always, begging my thoughts to leave me in peace.

Only after thirty-five days did I learn of anything beyond my own thoughts.

The first time Saba came to me I only stared at him beyond the bars, wondering if I was imagining him. His skin was clean and his head gleaming by the torchlight, and he looked at me.

"Maviah..."

And then I knew that he was real and tears rushed into my eyes unbidden. But I still could not move.

"My queen," he said. "What they do to you will earn retribution beyond any they have known. This I swear."

He'd called me his queen. Such a strange word.

"Do they feed you well?"

"How is Judah?" I said.

He placed his fingers around the bars and cast a glance back down the passage, then spoke to me in a hurried, soft voice.

"They say nothing of Judah. Every day Phasa inquires, but they say nothing. The Nabataeans are insane. I remain with Phasa only for your sake, you must know this."

I approached the bars and stared at him. His eyes were misted and his jaw flexed.

"Am I your queen, Saba? I have never been your queen."

He hesitated. "Now you are my queen. To the end of my days, I swear it."

Why was I speaking to him of queens? I should demand to know when I would be set free. But he would have told me everything he knew. So instead I was speaking to him about queens.

"You are mistaken," I said, finding the words thick on my tongue. "The Bedu have no queen. The woman who stands before you is only a slave."

One of the guards standing in wait down the passage approached. "You've seen what you came to see."

Saba spoke with a conviction as deep as the color of his skin.

"Do not lose hope, my queen. The fate of all Kalb now rests with you. The Thamud know no mercy. Keep yourself strong. Eat. Walk. Move!"

"Come!"

"Remember who you are," he said.

And then they took him, leaving me alone once again.

I crossed to the bench, sat heavily, lowered my head into my hands, and wept, overwhelmed. He had called me a queen!

Saba, the strongest of all warriors, perhaps stronger than Judah, unbending in his ways, servant to none but my father, had called me his queen. And yet he could not know how weak and worthless I felt in that hole.

He had placed his hope in a woman who had known only slavery all her days. A woman who could not honor her own father nor save even her own son. A woman who had not fooled Herod, nor Aretas, nor any of the gods, nor any living soul.

A woman who had fooled only herself by daring to believe, if only for a short time, that she was worthy of a man's task.

Nevertheless Saba's first visit gave me some hope, if only in knowing that he was alive and well. And I did begin to eat every scrap they set before me, and walk much of the day, and keep my arms as strong as I could, if only to distract myself from the voices in my head.

But his words also filled me with dread, for the burden of all Kalb was carried upon my shoulders.

He came once a week, each time for less than a minute, only to see that I was not mistreated. Each time he gave me the same word, begging me to remain strong, vowing his eternal service.

Each time I saw the rage on his face.

Not once did he give me any news about Judah or offer me any further word from the court.

To the best of my counting, I lived in the dungeons of Petra for eleven weeks all told, one of those in total darkness, seventy-one days in the second cell, never knowing what fate awaited me or Judah.

I was sleeping when the door swung open with a terrible squeal.

"Wake up."

I jerked up from the mat, mind yet clouded by dreams. The older guard who often smiled at me stood in the doorway, grinning. A second guard whom I did not recognize stepped around him.

"The court awaits you."

"Now?"

He grabbed my arm and pulled me to my feet. I stumbled after him into the passage, where two more warriors waited. They bound my hands in shackles, shoved a bag over my head, and led me from the dungeons by a chain.

I was barefoot and dressed in clean undergarments and a short, filthy tunic, but none of this concerned me. My mind was preoccupied with my fate.

This time I did not walk with my head held high. This time I was not fueled by rage, nor filled with purpose. This time I could not gather my thoughts, and I could not see, and I tripped twice up the steps leading into the daylight, which I could see only as pinpricks through the cloth over my head.

I wasn't bound by fear but by a great uncertainty, for in that cell I had lost my way. Questions flooded my mind. I resolved only to follow the guard and accept whatever fate awaited me.

They lifted me onto a camel, still hooded, and led me some distance away from the heart of the city, for the day grew quiet. The fresh scent of clean air filled my nose and lungs and the sun's warmth gave me some courage. Then they couched the camel and ordered me off.

I stood without sandals on hot sand for a moment before they tugged me forward, onto a stone path, up four steps, and into the cool of a building caged in silence.

The hood was pulled from my head and I blinked in the dim light. They were there. Aretas and his queen, Shaquilath, sat behind a wide stone table fifteen paces in front of me. We were in a large circular room with a domed ceiling supported by tall limestone columns. Stone benches behind the pillars rose to an outer wall. Small windows permitted a little light. The floor under my feet was made of stained stone slabs set in loose sand.

Apart from Aretas and his queen, only I and perhaps ten Nabataean warriors stood in the small arena. The soldiers, stationed to my right and left, all bore arms and awaited orders.

Behind me the heavy door slammed shut, closing off the outside world.

"Remove her shackles."

I turned to Aretas as the guard released the irons from my wrists and pushed me into the center of the room.

The light streaming in from the small windows that ringed the arena was joined by the light of six tall torches, three on either side of the stone table. A single wooden door, now closed, led deeper into the building behind it. There were no other appointments in the room.

Aretas slowly pushed himself to his feet and walked around the table, right hand at his beard, elbow supported by his left forearm, which lay across his chest. Today he wore a blue robe and a headband of leather inlaid with silver. Shaquilath remained seated, hair piled high as before.

Wind moaned through the narrow windows above us. Why had they brought me here, to an arena that appeared rarely used, or abandoned?

The king stopped in front of the stone table and studied me. "I see you are no worse off for your visit with us. As promised." He glanced at the domed ceiling and indicated the room with a lazy hand. "Do you know what this is?"

When I didn't answer he told me.

"Many years ago, after the death of Alexander the Great, when the Greeks were thrown into chaos, Antigonus the One-eyed ordered Athenaeus to crush the Nabataeans at Petra, for the whole world knew of our great wealth. They came at night, four thousand foot soldiers and six hundred horsemen. But my ancestors, rather than rush into battle, hid in the vast cisterns while the Greeks raided the city, thinking it abandoned. The Greeks took much frankincense and myrrh and five hundred talents of silver and retreated into the desert two full days' march before encamping to celebrate their victory. Surely you have heard of this great battle."

He waited for me to respond, and I cleared my throat. "No."

"No? The Nabataeans bode their time before descending on the Greeks while they slept. We slaughtered all four thousand foot soldiers and all but forty of the horsemen, so that they might take news of their defeat back to the Greeks as a warning. Did the Greeks learn? Of course not, but that is another tale."

He flashed me a grin and tapped his head with a thick finger.

"Strategy, daughter of Rami. This was three hundred years ago. Ever since, the Nabataeans have ruled with superior cunning and strategy. Always patient, always allowing the enemy to succumb to their own greatest weakness. I'm sure you can appreciate such wisdom. It's a matter of survival in this ruthless desert."

I gave a shallow nod.

He scanned the walls. "We now stand in one of the great underground cisterns in which my ancestors hid from the Greeks. Many years later, our king Obodas reinforced it with these columns and made it a treasury. When our greater treasury was completed, he then exposed its walls and made it an arena for training and sport. Much blood has been shed in this room. Mostly that of our enemies."

The floor was stained with blood, then.

"But this is not the point," Aretas said. "There is too much blood spilled in the desert already. The point is that the Nabataeans have always outwitted those who would undermine our kingdom. And I have no choice but to do the same today in the matter concerning Herod."

Growing impatient, his queen, who'd watched us without any discernible expression, spoke directly.

"It seems that your judgment of Herod was correct," she said.

"He's officially taken Herodias as his wife. We've decided to grant you your wish."

A flicker of annoyance at the interruption crossed the king's face, but he let it go. "Yes," he said. "We've decided to grant you your wish."

"With a few conditions," Shaquilath said.

"Naturally. With a few conditions." Aretas paced to his right, stroking his beard again. "Assuming, that is, that you're still willing." He faced me. "Or has your time alone cast doubt on your proposition?"

It had, of course. But I saw no alternative path to honor, and hearing that they had decided in my favor gave me some courage. At the very least I would be rid of Petra. I had come to despise what I knew of their city.

"My offer stands as spoken," I said, gathering strength.

"Then you have lost none of your resolve?"

"None."

"And you still believe you possess the strength necessary to approach Herod with all the cunning of your father?"

The fog in my mind was clearing and I slowly drew breath to settle my focus. I was sure to be joined by Judah and Saba once again— together we would find a way.

"Would I have presented the proposition if I doubted myself?"

He smiled. "No, I suppose you wouldn't have." He turned and walked toward the table again. "So, then, you may take to Herod my demand for payment of one hundred talents of gold. We will supply all that you need for the journey, including a sealed letter from me, explaining my terms."

"And if I succeed?" I asked, finding more courage.

Aretas reached his chair behind the stone table, seated himself, and stared at me.

"Return to me with this payment, and you will be properly honored."

His words did not reflect what I had requested per se, but they were enough for the moment. I dipped my head in acceptance.

"And if you fail," Shaquilath said, "there will be equal consequence."

"As I said, I accept my risk with Herod."

"I'm not speaking of your own life. Do you think we would send you to Palestine without a guarantee?" She motioned to one of the guards with her finger, and he strode for the door behind the table. "What is to keep you from fleeing your duty once it is agreed to? Only the leverage that we hold over you."

I watched as the door swung wide. First Judah, then Saba was led from darkness, both in chains, wearing only gags and loincloths.

My heart crashed against my breast.

Judah had lost some of his color and he wasn't as full in the chest. And yet his eyes were bright and full of courage as he looked at me. There was no sign of suffering on his face, nor regret.

I knew immediately that the only way the Nabataeans could have my mighty Bedu warriors in chains without sign of struggle was by holding my well-being over their heads. Judah's and Saba's allegiance to me had put them in these chains.

"Saba will go with you," Shaquilath said. "Phasa will throw a tantrum, but you will need your dark slave."

Saba remained between two guards near the door as they led Judah across the floor.

"And Judah?" I demanded.

"Judah. The one you love will be held for your safe return, of course."

"How dare you!" I cried. My mind felt loosed of its tethers. "I cannot leave without Judah!"

"Oh, but you must."

The large entrance door swung open and a man walked in. He stood in the light, dressed in the black fringed thobe of the Thamud. On his head a red-and-yellow kaffiyeh was bound by a black agal.

For a moment I could not breathe.

Kahil bin Saman.

This was the son of the Thamud sheikh who had crushed my father. This was the man who had flung my son from the window in Dumah.

My fingers began to tremble as he walked forward, first eyeing me, then stopping and bowing to Aretas and his queen.

"You must," Shaquilath said again. "And if you fail or defy this king in any way, your slave will be put to death."

I could not speak.

She nodded at Kahil, and he returned the gesture. The two guards restraining Judah seized his arms behind his back and held him still.

"So that you remember how serious this matter is..." the queen said.

Kahil walked up to Judah without ceremony, withdrew his hand, and struck him in the face with a fist. Judah's head snapped back with the impact. A white gash appeared over his right eye and immediately filled with blood, which flowed down his face.

When Kahil drew his arm back for a second blow I could see that his knuckles were wrapped in hardened pitch.

I had clung to my sanity for eleven weeks in Petra's dungeons, but there in the arena it left me completely.

I heard Saba protesting through his muzzle the moment I launched myself toward Kahil. It was only a cry, but I knew he was demanding I hold my place. Even I knew I should remain. Even I knew that any attempt to save Judah would end badly for both of us.

And yet I could not stop myself.

I hurled myself at Kahil's back as taught to me by Johnin in Egypt. His hand was drawn for a third blow when the crown of my head struck the small of his back.

Caught flat-footed, he roared in pain and arched backward.

I was weak from their dungeons, and the blow stunned me, but it didn't dull my instincts. Even as he staggered, I clawed at his face with my nails. Found his beard with my fingers. Yanked my hand away with all my strength. Heard the ripping of his hair.

Kahil screamed.

Then my hand was free and I plunged to the ground before rolling back to my feet and spinning back to him.

Held upright by the two guards, Judah sagged, oblivious to the world.

I went again before Kahil could recover.

The Thamud prince was not prepared for such a scorned adversary. Despite my weakness, I would have torn his eyes from their sockets had the blow not struck me from behind.

One of the Nabataean warriors reached me before I could strike again. His sword struck my head broadside. A dull pain flashed through my skull.

I instinctively planted my left foot forward, then spun my right leg up and around, high, so that my heel caught the warrior on his jaw. He dropped to the ground with a soft grunt, sword clattering on the stone beside him.

But the distraction had gained Kahil his time. He grabbed my hair from behind and slammed me to my back. Then he was on me, gripping my face with fingers of iron.

I tried to free myself, but his weight was too great and his arms too strong. He held my face with one hand and slapped me repeatedly with the other, cursing bitterly. His fingers tore at my cheeks.

Kahil surely knew that Aretas wouldn't allow him to kill me. So he did what came naturally to a brutal man. He set his intentions upon maiming me.

He snatched up sand from the floor and ground it into my eyes using his thumbs. His face was only inches from my own. I could feel his hot breath and his spittle as he screamed obscenities.

Pain such as I had rarely felt cut through my eyes, and I realized that he was trying to blind me. Yielding to panic, I flailed and struggled to keep my eyes shut, but no matter how tightly I clenched them, the pain spread.

"Enough!" Aretas roared.

Who pulled Kahil off me, I don't know, but he went with a roar of indignation.

"The whore has ripped my beard!" he cried.

"Enough!" Aretas thundered.

"I have full right to take blood for blood!"

"You've already taken it, you fool! Was it not her child you killed?"

I lay on the ground, short of breath. When I tried to open my eyes, I could see light, but the world was only a fog.

I heard Shaquilath's voice, soft-spoken and intrigued. "You are fortunate to be alive, Kahil. This one is a warrior. If she were not so weak, you would be dead."

"By this dog? She is a woman who eats the bones of carcasses. Abysm!" Kahil spit to the ground. "The death of her son honors all men."

"Be careful or she may crush your bones."

The queen's challenge hung in the room like poisoned smoke. Kahil was slow to respond, and when he did, there was no bottom to his bitterness.

"You dishonor me—"

"And you are servant of my queen," Aretas said. "Are you so eager to die?"

Silence.

"Take the slave Judah to Dumah," Aretas said to Kahil. "If I learn that you have maimed or killed him, I will cut your throat myself." He let the command set in. "Do you understand what I have said?"

Kahil did not respond.

"Are you deaf?"

"No."

"Then answer me! Do you understand what I have said?"

"Yes."

"Leave us!"

I heard shuffling feet and I pushed myself up with my arms.

"Judah..."

My voice was weak, no more than a whimper from a dying dog. But I knew that he could not have heard me if I'd screamed.

Then the door was closed and Judah was gone.

For a few moments, no one spoke.

"The Thamud are mindless animals," Aretas said.

He took a great breath, as if cleansing himself of his troubles before addressing me.

"You will remain three days to gather yourself. Then you will journey to Herod with Saba. Return to me as proposed and I will see you honored. If you have not returned within thirty days, then both your father and Judah will be put out of their misery."

CHAPTER TWENTY-TWO

JUDAH. MY mind was possessed with images of Judah. He, the lion, reduced to a sagging lump of flesh, chained by the same monster who had thrown my infant son from the window.

Judah, who had rescued me from my misery and brought his stars into my eyes. Judah, who'd held me tenderly and kissed me with abandon. Who had cut down Brutus before the beast could lay a hand on me. Who could walk through the Nafud and weather any storm, who could surely lead a thousand men into war and remain standing, who could shrug off the wounds upon his back and laugh at his torment so long as I was safe.

Judah, who had obsessed after his Galilean mystic as a Bedu boy might obsess after his first victory in battle. Who had followed me to Petra rather than follow his own destiny at the feet of that mystic, Yeshua.

Judah, whom I had sentenced to death.

And more, I had sentenced myself to death. Which meant there was no hope for Judah or me or the Kalb. I knew as much three days after Kahil blinded me, because my eyesight was still fogged and showed no sign of improvement.

The Nabataean physicians had cast their spells over me in Petra, beckoning their gods to heal, and they'd applied their salves to my eyes, but their chanting only quickened my hatred for all gods, and their ointments only increased the sting.

Still, the greatest pain lived in my heart, for it was enslaved to bitterness and dread. I could not rid myself of these, no matter how firmly I set my intention. My failure to rise above darkness made the pain worse, for it made a mockery of this blind queen in rags who came from a pathetic tribe of dogs deep in the barren desert.

After three days in Petra, we set out for Palestine, and I wore my dread like a cloak. Try as I might, I could not find hope. Day by day my fear grew, like a monster that could not be chased into hiding.

It became too much. I stopped Saba on a tall hill overlooking Palestine, overcome with unrelenting fear. It was then that I told him we could not go to Herod.

He said nothing. I could not tell if he agreed with me or hated me.

Tears flooded my eyes and there upon the camel I wept like a child. I was blind. It was too much! I could not overcome my fear. I would be thrown out because of my fear—I knew this as I knew my breath. Hadn't Yeshua said as much in his parable of the harsh taskmaster?

Wasn't I destined to be crushed?

I faced Saba with unbending resolve, tears still streaming from my pale eyes.

"We must find Yeshua."

"We go to Herod," he said, unsure.

"No. We have to find Yeshua first."

"We don't have time to—"

"Then I will go to him alone."

He considered my desperation for only a few moments before speaking.

"We will find Yeshua."

There was no more discussion. We would find Yeshua, who had spoken to me of my fear. Then we would go to Herod.

But my fear did not abate. With each passing mile it seemed to press deeper into my bones. I was going back into the jackal's lair, I thought. This time I would not emerge.

Six days after leaving Petra, my camel padded over the rocky ground two lengths behind Saba's, close to Sepphoris. We were weary from so many days in the hot sun, pushed by Saba's driven pace, for Saba was always of singular purpose. It was clear that he served not one, but three now: Rami as before, but also his queen, Maviah, and his brother, Judah.

The weight of the tallest mountain was upon my shoulders, but Saba bore it as well.

There was Rami, there was Judah, there was Saba, there was I. The fate of the desert awaited us four.

But there was more.

There was Yeshua.

The sun was slipping down the western sky to our left as we rode—night would be upon us in a few hours. Only at my hands and feet was my flesh exposed. Like a mummy resurrected from an Egyptian tomb, I was wrapped in a woolen cloak from shoulders to ankles. My head was hidden beneath a mantle and sheer scarf that covered my eyes.

Yet even without the veil, my vision was clouded so that the whole world seemed to be made of jinn and fog. I could see well enough by day to make out Saba's blurry form, well enough to function with careful estimation, but hardly more.

Saba led me faithfully, surely aware of the depths of my misery, but he allowed me to abide without offering advice.

Nine days of torment, and now Sepphoris was near.

Entering a sandy wash, he slowed his pace until I was beside him. For a while we matched stride, and finally he spoke, voice soft.

"I would tell you a teaching I once heard in the East," he said. "With your permission."

"A teaching, Saba. This is unlike you." We plodded on. "As you will."

"There is a woman on a path, wandering aimlessly. But a beast leaps from the rocks and she runs for her life, terrified. Sure to die, she reaches a cliff and leaps off to snatch a vine. Now out of the beast's reach she hangs, momentarily grateful. But looking down she sees at the bottom another beast waiting to devour her. Now she is trapped."

He was talking of me, I thought. Naturally.

"And above her the woman sees two mice chewing on this vine, one white and one black. Clinging to this vine she trembles, fearing for her life, for soon the mice will eat through the vine. Is not her fate sealed?"

"So it seems."

He took a deep breath.

"Only then does she close her eyes and calm her mind. And when she opens them, she sees strawberries on the cliff. Thus she picks one of the strawberries and eats it. And how sweet is that berry."

He stopped, as if finished.

"This is your teaching?"

"Not mine. Only one I once heard at a fire. Whenever I am in battle this teaching speaks to me."

I considered the tale and understood parts but not the whole.

"So, then, tell me what it means," I said.

"The beasts are all that we believe threatens us. There is no way to stop troubles from coming in this life. The mice, one white, one black, are day and night, the passing of our days. Neither can this be stopped. And yet, if one can calm the mind, take her eyes off the beasts, and release her fear, she might see what is before her."

"The strawberries," I said.

"And how sweet they are." He paused. "It is similar to the teaching of Yeshua and the harsh taskmaster, yes?"

Yeshua also had spoken of being able to see the light. But hearing Saba say it, I was seeing only darkness. There were no strawberries and there was no light. I was bound by fear of the beasts all about me.

"There is a beast in Dumah, far behind us," Saba said. "And one in Herod, ahead. Only by releasing your fear can you partake of what good stands before you."

"And if the woman on the vine is blind? What then, Saba?"

"Is blindness of the eyes or the heart?"

Anger welled up in my breast and I turned to him.

"Look at me, Saba," I snapped.

His head turned and I lifted the veil from my eyes.

"Tell me, are my eyes clear? Are these the eyes that Herod once saw?"

"It is not—"

"Answer me! What do you see? Are my eyes clear?"

He didn't speak, so I let the veil fall and faced the wash ahead of us.

"I cannot see, Saba." A great weight smothered me and I struggled to maintain my composure. "I've done everything the world has asked of me and now I find myself blind to it."

"This will pass," he said.

"So you said nine days ago." I was disgusted with myself for having so little strength. Was not the whole world faced with suffering? I had to shed my own self-pity before it swallowed me entirely, but I was powerless to do so.

Stinging tears came to my eyes.

"Forgive me."

"It is a difficult thing asked of you, Maviah. I spoke too quickly with this teaching."

"No." I exhaled slowly and gathered myself. "No, I am grateful for you. Please...forgive me."

"There is nothing to forgive," he said.

Always the rock, I thought. Judah the lion, Saba the pillar.

"I'm afraid for Judah. Even if we succeed..." My emotions choked me.

"When we succeed, we will return to Dumah and crush the Thamud."

Saba seemed to have adopted Judah's optimism. But I could not believe in any such future.

"I'm afraid, Saba."

He brought his camel to a halt and faced me.

"Then the mystic will give you courage," he said.

Yeshua.

We'd decided that Saba would go into Sepphoris and find the woman named Joanna—the disciple of Yeshua who was married to Herod's chief steward, Chuza. Nicodemus, who was pure in heart, had told me I could trust her, and so I would.

Joanna would know Herod's state of affairs. Nearly four months had passed since I last saw the king, and much had changed. She would tell us how to make an entrance to his courts. More importantly, as a follower of the mystic, she could tell us where to find Yeshua, who traveled often.

"We will make camp here," Saba said. "Sepphoris is only two miles."

So, then...the time had arrived.

"It is still your wish that I go alone?" he asked.

"It's the only way. Don't worry about me. I can fend for myself for a day. We are far off the road, are we not?"

"Yes."

"Then I will be safe."

"I will gather wood," he said.

"No, Saba. Go while there's still light. If you cannot find Joanna then find the other one, Stephen, son of Gamil. Trust no one else."

"I understand."

"If you find Joanna, I must know all she can tell you about this woman, Herodias. I need to know when she is with Herod and what influence she has in matters of state. I also need to know if Herod is bullheaded or cautious. I need to know what his court believes in regard to Phasa's flight. I need to know—"

"Yes, Maviah. I remember all that we spoke about."

But I was still anxious.

"Everything?"

"I know even what we have *not* discussed."

I nodded. "You will try to return by morning?"

"No later than one day, even if I fail."

"Don't fail."

"No."

"Good."

We sat for a few moments, he reluctant to leave his charge, I with nothing more to say.

"Then I go," he finally said.

I nodded. "I'll be here. Don't lose your way."

He didn't bother responding, for it was an absurdity.

"Be safe, my queen."

Queen. The word stung me.

He tapped his camel's neck with his riding stick. The beast protested with a soft grunt but obediently plodded forward.

"And Saba?"

He twisted back in the saddle. "Yes, Maviah...?"

"Remember to keep your head covered, it's far too distinguishable."

My vision was too clouded to see if he smiled, but I heard mirth in his voice.

"You must not worry, Maviah. Walking among the enemy is like drinking milk for me."

Who could instruct a Bedu warrior in matters of raiding?

"Milk is white," I said. "You are the color of pitch. Please be careful."

"Of course." And then he left me alone in the wash.

I stared at the hill over which Saba had vanished, feeling strangely comforted by his assurance. Was there any other man as dependable as the black tower from the east? Only Judah, I thought. If anyone could succeed, it was Saba.

My only task now was to wait.

And so I did. First on my camel for a long while, then in gathering wood for a fire as the camel grazed on bushes nearby. I prepared a simple meal of figs and bread baked in the sand, as Judah had shown me, and I drank milk Saba had collected that morning, for I was too worn to pull at the she-camel's udders.

Finally, when darkness hid the world and there was nothing more to be done, I lay on my bedroll near my camel and listened to her chewing her cud. Alone in the night, I began to cry.

I cried for Judah.

I cried for my son.

I cried for my shame.

And finally...I slept.

"THIS IS THE WOMAN?"

I heard the words in my dreams, thinking I was being accused.

"She looks like no queen from the desert..."

"As I said," Saba's voice responded. "She has seen great suffering."

"Then we must help her."

I was a woman in need of help, I thought. I was worthless now.

"Maviah."

A hand shook my shoulder and in my dream I opened my eyes. Day had come and a figure knelt over me, its blurred form wrapped in white cloth. The notion that this was a ghoul crossed my mind before it occurred to me that perhaps I *wasn't* dreaming.

I sat up and looked about, trying to blink the world into focus. Then I recalled all. I was partially blind. We had come to Sepphoris. Saba had gone to find Joanna.

"Saba?"

"It is Stephen!" the man said. "Son of Gamil. Joanna has asked me to come with Saba and so I have."

He immediately reminded me of Judah, for his voice was full of courage.

I pushed myself to my feet and looked past him. Saba stood beside a camel that bore a woman. I realized then that I did not wear my veil and they could see my eyes. They were the first in Palestine to see me as I was, and I felt naked.

I glanced down to where my covering lay on the bedroll.

"There's no need to cover yourself," Stephen said. "Your eyes will soon see, it is certain."

Was the clouding in my eyes so obvious?

"You've brought Joanna as well?" I asked Saba.

"No," he said, stepping forward. "The woman's name is Sarah."

"I bring Sarah," Stephen quickly announced. "She too must find Yeshua and so I take both of you. We will go to the sea and then north by boat to Capernaum. If he isn't there now, he will be soon."

He saw my hesitation, and continued.

"Do not worry, desert queen. You will see the world as it is soon enough, and then no king will stand in your way. The earth itself will bow before you; the stars will see one who believes and all the world will rejoice."

"You know him?"

"The king?"

"Yeshua," I said.

"As a brother!" he cried. Then, careful not to mislead: "Though I do not claim to be one of the twelve." He lifted his finger. "But I surely follow the teacher to whatever end."

"And you know Nicodemus?" I asked, for I wanted to be sure.

"But of course! It was I who told him to seek out Yeshua. Speak to him, Uncle, I said. Speak to him and all of your madness will fall away. You cannot reach God by washing your hands any more than you can see him by bathing your eyes. Yeshua gives new eyes and new hands. Those who follow him walk in a new power even now, where heaven has come to the earth. And now I, Stephen ben Gamil, will take you to him straightaway. With Sarah."

My spirit was lifted by Stephen's exuberance. There was nothing more I needed to know.

He headed toward his camel, walking past Saba. "You will see," he said, mounting. "And you too, warrior. Today will be your day of glory. If not today then tomorrow. Or the next day. But you must hurry, there is no need to linger."

This was how I first met Stephen, that young man of great faith. Indeed, he led us with his courage—even Saba.

I decided not to wear the veil now, for I was safe in this company. We had only just mounted when Stephen turned in his saddle and spoke to me.

"You must not fear Sarah. She is said to be unclean on account of her blood for twelve years, and she is understandably shy so prefers not to speak. I've told her that Yeshua does not see those who follow him as unclean. Still, she too will be made whole at his hand. She must only have faith."

Having made his proclamation, he turned and led the way up the slope.

I was mortified for the woman who followed me, for even among the Bedu a woman's cycle of blood brought her shame. As I understood it, those women who worshipped the god of the Jews suffered even greater shame.

So I slowed my mount until her camel drew abreast. I couldn't see her face clearly, but I could feel her silent humiliation as if it were my own. And was it not?

"He means well," I said.

She rode on, face fixed forward, and I wondered if I only added to her disgrace.

"I was born an outcast in the desert," I said. "Not unlike the lepers in your country. So perhaps we are sisters."

She offered no comment.

"You are safe with us," I finally said. "Saba will allow no harm to come to you."

I was about to prod my camel to move on when she finally spoke. Her voice sounded like a young girl's, though I knew she had to be more than twenty if she'd suffered bleeding for twelve years.

"You've met him?" she asked.

I turned to her. She was surely speaking of Yeshua.

"Yes."

"He is as Stephen says?"

"What does Stephen say?"

She hesitated before answering, voice still faint. "That he brings new life with a single word. That the blind see and the lame walk."

I was struck by the desperation in her meager voice. The world was full of kingdoms vying for power and glory, and yet were not kingdoms gatherings of people like Sarah, who only wanted to escape their fear and pain? Did not each one seek peace and love?

For more than a week I had wallowed in a stupor, pining for my own deliverance, but surely every common man and woman suffered, each mastered by their own fear. Who was I, then, to waste away in my own predicament?

Because Yeshua's kingdom was a kingdom of people, not of land or gold or anything that could be protected by armies.

Because Yeshua lived to restore Sarah.

"It is true," I said. "I've seen it with my own eyes."

Then why was I still afraid?

She fell silent again and I spoke no more, because I didn't know what else to offer her. I moved up to Saba, who told me of his visit to Sepphoris.

It had taken him much of the night to find Joanna in her home at the north end of Sepphoris, but she had withheld nothing from him because she already knew who he was. Rumors of the tall black desert slave who had accompanied Phasa on her flight had spread through the palace like fire. Surely, Herod despised Saba as much as he despised Phasa.

Herod was no longer at the palace in Sepphoris. His new wife, Herodias, refused to live in a city built for a Nabataean queen. The palace in Tiberias would be her home, far from any memory of Phasaelis.

Saba also learned that John, called the Baptizer, had spoken out against Herod's marriage to Herodias, for she had been married to Herod's brother. Inflamed by Herodias, the king had arrested the Baptizer and imprisoned him in his fortress at Machaerus.

Since that time Yeshua had gathered large crowds and spoken with even greater boldness for all to hear. Wherever he went he left awe and wonder. The teachers of the Law had sent their emissaries, who found mounting offense in Yeshua's teaching of the way of salvation—this way into the kingdom of heaven for all who would release what had once been written and follow him.

Yeshua had gathered twelve disciples to his side, but many others also followed, women as well as men, sinners and outcasts whom he forgave with a word.

"He brings great danger to himself," Saba said quietly as we rode. "Many fear he will be silenced."

As his mother, Miriam, feared. Stephen overheard and now turned on his mount.

"Yeshua finds no threat in this rumor!" he proclaimed, lifting a finger. "You will see, he holds no grievance. So, then, we too must hold none. Rome only does what Rome knows. Herod only does what Herod knows. But we must offer them no judgment. All grievance comes from fear of harm. To release grievance is to believe in God and the one he has sent. Do only this to be saved. This is the way, you will see."

I found in Stephen an almost childlike acceptance that was at once endearing and naïve. But his words echoed what I'd heard from Yeshua.

How could I hold no grievance against Aretas and the Thamud? Surely Yeshua judged those who smothered the poor. And did he not also judge the teachers of the Law?

As if anticipating my objection, Stephen added to his sermon there upon his camel.

"Even the Pharisees are only whitewashed tombs," he said, "vipers who have lost their way. Yeshua does not judge them, he only corrects their way of thinking so that they too may see, even as Nicodemus now begins to see."

"And will they?" I asked.

"I think not," he said, after a moment. "I think they are too busy worshiping in their temple. Yeshua's way would empty their coffers, surely, and then who would pay for their beautiful robes and lavish homes?" He chuckled and I could not help but smile with him.

After the noon hour we reached the crest of a hill overlooking the Sea of Galilee. Though I could not see clearly, I remembered the vast expanse of water.

But it wasn't the sea that captured my interest. It was the city that hugged that sea below us, like a behemoth in my murky view.

It was Tiberias.

There, behind the great outer walls, deep within its stone heart, waited Herod and his new queen, Herodias.

I sat upon my camel and stared, trying desperately to see more. Aretas had been clear. If I did not return to Petra with payment as agreed, he would allow the Thamud to execute both Judah and my father.

And yet how could I, now broken, stand before such a king and his jealous wife and demand one hundred talents of gold? If I had my sight, at least, I might present myself with wise words and boldness fitting of Aretas's authority. But even if not blind, how could I expect Herod to believe me?

How could a woman such as me win the ear of a king?

The terrible fear descended upon me again, and a tremor came to my fingers. I wanted to run. And if I could not run, I would throw myself at Herod's feet and beg for mercy, knowing he would offer me none.

Then my troubles would end, at the end of a sword.

"Maviah."

I turned to Saba, who was watching me.

"We must go while there is still light."

Yes. We must go. To Yeshua.

But in that moment, I forgot why we must go to Yeshua. My fear had washed all belief from my mind.

"You will see," Stephen said, urging his camel down the slope. "You will see!"

It was then, hearing Stephen's bold proclamation, that I knew he was wrong. I would *not* see. I don't know why I was suddenly so certain of this fact, but I was. Perhaps the mystic had spoken to my heart from far away and told me that my eyes would not be opened.

Or perhaps I was wrong. Perhaps I was only going mad.

I nudged my camel and followed the others down the hill toward the Sea of Galilee.

BETHSAIDA

"Truly I tell you, if anyone steadfastly believes in me,
he will himself be able to do the things that I do;
and he will do even greater things than these..."

Yeshua

CHAPTER TWENTY-THREE

WE WERE at the heart of the sea, halfway to the north shore, when the wind began to blow. But to say that it blew is like saying the wind had blown in the Nafud when the sands smothered us and swallowed my she-camel, Shunu.

With Saba's encouragement Stephen had found Elias, the same fisherman who had delivered us to Capernaum nearly four months earlier. He remembered me clearly and, though he said nothing, he stared at my face, wary, before Stephen assured him I was not a leper.

Once again we offered him a fair sum. Once again he was delighted to show his great value, promising us swift passage to the north shore. Once again Elias demonstrated his great passion for talking, this time with a willing partner in Stephen.

When it became clear that Elias dismissed the tales of Yeshua and was interested only in his fair share of fishing coin, Stephen didn't press his own passions. He spoke instead of fishing and the Romans and made small talk to pass the time.

The sky was cloudy when we left and turned dark soon after, but Elias assured us that there was nothing to fear.

"These clouds come often," Elias said, waving his large, callused hand at the sky. "They mean nothing. Rarely do they produce more than a brief squall. You must trust Elias."

"You see?" Stephen eagerly agreed "We can trust Elias. He's the best fisherman in all of Galilee."

"Everywhere, all fishermen know that what I say is the truth in matters of fish and sea," Elias quickly added. "There can be no doubt."

"There you are," Stephen said. "There can be no doubt."

Saba and Stephen sat opposite each other at the boat's center. I huddled next to Sarah at the bow, as far from Elias as possible, as was customary, for we were women. If he'd known of her condition, he might not have taken us, but no one made mention of it.

I could not see Sarah's face clearly but wondered if she was more familiar than I with these dark clouds.

"Do you know the sea?" I asked.

"No." By her voice I knew that she was terrified. So rather than find comfort, I sought to offer it.

"My sea is the desert," I said, "but I've been across this water with Elias twice. I'm sure it is safe."

"The wind is growing stronger. How will this boat not fall over?"

"It is made for seas, even when the wind blows strong."

"I can't swim."

"Swim?" The thought sent a chill down my back, for I knew that I too would sink straight to the bottom. "That's why we are in the boat, so that we don't need to swim," I said, offering a stilted laugh. But my concern grew with hers as gusts began to rip at our clothing.

"There is nothing to worry about," I assured her.

A rather large swell lifted the boat, and she took hold of my knee. The bow splashed down into the wave's trough, sending a spray of water over our heads.

Sarah cried out, and I would have as well had I not persuaded myself to be her strength.

From the back, Elias laughed defiantly. "It is nothing! The water will cleanse you and make you strong! There is nothing to fear! This sea is no match for Elias!"

"You are frightening them!" Saba chided. "Keep the boat straight."

"Straight? But we are straight! Straight into waves, as the camel goes over the sands."

I knew that Saba, too, was challenged by these waters. Sarah's hand was shaking, and I gripped it with one hand, using my other to hold the side of the boat, swells now slapping against it as wind howled overhead.

"It's all right, Sarah," I said. "Think of the sea as your own shame and it will be all right."

"What do you mean?"

"Have you not lived with this illness for many years?"

"Yes. Yes, but——"

"And yet you are alive."

She hesitated, so I finished the thought for her.

"So then, you will still be alive when this storm has passed. This is only the same storm we have faced all of our lives."

The wind moaned and the boat rocked and Sarah remained silent.

"Is it not so?" I demanded, seeking my own reassurance.

"Yes," she said.

"Well then," I said. "This is the same."

But it was not the same. No sooner had I offered my courage than a towering swell rushed us. I saw it in my blindness as a rolling fog, a ghoul from a nightmare.

Thunder crashed over our heads, and the sky stuttered with bright light. Then the wave threw us high and sideways, and I was certain that we would be crushed under that wall of water.

Sarah screamed and threw herself from the seat. The water swept over the bow, nearly tearing me overboard.

"Hold on!" Elias laughed. "It's only the sea, toying with us! Nothing to worry——"

But his voice was drowned out by a roar and more peals of thunder, for we had entered nature's full fury. I was sure the boat would be smashed to splinters.

I was already in the hull, clinging to Sarah and the beam beneath us. Saba had thrown himself over us both, to protect us.

"God save us!" Elias cried, now in terror. "He unleashes his wrath!"

Like a cork we bounced from wave to wave, sure to capsize at any moment.

"Have mercy!" Elias was now alone in his plea, for the rest of us were hugging the hull, too terrified to pray. "Forgive our great and terrible sins!"

But Elias's god wasn't listening.

The wind was the greatest enemy, for it howled like a jinn, mocking us in its rage. Water rushed into the hull, soaking us all to our skin. Rain fell now in sheets.

Above it all I heard Elias's cries, begging for his god to save him, confessing all matter of uncleanliness. And yet the sea raged, throwing us forward and to the side and swamping us with its fury.

The storm had come up so suddenly that I was tempted to believe the Jewish god had indeed determined to cleanse us of life itself.

Still the storm raged. Still we clung to life in that hull. Yet now even Elias had been silenced. In his stead, I heard Stephen crying out.

Not crying out so much as howling, I thought. Laughing.

I lifted my head and saw the blurred image of an upright man clinging to the mast, with one hand thrust into the air.

"Be not afraid!" he was screaming. "Have faith! This too shall pass!"

He had lost his mind!

But then the boat was thrown high in the air and he quickly found his sanity, collapsing to the mast's base, hugging it tight, terrified once more.

The boat landed with a crushing blow and I was sure we would perish in that sea.

It is difficult to explain what happened next, for I was at the bottom of the boat, struggling to keep my face out of the water that had filled the hull.

I remember hearing a roar louder than the storm itself, and I was thinking we had finally been overturned. But the roar passed over, rolling from one end of the sky to the other like the thunder of drums beating directly upon us.

And then the wind was gone, as if the roar had taken it and left. The rain stopped, not slowly, but as if the clouds had never opened. We pitched, but no wave rolled under us and the boat quickly settled.

I jerked my head up and the sight before me took my breath away. My vision was clouded, but this much I could not miss: a wall of rain and black storm clouds the size of the sky itself was fast retreating to the horizon, rolled up like a sandstorm in the desert. And in its wake, a perfect calm.

I turned my head and saw a light fog swallow us like a soothing breath. The storm had set upon us swiftly, but the calm chased it away far more quickly, like a nightmare vanquished by waking.

Stephen sprang to his feet, and Elias too. Then Saba. But none seemed able to speak. The gentle fog moved over the water, which was now like glass, without a wisp of wind.

"What in the name of—"

"Be quiet, Elias!" Stephen whispered, snatching his hand up to silence the fisherman. "Listen."

I could hear nothing but the gentle slap of water against our hull.

"There!" Stephen held on to the mast with one hand and thrust the other into the fog. I heard it then, the sound of voices across the water. We were near the shore?

But as I strained for vision, the dull image of a boat drifted into view, not a hundred paces distant. Then another beyond it. The voices of exclamation came from there.

And then a single voice, chuckling softly, stilling the others. I felt the hair on my neck rise, for there was something about that voice...

"Why are you so afraid?" it said.

The master.

I could not mistake the voice that had spoken to me in Capernaum. It was Yeshua. And now I could just make out his form standing in the boat among huddled men.

My heart soared with hope.

"Do you still have no faith?" Yeshua said.

For a long moment, only silence. But I could not contain myself after so many days in darkness.

"Master?" My voice echoed over the water.

There was no reply. He wasn't responding to me. Had he not heard me?

Stephen was not so meek. "Master!" I saw him throw himself from the boat. He landed on his belly with a mighty splash and immediately began to flail about, struggling to stay afloat.

For a moment we all just watched, taken aback by his impulsiveness.

Stephen twisted back for our boat, grasping at the water. "Help me!"

"Grab the oar!" Elias cried. "He can't swim!"

Saba grabbed the oar and quickly unwound the tethers that secured it.

"The oar, Stephen!" Elias cried. "Take the oar!"

Saba thrust it out and Stephen clung to the carved blade, kicking his feet to keep his head above water. Together Elias and Saba hauled him over the side, and he sloshed back into the boat like a great landed fish.

He immediately sprang to his feet, gasping, spinning back to the boat in the fog.

"Master," he called. "It is I, Stephen!"

"I see..." Yeshua's voice was only curious. "Stephen the brave."

Stephen glanced at me, and even in my blurred vision I saw him beaming. I looked across the water and saw we were drifting farther from each other, carried by momentum.

Why had Yeshua not answered my cry?

"I bring two for you, master! Elias can steer the boat next to yours. I bring... you can speak to them even now!"

"You could," Yeshua said, voice intrigued. "Wait for me in Bethsaida, my friend. I will return soon."

"Yes, of course. Bethsaida."

"Bethsaida," Yeshua said.

"We will wait for you in Bethsaida!"

Then I would see Yeshua in Bethsaida. My hope surged once again.

Stephen watched the boat as it drifted away, then turned to us, looking from one to the other.

"You see?"

None of us responded, yet my mind was swept away with what I had seen. Though I had felt Yeshua's presence as if it were a power unto itself, though I had wept at his words over me, though I had watched him touch a boy's shriveled hands and seen them made whole before my eyes—what kind of man could also command nature? Was he a god in the form of a man? And who was this Father who gave him such power? Who was this god who did not judge, as he himself had said?

I felt light-headed. My fingers tingled with the mystery of it all.

Stephen faced Elias. "You see?"

The fisherman stared after the other boats. A new breeze swept away the sea of fog and carried us away from each other. Above us the sky was blue once again. Elias was silent, for he could not make sense of what he had seen. Who could?

"Now you must see," Stephen said. "Take us to the shore near Bethsaida."

BETHSAIDA WAS east of Capernaum, a short walk inland from the sea, and after we came ashore Stephen took us there right away, before the sun set.

When we arrived, Stephen took us to a home at the edge of the village. It was occupied by an old man named Simon whose wife had recently died. Sarah and I were permitted to sleep in a room off the courtyard, but Simon was a religious man and would not allow us to eat with the men.

It didn't matter. We were both silent and withdrawn, each to our own thoughts. Even Stephen was silent. I could not help but think that we were waiting for yet another storm to fall upon us.

Was not Yeshua himself a storm? A storm of new understanding. A storm that would upend all that was known of the world.

We waited in Simon's home on the edge of Bethsaida for three days before Saba reminded me that nearly half of our allotted time had passed. We must make our return to Petra within a week, for it would take at least seven days to make the journey, more if we carried gold.

But the notion of securing Herod's agreement seemed impossible to me.

I did not venture into the town but kept to myself, near Sarah and Saba. I did not inquire of Stephen nor ask for more than what I was offered in way of water and bread, for Simon was poor.

In a fog I pondered my life, seeing the world as dimly with my eyes as with my heart.

Far away, Judah suffered in the torturous grasp of the Thamud. The thought made me ill.

Even now my powerful father wasted away without his tongue. Even now Aretas and Shaquilath protected their kingdom without care whether I lived or died. Even now Herod ate his grapes and drank his wine with a new queen who had stolen his mind.

But even as I considered these things, the voice of the one who commanded the sea called to me in the same words he'd spoken to his disciples.

Why are you so afraid, Maviah?

I am afraid because I cannot see. I am afraid because I am a woman and alone. I am afraid because all who have loved me are dead. I am afraid because I am surely not who I must be.

Do you still have no faith?

But you see, there was my truest conflict. What was faith? And if Yeshua's own disciples had no faith, having been with him for so long already, how could I possess it?

So on the fourth day, I approached Stephen.

"May I speak with you, Stephen?"

He looked about, and I knew that he was concerned with custom, for I was a foreign woman and he a Jew.

"With Sarah, naturally," I said.

"Yes! Yes, of course. We will sit there in the shade of the tree, yes?"

So I fetched Sarah, who agreed to sit with us.

"You will see, Maviah," he said, seating himself. "And you, Sarah. You too will have eyes to see."

"My vision is ruined."

"Vision? It is said in our scriptures, 'Without vision, my people perish.' This vision is to see the world as it truly is. He will give you new vision to see the world in a new way. The true world vision."

Always the same with Stephen. He would wait in Bethsaida for many days just to see with this vision. And wouldn't I? Yet I didn't have many days.

"Now," he said, "tell me what concerns you."

"Yeshua speaks of faith...what does it mean to you?"

He went still, as if I had knocked on a door that contained his greatest secrets. "Faith?"

"For the Jew, what does it mean to believe?"

"It is to trust. Not only to believe, for surely even the devil believes the truth and trembles. But to trust...that is everything!" He spoke urgently but in a soft voice, with a finger raised. "You are very wise, Maviah! This is what few understand. And you, Sarah; you must have faith. You too must believe."

"Do the disciples of Yeshua have so little faith, then?" I said.

He hesitated. "You speak of the storm."

"Yes."

He thought for a moment, then answered with care. "I was raised by my uncle in Judea for many years—"

"Nicodemus."

"Yes. He has always been one to think beyond the normal way of speaking. This is why he became a Pharisee, to find the truest way to God. To follow the last letter of the Law so as to find favor with God. I did not choose his path, but he taught me to think in new ways. Also, I studied with the Greeks and have traveled far. So..." He seemed reluctant to speak outright. "So perhaps I see things with a different eye."

"See how?"

"With the heart," he said. "The eyes are truly the heart and mind. As I hear the master, life is about what happens inside a man. To even think angry thoughts is no less than murder, he says. The world then is filled with murderers. And why does man get angry? Because he feels threatened or wronged. And why does he feel threatened? Because he does not believe he is safe. Why? Because he is afraid of God and so cannot trust him."

I followed his logic but had no concept of how to trust any god.

"This is the work of God, the master says: to trust in the one God has sent. To trust Yeshua and his way, Maviah. To trust that you too may calm this storm!"

"To say I believe this tree is a tree—"

"This is not belief as Yeshua means it!" he interrupted, terribly excited. "He means to trust what these human eyes cannot see. Belief *of* Yeshua is not belief *in* Yeshua."

I glanced in Sarah's direction but could not see her expression.

"Perhaps it is better to understand faith by your fears," he said. "Why did we fear the storm?"

"Because it threatened us," I said.

"There are those who say the storm does not exist. That it is evil. That this secret knowledge will save you. This is the gnostic way, Nicodemus tells me. But they are wrong. The storm is real, but it did not threaten us. Did you not hear Yeshua ask why the others were afraid?"

"They were afraid because the storm was about to crush them," I said. "We were all afraid."

Stephen lifted his finger, blurry in my sight. "Exactly! But only because we did not trust the Father to keep us safe as he sees fit. Our trust was in the boat instead! We put our trust in wood and pitch and flesh and blood and wind and water, and so the storm has dominion over us. Don't you see? We must let this world go and see no threat. This is what it means to believe *in* Yeshua!"

"The danger is real, not imagined! What you suggest is madness!"

"Madness!" he cried, delighted. "Of course the storm is real. In the eyes of children who trust their Father, there is no threat. No grievance against the storm. With faith, Maviah, you can see that nothing threatens you. Then you will fear no storm—you will master it. Only when you trust the Father can you let go of your fear and all grievance. This is why Yeshua told those in the boat that they had no faith, surely."

The teaching seemed too much now, for I was drowning already.

Stephen continued. "When the religious man argues with great passion, desperate to be right, does he not secretly harbor a grievance against the one who threatens his knowledge? This too is fear, but Yeshua does not argue in this way. There is no threat in the storm of words—his Father keeps him safe! This is his way."

"You speak as though letting go of grievance is nothing more than letting a stone fall from the hand."

"Ah . . . but this is the meaning of forgiveness, is it not? To let go. To forgive the world." He swept his hand through the air. "All of it! To let go of all blame."

The first hints of a greater meaning registered in my mind.

"And do you forgive?" I asked.

He stilled for a moment, caught off guard. Then he settled back down and sighed.

"Me? I am only a common man who thinks about these things. I cannot say that I believe any more than the others or I too would calm the storm. But I believe I am learning." Stephen leaned forward. "Do you know he has promised that all who follow him will do as he does and greater?"

"And do they?"

"Not yet." He sat back. "Perhaps because no one truly trusts. Many are called but few are chosen, he says. Narrow is the gate. Yet there are those who want to trust in him fully. Peter, James,

John, Sons of Thunder. The others as well. And some close to me in Bethany—Philip, Lazarus, and his sisters Mary and Martha. We all seek to know this way. As must you. And you, Sarah."

I could not doubt his sincerity, but how was it possible to hold no grievance and find no threat in the world? Such a person would indeed rule the heart with great power.

I blinked. *The kingdom of heaven, within.*

"When you listen to Yeshua, listen for what he tells you *not* to put your faith in," Stephen said, cutting my thoughts short. "Will a husband give you security? No! Will food save you from suffering? No! Will wealth save you from death? No! Nothing on earth will offer you salvation from the storms of this age or the next. Rather give what you have to the poor, for to give is to receive in his kingdom."

"My kingdom is not of this earth," I said quietly.

"Yes! Yes! Yet among and within us now! Where did you hear this?"

"He said it."

"Then you know! If you search your heart and find any grievance, even against the Romans, it exposes your lack of faith in the Father, who abides in the heart, for this is the kingdom of heaven as well. But believe in him and his way and you will be saved, because nothing that happens in this world threatens you. Let go of this world to master it. Seek his kingdom first and all will be added—or not, it doesn't matter. Do you see?"

Only with the dimmest vision, I thought.

"Yeshua says always: be anxious for nothing. And what is anxiousness but what the Greeks say? It is *merizo*, 'to divide,' and *nous*, 'the mind.' To have a divided mind, torn between security and fear. But we will only be anxious until we release all that we believe will save us, even knowledge, for faith, not knowledge, saves. *This* then is true salvation from all of life's suffering in this age and the next."

He grinned, nearly ecstatic.

"This is his meaning when he teaches that no one can serve two masters. There are two masters calling for your attention in every hour: the kingdom of this world symbolized by money, and the kingdom of heaven, which is spirit. Both are here—within and among us. You must choose to see the kingdom of heaven and abide. Until you forget and serve the other once again."

"Forget?"

He hesitated. "Unfortunately, yes. We forget far too often. But Yeshua's teaching calls to us still and we remember." Again, with his finger lifted. "If enslaved to the desire for wealth, let this go. If enslaved by grievance, turn the cheek. If your significance is in being mother or father or wife or husband or child or in having any of these—indeed, if you cling even to your own life—these too let go. Have instead a new mind set upon the kingdom. Do not be anxious, but rather repent—see beyond your old mind, you see? Only have eyes to see what is true beyond what you think. Trust the Father. Then you will master this world with pleasure rather than be mastered by it. Then you will find the power to command any storm."

Stephen was a master with words, I thought. He should one day stand before the crowds.

"You do this?" I asked. "You trust?"

Stephen stared at me, then shrugged. "As I said, I am only a common man with simple thoughts prone to forget such a simple truth far too often."

"I trust," Sarah said quietly.

We both turned to her. She'd been sitting as quiet as a flower, minding her own thoughts. And now her tone betrayed no doubt.

She faced us and spoke in hardly more than a whisper. "I think I trust."

"Then you will walk in his kingdom, Sarah," Stephen said. "There can be no question."

The breeze brushed my face. I felt as though I had entered a dream of impossibilities. And yet had I not seen the storm calmed?

Stephen stood and brushed the pine needles from his cloak. "Now I must prepare."

"Prepare for what?"

He turned to me. "You haven't heard? For Yeshua, of course. A great many know that he comes today. Today is the day, you will see."

CHAPTER TWENTY-FOUR

I WAS LYING on my back, staring at the ceiling of our room, when I first heard the commotion. Sarah was with me, and Saba appeared at the door.

"He is here already, on the other side."

Gathering ourselves, we rushed from the house and stopped short at the view. There, just beyond the town, hundreds were hurrying. To where, I didn't know, but it could only mean he had arrived.

Sarah was the first to run, and then I, on her heels.

"Stay close, Maviah!" Saba said. "Stay with me."

But I hardly heard him, for I was already caught up, rushing to stay with Sarah, who seemed to have forgotten that she was weak from her illness.

"Sarah!" I had to follow her—she was my eyes.

She ignored me, desperate to reach the same destination as everyone else.

Then we broke over a grassy slope west of the village and Sarah pulled up sharply, so that I ran into her.

Even with milky vision, the sight took my breath away. A thousand at least had already gathered. More streamed from the slope beyond. Only three months earlier in Capernaum there had been hundreds—now there were sure to be thousands.

How they loved him! Because he loved them as himself, as if they were he. *What you did not do to the least of these, you did not do for me.*

The least among them were those who'd sinned by breaking the law and were now outcast in accordance with their Law as given in their religion. Were they not the sexually deviant and lepers and hungry children and the poor and diseased and sinners of all types that crowded close? Yet Yeshua loved them and honored them— all except those who judged from afar whom he called hypocrties because they were no better deep inside.

Would he remember me and love me so? At such a distance I would not see his face clearly enough to know. And there were so many.

They hushed and settled down when they saw the teacher sitting on a large boulder. I too saw, just enough to see that he rested one foot on the rock, knee within the crook of his elbow, allowing the other foot to hang over the edge. He was speaking already, as if addressing only friends on a lazy afternoon. How long had he been here?

His voice reached me, and I stilled my breathing to hear.

"Have you not heard me say, no one can serve two masters? Is this not true?"

No one responded, for they, like me, were held in the grip of his presence already. His voice carried the kind of authority one would not dare resist. They had come to feed on his words and his power, I thought.

"Either you will hate the one and love the other, or you will be devoted to the one and despise the other. You cannot serve both God and mammon. Therefore I tell you, do not worry about your life, what you will eat or drink; or about your body, what you will wear."

Stephen's words echoed in my mind. Clearly, Yeshua spoke these truths often.

He spread a hand wide to indicate the sky.

"Is not life more than food, and the body more than clothes? Look at the birds of the air; they do not sow or reap or store away in barns, and yet your heavenly Father feeds them. Are you not much more valuable than they? Can any one of you by worrying add a single hour to your life?"

How true were those words, I thought. Still, I could not fathom a life so free of worry.

But he wasn't done with the matter.

"And why do you worry about clothes? See how the flowers of the field grow. They do not labor or spin. Yet I tell you that not even Solomon in all his splendor was dressed like one of these. If that is how God clothes the grass of the field, which is here today and tomorrow is thrown into the fire, will he not much more clothe you—you of little faith?"

The words crashed through my mind. I craved this faith as I had craved water in the Nafud.

"So do not worry, saying, 'What shall we eat?' or 'What shall we drink?' or 'What shall we wear?' For the pagans run after all these things, and your heavenly Father knows that you need them. But seek first his kingdom and his righteousness, and all these things will be given to you as well. Therefore do not worry about tomorrow, for tomorrow will worry about itself. Each day has enough trouble of its own."

A slight murmur rose at this, for trouble was the way of the Galilean under Rome. I couldn't tell if they agreed or disagreed with him, perhaps both. My heart was pounding.

Yeshua still sat on the boulder, one leg cradled in his elbow, the other hanging over the edge. He was tired, perhaps. Or only comfortable.

"You have heard me say to love your neighbor as yourself, for he too is your brother. I have said to judge not lest you be judged, for the Father judges no man."

He paused, looking at those gathered.

"You have heard me say, 'Ask and it will be given to you; seek and you will find.' If you know how to give good gifts to your children, how much more will *your* Father in heaven give to those who ask him!"

My mind filled with this new teaching. Yeshua's Father was also mine—he'd just said as much. And could I ask him for a gift? How? Must I build an altar?

"Today I will tell you a story about the Father and his sons, two brothers."

He unfolded his leg and pushed himself to his feet, now standing tall upon the rock. Then he lifted a finger and began.

"There was a man who had two sons. The younger one said to his father, 'Father, give me my share of the estate.' So the father divided his property between them. Not long after that, the younger son got together all he had, set off for a distant country, and there squandered his wealth in wild living."

The moment I heard his words, I found myself in the story, for, though not a son, I was a daughter bound to my father's name.

"After he had spent everything, there was a severe famine in that whole country, and the younger son began to be in need. So he went and hired himself out to a citizen of that country, who sent him to his fields to feed pigs. He longed to fill his stomach with the pods that the pigs were eating, but no one gave him anything."

He paused. The hill was silent.

I too was desperate to be fed, so far from my father and in desperate straits.

Yeshua spoke. "When the son came to his senses, he said, 'How many of my father's hired servants have food to spare, and here I am starving to death! I will set out and go back to my father and say to him: Father, I have sinned against heaven and against you. I am no longer worthy to be called your son; make me like one of your hired servants.' So he got up and went to his father."

Tears filled my eyes at his words. What I would give to be accepted into my father's house! I too had shamed my father in being who I was, and longed only to be honored in his house. All my life I had longed for it.

And yet I was a daughter, not a son. I was a woman made lower by slavery.

"But while he was still a long way off"—his voice came louder now, reaching far—"his father saw him and was filled with compassion for him; he ran to his son, threw his arms around him, and kissed him. The son said to him, 'Father, I have sinned against heaven and against you. I am no longer worthy to be called your son.' But the father said to his servants, 'Quick! Bring the best robe and put it on him. Put a ring on his finger and sandals on his feet. Bring the fattened calf and kill it. Let's have a feast and celebrate. For this son of mine was dead and is alive again; he was lost and is found.' So they began to celebrate."

I could not stop tears from slipping down my cheeks. A terrible knot filled my throat, for I had never known of such a father. Surely the story was about Yeshua's Father, not my own, nor any other, for Yeshua's Father did not judge his son.

A murmur again spread, for the story seemed to be finished. But Yeshua lifted a hand.

"Meanwhile, the older son was in the field. When he came near the house, he heard music and dancing. So he called one of the servants and asked him what was going on. 'Your brother has come,' the servant replied, 'and your father has killed the fattened calf because he has him back safe and sound.' The older brother became angry and refused to go in. So his father went out and pleaded with him. But he answered his father, 'Look! All these years I've been slaving for you and never disobeyed your orders. Yet you never gave me even a young goat so I could celebrate with my friends. But when this son of yours who has squandered your property with prostitutes comes home, you kill the fattened calf for him!' "

Yeshua paused, pacing upon that rock, and not a soul dared make a sound. The good son was angry and judged his brother, and therefore refused to go into his father's house. So now *both* sons had rejected the father, each in his own way. But would the father judge his firstborn?

" 'My son,' the father said, 'you are always with me, and everything I have is yours. But we had to celebrate and be glad, because this brother of yours was dead and is alive again; he was lost and is found.' "

The master paused.

"He who has ears to hear, let him hear."

Now a cacophony of questions and exclamations rustled through the crowd. The story was over.

A ringing sounded in my ears and I felt as though I could not breathe. Three truths seared themselves into my heart at once. The first, that though the sons had separated themselves from their father's table, first the younger and then the older, both remained sons of their father, possessing everything that belonged to him, for he judged them not and embraced them with equal joy.

The second, that both sons would find themselves only by letting go, as Stephen had said. The younger son, by letting go of what he thought might make him happy apart from his father. The elder son, by letting go of his grievance against his brother.

And the third, that I too would give all the life I had to be such a son. Though lost, to be found. And to have such a father. To sit at his table, sharing in all his great honor.

I was only half aware that one of the disciples had approached Yeshua and quietly spoke to him. Dazed, I watched Yeshua step off the rock and make his way up the far slope. Those seated there scrambled to make a way for him.

Sarah was already four paces gone when I became aware that she was rushing forward, hurrying through the crowd as Yeshua walked away.

"Sarah!"

I ran after her, flogged by worry. There were many people and she was moving quickly. What did she intend to do?

Saba spoke from my elbow. "We should return, Maviah. He leaves!"

"Sarah!" I ran faster, determined to stay with her. She seemed to know something I did not.

Perhaps I hoped that I could share what she had already found.

We were already running up the far slope when she reached the thick of the crowd and slowed to a fast walk, weaving past people.

"Maviah, we will come back!" Saba insisted. "There are too many!"

I pushed forward, close on Sarah's back, and when I finally caught her, I grabbed on to her cloak.

She pressed on, now clambering into the throng like a rabbit desperate to make its burrow. I couldn't see Yeshua—there were too many people on all sides, many who were poor and ill and foul-smelling. None of this mattered to Sarah.

"Sarah? Please..."

And then we were upon the inner circle, with many pressing close to Yeshua, touching his arms and garments while his disciples tried to keep a semblance of order about their teacher. He seemed unwilling to send any away.

There were two women in front of Sarah, between her and

Yeshua, and I thought she would push them aside, so desperate did she appear. Instead, being slight, she bent low and shoved her arm between them, and reached for the tassels of Yeshua's woolen tunic.

I let loose of her then, surprised by her boldness. And though my vision was blurred, I could not mistake what happened.

Sarah, having reached far, then stumbled and fell to her knees, panting, with me now several paces behind, Saba by my side. If Yeshua had not stopped, the crowd might have trampled her.

But he did stop, abruptly, lifting up an arm and looking about.

"Who touched my clothes?" he asked.

The crowd hushed and Peter, who stood close enough for me to recognize, looked about.

"You see the people crowding against you, master. Are they not all touching you?"

Yeshua turned, searching, and those near him backed up, giving him space. Sarah was on her knees, but at least ten others stood between her and Yeshua.

I saw her body quietly shaking with sobs.

I saw Yeshua looking about.

And I knew already why he was so determined to know who had touched him, though so many had. The thought sent a chill through my bones.

"Who touched me?" he asked yet again. "I must know. Who?"

Unable to contain herself, Sarah lunged to her feet and stumbled forward, pushing past the others, then falling to her knees again before Yeshua.

"It was me, Lord," she sobbed, clinging to his garment. "Please forgive me." She lifted her face to him. "I knew. I knew that even touching the hem of your garment would free me. I touched you."

For a moment, no one moved.

"And I felt it leave me as I did," she wept. "Forgive me. I beg you."

I wanted to rush forward and throw myself at his feet too, but I was terrified that I did not have Sarah's faith. Not even Stephen seemed to.

Yeshua reached down and touched Sarah on her head. He spoke in a tender voice, as a father might speak to his young child.

"Daughter, your faith has healed you. Go in peace and be freed from your suffering."

The words crushed me. He had called her *Daughter*.

Daughter, your faith has healed you. Yeshua had saved her from her suffering.

Sarah was weeping with gratitude now, bowed low.

I was about to run to him, terrified and desperate at once. But one of the disciples took Yeshua's arm and whispered something in his ear.

The master nodded, looked at those about him once again, then spoke plainly.

"I must go now, along with Peter, James, and John. Remember what you have heard and seen here today."

And then he turned and left. The people parted for him in silence, as if none could resist his will. "Jairus's daughter is dead," I overheard someone say. "He goes to see the daughter of the synagogue's ruler."

But I too was a daughter, and I too would surely be dead soon.

A terrible sorrow swallowed me.

Yeshua was gone.

SARAH had been made whole.

We returned to the house and it took her a long while to find the words to speak of the power she'd felt flowing up her arm and down her spine. Like no sensation she had ever felt, she said. It was a fire that had swept through her body, burning up every trace of her affliction. She still spoke in a meek voice and was yet a frail woman, but in every other respect Sarah seemed to be a giant in my eyes. She seemed to see the world with new vision.

But she couldn't find the words to explain how one could gain the faith that had made her whole. Though she could see with new eyes, I was still blinded and outcast.

Stephen suggested that this display of the master's power should chase away all my doubts and fill me with great courage. Instead my fear only deepened.

For I had not been made whole. I had not rushed to touch the hem of his garment. I had failed even here, north of the Sea of Galilee.

Many were called, as Stephen had said, and I was terrified that I was one of those who could not find the faith to follow.

When the sun was setting, Saba, quiet from all that he had seen, approached me to ask what I now planned. We didn't know when Yeshua might return, and Stephen wasn't to be found, so I didn't know.

"I need to be alone for a while, Saba."

He dipped his head. "As you wish. But then perhaps we might find another way. Aretas waits."

"Do you think I don't know this?" I snapped.

"The tiger crouches. You find yourself lost in fear."

"The tiger is Aretas and it is *you* who remind me of my fear!"

"Then you must believe the mystic with full confidence. He is truly a man who can command your troubles."

But I wasn't the queen Saba thought I was or could be. Truly, I despised my weakness.

"I know you mean well, Saba. But I'm forever enslaved."

I couldn't even see his eyes to know his reaction.

"Please...leave me."

"As you wish." He left me to my own torment.

Sarah was in the courtyard and must have overheard, but I wasn't interested in her telling me that I needed to trust Yeshua. I only wanted to be alone. So I gathered my shawl and wrapped my cloak around my shoulders, then I slipped out the back.

Under a full moon, the night was still save for the chirping of insects and the distant sound of a dog barking. There was a grove of olive trees on the rise behind the house and I headed to it, knowing I would find solace there, where no man walked at night.

Alone under a tree at the center of the grove, I sank to the ground, pulled my legs up under my chin, and I let myself mourn as I had in the dungeons of Petra.

I mourned for my dead son and for Judah and for Rami. But now I mourned mostly for myself, proving the fullness of my weakness.

The burden that the world had placed on me as a daughter to the wrong mother was too great. That same burden now crushed me as Maviah, daughter of Rami, from whom far too much was expected.

For a long time, I rocked there beneath the tree, counting up all the evidence that blamed the world for my misery. Yes, I was gathering grievances, but it gave me the only meaning I could find.

I fed my self-pity with hot tears of anger.

Overcome with sorrow, I settled to my side, lay my head on my hands, and let my tears flow until merciful sleep stole my mind.

THE DREAM CAME after many other smaller dreams, each accusing me of my faults.

I was in Elias's boat, and the dark seas raged about me like crouching jinn, snarling and foaming at the mouth. I spun around and saw that I was alone. The sky had turned black and the wind howled like rabid dogs with jagged teeth to shred the boat and rip the flesh from my bones.

Trembling, I clung to the mast with both arms, terrified for my life.

"Save me!" I cried, but the storm crushed my words with cracking thunder, denouncing me for my weakness.

Images rose up from those waves. My father, cursing my mother and throwing me to the slave traders as an infant. My master in Egypt, banishing me and sending me into the desert. Kahil, tossing my son from the window. Judah, beaten and bloody. A dungeon, imprisoning me in Petra. Sand pressed into my eyes, blinding me.

My own blood flowing, reminding me that I was only a woman.

The waves fell upon the boat and tore me from the mast, throwing me into the bottom of the boat. I gasped, gulping water. I would drown! It was too much for me. I was going to drown!

And then, in the way dreams can change, the water became my own tears, and I was drowning in wretched sorrow and self-pity. But I could not stand it, so I turned my sorrow into anger, then into such rage as I had never known.

I faced the black sky and I screamed my grievance, one arm around the mast again, one fist raised over my head. "I curse you, Rami! I curse you for throwing me away! I hate you!"

My words surprised me, for I had never allowed myself such words.

"I curse all the kingdoms who crush me! I curse the gods and the kings. I curse all men for enslaving me! I curse..."

The sea rose up beneath the boat like a mighty fist, thrusting it high, and my words caught in my throat. I could see that still larger waves were fast approaching, sure to hammer the boat to splinters.

Thunder roared. The wave fell away. The boat dropped and slammed into the sea with a shuddering blow.

And with that blow, a moment of calm came. I heard a gentle, consoling voice behind me at the bow.

"Maviah..."

I twisted to see Yeshua standing at the bow, feet planted—one upon the wooden seat, the other upon the leading tip of the boat. He was, gazing out at the horizon as if there were no storm.

Once again the wind blew, lifting his hair and tearing at his cloak. If he noticed, he showed no sign of it.

"Maviah...the one who feels so lowly among women. A slave among men. The least of all, so unworthy and afraid."

I was too stunned to speak.

"Do you still see all of this as great trouble where I see none?" he asked, slowly turning to face me. "Only because you see with a plank of judgment in your eye."

In that dream my vision was clear and I could see Yeshua's eyes, wells of endless peace and power, beckoning me to enter another realm. But he was saying I still could not see.

"In these waves that threaten to crush you, you still perceive darkness, and how deep is that darkness."

I could not speak. His teaching from Capernaum haunted me. *The eye is the lamp of the body. If your eye is clear, your whole body will be full of light. But if your eye is bad, your whole body will be full of darkness.*

"Why do you fear, Maviah?"

He smiled as if addressing a child distracted by her own silliness.

"Why do you hate?"

Hate? Did I hate?

"I..." It was all I could muster.

"Because you see only darkness. You are blind." He set his foot down into the hull and took a step toward me, shifting his gaze to the raging waves, unconcerned. "So you suffer. And how deep is that suffering. But this is the path you too must follow."

When he faced me again, the compassion and power in his eyes seemed to swallow me. I could not doubt that I was looking at more than a mere man.

"To the Hebrews it will one day be written of me: 'During the days of Yeshua's life on earth, he offered up prayers and petitions with fervent cries and tears...and he was heard because of his reverent submission.' "

A hint of sorrow crossed his face.

"Tears and submission, Maviah. Can you too submit your fear of death to the Father? Can you learn to trust? Can you follow the way into the kingdom of heaven where nothing can harm you?"

I must, I thought. I must...but I couldn't speak.

"They will also write of me: 'Son though he was, he learned obedience from what he suffered.' It will be written that I too learned to obey because it is true. What then do you think is my advantage over you? If my path is with learning and tears and submission, can you not follow that same path? You too can learn. You too can see past your troubles. They are like the waves you believe threaten this boat. You too can find freedom from the storm. You too can walk on troubled waters. Only then you will see that my yoke is easy and my burden is light."

In those words I found my first measure of comfort, because it meant he was like me. If he did it, could not I?

"Follow me, Daughter. Follow me on the narrow path so few ever find. Follow me because I *am* the way."

I suddenly wanted only this. I wanted to follow this teacher, this mystic, this son of the Father, this man who was surely more than a mere man, though he suffered as did I. Nothing else seemed to matter, for I understood that he too had followed the path of surrender and found great power. I could see this in his eyes, brimming with adventurous challenge and unquestioned acceptance rather than fear of the storm.

I wanted to run to him and throw my arms around him and cling to him, vowing all of my life. I wanted to trust him to find his yoke easy and his burden light as I surrendered my very breath. I wanted to rest in the arms of the Father, who loved without condition and did not judge me, as Yeshua taught. My hands trembled with that sentiment; tears streamed down my cheeks.

The storm was still raging about us but he could as easily step from the boat and walk on water as command these seas, I thought.

Could I as well?

"How?" I asked. Then with more clarity, finding my voice over the wind. "How do I surrender?"

He smiled and tilted his head slightly, as if daring me to hear him. He faced the storm and spoke in a soft voice, as much to himself as to me, I thought.

"Forgive," he said.

Just that one word, but it promised to unlock the secrets of the stars.

"Master..." I didn't know what to say. How could I forgive?

"Let go of your right to take offense at all that ever threatened you and all that threatens you still. Release the fear your understanding shows you in this storm. Turn even the other cheek."

Though I could not understand their full meaning, his words pulled deeply at my heart. To be able to see no offense so as to turn my cheek to all that threatened...this was forgiveness? What power he had! Could I then have this power?

"How?" I asked, voice thin in that dream.

He turned his head, eyes bright and fearless and daring.

"By trusting me instead. Put your faith in me, not the storm, nor the boat. I and the Father are one. Surrender to the Father even your need for life. You cannot truly forgive until you surrender your belief in this storm and trust in me instead."

Clarity came to me like the clearing of dark clouds. *In him!* Not by believing the truth *about* him, but by surrendering *to* him and trusting *in* him, I would have no need to protect myself from this or any storm. Would it then matter what happened to me, if my life was submitted to him? My fingers trembled with the power of what he was suggesting.

A faint, knowing grin twisted his lips. "Seventy times seven," he said. "Forgive the world of offense seventy times seven."

Seventy times seven. Not a number but the meaning of always, without ceasing. Yeshua's way was to abide only in forgiveness. And he was the power of that forgiveness.

"Would you like to see, Maviah?" he asked, stepping toward me.

Yes, I thought. I could see with my eyes, here in the dream. But he was referring to different eyes—the eyes of my heart. The lamp of my body that could see light instead of darkness.

"Yes," I said.

He stopped in front of me.

"Will you lead them into the way that I will show you?"

He was speaking of the desert, surely. Tears filled my eyes.

"Yes…"

"Will you follow my path and be the light of the world to shine in that darkness?"

"Yes…"

"Then your faith will heal you, Daughter."

He lifted his hand to my face and I closed my eyes.

"Peace…" The moment his fingers touched my eyelids, a blinding flash filled my mind.

"Be still…" Immediately the wind stopped. In one breath the boat became still. As if it had never been, the storm was gone.

Only blinding light remained, filled with a word that echoed through my mind.

Forgive. Release any offense, not only against others but against the world. Find no offense in the waves. Trust Yeshua instead.

I was thinking of the wonder in that word—*forgive*—when the dream was taken, leaving only darkness.

My eyes fluttered open. My vision was still blurred.

I'm awake, I thought. I'm awake and it's dark and olive branches reach for the sky above me, like fingers crawling from the dream.

I gasped and jerked up my head, straining for view. I was in the grove, under the tree where I'd fallen asleep. The eastern sky was only just beginning to gray, close to morning.

Nothing had changed here in the grove above Bethsaida, where my world was falling apart. My mind had found expression in a dream written from all I had heard Yeshua teach. All that Stephen had spoken under the tree.

But a dream of my own making.

"You sleep deeply, Daughter."

My heart leaped and I twisted to the sound of his voice.

He was there. Yeshua! His face turned toward the graying sky. How long he'd been with me I didn't know, but surely during my dream of him.

I scrambled to my feet, now fully awake. No one else was near.

"I come here often to be alone with my Father while the world sleeps," he said. "I find the trees calming and the silence comforting. It's here that I pray his kingdom come. His will be done, on earth as it is in heaven. It is here that I learn of forgiveness."

The kingdom within and among and at hand, even now.

He turned his head to look at me and, though my sight was not clear, I imagined the same spark of wonder in his eyes I'd seen in my dream.

"You are still blind, are you not?"

He said it with such compassion. His voice did not accuse me. He only pointed out my state of being, for I was blind in more ways than one.

"Yes," I dared to whisper.

"But to follow the narrow path ahead of you, you must be able to see."

I nodded. Tears rose to my eyes, unbidden. A part of me was still on that boat tossed by the storm, which had become all the challenges and fears I faced. Yeshua alone was my savior, now offering me sight.

"Yes," I said. I wanted to say more but could not.

"You must remember...what you will see now is only the half," he said. "There is far more to be revealed in time. Only then will you be able to follow where I will go. This is the way, and even so, it will become forgotten."

Yeshua turned to me and stepped forward. And with each step he took, my anticipation quickened. I knew. I simply knew. I knew faith, for in that moment I would do whatever he asked without the slightest question.

"Today you can only follow where I have been. But then, you will follow where I go."

I could not keep the tears from rolling down my cheeks now. His every word was water to my scorched soul, the bread of life itself.

He stopped before me. "Daughter..."

There was such tenderness now. My knees were too weak to hold me and I felt myself sinking to my knees, trembling under his power. With everything in my being, I was desperate to reach out and cling to him. To offer my life to him. To trust him without reservation.

"Master..." I breathed.

"Now you see already."

His hand touched my head and I felt heat rush over my crown and spread down my spine, then through my arms and legs.

There on my knees I closed my eyes and wept like a child. The sorrow I had carried for so many years was washed from my mind and heart, which were flooded instead with light and love. I knew without a shadow of doubt that I had found not only myself, but in Yeshua my master, and through him my Father.

A groan broke from my throat and I began to shake with sobs, overwhelmed by such exquisite relief, for I, like the son in his parable, had been lost, but now I was found.

Waves of light seemed to sweep over and through me, filling my veins and my bones with warm love. I was awash in the kingdom of heaven. And there was no end to those waves of light...they were eternal. Time had vanished.

He was gone, I finally realized. And yet he was still with me, as near as my own breath.

I don't know how long I wept; I only know that when I then sighed a great breath and opened my eyes, morning had come.

The sight offered to me by my two eyes was still blurred, but this was of no consequence. I was seeing with new eyes. Eyes that did not require the light of the sun in this sky.

The light of the kingdom of heaven was bright within me.

I stood unsteadily, slowly gathered myself, looked once more about the grove to see that I was still alone, then walked down the hill.

The time had come to save Judah.

CHAPTER TWENTY-FIVE

I FOUND IT strange, my return to the house in Bethsaida where Saba, Stephen, and Sarah waited in the courtyard, eating bread. Strange because I saw the world differently now. Not as I once had been, but as I now was.

I still could not see them with clarity, but I had an uncanny idea of what was around me. By some unknown sense, I was more aware of my surroundings.

When I walked into the courtyard, all three stood up at once, anticipating me, for they knew I had been alone all night. Perhaps they also knew that Yeshua had gone to me. I don't know.

But there was nothing to report in words that might make sense to them, I thought. I was only to be who I was, the daughter of my Father in that kingdom now so real to me.

My body's eyes had not changed—they were still fogged and half blind. But something about my countenance moved my companions.

"He came to you," Stephen said with wonder.

I nodded. "Yes."

He was silent.

"We must leave for Tiberias immediately," I said.

Elias had waited on the north shore, I learned. Having seen the storm calmed, yesterday he had gone to hear with his own ears the teaching of this teacher.

Our passage back to Tiberias was quiet, for each of us was still lost in the mystery of all we had seen.

Sarah took my arm as we sat at the bow, and she pulled me close. I placed my hand over hers and we became like sisters there, without speaking a word. We shared Yeshua's power like a secret too great to be announced.

Only when we landed and Stephen was to take Sarah back to Sepphoris did we four speak with more than words in passing. Our paths diverged on the hill overlooking Tiberias.

"You are certain you need nothing more from us?" Stephen asked.

"You have given more than we can ask," Saba said. "Maviah will follow her own way now."

"*His* way," Sarah said.

I looked at her, then gently placed my hand on her arm. "His way."

"And what is his way, then?" Stephen asked, for he'd been eager to hear more since leaving Bethsaida.

"But you know, Stephen," I said. "You told me yourself."

His eyes lit up. "Then I was right."

"Perhaps more than you can know."

He stepped up to me and fell to one knee.

"Then you are blessed, Maviah! Few among my people bow before women, but my eyes now see a queen who is blessed by Yeshua!"

I wanted to tell him to stand, or to kneel with him, for I was no more a queen than he a king. But I remained as I was, for all that I had once taken as truth was now suspect. Was I not a queen? A new truth had entered my mind, and much of it was still a mystery to me.

"Do we not both follow Yeshua now?"

He stood slowly. "Yes."

"And I," Sarah said.

I looked at Saba.

"And I," he said, bowing his head.

"Then we will part ways," Stephen said. "And one day, by his grace, we will join again, followers of Yeshua's way."

Though we had been strangers only days ago, there on the hill we stood as one.

"He said something to me." I looked in the direction of Tiberias spread out below us. "He said there is far more to be revealed in time. Only then will we be able to follow where he goes."

"And where does he go?" Sarah asked.

"We don't know. But what we have seen is only the half of it."

"The half of it!" Stephen said. "This is only the beginning. The world will not contain those who calm the seas. This is his way."

And it was, I thought. To calm the seas and walk on water— Yeshua could surely do both if he pleased.

I looked at Stephen, remembering the rest. "And his way is easily forgotten. He said as much."

To this no one replied.

"Take me to Herod, Saba," I said.

We parted ways then, but I was sure our paths would cross again, for it was no mistake we had come into such a knowing together.

HOW TO GAIN entrance into the king's courts was not a concern to me. I only knew that I would, and I rode into Tiberias without care of what fate might befall me. My course was set and Saba never questioned it.

We entered the city on camelback through the front gate as two common Bedu wrapped in desert clothing, one with clouded eyes, for I did not cover my face.

My sight was only for the palace, and I paid little attention to the city itself as Saba guided us through.

When we reached the inner gates before the palace grounds, I felt no fear, only confidence, though the guard stood in my way.

"What is this?" he demanded. "A woman with leprosy?"

I looked at him and said only what I had come to say.

"My name is Maviah, daughter of Rami bin Malik. Herod eagerly waits for the message I have come to deliver."

He stared back as if trying to think of how to contest me, but I offered him no resistance. He too was like the wind and the waves, ferocious until calmed with acceptance rather than fear.

The guard then turned and ordered another to take word to Herod. What then was this power that I could stand like a pillar before men who would otherwise challenge me?

We waited only a short while before they took us through the gate, then to the palace and into Herod's courts. Much had changed since my first encounter with the tetrarch of Galilee in Sepphoris. I did not feel like that woman now.

This time I could not see the display of Herod's wealth, but I judged his court in Tiberias by size alone to be even more grand than the one in Sepphoris. My blindness forced me to see in a new way, and perhaps that was now my greatest gift.

Herod was waiting in his new court. With a woman. This was his new queen, Herodias. She stood by the window across the room, arms folded, staring at me. Part of me wanted to see her face more clearly. I was curious about the woman who'd captured Herod's heart. Who could be more beautiful than Phasa?

"Leave us," Herod ordered the guard.

They closed the door, leaving Saba and me with the king and his new queen.

"It is true then," Herod said, approaching. "Maviah returns to the den of the lion."

"She is blind?" Herodias asked.

Herod made no response, circling me.

The queen lowered her arms and crossed the room. "And mute as well," she said. "A mangy dog from the desert who limps back to be punished for her betrayal."

Fear whispered to me for the first time, accusing me of weakness. I shifted my focus to the calm seas inside, where nothing could threaten me.

"Is it contagious?" she asked, then faced Saba. "Speak up."

"She was blinded in the court of Aretas," Saba said. "She can see, but poorly with these eyes."

It was true—he was reminding me. I could see more clearly than any of them. But a part of me was beginning to doubt in the face of one so sharp as this woman. She reminded me of Shaquilath in Petra.

Still I said nothing.

"And why did Aretas have her blinded?" the queen asked.

"It was the prince of the Thamud," Saba said. "He felt threatened by her."

"Threatened? By this?"

Silence settled over us. And then words came to me.

"Do you not feel threatened, Herodias?" I asked, voice calm.

"By whom?"

"By the Baptizer," I said, looking now at the king. "I understand you have imprisoned him, a sage who holds no sword."

I walked to the window, where the greater light allowed me to see to the horizon, however fogged. Herod made no attempt to stop me.

"Aretas's queen, Shaquilath, first felt threatened by me." I turned to them. "All kings and queens struggle to protect what is theirs, do they not? The Baptizer, John, speaks out against your marriage, so you have put him in a dungeon. Perhaps you would prefer him dead."

"Perhaps we would prefer the same of you," Herodias said.

I knew then that Herodias would not rest until John the Baptizer was dead. And she was as capable of killing me.

"Perhaps," I said, approaching again, now crossing my arms. "We see ghouls where there are none but our own selves, haunting us in the darkness. It is your own fear, not the Baptizer, that chases you, Herodias."

She was silent.

"As for me..." I faced Herod. "A blind woman presents no threat to the king of Galilee and Perea. I come only to help you protect yourself from the one who does."

"The Baptizer is a fool," Herodias said. "What can you know of him?"

"I speak of Aretas, not the Baptizer."

"Aretas is no less a fool."

I dipped my head and addressed only Herod now. "A fool with an army capable of crushing Tiberias. Did you think he would simply accept your divorce of his daughter?"

"And do you think I am powerless?" Herod said, but there was some respect in his voice. "Or that I know nothing?"

"No. You know that the king who kept me in his dungeon for three months is heartless. You know his fury is not easily quenched."

"And why does this ferocious king send a blind woman to us?" Herodias demanded.

"Because I insisted," I said. "Is it not the safest way for you? To give a payment in secret?"

I knew that I had Herod's undivided attention. Herodias's also, but for a different reason. She was still too self-important to be reasonable, I thought.

"Why would we pay Aretas?" she demanded.

"Please, my queen." Herod faced her. "Not now. When the time comes, you will have what you want. Today I will be king."

She considered his admonition, then submitted to him. "As you wish. Come to me soon."

"Of course. Can I ever deny you?"

"No," she said. "Remember that."

"Always," he said.

She was stronger than Phasa, I thought. This was what had attracted Herod. He longed for this kind of strength to satisfy his needs, having been raised under his father's fist. So, then, perhaps they truly deserved each other in a way Herod and Phasa did not.

Herodias turned and left, leaving me behind closed doors with her king.

"What is it about you?" Herod said, coming closer now. "What has become of the queen who once trembled under my touch?"

"She sees Herodias's slave," I said.

"Then she sees far too much. And with wounded eyes."

Herod had once shown his fascination for me as a woman. I thought he might now as well, but his resolve had already been rattled.

"You surprise me." Herod turned away and paced. "So tell me, queen of the desert... what is his price?"

"One hundred talents in gold."

He looked up. "Gold?" It was a massive sum of wealth.

"To be taken by me tomorrow. If I do not return within the week, you will face a bloody war."

"I see. And if I agree to this price? What guarantee do I have?"

I had come to deceive Herod. I had come to save my own life and retrieve the gold so that I might find mercy in Petra. Judah's life depended on it.

But now, deception seemed to be a mistake.

"None," I said.

"None? Aretas sends me a demand for payment without offering any benefit for that payment?"

"On the contrary, Aretas sends assurance that one hundred talents of gold will free you of any further obligation. But he intends to deceive you and wage war regardless."

"Is that so?"

"It is."

"Then you betray him by telling me."

"Do I?"

He paced.

"Do you have his seal on this false assurance of his?"

"Show him, Saba."

Saba withdrew the letter from Aretas and handed it to Herod, who broke the seal and read the contents. In it Aretas swore to wage no war if he received the price. The fabrication had been my idea.

"And you say that this is a lie?" he said, lowering the scroll. "Why do you tell me?"

"Because I serve neither you nor Aretas," I said. "And because I know that you will still give me the gold as well as a guard of fifty men to see its safe passage to the border at Perea."

Herod seemed amused. "Now she reads minds as well?"

"If you don't, you heap salt in his wounds. Are you ready to wage war this month? Are the Romans ready to die in battle to defend you over a woman?"

"The emperor gave his consent."

"But not his army."

He stared at me for a long moment before speaking in a soft voice.

"So you think I will pay Aretas only to delay him?"

"Yes."

"And how long do you think one hundred talents will buy me?"

"I don't know, but he's a patient man. A year? Two. Three, per-haps. Then Aretas will come. Or you can refuse payment now and immediately face a show of great force."

He absently pulled his fingers through his beard.

"I see. And if I refuse, what of you?"

I shrugged. "He will kill me. With Judah and Rami, both held by the Thamud for leverage."

Herod was silent, knowing well the full landscape now, for he understood the ways of kingdoms on earth. He finally turned and walked to the window to gaze out upon his own.

"What a queen you would make, Maviah, daughter of Rami. What a queen indeed. I don't think I've ever heard an emissary speak the truth so plainly before. They all lie, you know. Politics is only a game of lies and treachery. You do realize that Aretas may now kill you for telling me the truth, even with my payment."

"That is my concern, not yours."

"Indeed." He faced me and sighed. "I will give you his payment on the condition that you be as truthful with him. He must know that I expect his attack even now and am prepared."

I'd already decided I must.

"Of course."

"Well then, my fate is in your hands as well."

"Perhaps."

He hesitated.

"Spend the night," he finally said. "Dine with us at my table. You can leave in the morning."

I considered his request briefly but felt no desire to spend more time in his wife's company.

"We will wait for your contingent beyond the gates, as the sun rises."

"A pity." Again he sighed. "As you wish. Sunrise it is."

I offered him a shallow bow. "Thank you." I turned to leave, then realized I wasn't yet finished, so I faced him again.

"There is one more thing."

"I hate to think—it's a heavy payment already."

"It's about the one who comes after the Baptizer."

He responded slowly. "What of him?"

"He speaks of a new way for the heart—Jew, Roman, or Bedu, it doesn't matter. Does this threaten you?"

"The Baptizer denounces my marriage."

"Does Yeshua?"

Herod hesitated and I spoke before he could respond.

"You will find no fault in him when the time comes."

"You've met him?"

"He changed my life," I said.

And then I left Herod's courts.

CHAPTER TWENTY-SIX

IT TOOK our caravan of twenty camels four days with a guard of fifty to reach the Nabataean border, and another three days with twenty of Aretas's best warriors to reach Petra once again. How Aretas knew to have the warriors ready at the border didn't matter so much to me. Nor did it matter why Petra was prepared for our arrival—not just the rulers, but the entire city, as if Herod himself were making a grand entry.

My mind was preoccupied with other thoughts. Thoughts of Yeshua. Thoughts of Stephen and Nicodemus. Thoughts of what the master's way truly was, so far from Palestine.

And thoughts of why the clarity of my experience with him was so quickly fading, with each mile and each day, it seemed. So I clung to my thoughts, determined not to let his power slip away.

I knew little of Yeshua's full teaching, for I had spent only a few days with him. I had learned much from Stephen, but Stephen was still learning himself.

And yet all that I had seen and heard was so very simple that even a child might understand it, I thought. So simple that it rattled the mind, for Yeshua's way was wholly contrary to the ways of the world, in particular the laws of religion and the kingdoms on earth.

Religion offered reward and punishment through laws of eating and drinking and daily activities. Failing these laws plunged one into shame and guilt. But Yeshua seemed to ignore such laws and spoke of love and of something far more offensive to the religious mind.

Faith. A child's faith. When the storm came, to trust in Yeshua who was one with the Father, even as a young child might trust a perfectly loving father. This was what it meant to believe.

Did I trust, then? This was the question that haunted me those many hours upon the she-camel as it plodded over the terrain.

Did I trust the Father who, according to Yeshua, would give to me more than any earthly father might give to his child?

I heard his words still: *If you have faith as small as a mustard seed, you can say to this mountain, "Move from here to there," and it will move. Nothing will be impossible for you.*

Did I trust?

And more: *If anyone steadfastly believes in me, he will himself be able to do the things that I do; and he will do even greater things than these.*

Did I trust? Did I have faith? Did I believe in this way?

But I now had at my disposal a way to *know* if I trusted. By only listening to my own heart, I would know if it placed its faith in the storm or in Yeshua, who was the way.

If I feared the storm, my faith was in *its* power.

If I feared for my body, my faith was in that body, what I would eat or drink, how it might survive and be satisfied.

If I feared for Judah's life, I put my faith in death and in him.

If I feared Aretas, I put my faith in his ability to hurt me, like any storm.

If I feared my own misunderstanding, I put my faith in my own ability to know the mystery beyond me.

This was the way of the world, protected by position and sword and gold and knowledge. Yeshua's way was to protect nothing and let go of all grievance, as Stephen had said.

His way was faith, dismissing the Gnostics' expectation that knowledge would save. His way was to *be* the kingdom among those who suffered on earth.

His way was to turn the other cheek when the evil one came. His way was to forgive seventy times seven. His way was to let go of the belief that the storm threatened, and to offer it peace through a child's faith.

His way was to offer love rather than offense at every turn, for offense only empowered the storm.

You of little faith.

Was I one of little faith? What kind of power might be seen among those who truly followed Yeshua's way and trusted him as that way? This was now my path, for nothing could compare to what I had seen.

According to Nicodemus, letting go of belief in the world's way was like being born once more with the simple trust of a new child. And now I understood why: the old heart could see only offense and fear when the sword was raised against it or when unfair treatment stormed the gates of one's mind and body.

But the newborn mind saw in spirit, having not yet learned offense. It then could return love instead of fear. Why would it fear a storm if it drew no offense from that storm?

What then were my storms to fear?

Aretas. Rami. The Thamud. The loss of Judah. My own failure, should I waver.

You of little faith.

"Father..." I whispered under my breath. "Give me Yeshua's eyes to know you and follow his way. Give me your hand on this earth, to be your daughter and show your power." Then I whispered that word again, lost in its wonder.

"Father..."

The word sounded foreign to me. And yet my fingers tingled with the raw power I felt in uttering such an intimate understanding of God, for he ruled the realm within me, as Yeshua had said so many times.

As we approached Petra this is how I understood Yeshua's way, knowing that I had only seen the half of it, as he himself had said. But the half he'd shown me was true.

Our column of twenty camels, each heavily burdened with five talents of gold, was not the largest to enter Petra. A caravan of over three hundred camels came from the south that same hour, bearing spices. But so much gold had not been brought to Petra that year, nor the one before, I was told by the guard.

Among the Nabataeans, wealth and power were displayed for all to see. Nothing mattered to Aretas as much as his reputation, for this kept his enemies far away.

The king's warriors had given me garments for my entry—a blue tunic with a golden shawl and sash. Gilded thongs held the fabric close to my legs so as to give me freedom on the camel. My sandals were leather inlaid with silver.

I had veiled my face for the journey and none of the warriors, neither Herod's nor the Nabataeans', had seen my eyes. The head covering I wore now was black with a golden cord, and the lace before my eyes as dark.

I knew, then, that they wanted me to come as a victor, not as a slave. But Aretas had gone to extraordinary lengths to receive me.

The children ran out to greet us a mile before we reached the city.

"Maviah comes with gold!" they cried, running alongside. "The queen of the desert comes with gold for Aretas, friend of his people!"

"They know too much!" Saba said, scanning the cliffs. If these children knew, the whole city must as well. "He wishes for us to be robbed?"

But we both knew that any fool who attempted such a feat would quickly perish.

Women stood along the cliffs, sending their ululating voices through the canyons, announcing our arrival for all. Men and women of all ages soon joined the children, watching from the side of the road as we approached, then surging alongside to match our pace. I rode in silence, swaying with the camel's plodding gait, keeping my mind on the scope of my mission.

Like the good stewards in Yeshua's parable, I had seen past my fear to bring these talents of gold to Aretas. And yet so far from the hills of Galilee, his way now seemed distant.

I had expected to be led through the streets of that great rock fortress to the columned temple where the king and his queen had first put me on trial. Instead we were funneled to the arena built into the cliffs on the city's southern perimeter. It was into this arena that thousands of Petra's inhabitants now flowed.

"He wishes to make a spectacle," Saba said, riding by my side, tall and naked to the waist. His muscles were taut, glistening like crafted onyx under the hot sun, and the hilt of his broadsword lay by his hand, ready for the least of threats.

"Better a spectacle than a prison," I said.

"Unless the spectacle becomes your prison."

My smile was faint and forced. "I appreciate your worry, Saba, but you must now have faith."

"I do not trust him."

"Then trust me, if you must. Are we not here, with the gold?"

He was silent before offering me a nod. "Perhaps I speak too soon."

"See the strawberries, Saba. Take your eyes off the beasts. Isn't that what you told me?"

"As I said, I speak too soon."

I nodded.

The guard parted as we reached the gates, making a clear path for Saba and me abreast, followed by the twenty camels burdened with Herod's gold. We passed beneath arching stonework intricately carved to pay homage to the gods.

The moment we crossed into the arena, my breathing thickened. I could not see their faces, but the sheer number of those gathered pressed down on my heart. Many thousands filled the stone benches that rose from the circular arena floor to a height as tall as two temples.

A roar erupted as the throng stood. I could not miss the stage at the north end, graced by six in tall gilded chairs. Three of them I knew by their stature and dress: Aretas and Shaquilath, seated, and Phasa, standing.

I came to a stop and gazed at the people, for the moment taken aback. Saba said something, but his voice was lost in that cry. Why had Aretas gone to such lengths? Surely not simply to impress his people.

It was the way of kings to take full advantage of any opportunity to show their dominance. At times this was better demonstrated by taking gold than by shedding blood. And was this not Herod's gold, delivered now to Aretas by great cunning?

I was only the messenger, I thought. The gold behind me was their victory, and I its honored caretaker.

I tapped my camel and nudged it toward the great platform, ignoring the crowd. Not until I had come to a halt ten paces from the stage did Aretas slowly rise and lift his hand.

The roar quieted quickly, leaving reverent silence in its wake.

Phasa hurried to the platform's leading edge. "I knew you could do it! Isn't this what I said, Father? I knew with Saba, you would best that old scoundrel!"

Aretas turned his head to her. "Phasa..."

"What did he say of me?"

"Sit!"

"Give me a moment to—"

"Now!"

"We will speak soon, Maviah," she said, withdrawing. "And you, Saba."

She hadn't been heard by the crowd, I guessed, for she had not raised her voice.

Aretas walked to the steps and descended to the arena's floor. He passed Saba and me without so much as a glance, focused on the camel immediately to our rear. The heavy leather bags sagged on either side of the beast to keep the weight low, and their straps were cinched tight by buckles. These Aretas quickly released before opening the flap of one bag.

The crowd waited as though without breath, eager for his verdict.

Aretas shoved his hand into the bag, then pulled it out, fingers wrapped around a fistful of gold coin. This he thrust into the air, turning about to show all gathered.

At once their roar shook the arena.

"No one defies me!" Aretas shouted. "No one!"

They raised their fists with him, taking refuge in their king's unquestioned power.

"Is your king not the friend of his people?" he cried.

Their thundering agreement made words unnecessary.

Aretas lowered his hand and let the gold fall from his grasp as he stepped toward the chief guard, who stood beside my camel. A dozen coins plopped into the dust at his feet.

"Hold the camels at the wall." He looked at me. "Set up the perimeter."

The warrior barked formation orders, and fifty more warriors trotted into the arena armed with spears and swords. Under further commands, half took the camels' ropes and led them to the wall, where they were placed in a long row for all to see.

The other half formed a quick half circle behind Saba and me, still seated upon our camels. I wasn't sure if they were our guard or a new enemy. I could not see their expressions to judge their intentions.

Aretas had taken the stage again and now faced me, basking in the rhythmic chanting of his people.

"Aretas, Aretas, Aretas, Aretas…"

He lifted his hand again and the cries quickly faded.

"Today we have our victor." He thrust his hand toward me. "I present to you Maviah, daughter of Rami bin Malik!"

Their praise crushed my ears. And Aretas let the cheer endure for a full minute before he finally motioned for their silence.

For a few moments nothing seemed to happen.

"He beckons you closer," Saba said. I had missed his cue.

Rather than dismount, I approached the stage on camelback, so as to speak with him face-to-face.

"Welcome to my home, queen of the desert." His soft words were not meant for his people. "It seems we may have underestimated you after all."

He'd called me a queen. I dipped my head in respect. "Thank you, my king."

"For all of this, I offer you honor, as I promised. Hear the people's love for you."

"I seek only your own."

"Yes. Of course." He looked past me. "And do you bring me anything other than gold?"

"Only word from Herod."

"Naturally. Word. Word from the devil himself." He looked back at me. "And?"

"He would have you know that he prepares for your armies even as we speak. He knows that this gold won't stay your hand."

"Does he? And what would lead our enemy to draw such conclusions?"

"I told him," I said. "In doing so, I earned his respect and your gold. I also learned his state of mind, as you requested. As such, I have fulfilled my obligation to you."

He stood still for a few seconds, then chuckled softly.

"Your cunning matches only my own queen's. Well then, as you say . . . you have satisfied my requirements and proven yourself worthy. Honestly, I'm quite impressed."

"Thank you."

Shaquilath stood and approached to stand just behind her husband, on his right. "Will you remain veiled before your king?"

So, then . . . they would see.

I lifted the veil from my face and stared at them through those milky eyes.

"Forgive me," I said.

"Your blindness lingers?" Aretas asked.

"I can see what I need to see. All I ask for now is your blessing to return to Dumah."

"Yes . . ." He lifted his finger. "Dumah. Of course. I would give you my blessing as promised."

He was going to return me with honor? I could not have hoped for more.

"Thank you." I bowed my head.

"Unfortunately . . . I am not the only one you must satisfy," he said.

Shaquilath stepped up to her husband's side and stood tall, like a statue before her people, making no secret of her power.

"You surprise me, daughter of Rami. In all the desert I have not known a woman like you." Her tone was sincere. "It's a pity, the way that brute Kahil blinded you. And yet you had your way with Herod."

They had kept the crowd in silence for several minutes now. What were they waiting for?

"You would restore the honor of your father in Dumah?"

"Yes."

"You would return to your home with the seal of Aretas to save your father?"

"If the king agrees."

"You would rescue the slave Judah from all of his torment..."

I hesitated, because there seemed to be a challenge in her tone.

"Yes," I said.

"You would then be a savior to your people. A true queen of the desert."

"I only wish to restore——"

"But there is room for only one Kalb to command," she said, cutting me short. "And the king has given his approval to another."

She nodded to the chief guard on my right, and he lifted his hand, relaying an order to the warriors behind me. I glanced back to see them spread wide.

"To whom?" I asked, turning back to the queen.

"To the son of Rami, of course. The one who has made alliance with the Thamud on the behalf of all Kalb."

My half brother. *Maliku.*

A knot gathered in my chest.

"Maliku," she said. "We cannot support both you and your brother, who publicly defies you. Prove yourself by killing the one who betrayed your father, then we will support you. We will order Judah set free and support whatever outcome you can arrange in Dumah."

Kill him?

Surprisingly, the notion made sense to me. In the ways of justice required by the Bedu, Maliku had already sentenced himself to death by betraying Rami. He was a cancer to all Kalb now—any restoration of honor and order among the tribes would demand his death.

But I wasn't the one to do it, even if I could.

"You overestimate me," I said.

"Oh, but I don't think I do. The woman I saw throwing herself at Kahil knew more than mothering. You have been trained in arts unknown in the desert."

"As I said, you overestimate me."

"We shall see."

No. I can't see, I thought, and that too is a problem.

"Even if I find Maliku in Dumah and kill him, you wouldn't know whether I wielded the sword. If you must have him dead, arrange for it yourself. I'm sure if you ordered your servant Kahil of the Thamud, he would be more than happy to kill one so familiar with betrayal."

"But you too are fluid in betrayal," Shaquilath said. "As I see it, you have betrayed both Herod and Aretas."

It wasn't entirely true, I thought. But the king beside her said nothing, content to let her fulfill her own demands in the matter.

"We would know your loyalty to Aretas only if you killed Maliku, as ordered by the king you would serve."

The reasoning behind her demand for justice and loyalty was too sound to dispute. I had to earn myself more time.

"Then send me to Dumah and let me win the king's loyalty."

"There will be no need for that," she said, lifting her head to gaze past me. "You will fight him now, in this arena. Only one of you will return to Dumah alive. That person will have the king's full support."

I jerked my head around and saw. I could not mistake the posture of the one who so despised me.

Maliku stood at the center of the arena, dressed in full armor, leaning on his sword.

"Maviah, champion of Aretas, will fight!" Shaquilath cried, fist thrust over her head.

Ten thousand voices joined in a cry of approval that shook my bones.

I knew then why they had come.

CHAPTER TWENTY-SEVEN

SABA WAS the first to move, dropping from his camel and snatching up his sword in one fluid motion. He had taken four running strides toward Maliku before I spoke.

"Saba, no."

He pulled up, a panther poised to strike.

"She defends the honor of Aretas!" Shaquilath cried, voice just above the din of the crowd. "They fight to the death!"

I stared at Maliku's blurred image, unexpectedly filled with rage. Because of Maliku's betrayal, the Thamud had crushed Dumah and cut out Rami's tongue. Because of him many Kalb women had been raped. How many were dead due to this vile creature's passion for power?

Twenty days had passed since they'd taken Judah—just enough time to go and return at a fast pace. Shaquilath had ordered they send Maliku to Petra then, in the event I returned with the gold. They had planned for this meeting all along.

"If you refuse," the queen said, "then he will cut you down on this very ground. He cannot refuse."

If I refused? Surely they did not expect me to better a man who'd trained his whole life to kill. Maliku was twice my size and strength.

And yet Shaquilath was correct: the path of my people's liberation now ran through Maliku. If I died today, he would return to Dumah and rule with the Thamud uncontested.

Judah's words filled my mind: *We must turn the other cheek, but only to our brother.... Let the Romans reap the same end they have sown. If a man comes to take your life, am I to allow it?*

I did not know if this was Yeshua's meaning. But facing Maliku, I made it so. Maliku was no longer my brother.

I have not come to bring peace, but the sword to divide, Judah had said, speaking of Yeshua's teaching. And in that inflamed state, I embraced the teaching.

Saba trotted back to my camel. "Maviah, you must not fight him. He is too strong."

I slipped from my mount and landed on the dusty ground, jaw set.

"Give me your sword," I said to Saba, eyes fixed on the shape of my half brother.

"Maviah—"

"Now, Saba!"

He reluctantly held the blade out and I took it from his hand, then snatched up the dagger he handed to me.

"Stay here," I said, shoving the knife into my sash.

An image of Johnin crossing the arena floor, heavy sword in his veined hand, filled my mind. Our swordplay had been born out of intense attraction, and for months it had been the only way for us to spend time together. He'd shown me much, but it was his words that came to me now.

Show them no fear, and they will find their own.

Fear...that word again.

Speed is twice the friend over strength.

But I walked slowly toward Maliku, dragging the tip of Saba's great curved sword in the dust behind me.

You're smaller. Use the weight of the sword for you, not against.

The crowd quieted—Shaquilath wanted to hear. And so now they heard the scraping of a sword behind a frail woman who dragged the heavy blade to her own death.

But I was not ready to die.

Was Maliku smiling? I don't know because his face was only a blur. But then he spoke and I knew he hadn't changed.

"The whore has survived," he sneered. "I don't know what that dog Judah sees in such a pathetic scavenger as you."

Darkness swept over me. My hand tightened on the sword's leather-wrapped handle. He was now only seven paces off and still leaning on his sword.

"The slave is alive. But he cries for you through broken teeth."

His words stalled me four long paces from him.

"Greetings, Sister."

I gave him a shallow nod. "How is our father?"

"He is silent. And now you see though leprous eyes."

"I see clearly now. I see that your heart is as black as tar burned for fire."

He chuckled. "A fire that will consume all—"

I leaped forward at the word *consume* and was halfway to him with blade drawn back before my sudden movement stole the words from his mouth.

I meant for that first blow to cut into his head, if only to silence the poison flowing from his mouth, but he spun away from me, a simple but effective evasive shift.

I adjusted the arc of my blade, now borne by my full weight as I twisted to bring its tip across his back. I felt the contact of sharpened edge and leather. Heard my scream rending the silence.

Then felt the piercing of flesh as the leather yielded.

Maliku grunted and stumbled before catching himself. I saw him instinctively reach for his back to check for damage even as my momentum carried me to the ground.

When they are distracted, Maviah. Johnin's words again.

I released the heavier sword and grabbed the dagger from my waist while I rolled. He was there, with blood on his fingers, when I came to my feet. I let loose the knife then, while he was still confused by the fact that I'd cut him first, and it was halfway to him before he saw it coming.

He was too late to avoid it. The blade sliced into his side, below his armor. He staggered back again, like a struck bull.

The crowd erupted and I drank their courage, sweeping up Saba's blade once again. In quick succession I had wounded him twice.

But Maliku only ripped the knife from his side.

"The whore can scratch." I could hear the amusement in his voice.

He reached across his chest and jerked the cords that held his armor in place. Flung the leather molding to the side to bare his arms and chest for easier movement.

"So, then...we fight!" he said.

The crowd was chanting now, demanding I strike again. But I no longer had the advantage of surprise.

Watch their eyes, Maviah. You can see them move in their eyes first.

But I couldn't read his eyes or face to anticipate his next move. How many hours had Johnin and I locked eyes to learn the subtleties of intention and more? It meant nothing now.

My blindness suddenly loomed like a mountain and fear reached into my bones.

Maliku came for me then, in long strides, running on the balls of his feet, crouched over with his sword held lightly.

His blow, when it came, was like lightning, and I jerked to my left to narrowly avoid his blade. Then I swung my own, when his side was exposed.

But Maliku was ready this time. He stepped into my swing, swept my arm wide with a thick forearm, and brought the heel of his free hand into my chin.

I felt my head snap back. Heard my teeth crack together.

The blow lifted me off the ground and dropped me onto my seat with enough force to knock the breath from my lungs.

He was still coming.

I threw myself to my right, rolling away. As I turned, his blade smashed into the ground, sending stinging dust into my eyes.

My eyes.

I blinked, frantic to see, but the world only darkened. My half-blind eyes had accepted the dust without closing for protection.

Screaming now, I wildly swung my blade at his legs, which I struck, but without power, for I was still on the ground and had no leverage.

The world was in a brown fog thickened by my panic. I had to clear my vision!

Rolling to my feet, I ran to my right, knowing he was to my left only because I could hear him. When I looked, I saw only a dirty fog.

Now flooded by fear, I tried and failed to blink my vision clear. I wiped the back of my hand across my face, desperate to see more than I could—a form, arms and legs, an enemy, anything that would give me the dimmest ray of hope.

I was only a hobbled woman for Maliku's blade.

This is who you are, Maviah. Only the shamed daughter of a whore.

Where was he? The crowd was still cheering, oblivious to my predicament. They'd come for a spectacle. Now they would see a slaughter.

This was always your destiny, Maviah.

I backed on my heels, breathing in long pulls, expecting a blow. But Maliku wasn't ready to cut me down. His soft chuckle, close to my left, said as much.

Swinging my blade in his direction, I found only the emptiness between us. Again, panic mounting. I could hear him breathing, hear the amusement in his soft grunt, hear my own heart pounding in my chest.

Maliku's fist landed then, on my cheek, hard enough to spin me around.

Terror washed through me.

It's over.

I began to swing my blade again, even without a target. But Maliku landed another blow, an open palm upon my left cheek. The crack of it filled my head with ringing.

It is over…

Only when I stepped back and let Saba's blade fall from my fingers did the crowd realize the depths of my trouble. Their cries faded. Silence settled over the arena, punctuated by only a few calls, urging us to fight.

"Maviah!"

Saba…Saba was calling from my right.

Shaquilath stilled him with a quiet warning. My fate was in my own hands. She had sentenced me to death, I thought. Shaquilath, not Aretas.

I would let Shaquilath see what she had ordered.

Distraught and drained, I began to walk toward the sound of her voice, knowing that Maliku's blade would cut into me at any moment.

"She runs to her black slave?" Maliku taunted.

But he didn't understand. *I* was the slave. And blindness once again my master.

I kept walking, but now a terrible sorrow welled up from deep within me and I felt as though I might weep.

Do not allow fear to bind you up, dear one.

I was simply placing one foot in front of the other, expecting a blow from behind, when Yeshua's tender words, spoken that first night in Capernaum, whispered again to me there in the arena. And with those words, the world shifted.

Or I might say quieted, because Maliku said something behind me and he sounded far away. So did the calls from the arena.

But the shift wasn't only in sound, it was also in speed, for the world seemed to slow. My pace by half, my arms swinging at my sides as though in water.

You will only lose what you already have.

What do I have?

I heard a very soft laugh that immediately reminded of Yeshua on the boat in my dream, unaffected by the storm. And I knew the answer to my own question. I knew what I had. He had given it to me in the olive grove.

Sight.

Sight to see all that I could not see with the eyes in my head. Sight to see that the storm did not threaten me. Sight to see that I dwelled in that kingdom called heaven. Sight to see my Father, who did not judge me. Sight to see that there was nothing to be afraid of. Ever.

Sight to see Yeshua and his way.

I took one more step, but now even my heart seemed to have slowed and I stopped there, in the middle of the arena.

His words came to me again, the same he'd said to his disciples after calming the storm.

Why are you afraid?

His truth flooded me. Was I not the daughter of Yeshua's Father? Had he not made the sea? Was the desert not his resting place?

Had I forgotten so quickly? I had believed in Yeshua, yes, but had I known his Father? And was this not truly *my* Father?

I could hardly breathe for the emotion that choked me.

"Abba?"

The word came to my lips as the simple question of a young girl looking up into the eyes of a king to know if she was his. The mere call of a sparrow.

But it seemed to fill the whole world, now silenced and enshrouded by mystery.

I could hear nothing except my own heartbeat. The entire arena seemed to have faded into a distant realm. In a faint whisper, daring to believe, I spoke again.

"Father..."

His response came from the stillness. A breath.

His breath, flowing over me like life-giving water in the deepest sands. It washed over my face and down my neck and arms. Over my chest and belly and down my legs.

You are mine, his breath said.

"Yes," I whispered, closing my eyes against tears that welled. "Yes..."

Trust me.

I felt my knees shaking. My tears spilled over and now trailed down my cheeks. I knew that thousands were watching me in the arena, and that Maliku might even now be raising his sword to deliver his final blow.

Of all this I was aware, but only as a distant abstraction. For I was now seeing through the eyes of belief in a different realm full of mystery and wonder to be embraced as only a child can embrace.

I was that child, made clean and perfect in the presence of her Father.

In me there was no shame, for I was now born into honor. I was

Rami's daughter only in name. And even now I would put my faith in a new name, born of a new Father who saw only honor in me.

A burning heat swept over my face, and there with my eyes closed, I saw more.

I saw them all, crying out to know and be known. I saw Judah. I saw Saba and Aretas and Shaquilath and Rami and Herod and Phasa. I saw Maliku. Children, like me, crushed by the desert, longing for love.

But they had not learned.

I saw Yeshua and I wept. I wept because he too had suffered and so had learned submission, and then he had shown me the way to follow. I wept because I knew that his suffering was not yet complete, however it might come.

But even more, I wept because Yeshua had finally shown me who I was.

I was the daughter of my Father. No harm could come to me. Ever.

Do you have faith, Daughter?

"I see..." I said, speaking through my tears. "I see..."

It is only the beginning.

The half of it, I thought. That half of Yeshua's way was letting go of this troubled world to see another of peace and power. And how easily forgotten was that way. Had I not forgotten?

The air was perfectly silent.

But now I remembered.

I stilled my breath and opened my eyes.

I saw the arena swimming in my own tears. But the view was no longer milky.

I could see?

So I blinked. Then twice. The image of Maliku, not so far away, came into sharp focus. Shaquilath on the platform, much closer than I had assumed she'd be. Phasa and Aretas, beside her, staring out.

Saba beside the camels. The guards with their tall spears, lining the walls, facing me.

My sight had been fully restored.

I turned my head and gazed at the arena. They were watching, uncertain and silent.

"Your eyes..." Maliku was staring at me in confusion.

In him I saw only a storm. A black cloud rising in anger to throw my boat over and drown me in shame.

Was not the whole arena but another storm?

Forgive, my master had said. *Seventy times seven, forgive.*

Stephen's thoughts came to me. To hold no grievance—this is to forgive. To take no offense at the fist raised against you. Only then can you turn the other cheek. This is the way of mystery. This is the way of great power.

I looked at Maliku and saw no threat in him. Was he not only lost, as I had been? Was he not only looking to be honored?

And Shaquilath, who stood on the platform not fifteen paces away, eyes wide. Did she not long for the same? Aretas as well. Though lost, had they not also been fashioned by my Father? Were they not my brother and sister?

I saw the queen's eyes shift and I followed them to see that Maliku was running for me. It was strange to see him so crouched, face twisted with rage, eyes fired with hatred. Strange because it seemed absurd.

Such was my belief as I stood before them all.

He angled directly for me, sword drawn and then slicing through the air. I could hear every piece of emptiness cut by that blade as it approached my head. See its movement as though in a dream.

To avoid the blade, I needed only to step aside. So I did, watching it slice more emptiness, buffeting air across my face.

Maliku's momentum spun him, but he quickly adjusted his weight and brought the blade around for a second blow, this one aimed for my midsection, accompanied by a full-throated cry.

Once again I stepped out of the way of his sword. I might have been able to do it with my eyes closed, I thought.

And another thought, plain to me: Judah was wrong about Yeshua's teaching on the sword. The master had indeed come to bring a sword, but that sword would be wielded by those who would take it up in anger. They would be angry because his way of love and forgiveness was threatening to those who did not embrace it. His way would divide even brother from sister, daughter from father. The sword, then, would be swung by those like my brother. It was not for the followers of Yeshua.

I could not explain how these things were so plain, nor how my power over Maliku was gaining strength—I only knew it could, it would, it was. The spirit was like the wind, blowing where it willed—had not Yeshua said so?

It was the way of mystery and wonders.

The way of the mystic.

When Maliku struck a third time, I thought he would harm himself with such twisted effort. So this time I reached out my hand and caught his sword arm at the wrist.

His superior strength should have smashed my hand out of the way. His blade should have run through my chest.

Instead, with little force, my hand stopped his arm as if it were a blade of grass.

"No more, Brother."

He stared at his arm, trembling in my grasp. Then at me, eyes round with terror.

"No more." I plucked the dagger from his belt. "It is over."

My words washed over him and he staggered back, releasing his blade, which landed heavily on the ground.

"Jinn!" he cried, still backing up. "She is possessed!"

A murmur spread through the crowd, for this was a harsh accusation. It was said that these demons could give a person great power. Had not Yeshua been accused of the same?

"She is possessed by the jinn!"

We both knew that I could have picked up the sword at my feet and removed his head from his shoulders. But I had no such desire. I only pitied this lost jester.

"Kill him," Shaquilath said. "You cannot both live!"

"She is possessed by the jinn!" Maliku cried, spinning to the queen. "She must be burned!"

"Kill him!"

In that moment I could not. My place was only to forgive him, perhaps because he was indeed my brother. I wasn't sure I could kill anyone in that state.

But the queen could not fathom such sentiments. So I turned to the crowd and lifted Maliku's dagger in my right fist.

"I have Maliku's dagger." My voice rang out for all to hear. "He is mine to kill. As easily as Kahil of the Thamud killed my infant son, I can take the life of the one who betrayed my father, Rami bin Malik, great sheikh of Dumah. This is my right."

Agreement rose on strained voices, crying for justice.

"But he is my brother!" I cried.

They quieted.

Lowering the blade, I sliced my left palm and watched as blood seeped from the wound. I closed my hand, allowing the blood to leak between my fingers. Lifting my bloodied palm, I extended mercy as I'd seen Judah do with Arim, the Thamud boy.

"As is the way of all Bedu, I offer my blood in his stead."

My words robbed the arena of its breath.

"I invoke the Light of Blood," I said. "Maliku's death is now on my head, paid for by my own blood in the way of all Bedu. No man may harm my brother without harming also me. In this way I, Maviah, queen of the Kalb, offer mercy to my own brother, even as the mighty Aretas, friend of his people, offers mercy to all who are Nabataean."

For a long moment, the arena remained gripped by silence. And then a woman raised her voice.

"Maviah, queen of the Kalb, the merciful! Maviah, queen of the Kalb." In an instant it was joined by a hundred voices. Then by a thousand. Then by all.

Five thousand souls who knew that only a king's mercy could give them life. On any day, Aretas could as easily kill them as allow them to live.

But I had offered mercy through my own blood, as was the Bedu way. The Nabataeans also honored this same way.

The roar had become my name only now, chanted over and over:

"Maviah...Maviah...Maviah...Maviah..."

Even then I was only Daughter. Daughter of Yeshua's Father, who was also my own.

I lowered my bloodied hand and walked toward the stage. And still they cried my name.

"Maviah...Maviah...Maviah..."

My camel had joined those bearing Herod's gold. Saba dropped to one knee as I approached and I let him give his honor to me. My attention then turned to Maliku, who stood by the stage, confused and frightened despite his show of bravery.

I still didn't know how I had gained such strength or whether it would last. I only knew that I had surrendered to a higher truth found in Yeshua. To my Father and his kingdom.

Five paces from the stage, I stopped and looked at Aretas, who could not hide a thin smile. Then I lowered myself to one knee, placed Maliku's blade in the dust before me, and bowed my head.

I was Maviah, daughter to another king in a kingdom they did not know, but today I was also subject to this king.

The crowd quieted at his raised hand.

"Stand."

I stood and looked at king and queen. Shaquilath, in her red silk dress wrapped tightly as was her way, towered in majesty, face set. But there was no anger in her eyes. Only wonder.

"Your cunning knows no end," Aretas said quietly. "The Light of Blood. Indeed."

I dipped my head. "Indeed." He could not disregard the sacred tradition among a people so bound by it. Maliku, on the other hand, could even now take a blade and try to kill me. He was under my protection, not I under his.

But any attempt on my life now would make him look foolish. As well, he would fail miserably.

Aretas glanced at the queen, then sighed. "Well then. It seems you have earned what you sought. The power of a kingdom and the love of a people."

"I seek no power in your kingdom," I said. "Mine comes from another."

"Oh? The kingdom of the Kalb has no power for you. It has been crushed."

"The kingdom of heaven."

His brow arched. "You are now a god?"

"No. But I serve one. His kingdom is within, and his will is going to be done on earth as it is in heaven."

He studied my face, my eyes.

"This kingdom gives you the power to see once again..."

"Clearly."

He evidently didn't know how to respond, but Shaquilath took advantage of his silence.

"You are truly blessed among all Bedu, Maviah. Never have I seen such resolve and courage in one such as you."

She looked down at Maliku.

"Your sister has spared your life, I suggest you use it well. Leave Petra. If you return, I will personally run a sword through your gut."

He started to protest.

Shaquilath shoved her finger at the arching entrance. "Leave us!"

Maliku cast me one last look, then turned and jogged from the arena, looking back once at the arch over the entrance before vanishing.

"Your troubles with him are not finished," the queen said. "He is your great enemy now."

"As he always has been."

She nodded, then looked at her subjects lining the stone seats in the arena.

"When seeking greatness, one must face great challenge, you understand?"

This was her apology, I thought.

"And so you have," she said. "And now you will be honored." Shaquilath looked down at me. "I find in you a queen and a sister today."

I bowed my head. "I am humbled."

"Never cross me again."

This I could not promise, so I held my tongue.

"May you find Dumah yours," she said.

Find it? I wasn't sure what she meant.

"Under what terms?"

The king clasped his hands behind his back and paced to his right, then back.

"You may return to Dumah as you wish. I hereby withdraw my support from the Thamud and from all tribes in Dumah. So long as I receive my tax, I will not meddle. Find your way. Wage war if you must. May the Bedu most deserving rule the tribes of northern Arabia."

"And Judah?"

"He's alive. Find him. Save him. You seem quite adept."

"Rami—"

"Is still alive. I suggest you leave soon."

So . . . I had no Nabataean warriors, only their honor.

"Then I go alone."

"You go with Saba."

"Father." Phasa stepped forward, concerned. "You promised—"

"The slave goes with Maviah!" he snapped. "My word is final." Then, turning to me, "Even the gods know that a queen needs at least one subject."

It was settled then. I wasn't sure what to think, but I felt no fear.

"Today," Shaquilath cried out for all to hear, "Petra honors a new queen in the desert. Maviah, daughter of Rami bin Malik, we salute you."

The massive stone arena built into the cliffs at Petra shook with the response.

Maviah.

Queen.

CHAPTER TWENTY-EIGHT

I HAD HEARD of kingdoms far beyond the oasis that give birth to life where none should be, kingdoms beyond the vast, barren sands of the Arabian deserts.

I had lived in one such kingdom beyond the great Red Sea, in a land called Egypt, where I was sold into slavery as a young child. I had dreamed of the kingdoms farther north, where it was said the Romans lived in opulence and splendor, reveling in the plunder of conquered lands; of the silk kingdoms beyond Mesopotamia, in the Far East where whispers and magic ruled.

But none of these kingdoms were real to me, Maviah, daughter of the great sheikh of the Banu Kalb tribe, which presided over Arabia's northern sands. None were real to me because I, Maviah, was born into shame without the hope of honor.

But there came into that world a man who spoke of a different kingdom in words that defied all other kingdoms.

His name was Yeshua.

Some said that he was a prophet from their God. Some said that he was a mystic who spoke in riddles meant to infuriate the mind and quicken the heart, that he worked wonders to make his power evident. Some said that he was a Gnostic, though they were wrong. Some said that he was a messiah who came to set his people free. Still others, that he was a fanatical Zealot, a heretic, a man who'd seen too many deaths and too much suffering to remain sane.

But I came to know him as my master, the one who saved me. Yeshua, who showed me the way into a far greater kingdom within and among and at hand, full of power and wonder. Yeshua, who through tears learned obedience and so commanded the waves with stunning power and authority.

Yeshua, who introduced me to my Father, who did not judge me but cherished me even among the least as his prized daughter.

Saba and I sat upon our camels at the high point five miles east of Petra, gazing at the desert sands, which slept under the watchful gaze of the hottest sun.

"Tell me, my queen," he said. "Which kingdom rules your mind now?"

"At this moment?" I would not deceive my only trusted servant. "The kingdoms of the earth. But with a weak hand."

He kept his gaze fixed toward Dumah.

"There will be much bloodshed in these kingdoms," he said.

"There may be."

"We are ill equipped."

"We have all we need."

"The Kalb will hate you."

"I will love them."

"Kahil knows you come and gathers his armies already."

"Mine too waits, unseen."

"It may take many months to gather all the tribes."

"I have no other engagements."

A smile tempted his face. My pillar, my servant, my strong right arm, my Saba. But my heart ached for Judah.

We were silent for a few moments before I spoke.

"Your kingdom come, your will be done, on earth as it is in heaven," I said, quoting Yeshua. "This is why we go, Saba. To be awakened and to awaken that kingdom of the Father on earth."

"You are asleep?"

"Are you, Saba?"

He gave me a nod. "I am awakening."

His tone was sure, resonating from a place deep within him. It was then that I first became aware that the quiet, stoic Saba had been profoundly changed in a way not yet seen by the world. His day would come, I thought. This is only the beginning for him.

"The way we have seen is only the half of it," I said. "There is more to learn. Much more."

"And yet even this half is easily forgotten."

His words struck me. So, then, Saba had seen how easily I had misplaced my own faith in Yeshua before remembering in the arena.

"The forgotten way of Yeshua," I said. And even in saying it I realized I might very well forget again.

"Tell me, Saba. In your understanding, what is that way so easily forgotten?"

He hesitated then spoke in an even tone, as if well-practiced already.

"There are two realms: the kingdom of heaven and the kingdom of earth. Yeshua's treasure is the eternal realm of the Father, also called heaven, manifested in great power also on earth. It is within and among us even now. Abiding in there, one finds salvation from all that threatens in this life and in the life to come."

He paused.

"And?"

"The path into this eternal realm is faith—belief in, not *about*, Yeshua. Intimately knowing the father, not merely knowing *about* him with the mind. Even the devils know all about God and it profits them nothing. Even calling him Lord and doing many miraculous works in his name means little. Only knowing him intimately, as an infant knows."

I nodded, surprised by how succinctly he put what we had heard.

He continued. "The means to such faith is sight. Not sight as seen by earthly eyes, which shows much trouble, but perception of the light of the world, which shows peace in place of the storm. Yeshua has come to bring sight to the blind so the eyes of our hearts might be opened to see the eternal realm of the Father, even now. This he also calls rebirth—to see the kingdom of heaven."

I nodded. "Yet even seeing, one can easily see darkness instead of light and so become anxious once again," I said. "Any day, any hour. And how deep is that darkness that crushes like a storm."

"How deep is that darkness. But there is more."

"More?"

"The expression of that realm is love. The love of the Father who does not judge, and of Yeshua who does not accuse. And love of all as yourself. Love, even, of any enemy."

The enemy. *The Thamud. Kahil. Maliku.*

"Even of the enemy," I said.

Saba faced me.

"You will return to Palestine to find him?" he asked.

Yeshua's words came back to me. *There is far more to be revealed in time. Only then will you be able to follow where I will go.*

And where will you go, master? Where will you lead me?

It was a mystery. I would trust, absent of that knowledge, for this was faith.

I had wondered on occasion why he would reveal himself to me as he had. Perhaps I could accept his teaching as I had only because of my ignorance of deep Jewish convictions, so dear to those Galileans to whom he spoke. But none of that mattered now.

He *had* revealed himself to me. And I would never be the same.

"Yeshua and I will meet again," I said. Then I tapped my camel and took us into the sands.

Toward Dumah.

Toward Judah.

To my fate.

COMING FALL 2015

A.D. 33

AUTHOR'S NOTE

Every teaching spoken by Yeshua in *A.D. 30* is taken directly from the record of his teachings, referenced in the appendix below. How his teachings were understood by various characters in the story is a matter of their interpretation.

In addition, though I have fictionalized Maviah's journey, none of what otherwise occurs in *A.D. 30* contradicts well-supported historical records of what happened within the scope of this novel. Among many others, these events include the suppression of the rebellion in Sepphoris by Varus and Aretas's army of Bedu (though his dagger is my addition); Herod's divorce of Aretas's daughter, Phasa; the imprisonment of John the Baptist following Herod's marriage to Herodias; and the events surrounding Yeshua's ministry, including his referenced meeting with Nicodemus, the calming of the storm, the healing of the woman with the issue of blood, and his teachings in the hills of Capernaum and Bethsaida.

Scholars agree that Yeshua would have repeated his teachings many times throughout his ministry from beginning to end, yet I have focused primarily on those teachings recorded early in the gospels, because his emphasis shifted toward the end of his life, as we shall see in *A.D. 33*.

Please note that there is little agreement in the scholarly community regarding specific dates for certain events—whole books have been written to argue various points of view. But in the end, the lack of consensus about the specific timing of some events has little bearing on the significance of those events. I contend that *when* an event occurred is not nearly as important as the fact that it *did*. I have thus chosen a scholarly calendar that best facilitates Maviah's story.

And this is only the beginning...

APPENDIX

References for the teachings of Jesus. Unless otherwise noted, all references are from the NIV.

Dumah: Matthew 5:39 "I tell you, do not resist an evil person. If anyone slaps you on the right cheek, turn to them the other cheek also."

The Nafud: John 12:24 "Very truly I tell you, unless a kernel of wheat falls to the ground and dies, it remains only a single seed. But if it dies, it produces many seeds."

Galilee: Matthew 11:25 (NASB), 18:3 (NIV) "At that time Jesus said, 'I praise you, Father, Lord of heaven and earth, that you have hidden these things from the wise and intelligent, and have revealed them to infants.' . . . And he said: 'Truly I tell you, unless you change and become like little children, you will never enter the kingdom of heaven.'"

Capernaum: Luke 17:20, 21 (NKJ) "Now when He was asked by the Pharisees when the kingdom of God would come, He answered them and said, 'The kingdom of God does not come with observation; nor will they say, "See here!" or "See there!" For indeed, the kingdom of God is within you.'"

Petra: Matthew 6:22, 23 (NASB) "The eye is the lamp of the body;
   so then if your eye is clear, your whole body will be full of light.
   But if your eye is bad, your whole body will be full of darkness. If then the light that is in you is darkness, how great is the
   darkness!"

Bethsaida: John 14:12 (AMP) "I assure you, most solemnly I tell you,
   if anyone steadfastly believes in Me, he will himself be able to
   do the things that I do; and he will do even greater things than
   these, because I go to the Father."

Chapter 16

1. The kingdom is within you: Luke 17:20, 21 (NKJ) "Now when
He was asked by the Pharisees when the kingdom of God would
come, He answered them and said, 'The kingdom of God does not
come with observation; nor will they say, "See here!" or "See there!"
For indeed, the kingdom of God is within you.' "

2. Jesus speaks of the sword: Matthew 10:34–36 "Do not suppose that I have come to bring peace to the earth. I did not come to
bring peace, but a sword. For I have come to turn 'a man against his
father, a daughter against her mother, a daughter-in-law against her
mother-in-law—a man's enemies will be the members of his own
household.' "

3. Abolish the Law, fulfill the Law: Matthew 5:17–19 "Do not
think that I have come to abolish the Law or the Prophets; I have
not come to abolish them but to fulfill them. For truly I tell you,
until heaven and earth disappear, not the smallest letter, not the
least stroke of a pen, will by any means disappear from the Law
until everything is accomplished. Therefore anyone who sets aside
one of the least of these commands and teaches others accordingly
will be called least in the kingdom of heaven, but whoever practices

and teaches these commands will be called great in the kingdom of heaven."

4. The law concerning an eye for an eye: Exodus 21:12–17, 23–25 "Anyone who strikes a person with a fatal blow is to be put to death. However, if it is not done intentionally, but God lets it happen, they are to flee to a place I will designate. But if anyone schemes and kills someone deliberately, that person is to be taken from my altar and put to death. Anyone who attacks their father or mother is to be put to death. Anyone who kidnaps someone is to be put to death, whether the victim has been sold or is still in the kidnapper's possession. Anyone who curses their father or mother is to be put to death.... You are to take life for life, eye for eye, tooth for tooth, hand for hand, foot for foot, burn for burn, wound for wound, bruise for bruise."

5. Reversal of the law of an eye for an eye: Matthew 5:38–42 "You have heard that it was said, 'Eye for eye, and tooth for tooth.' But I tell you, do not resist an evil person. If anyone slaps you on the right cheek, turn to them the other cheek also. And if anyone wants to sue you and take your shirt, hand over your coat as well. If anyone forces you to go one mile, go with them two miles. Give to the one who asks you, and do not turn away from the one who wants to borrow from you."

6. Speaking parables so that they do not understand: Matthew 13:13 "This is why I speak to them in parables: 'Though seeing, they do not see; though hearing, they do not hear or understand.' "

7. Pharisees accuse Jesus of coming from Beelzebul: Matthew 12:22–24 "Then they brought him a demon-possessed man who was blind and mute, and Jesus healed him, so that he could both talk and see. All the people were astonished and said, 'Could this be the Son of David?' But when the Pharisees heard this, they said, 'It is only by Beelzebul, the prince of demons, that this fellow drives out demons.' "

8. Rebirth is like the wind, unseen: John 3:8 "The wind blows wherever it pleases. You hear its sound, but you cannot tell where it comes from or where it is going. So it is with everyone born of the Spirit."

9. One cannot see the kingdom unless they are born again: John 3:3 "Jesus replied, 'Very truly I tell you, no one can see the kingdom of God unless they are born again.'"

10. Few will follow the narrow way to life: Matthew 7:13, 14 "Enter through the narrow gate. For wide is the gate and broad is the road that leads to destruction, and many enter through it. But small is the gate and narrow the road that leads to life, and only a few find it."

11. Jesus is the way: John 14:6 "Jesus answered, 'I am the way and the truth and the life. No one comes to the Father except through me.'"

Chapter 17

1. Revealed the truth to infants: Matthew 11:25 (NASB) "At that time Jesus said, 'I praise you, Father, Lord of heaven and earth, that You have hidden these things from the wise and intelligent and have revealed them to infants.'"

2. Unless you change and become like a child: Matthew 18:3 "And he said: 'Truly I tell you, unless you change and become like little children, you will never enter the kingdom of heaven.'"

3. Treasure in the field: Matthew 13:44 "The kingdom of heaven is like treasure hidden in a field. When a man found it, he hid it again, and then in his joy went and sold all he had and bought that field."

4. Pearl of great value: Matthew 13:45, 46 "Again, the kingdom of heaven is like a merchant looking for fine pearls. When he found one of great value, he went away and sold everything he had and bought it."

5. Treasures in heaven: Matthew 6:19–21 "Do not store up for yourselves treasures on earth, where moths and vermin destroy, and where thieves break in and steal. But store up for yourselves

treasures in heaven, where moths and vermin do not destroy, and where thieves do not break in and steal. For where your treasure is, there your heart will be also."

6. The kingdom is at hand: Matthew 4:17 "From that time on Jesus began to preach, 'Repent, for the kingdom of heaven has come near.'"

7. Faith to move mountains: Matthew 17:20 "He replied, 'Because you have so little faith. Truly I tell you, if you have faith as small as a mustard seed, you can say to this mountain, "Move from here to there," and it will move. Nothing will be impossible for you.'"

8. Greater things: John 14:12 (AMP) "I assure you, most solemnly I tell you, if anyone steadfastly believes in Me, he will himself be able to do the things that I do; and he will do even greater things than these, because I go to the Father."

9. Parable of harsh taskmaster: Matthew 25:14–30 "Then the man who had received one bag of gold came. 'Master,' he said, 'I knew that you are a hard man, harvesting where you have not sown and gathering where you have not scattered seed. So I was afraid and went out and hid your gold in the ground. See, here is what belongs to you.' His master replied, 'You wicked, lazy servant! So you knew that I harvest where I have not sown and gather where I have not scattered seed? Well then, you should have put my money on deposit with the bankers, so that when I returned I would have received it back with interest. So take the bag of gold from him and give it to the one who has ten bags. For whoever has will be given more, and they will have an abundance. Whoever does not have, even what they have will be taken from them. And throw that worthless servant outside, into the darkness, where there will be weeping and gnashing of teeth.'"

10. The beatitudes: Matthew 5:3–11 "Blessed [also translated 'happy'] are the poor in spirit, for theirs is the kingdom of heaven. Blessed are those who mourn, for they will be comforted. Blessed

are the meek, for they will inherit the earth. Blessed are those who hunger and thirst for righteousness, for they will be filled. Blessed are the merciful, for they will be shown mercy. Blessed are the pure in heart, for they will see God. Blessed are the peacemakers, for they will be called children of God. Blessed are those who are persecuted because of righteousness, for theirs is the kingdom of heaven. Blessed are you when people insult you, persecute you and falsely say all kinds of evil against you because of me."

11. You are the light of the world: Matthew 5:14, 16 "You are the light of the world. A town built on a hill cannot be hidden."

12. The eye is the lamp of the body: Matthew 6:22, 23 (NASB) "The eye is the lamp of the body; so then if your eye is clear, your whole body will be full of light. But if your eye is bad, your whole body will be full of darkness. If then the light that is in you is darkness, how great is the darkness!"

13. Take the plank out of your eye: Matthew 7:4, 5 "How can you say to your brother, 'Let me take the speck out of your eye,' when all the time there is a plank in your own eye? You hypocrite, first take the plank out of your own eye, and then you will see clearly to remove the speck from your brother's eye."

14. Do not resist an evil person: Matthew 5:38–42 "You have heard that it was said, 'Eye for eye, and tooth for tooth.' But I tell you, do not resist an evil person. If anyone slaps you on the right cheek, turn to them the other cheek also. And if anyone wants to sue you and take your shirt, hand over your coat as well. If anyone forces you to go one mile, go with them two miles. Give to the one who asks you, and do not turn away from the one who wants to borrow from you."

15. Love your enemies: Matthew 5:43–45 "You have heard that it was said, 'Love your neighbor and hate your enemy.' But I tell you, love your enemies and pray for those who persecute you, that you may be children of your Father in heaven."

16. Judge not lest you be judged: Matthew 7:1, 2 "Do not judge, or you too will be judged. For in the same way you judge others, you will be judged, and with the measure you use, it will be measured to you."

17. The Father does not judge: John 5:22 "Moreover, the Father judges no one, but has entrusted all judgment to the Son."

18. I will not accuse you: John 5:45 "Do not think I will accuse you before the Father. Your accuser is Moses, on whom your hopes are set."

19. What you did not do to the least of these: Matthew 25:45 "He will reply, 'Truly I tell you, whatever you did not do for one of the least of these, you did not do for me.'"

20. Build your house upon the rock: Matthew 7:24–27 "Therefore everyone who hears these words of mine and puts them into practice is like a wise man who built his house on the rock. The rain came down, the streams rose, and the winds blew and beat against that house; yet it did not fall, because it had its foundation on the rock. But everyone who hears these words of mine and does not put them into practice is like a foolish man who built his house on sand. The rain came down, the streams rose, and the winds blew and beat against that house, and it fell with a great crash."

Chapter 23

1. Fear and faith: Mark 4:35–40 "That day when evening came, he said to his disciples, 'Let us go over to the other side.' Leaving the crowd behind, they took him along, just as he was, in the boat. There were also other boats with him. A furious squall came up, and the waves broke over the boat, so that it was nearly swamped. Jesus was in the stern, sleeping on a cushion. The disciples woke him and said to him, 'Teacher, don't you care if we drown?' He got up, rebuked the wind and said to the waves, 'Quiet! Be still!' Then the wind died down and it was

completely calm. He said to his disciples, 'Why are you so afraid? Do you still have no faith?' "

2. Anger and murder: Matthew 5:22 "But I tell you that anyone who is angry with a brother or sister will be subject to judgment. Again, anyone who says to a brother or sister, 'Raca,' is answerable to the court. And anyone who says, 'You fool!' will be in danger of the fire of hell."

3. To believe in the one: John 6:29 "Jesus answered, 'The work of God is this: to believe in the one he has sent.' "

4. Many are called, few are chosen: Matthew 22:14 "For many are invited, but few are chosen."

5. Narrow is the gate: Matthew 7:13, 14 "Enter through the narrow gate. For wide is the gate and broad is the road that leads to destruction, and many enter through it. But small is the gate and narrow the road that leads to life, and only a few find it."

6. Serving two masters: Matthew 6:24 "No one can serve two masters. Either you will hate the one and love the other, or you will be devoted to the one and despise the other. You cannot serve both God and money."

7. Disregard all, including self: Luke 14:26 "If anyone comes to me and does not hate father and mother, wife and children, brothers and sisters—yes, even their own life—such a person cannot be my disciple."

8. Give up all your wealth: Luke 18:22 "When Jesus heard this, he said to him, 'You still lack one thing. Sell everything you have and give to the poor, and you will have treasure in heaven. Then come, follow me.' "

Chapter 24

1. Serving two masters: Matthew 6:24 "No one can serve two masters. Either you will hate the one and love the other, or you will be devoted to the one and despise the other. You cannot serve both God and money."

2. Be anxious for nothing: Matthew 6:25–34 "Therefore I tell you, do not worry about your life, what you will eat or drink; or about your body, what you will wear. Is not life more than food, and the body more than clothes? Look at the birds of the air; they do not sow or reap or store away in barns, and yet your heavenly Father feeds them. Are you not much more valuable than they? Can any one of you by worrying add a single hour to your life? And why do you worry about clothes? See how the flowers of the field grow. They do not labor or spin. Yet I tell you that not even Solomon in all his splendor was dressed like one of these. If that is how God clothes the grass of the field, which is here today and tomorrow is thrown into the fire, will he not much more clothe you—you of little faith? So do not worry, saying, 'What shall we eat?' or 'What shall we drink?' or 'What shall we wear?' For the pagans run after all these things, and your heavenly Father knows that you need them. But seek first his kingdom and his righteousness, and all these things will be given to you as well. Therefore do not worry about tomorrow, for tomorrow will worry about itself. Each day has enough trouble of its own."

3. Love your neighbor as yourself: Matthew 22:39 "And the second is like it: 'Love your neighbor as yourself.' "

4. Judge not lest you be judged: Matthew 7:1, 2 "Do not judge, or you too will be judged. For in the same way you judge others, you will be judged, and with the measure you use, it will be measured to you."

5. Ask and it is given: Matthew 7:7–11 "Ask and it will be given to you; seek and you will find; knock and the door will be opened to you. For everyone who asks receives; the one who seeks finds; and to the one who knocks, the door will be opened. Which of you, if your son asks for bread, will give him a stone? Or if he asks for a fish, will give him a snake? If you, then, though you are evil, know how to give good gifts to your children, how much more will your Father in heaven give good gifts to those who ask him!"

6. The story of the Father and his sons: Luke 15:11–32 "Jesus continued: 'There was a man who had two sons. The younger one said to his father, "Father, give me my share of the estate." So he divided his property between them. Not long after that, the younger son got together all he had, set off for a distant country and there squandered his wealth in wild living. After he had spent everything, there was a severe famine in that whole country, and he began to be in need. So he went and hired himself out to a citizen of that country, who sent him to his fields to feed pigs. He longed to fill his stomach with the pods that the pigs were eating, but no one gave him anything. When he came to his senses, he said, "How many of my father's hired servants have food to spare, and here I am starving to death! I will set out and go back to my father and say to him: Father, I have sinned against heaven and against you. I am no longer worthy to be called your son; make me like one of your hired servants." So he got up and went to his father. But while he was still a long way off, his father saw him and was filled with compassion for him; he ran to his son, threw his arms around him and kissed him. The son said to him, "Father, I have sinned against heaven and against you. I am no longer worthy to be called your son." But the father said to his servants, "Quick! Bring the best robe and put it on him. Put a ring on his finger and sandals on his feet. Bring the fattened calf and kill it. Let's have a feast and celebrate. For this son of mine was dead and is alive again; he was lost and is found." So they began to celebrate. Meanwhile, the older son was in the field. When he came near the house, he heard music and dancing. So he called one of the servants and asked him what was going on. "Your brother has come," he replied, "and your father has killed the fattened calf because he has him back safe and sound." The older brother became angry and refused to go in. So his father went out and pleaded with him. But he answered his father, "Look! All these years I've been slaving for

you and never disobeyed your orders. Yet you never gave me even a young goat so I could celebrate with my friends. But when this son of yours who has squandered your property with prostitutes comes home, you kill the fattened calf for him!" "My son," the father said, "you are always with me, and everything I have is yours. But we had to celebrate and be glad, because this brother of yours was dead and is alive again; he was lost and is found.' "

7. Your faith has healed you: Mark 5:30–34 "At once Jesus realized that power had gone out from him. He turned around in the crowd and asked, 'Who touched my clothes?' 'You see the people crowding against you,' his disciples answered, 'and yet you can ask, "Who touched me?" ' But Jesus kept looking around to see who had done it. Then the woman, knowing what had happened to her, came and fell at his feet and, trembling with fear, told him the whole truth. He said to her, 'Daughter, your faith has healed you. Go in peace and be freed from your suffering.' "

8. Jesus quotes Hebrews on his obedience: Hebrews 5:7, 8 "During the days of Jesus' life on earth, he offered up prayers and petitions with fervent cries and tears to the one who could save him from death, and he was heard because of his reverent submission. Son though he was, he learned obedience from what he suffered."

9. Few find the narrow gate: Matthew 7:13, 14 "Enter through the narrow gate. For wide is the gate and broad is the road that leads to destruction, and many enter through it. But small is the gate and narrow the road that leads to life, and only a few find it."

10. Forgive seventy times seven: Matthew 18:21, 22 "Then Peter came to Jesus and asked, 'Lord, how many times shall I forgive my brother or sister who sins against me? Up to seven times?' Jesus answered, 'I tell you, not seven times, but seventy-seven times.' "

11. Thy kingdom come, on earth as it is in heaven: Matthew 6:10 "Your kingdom come, your will be done, on earth as it is in heaven."

ABOUT THE AUTHOR

TED DEKKER is a *New York Times* best-selling author with more than ten million books in print. He is known for stories that combine adrenaline-laced plots with incredible confrontations between unforgettable characters. He lives in Austin, Texas, with his wife and children.